PRAISE FOR
THE BONE KEEPER

"*The Bone Keeper* will corrupt your days and shatter your nights."

—Val McDermid

"A dark and brilliant thriller from a writer who just gets better and better. *The Bone Keeper* is tense, chilling, and hugely scary."

—Mark Billingham

"Luca Veste proves that you don't need to go to the Bayou or the Everglades to find something terrifying in the deep, dark woods... An entertainingly nasty piece of work."

—Christopher Brookmyre

"*Candyman* meets *The Silence of the Lambs*."

—Eva Dolan

"Terrifying, gasp-out-loud, totally compelling, and twisted... I loved it!"

—Miranda Dickinson

"Urban legend meets serial killer thriller—a terrifying book that walks the line between crime and horror."

—Stuart Neville

Also by Luca Veste

The Bone Keeper

THE
SILENCE

A NOVEL

LUCA VESTE

sourcebooks
landmark

Copyright © 2020 by Luca Veste
Cover and internal design © 2020 by Sourcebooks
Cover design by Ervin Serrano
Cover image © Reilika Landen/Arcangel, VolodymyrSanych/Shutterstock

Published by Sourcebooks Landmark, an imprint of Sourcebooks
P.O. Box 4410, Naperville, Illinois 60567-4410
(630) 961-3900
sourcebooks.com

Library of Congress Cataloging-in-Publication Data is on file with the publisher.

Printed and bound in the United States of America.
VP 10 9 8 7 6 5 4 3 2 1

FOR STEVE CAVANAGH—MY PODBRO, MY SHAKY
IDEA FIXER, MY GUIDE, MY CONFIDANTE,
BUT ABOVE ALL ELSE, MY FRIEND.

When it was over, there was silence.

It wasn't a calm type of quiet. Peaceful or tranquil. It was a suffocating stillness as reality settled over us all.

On me.

No turning back now. No changing our minds. No fixing our mistake.

I can still feel the mud under my fingernails. The blood that didn't belong to me on my skin. The smell of sweat and fear.

I could scrub myself clean over and over, and it would never be enough.

It would still be there. Ground down, seeping into my skin. Turning my blood black and cold.

The dirt.

The pain.

The evil.

This was my mistake. My fault.

In the beginning, there was a boy. A small, anonymous young boy, who you wouldn't look at twice. Quiet and thoughtful.

He would become a killer, but that happened later. For now, while he was a child, there was only the song.

> *Oranges and lemons*
> *Say the bells of Saint Clements.*
> *You owe me five farthings,*
> *Say the bells of Saint Martin's.*
> *When will you pay me?*
> *Say the bells at Old Bailey.*
> *When I grow rich*
> *Say the bells at Shoreditch.*
> *When will that be?*
> *Say the bells of Stepney.*
> *I do not know*
> *Says the great bell at Bow.*
> *Here comes a candle to light you to bed,*
> *And here comes a chopper to chop off your head!*
> *Chip chop chip chop the last man is dead.*

The children would sing that song and play their game—never including him.

That's how it began.

That's where he learned how to use it. The words meaning so much. Giving him something he never had.

He started with dolls. Removing their heads, lighting his candles.

Then, later, they didn't provide what he had needed.

It had to be something more real.

Chip chop. Red candles, lighting them to death. Endless sleep.

It gave him power. Revenge.

Relief.

Finally.

ONE

Our phones had pinged at the same time. A smile on our faces as we read the latest message in the group chat, turned to each other, and both agreed without saying a word. That's how we live our lives now. A series of moments, interspersed with cell phones vibrating or dinging away to let us know what is happening around the world. We're instantly contactable. When the world ends, we'll find out from a breaking news notification, I imagine.

There's a point when you know age has finally caught up with you. That you're not young anymore and time is marching on. Life is happening, and you have to make a decision to catch up with it or try to stop it somehow. That you are no longer in your teens or your twenties, that forty isn't that far away and you have to start growing up.

For me, it was when I bought my own house and went to a nineties-themed music festival.

The two were unrelated but happened in the same week.

The blurred line between nostalgia and my unfolding future. An invisible line, drawing the former to a close and starting the latter.

The music festival had come up as a link in that group chat. Chris had sent it; Michelle had replied with some emojis; Stuart took a day to respond with a thumbs-up and a list of bands he hoped would be there. Alexandra and I were already discussing whether it was too close to our move-in date, deciding within a few minutes it would be fine.

We had saved and saved, scrimping together every last penny for the deposit. The monthly payments were more than manageable, less than we had been paying in rent, strangely enough.

Now, it was ours. The very first place we could properly call home.

This belonged to us. It was only bricks and mortar, but when Alexandra and I had picked up the keys and let ourselves inside for the first time, there was a definite feeling of arrival. Into adulthood, home ownership, being.

It's bizarre the way inanimate objects can suddenly become the catalyst for relief.

The boxes were inside the house but remained firmly unpacked. All clearly marked and not by my hand. I'd come back to the rented flat we shared one day to find a load of boxes with different rooms noted on them.

That had always been Alexandra. I had no issues with organization, but when she was excited about something, I didn't stand a chance. I took a breath, and she'd already done it.

"Matt, have you seen the roll mat?"

I wondered for a second or two what the hell a roll mat was, then remembered just in time. I didn't want another lesson in camping if I could help it. I looked around the room, wondering how we'd manage to find anything and then spotted it wedged between two boxes marked LIVING ROOM. I shouted up a confirmation to Alexandra and continued making a playlist for the car.

Each song was a reminder of another time.

"Rhythm Is a Dancer," Snap! That one was from 1992—year

six in primary school. First dance I remember in school. I danced for the first time in front of people. I'd tried to avoid doing the same thing ever since. Same year as "End of the Road" by Boyz II Men and "Stay" by Shakespears Sister. Also "I Will Always Love You," but I'd rather forget that song and the film Alexandra watched on a yearly basis for some unknown reason.

1993. First and second year in high school. The year of Wet Wet Wet and that song that seemed to be Number 1 for the entire year. I wasn't a fan but stuck it on the playlist anyway. Also added Mariah Carey's version of "Without You," Pato Banton, D:Ream, and East 17.

1997. Year ten and eleven in high school. Puff Daddy missing Notorious B.I.G. Will Smith with "Men in Black." No Doubt, Natalie Imbruglia, and the Verve all got added. I stuck Hanson in for the laughs it would surely generate.

And the mass sing-along.

1998 and 1999. GCSE's and the start of A-Levels. The year the pickings in music became slimmer. Steps and S Club 7 had arrived. "Tragedy" had to go on there. As did Shania Twain. Then, it was the greatest pop song of all time—in my humble opinion—"...Baby One More Time" and the ridiculously young Britney Spears.

I smiled to myself, each song coming to mind instantly and vividly. The soundtrack of my youth. I threw some Cast and Space tracks on the list because they were ace and local to us. And they would annoy our mate from Manchester, Stuart, too.

The weekend was going to be filled with reminiscing and sore throats from singing songs we somehow still knew by heart.

"We've just bought a house, and now we're swapping that for a tent in a field," I said as Alexandra walked into the room. I stopped updating the playlist, looking up at her from the sofa that wouldn't stay in the position we'd dropped it in the day before. "I don't understand how this happened. We've got a proper bed here. And walls."

"Stop moaning," she replied, shaking her head and smiling to herself. "Where's your sense of adventure? We're not too old to be going camping, you know."

"I'm just saying, surely we've gotten to the point where we can afford to have proper walls now. Walls, Alexandra. They're this new invention that stops us from freezing to death at night."

"Sarcasm is your least attractive trait. And where's the fun in that? This whole weekend is about recapturing our youth, right? Well, that means we're going to be in a field with thousands of other people."

I took a breath, ready to argue my point further, but could see it was pointless. Truth was, I was just as excited about it. Still, it was October, and my feet never felt warm at the best of times.

"Did you put that thing under the car?"

I frowned, then remembered what she was talking about from the roll of her eyes. "I'm not sure it's a good idea. I don't like the thought of leaving a spare key fixed to the car. Seems to be asking for trouble, isn't it?"

"It's totally safe. And anyway, it's just a precaution. If you lose the car keys in some field near Bath, you'll be complaining for weeks after about the cost."

"Okay, okay, I'll do it when we get there." The little black box was on my desk. A combination lock and a spare car key inside. You could affix it in the wheel arch, and it was unbreakable apparently. I wasn't so sure. I used our anniversary as a memorable date to unlock it. Our *newest* anniversary date.

"Are you ready to go?" Alexandra asked, adding yet another

thing to backpack three—the other two were already in the trunk. "We've got to meet the others in fifteen minutes."

"Yeah, just finishing off now. Just trying to remember that song Michelle used to sing in science in year ten."

"'Saturday Night' by Whigfield."

"That's the one," I said, typing it into the search bar. Over two hundred songs on the playlist now. Mostly nineties-era music, with a few eighties power ballads thrown in for good measure.

"Well, hurry up," I said, then smiled when Alexandra came over to me and wrapped her arms around my shoulders as I sat in my desk chair. I leaned back and rested my head against her body. "You know how they get if we're late."

"I know. I'm just thinking though...we haven't christened this room yet."

I was grinning as I stood up, and like giggling teenagers, we closed the curtains.

We were late.

———

An hour or so later, we were making our way down the M6, singing along to Aerosmith at the top of our lungs. Michelle and Stuart in the back seat, Chris and Nicola in another car behind ours.

Michelle had always been the singer in the group. Now, she was blaring tunes from the back seat as if it were karaoke time at Coopers pub in town. Loud and almost never in tune. She'd cut her hair into a bob a week or so earlier, and it bounced around her face as she moved. I kept glancing in the rearview mirror and smiling through my own monotone delivery.

It had been Chris's idea to do this. Almost as if he knew that it was something we all needed—a way of drawing a line under our youth and accepting the fact that we were all now in our midthirties and it was time to move on with the next stage of our lives. Stuart and Michelle hadn't needed much convincing. For them, it was simply an opportunity to reunite and continue the longest on-again, off-again relationship since Ross and Rachel.

It was a music festival with a difference—every band booked had been either genuinely half-famous twenty years earlier or were tribute acts for the bigger names. No Way Sis for Oasis. Blurred for Blur. Slice Girls for... Well, I got the point quick enough.

As a group of friends, I suppose we all had a little arrested development. In our thirties and only just buying our own house. None of us were parents yet. We'd traveled the world instead, lived in rented accommodations, had jobs instead of careers.

We were the people tabloids liked to castigate with the term *millennials*.

None of us enjoyed avocado on toast, so we had that going for us at least.

Alexandra placed a hand on my thigh as I tapped the wheel in time to the music blaring from the car speakers. The GPS on my phone told me we still had a few hours traveling ahead of us. I looked across at her and grinned. She responded by placing her other hand over her heart and matching Celine Dion's voice echoing around the car.

If I'd believed in perfect moments—another nineties song—that would have been one. I wanted to capture it in a bubble and live in it forever.

Even as clouds drifted across the sky and darkened the day enough for me to prop my sunglasses on my head. Even when spots of rain splashed against the windshield. Even when Michelle and Stuart began bickering in the back seat...I kept smiling.

As if nothing bad could ever happen to us.

TWO

S tuart and his thinning blond mop of hair calmed down a little, unable to match Michelle's stamina beside him in the back of the car. I looked up in the rearview mirror and saw the approach of middle age written in the lines creasing his face. Around the eyes, mostly. His skin was still the color of bronze sand, the stubble perfectly sculptured on his face not graying as yet. I tried to imagine him as someone in their forties or fifties and failed. Simply accepting he was the same age as me was difficult enough, given he still looked like he was in his twenties.

The journey continued, carried along on a wind of nostalgia. "Here Comes the Hotstepper" and "It's Oh So Quiet" particularly loud highlights. Every hour or so, we'd stop at a gas station, and people would swap cars. Managed to turn a three- or four-hour journey into one closer to six and a half hours.

Not one of us stopped smiling the whole time.

On one of the stops, I stood with Chris, sipping on coffees in the October sunshine. Alexandra was passing a can of Carlsberg over to Nicola from a cooler bag. They'd be wasted by the time we arrived, I guessed. It wouldn't take long for Chris and me to catch up to them.

On the wall outside the entrance, there was a missing person's poster. A young man, late teens. The picture looked like a mug shot, and I wondered if he really was missing or had simply forgotten to tell his family he had been sent to prison for something. Someone had scrawled the words *Candle Man's got him!* across the picture.

"Candle Man?" I said, raising an eyebrow in Chris's direction.

He glanced at the poster and rolled his eyes. "You've not heard that story?" Chris replied, shaking his head with a snort of derision. His hair flopped over as he moved, becoming less copious by the day. There would be a time when his previous nickname of the Liverpudlian Hugh Grant wouldn't fit any longer. "That's that serial killer who is supposedly responsible for every missing person in the country. Someone went missing up our way a few months back, and the police actually had to come out and release a statement to try to stop the rumors spreading about it online. You work in computers; you should know about it."

"I don't know everything that happens on the internet because I work with computers, Chris."

"I know, I know. I just thought you might have come across it."

"I think I have," I said, something rattling away in my subconscious. "Was there a documentary or something?"

Chris shrugged his shoulders and sipped on his coffee. "Not sure. Michelle was telling us about it in the car. Apparently, a red candle appears or something, and there's a dude who has killed all over the country for years and years. Probably something that makes families of people who go missing feel better. Michelle reckons it's true and that the police are just trying to keep it quiet."

"Sounds like rubbish to me."

"To anyone with half a brain."

"Good idea this, mate," I said, patting Chris on the shoulder and changing the subject. "Just spent twenty minutes singing Spice Girls songs."

"Yeah, well, thankfully they won't be at this thing."

"You always had a soft spot for Baby Spice."

"That makes more sense than your Sporty obsession."

I laughed and shook my head. "It's only because of the accent."

"Reckon it's time we grew up?"

"We already have," I said, seeing Alexandra and Nicola walking back out and toward the car. We followed them across the parking lot, and I smirked at Chris. Tried to keep the excitement out of my voice. "We're gonna start trying for a baby. And, in preparation for that, I'm buying a ring."

Chris stopped dead in his tracks, and I had to shush him as he made a noise like an excited animal. "Are you serious?"

"Will you keep your voice down?" I said, unable to keep the smile from my face. "Yes, I am. It's time. We've just bought the house, we're doing well financially…and I bloody love the bones of her, mate. Why should we wait any longer? It's not like we're getting any younger. We've been talking about it for a while, but I don't think we were sure until the house went through."

"I can already see you with a kid," Chris said, holding back laughter. "Walking around with a baby sling and a membership for Chester Zoo."

"Well, when you put it like that…"

"I'm happy for you," Chris said, using the fingertips of his right hand to lift the flop of hair from his forehead. "I just don't envy you telling Stuart I'm going to be your best man."

"Cocky, aren't you?" I replied, laughing openly now. "You're so sure I'd pick you?"

"What are you two gossips talking about?"

We looked up as Stuart joined us. Chris glanced at me with a ridiculous grin on his face and motioned with his head. I sighed and told him what I'd just told Chris.

"Well?" I said when I'd finished, expecting the usual lecture about never settling down from Stuart. He had always been opposed to any notion of getting older and doing mature things. "Tell me I'm wasting my life and I should have stayed single. Again."

Stuart hesitated, then smiled at me. "I think it's great. About bloody time if you ask me."

I held onto Chris as I pretended to almost faint. "Are you serious? The great Stuart Johnson, thinking marriage and kids is a good idea? I don't believe it."

He gave me a playful shove and told me to shut up. "Listen, even I know we're not as young as we once were. And besides... maybe I've been thinking about settling down myself. Finally."

We followed his gaze toward Michelle and both broke out into oohs and aahs. He laughed, and we went back to the cars still joking around.

An hour or so later, after driving down an inordinate number of country roads that could barely be called that, we finally arrived at the festival. It wasn't until I was out of the car that I realized quite how in the middle of nowhere we appeared to be. We had driven past the odd farmhouse on the drive, but now it was a muddy field and acres of land all around us. We found a spot out of the way and pitched our tents as far away from anyone else as we could manage. Behind us, woodland stretched out for as far as we could see. Chris grinned at me the entire time we were setting up, and he suddenly looked ten years younger. I wondered if we all did. Michelle and Stuart were snogging like teenagers, being goaded by Alexandra and Nicola.

It was the way things had been, the way I hoped they always would be.

"Why this?" I said to Chris, as we both took a break and opened a can of lager for each of us. "I didn't think you went in for all that nostalgia stuff?"

"Look at us," Chris replied, swiping an arm to indicate the others. "This is our last chance before you and Alexandra get married and start a family."

"Now you say it out loud…" I said with a smirk, but Chris waved me off.

"We both know you can't wait to get started. You'll get married, have kids. Stuart will either wake up and realize Michelle is the one or go traveling again if he wasn't being serious. Me and Nicola will carry on as normal. Getting older and older each day. I saw this event and thought it was a perfect way of drawing a close on a chapter in our lives. Make sense?"

"I suppose," I said, knocking back a large glug from the can and noisily sighing with satisfaction. "Are you and Nicola going to be doing the same, then?"

"We're already married," Chris replied, chuckling to himself. "You were there, remember?"

"I meant having kids. I'm surprised you haven't before now."

Chris placed his hand on the back of his neck and seemed to rub some life into it. "Well, there's the whole not-being-able-to-conceive thing, Matt."

"I'm not saying that," I said quickly, annoyed that I'd put my foot in it. I remembered when he'd told me that they couldn't have kids. I didn't think he'd ever been as low as he was at that point. "I meant, you could adopt or whatever. I think you'd make boss parents."

"So do I," Chris replied, then shrugged his shoulders. "Who

knows? Nic is pretty focused on what we do have right now. We talk about it, but I don't know. I'll tell you what though—over twenty years we've been together, and I would still do anything to make her happy. And she'd do the same for me."

Silence fell over us for a second before I shook it off. "Mate, who knew getting old would turn us into sappy fools? Let's get drunk and stupid, like the old days."

Chris laughed hard and clunked his can against mine. "Agreed."

We were soon lost in the group and its madness.

Happy, laughing, shouting, telling stories. Remembering times when we were younger. The pacts we'd made, the drunken tales of woe, the shared experiences. They all fell out of us in a collective bout of togetherness.

We were young again for a final weekend.

It was the six of us. Had been for as long as I could remember. What had started as friendship had become more than that for almost all of us.

The darkness grew at night, and we laughed, we drank, we sang. We enjoyed ourselves as if it were the nineties again and we didn't have a care in the world.

And at night, when the silence fell, we didn't feel any different.

THREE

looked at Alexandra and smiled. "Worth it?"

"Worth it," she replied, stroking my arm and looking off toward the stage. The last band was playing, and even though they looked like dots from where we were standing, it was still some sight.

It was almost as if twenty years hadn't passed for any of us. Earlier in the day, I'd looked around and it was like we were all eighteen again. Bouncing up and down, laughing and singing along to songs we didn't really know the words to. Making our own up to cover the gaps.

We were wringing every last moment of joy from the experience. We may have been in our midthirties, but we could have been kids again.

Now, as the moon shone above us and the music came to an end, it felt like we could do this forever.

"What a weekend," Stuart said with the wide grin he always wore after drinking. His words weren't slurred yet, but I didn't think that would be far off. "So glad I came."

"Yeah, I bet you are," I replied, catching Alexandra's eyes as she linked her arm in mine. I nodded toward Michelle, who was staring with googly eyes toward Stuart. Alexandra giggled and covered her mouth. "Let's get back. It's a bit of a walk from here."

We walked in pairs into the darkness, the occasional fluorescent light above trying to guide our way. We'd pitched our tents on the very outskirts of the fields, wanting to be as far from the younger attendees as possible.

That was probably the only thing that had marked us out as part of the older campers that weekend though. Most of the crowd the festival had been targeted at—like us, the thirty-odd-year-old contingent—had decided against camping. Those who seemed to just want to dance to music they vaguely remembered as toddlers had filled the campgrounds.

"How many do you reckon we saw in the end?" Alexandra said, resting her head against my upper arm as we trudged through the field.

"Bands? I don't know. Over three days, maybe twenty, thirty?"

"Some of them looked proper old now. Still got the dance moves, but they're all a bit slower these days."

"We're all getting old," I said, drawing her arm closer to me with a squeeze. She responded with a playful punch to my arm.

"Speak for yourself. I'll still be going to festivals in my seventies, dancing long into the night."

I laughed softly, waiting for her to rest her head on me again. It was Sunday night. The end of a perfect weekend. Three days of drinking, singing, laughing, and talking.

"It's like being back at university," I said, watching Chris and Nicola walking ahead of us. Stuart and Michelle were behind us, doing what they seemed to have spent most of the weekend doing—slobbering over each other like lovestruck teens. "Carefree, young enough to not worry about the consequences of anything. Not having to get up at a ridiculous time in the morning for work…"

"Drinking too much, smoking too much…"

"Yeah, those things too," I said, looking over my shoulder and smiling at Stuart and Michelle. They were clinging on to each other, pausing every few steps or so to kiss and grope each other. "Do you think them two will actually make a go of it this time?"

Alexandra looked over her shoulder and then back at me. "It would be about time. It's obvious they're perfect for each other."

"And it's not like we haven't told them enough times."

They had been an on-and-off-again relationship for as long as I could remember. They never seemed to split acrimoniously—we never really knew if they were together or not. There were no arguments or cross words. No picking of sides. They were simply a couple one day and not the next.

It seemed to work for them.

"I suppose they're not like them two," Alexandra said, meaning the couple ahead of us. Chris and Nicola. "They're different, I guess. They found each other early enough to not allow any doubt to creep in."

I couldn't disagree. I'd known Chris the longest of everyone, but even then, I couldn't really imagine a time when he'd been alone. Nicola had been on the scene almost as soon as I'd met Chris. And they fell into a relationship just as quickly. "What about us?"

Alexandra stopped walking, reaching up to me and placing her arms around my neck. "It just took us a little longer than them two. That was all. And hopefully Stuart and Michelle will realize it like we did."

I smiled down at her and then kissed her.

"A perfect end to a perfect weekend," Alexandra said, her smile shining in the moonlight.

"Not going to get any disagreement from me."

It was past midnight by the time we all reached the tents we'd called home for the past few days. The nearest neighbors were a good distance away, but we could still hear soft music beating from that direction. Raised laughter every now and again. It wasn't loud enough to bother us. On the other side of the tents was the woodland that encircled the entire area. A mass of fields, in the middle of a seemingly unending forest. We'd taken advantage of the cover the trees afforded us, meaning we didn't have to go searching for Portaloos every few minutes. Late at night, it hadn't been as much fun, but I'd used the flashlight on my phone and not gone far past the tree line on the couple of occasions I'd had to relieve myself after the sun had gone down.

The first night, Stuart had attempted to tell us a ghost story that involved the woods, one of those old urban myths we'd all heard before. He hadn't got through much of it before our laughter at his awful storytelling ability became too overwhelming.

Still, bad stories aside, I hadn't wanted to go much farther into the woodland than was necessary. It gave me the creeps even in the daytime. Too many trees, too many hiding places.

Chris was already digging into his stash of food as we joined them. He threw me a bag of chips I caught with both hands, almost too hard. I passed them to Alexandra and then grabbed another myself. Sat down in the fold-up chairs we'd brought along with us.

"Nothing's been nicked," Chris said, his familiar refrain every time we'd arrived back at camp. "Successful weekend in that respect."

"I told you there was nothing to worry about."

"Yeah, well, I wasn't sure," Chris replied, reaching the end of his chips packet and pouring the crumbs into his upturned mouth. "You hear bad things about these types of places."

"It's not that long since we've been to a festival," I replied, shaking my head. "You're making it sound like we're in our fifties and reminiscing about Glastonbury or whatever."

"I'll be glad of my own bed," Nicola said, sitting on the grass near Chris's feet and resting her head against his knees. "That's something that's definitely changed since we were last on one of these. I can't deal with the lack of memory foam like I used to."

"I know what you mean," I replied, stretching my arm out over my head. "Back has been aching all day."

"Didn't seem to bother you when you were bouncing up and down this afternoon," Alexandra said, laughing as she reached for a can of beer and opening it. "We're not as old as you think. Stop making out like we are."

"I agree, Alexandra," Chris said, deadpan as usual. "You're only as old as you allow yourself to feel. I think I could still keep up with the eighteen-year-old Chris. Probably outdo him as well."

"Yeah, well, you've always been a slow drinker," I said, avoiding the kick from Chris I had expected. It was nowhere near me, and Nicola giggled in response.

I opened my mouth to say something when it was snapped closed by a noise from behind us. Back the way we'd walked.

"I knew it had been too good to be true," Chris said quietly, sighing around every syllable it seemed. "Always got to be a fight at a festival. No one can just come to these things and have a good time anymore."

"Shush," I replied, standing up and looking back out into the darkness. I was trying to work out what we were hearing. Raised voices, low and high. They were traveling from a good hundred or two hundred meters away, but we could hear them over our neighbors' music. "I think it's them two."

"Stuart and Michelle?" Chris said, getting to his feet and standing next to me. "Surely not. I've never heard them say a bad word to each other. It'll be one of those lot from over there, drunk or something."

Chris pointed toward tents in the distance, but I didn't think he was right. I could hear Stuart's voice, his Manchester accent drifting our way. I looked at Alexandra and smiled. "Maybe one of them made the mistake of trying to propose or something."

She didn't smile back at me. Instead, her brow furrowed as she lifted herself up to her feet and stepped forward. "It's getting worse."

I turned back in the direction of the raised voices and could hear them more clearly now. I was sure it was Stuart and Michelle—could hear them distinctly, shouting, arguing. All the time getting closer and closer to camp.

"Shall we pick sides now, or wait to hear what it is they're screaming about?"

Alexandra aimed a playful punch toward my shoulder but missed purposely, it seemed. "It could be serious."

"I doubt it," Chris said, taking a couple steps forward and then turning back to us. "It'll be something stupid, no doubt. Matt, come on. Let's go get Stuart and calm them down."

I hesitated, looking at Alexandra, who gave nothing away. I sighed and shrugged my shoulders, following Chris.

FOUR

I wasn't even sure what the argument was about at first.

It became clear soon enough.

Stuart and Michelle had appeared from the darkness, with no effort to disguise the fact they were in the midst of a major row. Now, everyone was involved, for a reason I could only assume had more to do with alcohol than strident beliefs.

"I thought we weren't going to pick sides?" I said, not for the first time, as Nicola made another jab toward Stuart. "It's not our fight to have."

"Yeah, well, you haven't been the one to pick up the pieces when he buggers off and leaves Michelle on her own again."

Nicola stared at me after she spoke, almost daring me to argue with her. She may have been the smallest in the group—just over five feet tall—but solid looking all the same, and I had always avoided any type of confrontation with her. Instead, I sighed and looked toward Alexandra for help, but realized she was trying hard not to be drawn in.

"Why don't we just chill out and have a drink?" Chris said, his voice still unwavering. He was always the one who tried to calm things down, but I didn't think he would succeed this time. "Let's not spoil the weekend with a disagreement. We can talk about it another time."

"No, Chris," Michelle said, arms folded across her chest,

swaying slightly as if an invisible breeze was moving her. "A drink isn't going to help the situation. All I said was that maybe it was time he grew up and made some final decisions."

Michelle pointed an accusatory finger toward a silent Stuart, who was edging away from the group with every passing second. He didn't look as surprised by her outburst as the rest of us, but seemingly didn't want to stick around to find out what the result of it was going to be.

"You've been all over me for days, then you're just going to run away again?"

"That's not what I meant," Stuart said, but even I could see the lie from a mile away in the dark.

"*Not what you meant?*" Michelle replied, her voice louder and mocking now. Desperately trying to hide the hurt too, I imagined. I wanted to pick Stuart up and throw him as far as I could at that moment.

Idiot.

"How about you go now and leave us alone? It's not like you don't lift out easy enough. Last in, first out. Isn't that right? Isn't that what you're afraid of? You've always wanted to finish things with me for good, but you don't have the balls to do it, because you know what'll happen if you do. Everyone in this group will choose me over you."

Stuart laughed humorlessly, but when he looked at the rest of us he stopped. At Chris, who averted his eyes and crossed his arms across his chest. Easy to read, as he always was.

"Michelle, maybe this is something that you and Stuart should talk about tomorrow with clear heads." No sooner had the words left my mouth than I realized they were falling on deaf ears.

Michelle moved toward Stuart, who stopped moving away

but had his head lowered. Staring at the ground with great interest it seemed.

"Tell them all," Michelle said, her voice echoing around the field. No doubt a few campers would be listening in with great interest, but if Michelle knew that it didn't seem to bother her. "Tell them what you've done to me over the years. How you've cheated and lied so many times. How you've broken promises and told me the same crappy story over and over. Tell them what you've been doing without anyone knowing. Tell them what kind of man you *really* are. You've been using me for years and that stops now. I've had enough. I can't stand your lies anymore. It's gone too far."

I listened to her voice get louder and louder, as she screamed accusations at Stuart. He seemed to take it all and not rise to anything. As if he knew he had no defense.

"And now, after you pretend to be normal with me all weekend, you lay this bull on me that you're not even gonna be around. You've been lying to me with your actions all weekend, then can't even wait until we're on the way home before discarding me like I'm just a piece of rubbish to you."

"Michelle, it's not like that—"

"No, Stuart," Michelle said before he had a chance to finish the sentence. She sniffed and stepped closer to him. When she spoke, her voice was quieter now. Steelier. "I hope you die. That's what you deserve."

"Come on," Nicola said, moving to Michelle's side in an instant and putting an arm around her. "You can sleep in my tent. Chris can bunk with him, and we can leave first thing."

I turned to Alexandra, who opened her mouth to say something to me, but then decided against it. She followed the other two women as Chris steered Stuart away from the tents.

I went with them, a few steps behind, as we walked in silence until we were far enough away to not be heard by the others.

"She's not thinking straight," Stuart said, looking at his feet instead of the two other men. "I don't know what she's going on about."

"Sounds like she's had enough, mate," I said, moving toward him and slapping a hand on his shoulder. "You've been on again, off again so many times, it was always going to be the case that one of you would eventually need some kind of commitment. That's just life."

"That's the thing though," Stuart replied, looking at me now. The whites of his eyes were dull in the darkness, but I could almost feel them straining to be believed. "It's never been casual for me. It was always her who pulled back. I wanted to be together properly for years, but she was never ready. Now, suddenly it's all being thrown back in my face."

"Mate, it's not like what she was saying wasn't true though," Chris said, his voice soft and calm. That was always the way he was. The voice of reason whenever any of us faltered. He gave a knowing look at Stuart. "We know you've not always been completely faithful."

"How is it cheating if we're not really together?"

I recalled a TV character from decades earlier shouting "*We were on a break!*" and closed my mouth so I didn't start laughing.

It was all so ridiculous. I felt like we were all in school again. Teenagers, arguing over silly little things that didn't matter. Perhaps trying to recapture our youth at a music festival had somehow sent us back twenty years emotionally too.

"I'm sure she doesn't really want you dead," I said, trying to ease the tension and probably failing. "Still, probably best to sleep with one eye open."

"Mate, I'm more worried that Nicola will take it as an instruc-tion," Stuart replied, nudging Chris with his elbow. "That girl scares me more than anyone else. When you're arguing with her, do you do it from another country just in case?"

Chris didn't rise to the joke, or take it as one, it seemed. "We never argue," he said, shrugging his shoulders and kicking at the dirt beneath our feet. "She's not that scary, is she?"

"No, course not," I said, nudging Stuart to say the same.

Chris seemed to accept the slight untruth.

"Everyone's had too much to drink and isn't thinking straight," I said instead, shaking Stuart's shoulder with my hand. "Tomorrow, it'll all be okay again. Maybe it's time to have an honest discussion with her about things. I know it scares you, and that's probably what's kicked this off. What did you say?"

"That I was looking at going abroad for a few months."

"Well, that'll do it. Stop messing about, mate. Tell her how you feel and decide once and for all whether you should be together or not."

"After that, I don't think she's going to want to hear it…"

"You don't know that," I cut in before Stuart had time to finish. At that point, I just wanted to go to bed. The weekend was catching up with me—the lack of sleep, the drinking, the noise. I didn't sleep well at the best of times, but I'd barely had more than two hours a night since arriving there. "It'll all be different by the morning. She'll have calmed down, and you'll actually have to talk this time."

I caught a glimpse of his smile in the dark before we all headed back. It was quiet when we reached our tents, but we could hear whispers coming from where Chris and Nicola had been staying together. I watched Chris and Stuart get into the tent that Stuart had been sleeping in without a word.

Inside mine, it was empty. I didn't have to wait long before Alexandra came back.

"Okay?" I said, my voice barely audible, even in the cramped space. "All calmed down?"

Alexandra nodded in the dim light of the electronic lamp I'd set up. "She was proper angry, but seems to have just slid into overwhelming tiredness now. More's the pity. Would have been interesting to see what happened if she'd attacked him."

"It would have been the end of the group, that's for sure."

"All things have to come to an end at some point."

I whisper-grunted in response but lay back on the floor and smiled as Alexandra came next to me. Draped an arm over me and curled a leg over mine.

"Promise me we'll never be like those two."

"I promise."

It was a promise I meant in the moment, but one I knew I couldn't well keep. I'd been in enough relationships—short-term for the most part, of course—to know that things can change quickly. In a second, sometimes. The things that don't bother us at the beginning can suddenly become the single most irritating action a person can do at any moment. The arguments that would never happen in the first few weeks can increase in frequency.

We never really know another person.

Eventually, sleep took me. I was looking forward to a real bed, but that night I drifted off quickly.

Then, at some point in the night, I was woken by a sound. Silence ending. The dead of night cut through with a blade of shock and awe.

A scream in the darkness.

FIVE

The scream seemed to be from another world at first. One that was blurred and distorted, dreamlike, an illusion of reality. I was convinced at first that I was the only one who had heard it, but when it happened again, I felt Alexandra shift beside me and speak softly into the night.

"What was that?"

I almost asked if she'd heard it too, but instead, I heard noise from one of the other tents. Between the screams, the silence was suffocating. Punctuated with heavier breathing from Alexandra lying next to me as we worked out what to do.

"Was it a person?" I said, whispering, though by now, everyone would have heard the noise. "What was it?"

My eyes were becoming accustomed to the darkness just as Alexandra picked up her phone and switched the flashlight on. The light illuminated us, and she opened her mouth to answer as another piercing screech destroyed the silence. Familiarity stung me.

"It's Stuart," I heard myself saying, but I was already scrambling out of the tent, the jeans I'd left crumpled up at the entrance to the tent halfway up my legs as I crashed out of it onto my knees. I struggled to stand up, as the others emerged from their tents around me. I was only faintly aware of them as I started running toward where I'd heard Stuart's scream.

It was in the woods behind our campground. I didn't think; there wasn't a conscious thought about what I was doing. I simply took off in that direction, ignoring the protests from my legs as I hurtled into the woodland. Somewhere at the back of my mind, I was glad of the socks I'd left on my feet to ward off the cold. My jeans were over the long boxer shorts I'd worn to sleep, but I was shirtless as I scraped my body against branches sticking out in the darkness.

My mind became a mess of thoughts within seconds. It began as broken images of Stuart in danger. Trapped. Lost in the darkness. Then, panic gripped me in a vise of terror and wouldn't let go.

Stuart's screams for help had been filled with one thing. Fear.

Behind me I could hear voices, but it was my own that took precedent as I shouted Stuart's name. I had been in the woods for less than a minute, yet it already felt like hours had passed. My body screeched with adrenaline, eyes desperately trying to become accustomed to the dark around me.

"Stuart!"

Another yell came back at me, and I switched direction and continued running. My own breathing, hard and heavy, echoed as I waded in farther, the woods becoming thicker and more dense.

Another cry of alarm was only yards away, and I raced up what was an incline in the trees. My feet scrambled for purchase as I fell forward, my hands feeling the soil underneath them. I brushed aside leaves and twigs. Kept moving upward as the top came into sight.

Below me was a clearing in the darkness. I could only see shapes in the shadows as the black of night enveloped me.

"Help," Stuart cried, and I stood still.

I always felt as if fear would be an ice-cold feeling. It would run through my veins and freeze me in place. Real fear, that is. The type you feel when you hear a noise in an empty house at night. Or a loved one goes missing. I had never considered myself brave or courageous. I always suspected I would turn to stone and become a useless block of that cold, frozen fear.

Now, instead of ice, I felt my temperature rise, my mind begin to almost clear, and some primal instinct take over.

I heard myself shout, but it was disconnected from me. As if it were someone else's voice, simply using me as a vessel.

It broke the spell, and I moved toward them.

And that's what it was, I realized suddenly.

Them.

Stuart wasn't alone.

I heard bodies crashing into each other. Shouts and screams, cascading down as they bounced off surrounding trees. All of it building and building to a wall of noise.

At first, I thought it was Chris pinning Stuart to the ground, but then I caught a putrid smell—unfamiliar and strange—emanating from one of the men and it broke the spell.

It was a stranger.

It was someone I didn't know.

He was hurting my friend.

I piled in, dragging the stranger from Stuart and flapping wildly with clenched fists.

There was more noise from beside me, then the familiar scent of the expensive aftershave Chris wore. It was still on his skin, lingering hours after he'd applied it. I felt comforted by the smell as it assailed and embraced me.

I no longer felt alone in the darkness.

Then, the world seemed to shift and reality came through

the fog I had been moving in. The darkness was punctuated by light from above, and I could hear Alexandra's voice. She was holding her cell phone up, flashlight shining from it. Another light appeared from a similar source, but I couldn't see who was holding it.

"No…"

I turned toward her, wondering why she disappeared almost instantly, replaced by a carpet of stars.

The sky was above me and my ears were ringing. The gentle thud of pain became a crescendo as the back of my head seemed to balloon in size.

There was a second when I didn't think I could move again, then something took over me. I knew there was danger in those woods. Right now. In that clearing. Something was trying to hurt us, and I couldn't let that happen.

I moved groggily to my feet and grabbed at someone for purchase. That smell still surrounded us, the rotting decaying scent that filled my nostrils and cleared my head.

"Matt—"

I heard Chris grunt my name and moved toward him. The lights from a phone were shining from above us, moving around as if we were in a violent disco. I could see a figure, large and imposing, gnarling and snarling as he gripped Chris from behind. Something else in its hand.

It was large. My first thought was that there was something wrong with his hand. Then I realized what it was.

It's a machete. He's trying to kill us all.

At their feet, Stuart had his head in his hands, swearing and breathing heavily.

I didn't think.

I had never been a fighter. One or two confrontations over

the years that were difficult to avoid. Most ended the same way. A dull thud of closed fist on jaw, usually partially blocked. Then, it was simply rolling around on the floor until someone broke us apart.

This was different.

This was about survival.

Someone was attacking my friends, and I needed to save them.

There was something hard on the ground beside me, and I grabbed it. A rock, smaller than a paving stone, heavy enough to do damage but not enough that I couldn't pick it up and raise it over my head.

I hit the attacker in the middle of his back. He let out a cry and collapsed to the ground with an exhalation of air. I heard another noise of metal striking stone. I dropped the rock next to him, then it all became a blur again.

There was noise. I heard Alexandra's voice beside me suddenly. Nicola's breathing. Michelle's crying. We were all together.

I don't know who did what to the man. My feet were hurting, meaning, at some point, I kicked him, but it was a mess of action and violence.

Bodies crashing together. Grunts of effort, of pain, of fear.

At once, they all coalesced until they became a blur of nothingness.

Then, there was only silence that seemed to last forever. No sounds, no breathing, nothing. Just a blanket of sudden calm and stillness.

The moonlight above us dipped behind clouds, as if it knew something dark had occurred and it needed to react. The sky was a little less dark, even as the moon disappeared.

Red sky at night, shepherd's delight.

Red sky in the morning...

I looked around, avoiding anyone's eyes. We were standing near a luscious green hill of some sort. Trees in autumn bloom surrounded us, no houses or roads in view. I realized I'd been there before. Earlier in the day, a couple of hours after sunrise, nursing a hangover and hoping I could walk it off before starting over again. I had stood at the top alone, and it had been almost as if I could see the entire world laid out before me. The palettes of greens and browns and oranges. The blue sky above me had seemed to stretch on forever.

No clouds at that point. A dull sun overhead, not overly impactful, not blaring or searing.

No darkness.

No death.

I could hear voices growing as panic began to set in. The silence was broken, but my mind tried to refuse to hear it. An arm went around my shoulders. Tried to pull me back, but I wanted to see what we had done.

I *needed* to see.

The sound of running, shouts flying in two different directions. Arguments breaking out. Cries and recriminations. Tears and anger.

I barely heard them all.

It was as if I were alone there.

I could no longer feel the hands pulling me back. It was only a few feet away from me now, and I couldn't stop myself.

The body made me pause. The blood on his face. Pooling around him as it seeped—no, *gushed* is the right word—out of him.

I imagined a panicked look on his face as I reached out to him.

His pain. His anguish.

His silent plea for help.

Those things were created in my mind, as he remained lifeless.

The dirt and soil on his face, mixing brown and red together. The angled features of someone for whom this was his kingdom. We had disturbed him in his natural habitat and yet he was the one dead. Not us.

A man. That's all he was. That's all that was left behind in a broken shell of a body. I couldn't think clearly, my mind a muddle of voices and noise. One single thought rolling and rolling around my head until it made me feel nauseated.

We had killed him.

We had killed him.

We had killed him.

SIX

Silence.

Not even breathing. We had all seemed to collectively hold our breaths for the past minute. Or ten. Or twenty. I wasn't sure how long we were standing there. With every passing second, it felt as if a lifetime were going by.

Then, something else growing among us.

The weight of understanding of what we had done. It became more real, the longer we were standing there in the quiet.

Someone spoke first, but I don't know who it was. I don't know if it was me. I heard the words, but it was as if they came through a thick fog of chaos.

"What have we done?"

It was the catalyst for the world to come back to life. I could hear sounds again. Choked sobs, heavy breathing, whispers. They all came into focus finally, and the first feeling I had was that I wasn't alone.

That we had all done it.

"Is he...?"

It was Alexandra, and my stomach fell the last few inches to the ground at the fear I heard in her voice. I turned in her direction, but I couldn't see her. The sky was lightening by the second, but my surroundings were still blurry.

I was crying. Tears were filling my eyes, and I couldn't control them. I felt cold, shivering against an unseen wind, even as sweat cascaded down from my forehead and mixed with the tears on my cheeks.

"What did you do?" It was Nicola's voice. No fear there. It was anger instead.

I was faintly aware of Stuart rising to his feet, a hand on my arm. A weight that was there and then gone in an instant. I looked back at the ground. At the man lying prone and not breathing.

"He was going to kill me," Stuart said, spitting his words in her direction. That was when the shouting began.

Nicola was suddenly upon us, words escaping her mouth, accusations and vocal blows flowing. "This is your fault. You've done this. What were you even doing out here? I always knew you'd ruin our lives. You couldn't just be normal, could you? Couldn't just let us be. We wouldn't be here if it wasn't for you. I didn't want to come. Chris didn't either—but that wasn't good enough for you. You made us come here, and now look what you've turned us into."

"I'm sorry... I didn't mean for this to happen."

I listened as it continued—Nicola's voice bouncing around the trees and settling over us all. I was confused by her lie about it being Stuart's idea to be there, but it was gone in another second of chaos. I wiped a sleeve across my face and moved slowly away and toward Alexandra. I wanted...needed her to see me.

Michelle was kneeling on the ground, arms wrapped around her body, rocking back and forth. She was muttering to herself, saying words I didn't understand.

"We have to stop this," Chris said, as I began to see a little clearer now. "We need to do something."

"Like what?" Stuart replied, almost laughing as he spoke. "It's a bit late to do anything, isn't it? He's dead. What can we do?"

"Call for an ambulance?"

"It's too late for that," Stuart said, rubbing at the back of his head. He looked at the palm of his hand when he took it away and then rubbed it down his leg. "It's over. It's all over."

"What happened?" Alexandra said before I could reach her. She walked past me as if I weren't there and moved toward Stuart and Chris. "Why was he attacking you?"

Stuart looked away and wiped his hands on the front of the shirt he was wearing. Looked at Chris and shrugged. "I came out to go for a piss, that's all. Then I just felt someone on my back. I thought it was one of them two trying to scare me, but the smell of him...I knew it wasn't Chris or Matt. It's all a blur after that. I just remember him on top of me, trying to wrap his hands around my throat, punching me in the head, so I shouted for help. Tried to stay alive. He cut me a few times...then you were all here."

"Who is he?"

"How am I supposed to know? Some freak in the forest who kills people, just going for a slash. That's my best bet."

"He wouldn't just attack you for no reason," Alexandra said, moving away from us now. "It doesn't make any sense."

"We should call someone," Chris said quietly, rubbing one arm as if to warm himself up. "They can come and help us. I'm sure they'll understand..."

"No," I said, speaking for the first time. I wasn't even sure I'd actually spoken out loud, but the way everyone turned to look at me suggested I had. I shook my head, thinking of everything that would follow. "Look at us. There's six of us and only one of him. Are they really going to believe what we say? We killed him—"

"We just tell them the truth," Chris said, coming up to me and placing his hands on my upper arms. He was shaking. "He attacked us, and we were defending ourselves, that's all. It was dark, and he was trying to kill Stuart."

"Chris, I hit him..."

"We all did. This wasn't just you." He picked up the blade the man had been holding and held it up to us all. "Look what he had. A bloody machete. He was going to kill Stuart. Me. You. We were just defending ourselves."

"It doesn't matter," I said, hearing my own voice echoing back from the trees around us.

The shout was loud enough to shock even Michelle into silence. She continued rocking back and forth, but she was no longer whispering to herself.

"All they will see is a bunch of people, alcohol in their system, drugs in their tent. That's all they'll need. We'll be screwed. Three on one. No, *six* on one. That's what they'll say. There's nothing to say that machete isn't ours. It'll have our DNA on it."

I wasn't sure if that was true, but it felt like it would be. The drugs were the main thing. It was only a bit of weed, but that wouldn't matter. I didn't smoke myself, but Stuart's eyes began to widen as soon as I mentioned it.

"What do we do then?"

"We do nothing," I said, wondering where this was coming from. I wasn't sure myself. This sudden conviction not to do the right thing. The normal thing. To call someone to help us. Yet I knew what this would look like. What it would mean for us all. It would become something we were synonymous with forever. We would never be allowed to forget what we'd done.

No one would believe us.

"There's no reason for anyone to suspect us," I continued as I became more convinced I was right. "These woods are massive. Our camp is close by, but that doesn't matter. There's no reason we have for being here."

"What if someone saw us all coming out here?" Stuart said, but I could see I already had him on my side. He wasn't saying no.

"It's four in the morning. It's pitch-black. No one can say anything for certain. We could just move him farther in. Make it look like some kind of accident."

"At the bottom of a tree or something," Nicola said, walking over to us now. Her voice was calmer, but I could see her eyes were dancing wildly. A sheen of sweat on her forehead. "Things like that happen all the time."

"It's not just a head wound," Chris said, moving his arm toward Nicola's shoulders, then seemingly deciding against it. "I had my...arm around his neck. Stuart...Stuart was punching him in his chest. There'll be bruises."

I risked another look at the man on the ground, seeing him properly for the first time. The color of his skin was like none I'd ever seen before. A mixed palette of blues, grays, and whites. I didn't check, but I thought about the marks on his neck—an autopsy that would maybe show he'd been asphyxiated. As well as a bunch of skull fractures, unexplained bruising, and who knows what else.

"I don't know what else we can do," I said, choking on the last word as more of the real world snuck into my consciousness. Adrenaline was slipping away from me now. "We can't just leave him to be found. We can't tell anyone."

"We bury him," Stuart said, staring at the lifeless body at our feet. "That's the answer. By the time anyone finds him, we'll be long gone. No one will ever know."

"Are we seriously talking about this?" Chris ran a hand through his hair and I could see blood drying on his knuckles. "There's no coming back from it if we bury him."

"What do you suggest," Stuart said, closing the distance between him and Chris. He was inches from his face, his voice more threatening than I'd ever heard it. "Do you want people out there thinking you're a murderer? Is that what you want? Everyone at your job, in your family, all judging you? Wondering if you killed a man in cold blood, because that's what they'll do. They'll never believe that six people came into these woods and defended themselves from a stranger. It'll be six people, drunk and high, killed someone because they wanted to. It's as simple as that."

I looked around the clearing, my heart threatening to beat its way out of my chest and try to make a bid for freedom. I wanted to be anywhere else. Not having to make these decisions. Already, I could feel myself changing. As if something was crawling from the tips of my fingers, up my arms, and into my chest. A darkness. An evil.

We should be calling someone. We needed help.

I spoke, sealing the deal we were going to make.

"We're going to need a shovel."

SEVEN

S tuart went off in search of something to use. So we could dig. Nicola told me the time was four thirty, and I was still unsure whether this entire thing was real or a lucid nightmare of some sort. I kept pinching myself to check, but it didn't seem to do anything but give me a dull pain for a second or two.

"We need to make sure he doesn't have anything on him."

I turned to Chris, who was becoming more ashen-faced by the second. His voice was shaking and quiet. "What do you mean?"

"What if he was watching us?" Chris replied, looking at me and then averting his eyes. "If he was after Stuart or one of the girls...or us, even? If he's ever found, they'll come looking for us."

I thought it over and wondered if there was any reason I could give for not rifling through a dead man's pockets. Nothing seemed worse than what we'd already done, so I turned my back and said, "Go ahead."

I couldn't touch him. Not then.

A breeze rippled through the trees, the sound like whispers of the dead. I wasn't religious, but I had the feeling of being watched and judged. By all those who knew us. My grandparents, great uncles and aunts, my dad. All gone. Now, they could be sitting atop some cloud, looking down on what they had created and what I had done.

My eyes closed to it all. The feelings, the thoughts, the guilt that was already rising to the surface. I wanted to wake up and see it was all a dream.

When I opened them again, nothing had changed. Alexandra was still pacing around the clearing. Nicola had gone with Stuart, leaving Michelle still on the ground, arms wrapped around her legs, still rocking slightly. She was the tallest of the three women, but she seemed diminished in size. Her carefully styled bob haircut was now wild.

I approached and laid a hand on her shoulder. She flinched at the touch and didn't look up at me. I could feel cold skin and bone through the thin T-shirt she was wearing. "Michelle…"

"Leave me alone. Please."

I moved away, hands palm out and in the air. Walked back over to where Chris was kneeling over the body but stopped a few feet away. "Anything?"

"Only a couple of weird things. No phone or anything like that. A fishing thing—a bait hook, is it called? A lighter. And some birthday candles. Look."

I risked another step closer and saw what he had in his hands. "Weird," I said, wondering why anyone would be walking around the woods with candles in their pockets. A spark of memory flashed in my mind but disappeared before I had the chance to consider it more.

"Nothing to say why he's here or where he's come from?"

Chris shook his head and got to his feet. Brushed down his trousers and then wiped his hands against the black T-shirt he was wearing. "Nothing at all. Maybe it's as Stuart said—he was just out here looking to hurt someone and Stuart was in the wrong place at the wrong time. If he's from around here, maybe he saw Stuart as a threat to his farm or something. Mistook him for a burglar, I don't know. It's that kind of place. Which means, of course, that they'll have plenty of people to back them that they're good people. That Stuart and the rest of us were drunk, drugged up, and set upon him."

"I don't need to be convinced any more, Chris. I just want to get this over and done with."

"Me too."

"I can't lose everything," I said, then faltered as I tried to speak again. "This is…"

"It's okay, mate. Everything will be okay. I promise. We just have to get through it. Then we can go back to our normal lives."

"Nothing's ever going to feel normal again."

I waited for a response from Chris: a protestation or disagreement. Nothing came. The smell from the dead man seemed less strong now, as if my senses had been heightened earlier and were now returning to normal. It wasn't as bad as before, but I doubted he looked after himself all that well. I wondered if he had a family. Living on some farm in this damn countryside. Waiting for him to return home. Maybe they'd wake up in a few hours and wonder where he was. What had happened to him. He could be a father, a husband, a brother, a son. He was all of those things in my head now. Part of a loving family, who would forever be waiting for him to come home.

Then, I saw the blade on the ground where Chris had left it, and I wondered what kind of man walked around with something like that late at night. Who tried to harm people with it.

I started moving soil away using the machete. It would take me days to make a hole big enough, but I had to do something. The black ground grew blurry, as my eyes filled up again. I blinked the tears away. Alexandra came to stand near me for a time, but stayed silent. I looked up at her at one point, but she turned away from me.

I could feel it all slipping away there and then. Everything that I'd been working toward. Our future. There was no big moment that I could see, simply a soft fading as the seconds and minutes passed in that silent forest.

Sometime later, Stuart and Nicola came through the tree line—Stuart holding what looked like a shovel in one hand. He half explained finding some farm outbuildings, but I was barely listening. I stepped back from the rectangular-shaped marked grave I'd carved into the ground and watched as Stuart wordlessly began to dig.

We took turns. None of us speaking. We all seemed to know that there were no words to say.

I wanted to talk. I wanted to stop this. It seemed like insanity had taken over the group and we weren't thinking clearly. There was some other way out of this, but we weren't seeing it right then. Instead, we were making a decision we couldn't come back from. One I had been at the forefront of, I thought. It would come to define us forever.

Maybe that was only fair.

Even in self-defense, we'd ended another person's life. There was never going to be a way out.

The only person who didn't watch as we moved the body into the grave was Michelle. She was still sitting in the same position. It seemed we had collectively decided to ignore her. No one tried to comfort her again, once she'd warned me off. Instead, we moved the soil and mud back over the body and watched it disappear.

"We can never talk about this," Stuart said when it was

over. When all that remained was a mound of earth that had been disturbed but would soon return to nature. "We can never tell anyone what happened. No one will ever understand what we've done."

"How do we ignore what happened here?"

Stuart turned to me, and I expected to see a flash of anger in his eyes. Instead, they were filmy and pleading. "We don't. We can't. We...we just have to try to get on with our lives, or someone will know. Matt, we didn't have any choice. It was do what we did or someone was digging a hole for us. That's all it comes down to in the end. Kill or be killed. It's not our fault we were put in this position."

"Not all of our fault..."

"I didn't do anything wrong, Nicola," Stuart snapped, turning on her. There was anger there in his eyes now. "I didn't ask to be attacked. I didn't ask to be almost killed. Would you rather he killed me than the other way around?"

Nicola stared him out as Stuart waited for an answer that was never going to come. I walked across and stood in between them.

"This isn't going to help anything," I said, as Nicola moved away finally and laid a hand on Chris's arm. He reached across his body and held onto it. "We can't turn on each other now. Stuart is right. This ends here, now, tonight. We don't talk about it. We don't tell anyone. We did what we had to do—what anyone else would have done in the same position. I don't know who he was, but it doesn't matter. He wanted to hurt us. That's enough for me. We all have to agree on this and anything moving forward. All six of us. No one does anything without the say so of everyone involved. That's the only fair way of doing this."

"A pact," Chris said quietly, looking at the mound of earth.

"Yes," I replied, my voice stronger than it had been in the previous hour. Wishing I were anywhere else at that moment than there. "We're in this together."

They all soundlessly agreed.

"We have to go home. Act as normal as we can."

I knew it wasn't going to be as easy as that. We would all carry the weight of what we had done forever. That was the type of people we were. We didn't get into trouble; we didn't have arguments with strangers. We kept ourselves to ourselves. The only thing I knew about the police and law came from watching television dramas.

We didn't know that world. Now, we were forever going to be connected with it.

I also didn't believe a word I'd said. Or Stuart's words, or Chris's. We had done wrong. And we would be judged for it. Not by some higher power, but by ourselves.

There was no way back.

I looked around the group as they stared at the ground. Nicola was whispering something to herself that sounded like the Lord's Prayer. Stuart fiddled with the hem of his T-shirt and I could see the marks on his arms. They would need to be cleaned up.

My eyes narrowed, ignoring the broken form of Michelle, still kneeling. Twisted on the spot, looking all around us.

"Where's Alexandra gone?" I said, but I was already moving as I said the words.

EIGHT

I was running, not thinking about where I was going or what I was doing. Not the movement, the direction, the course. It was Alexandra's face in the darkness that was running through my mind as I drove my body through the woodland. I could feel the pain from the rocks and undergrowth as they passed beneath my socked feet, but it was dull and easily ignored.

"Alexandra!"

Breathless as I jogged through the trees, taking turns and following paths that I couldn't see. I was running in circles without knowing. Over and over, I called her name.

"Alexandra?"

I was gasping for breath as the world closed in around me. I had no sense of direction, and all I could see were trees and bushes and soil and blood.

There was a sound from behind me, and my name being shouted. It was Stuart, trying to find me, trying to find Alexandra. I kept moving, slowing down and scanning my surroundings. The clearing where we had...we had done what we had done was over to my right-hand side. I moved forward and tried to think clearly.

Then, I heard her voice.

Quiet and scared. Filled with fear. Not far away at all. I covered the distance in seconds, brushing aside branches that flicked back and scratched my face. I squinted my eyes and slid down an embankment I didn't see coming.

I almost crashed into her.

It wasn't as large a clearing as the one from before, but smaller. It was completely closed in, flat ground covered in brown decaying leaves and broken twigs. They crunched under my hands as I got to my feet and grabbed Alexandra, who was facing away from me.

"Are you…"

I didn't get the chance to finish my sentence as she cut it off with a choked sob. I came to her side and followed where her eyes were transfixed on the ground.

The first thing I saw was the candle. Housed in a metal storm lantern. Burning. It was red. Blood red.

Like the blood on the young man Alexandra was standing over.

My first thought was that Alexandra had done this—that she'd run into someone else and managed to hurt them before they hurt her. Then, I realized that the person on the ground wasn't making any sound. Wasn't breathing.

Another death.

I staggered backward as I saw the scene properly for the first time.

The red candle, bleeding light from within its confined space.

The young man must have been around nineteen or twenty years old. Short blond hair that was dirtied by the mud underneath the head. His face turned away slightly, mouth open in one final exhalation. A gouge in his face that ran down from his temple. One that ran along the jawline.

I couldn't see the other side to see if there was a matching wound there.

There were other injuries.

Too many.

"Oh no…" I heard myself say, then bent over as my stomach contents threatened to release themselves. My throat burned, but nothing came out. My hands were on my knees as my legs grew weaker.

I wanted to collapse there. To roll up into the fetal position and never move again.

When I closed my eyes, I could still see it. The body. What had been done to it.

Then, I remembered Alexandra and forced myself to stand. I couldn't leave her there alone.

"Come on," I said to her as I placed an arm around her and tried to pull her away. "We can't stay here."

"Look at him," she whispered in reply. Her eyes were transfixed on the body. The sky was becoming lighter by the second, the color of it matching the candle burning on the ground. "We can't just leave him."

"He's gone," I tried, but I knew it was pointless trying to pretend we could just walk away. I could see the music festival wristband on the young lad's arm. Frayed at the edges. Spotted with blood. "There's nothing we can do for him now."

From behind us, the trees began to move and Stuart emerged into the small clearing.

"What the hell…"

I turned to look at him and held one hand up. "Alex found him like this. What is this, Stuart?"

Stuart hesitated, then stuttered out a reply. "How am I supposed to know?"

"A guy attacks you in the woods, then we find some lad dead only a few yards away? Did you know about this?"

"I was near here," Stuart replied, indicating the invisible woodland behind him. "Maybe I heard something...I don't know. I don't remember properly now. He was on me pretty quickly, and then I was just fighting for my life, or have you forgotten about that? Do you think he...did I..."

"You interrupted something," I finished for him. I released Alexandra from my grip, walking toward Stuart. "That's why he went after you."

There was more movement, and Chris and Nicola joined us, standing at the top of the embankment I'd fallen down. I spoke before they had the chance to. Both of them had clasped their hands to their mouths as they saw what was there. "This is why he went after Stuart."

"The man..."

"Yes," I said, facing Chris now. I looked at the three in turn before glancing back at Alexandra. She was still staring at the young lad on the ground "We need to call someone now. We can't deal with this on our own. My plan is no good."

"No," Stuart said, shaking his head. His hands were balled into fists now. "You were right. This won't just go away."

"We'll be heroes," Chris said quietly, but I didn't see any conviction in the statement. "We tried to save someone from... whatever this is. So what if he died?"

"You know what will happen," Stuart replied quickly, turning to Chris and unfurling his fists. The muscles straining at the arms of his T-shirt began to relax. He flicked a lock of blond hair away from his forehead, then moved his hand onto Chris's shoulder. "They'll find cracks in our stories. There'll be questions we can't answer. It won't take long for them to work out the truth. We killed him without knowing what he was doing out here. And then buried him. Did you forget that part?

Do you not think they'll notice that he's been six feet under the earth? They will be able to tell that we tried to cover it up. Then it's even worse."

"This is too much," Alexandra said, then repeated it again louder this time. "We can't just walk away from him. From all of this. We've got to tell someone."

"Alex…"

"No, Stuart." Her voice was a shout now. Loud in the quiet woods. I looked around, suddenly nervous that someone would hear us finally and discover us all standing around another dead body. "We can't, don't you see? We have to do something."

"I want to go home," Chris said, and he sounded like the boy I had first met in high school. Eleven years old. Quiet and scared. Not the thirty-odd-year-old I knew now. He was twenty years younger and wanted it all to be over. To go back to a normal that would never exist again. "We shouldn't even be here."

"Well, we wouldn't be if it weren't for you," Stuart spat out, disgust filling his features now. "I'm not going to let this ruin me. I have a life. So do all of you. What about your family? About work? This will ruin us all forever. Do you think they're gonna enjoy having us splashed all over the newspapers. And what about the internet? Social media will crucify us."

"We didn't do anything wrong," I said, pleading now. Every word was a stab at the heart of my life and all it was. "We just have to tell the truth. That's all."

"It won't matter. You think everyone will just believe we interrupted a killer and then made sure he couldn't do it again?" Stuart paused, breathed in deeply, as if to calm himself. "How do we explain that we buried him? That we were worried he was going to rise from the dead and get us before they came? It's ridiculous. They'll wonder why we're all here. Why we didn't call the police straightaway. That man back there...it's already over an hour since he died. Maybe longer. Even if we dug him up, cleaned him up, then put him near this body, they'll still know. They'll find his blood, our blood, everywhere. There isn't a story we can make fit with what we've already done. With every passing second, we look more and more guilty. They'll find witnesses. They'll find out the truth."

I opened my mouth to argue further, but I didn't have any words to say. I couldn't believe what we were doing. The relative calmness as we stood near two dead bodies. One we were responsible for, the other too late to save.

The world felt like a nightmare. Lucid and tangible, but not real. It couldn't be. This wasn't happening. Nothing made sense, yet when I closed my eyes and then opened them again, I was still in the woods.

"We have to get out of here," Nicola said finally, breaking the silence. "I'm not going to have my life changed because of what you've done. Nor is Chris. We're leaving and I'm not going to talk about this again."

"Nicola..."

"No, Alexandra," Nicola said, folding her arms across her chest. Her face was reddening and her nostrils flared with anger. Her face had become even more angular and pointed somehow. "Don't you get it? It won't be just them; it'll be all of us. I've worked too long and too hard for something like this to ruin it. I won't have it. Do you want your life turned upside down? Everything ends if we tell someone. We were too late to save this kid, but we're not too late to save ourselves. He's dead. Stuart obviously interrupted his killer and now he's dead too. That's all there is to it. We can't change what's happened, but we can change what happens next. I'm not going to let you all make a bad decision. It's as simple as that."

We let her words fall over us, and I could see that she was right. This was over, unless we made things worse.

Each of us, in turn, seemed to make the same decision. It was Stuart who spoke first.

"What do we do with him now? Do we bury him as well?"

I shook my head. "We leave him to be discovered."

"You know what this is, don't you?"

I turned to see Michelle standing in between two trees, almost masked by overhanging branches. She was dead-eyed, staring at the body on the ground. She stretched out a hand and pointed toward the body. Then above it, at the candle. "It's him."

"Who?" Stuart said, but Michelle ignored him as she came closer and stood over the body.

"They've been saying for months that they weren't connected."

"What are you talking about, Michelle?" Chris said quietly, as he released himself from Nicola and moved to Michelle's side. "You're not making any sense. Maybe you should go back…"

"No, don't you see?" Michelle replied sharply, making Chris take a step backward. "There was a documentary about it last year. It's been all over the internet since then, but the police keep saying it's not real. This proves it is. Look at it."

"Look at what?" I tried, glancing at the others, but they were looking anywhere but at the body or Michelle now. "Tell us what's going on."

"The candle. It's what he leaves in all of their houses."

"Who does?"

Michelle placed her hands on her hips and nodded her head. "It's him. We killed the Candle Man."

NINE

"What are you talking about?" Nicola said, looking at Michelle with an air of exasperation.

"It's this serial killer, who has been murdering people for years."

"Michelle, this isn't the time for conspiracy theories," Stuart said, folding his arms in frustration. "It's not the time."

"What is it time for then? Time to kill someone else?"

Stuart opened his mouth to shout back at her, but thought better of it. I moved closer to Michelle. "Talk to us."

"I can't…"

"I saw that thing on TV," Alexandra said, not looking at any of us. "There's all these missing people that have never been found. There's this theory that a serial killer killed them, going back decades. There's that documentary Michelle talked about and the podcast thing that was big for a while. Well, until they moved onto another urban myth. They reckon some of them are connected by something they found after they went missing."

"Red candles," Michelle said, pointing at the one on the ground again. "This means it's real. That…man. He was the Candle Man."

"I said this before," Stuart said, rolling his eyes at Michelle. "It's all been debunked. Some of the people reported as missing and dead are actually alive and well. They've turned up a few days later and that hasn't been reported."

"Yeah, but look at this." Michelle gestured toward the body and the candle still burning away at its head. "You think this is normal? It makes more sense than you disturbing someone in the middle of the woods while having a pee, then getting attacked with a machete for your troubles, doesn't it?"

"It does make sense," I said, a wave of nausea washing over me. It was beginning to fall into place.

We had killed a serial killer. Interrupted him while he was offing another of his victims and stopped him in his tracks. I had a sudden urge to giggle. To laugh myself silly with the ridiculousness of it all. Maybe that would make me wake up. Instead, I pinched the skin under my left bicep and again felt only a dull pain.

Still awake.

"I'm only telling you what I know," Michelle replied, turning her back on them all and walking back into the woods. I considered going after her, but thought she wanted to be alone.

"You think this could be..."

"A serial killer's victim?" I finished the thought for Chris. "I don't know. We're not exactly thinking straight, are we? It makes a weird kind of sense though, don't you think?"

"Maybe."

I forced myself to look again at the boy on the ground. Very late teens, I guessed. And when I let my eyes wander around the entire scene, it did look ritualistic. The way the candle was positioned, the marks made on the body.

"I think she's right," I heard myself say, then turned away from them and faced the trees for a few seconds. When I turned back, Alexandra was standing in the center of the group.

"It would make sense," she said, her voice cold and devoid of emotion. "That documentary might have been *A Current Affair* special, but there were a lot of coincidences in it. The candles being one of them. They had a couple of police spokespeople on it though, who weren't having any of it. But what if this is it?"

"Or a copycat?" I asked, knowing no one could give me an actual answer. We didn't really know what we were talking about. I suppressed the urge to scream, swallowed it down instead. When I continued, I was surprised at how calm my voice sounded. "Where were the missing people from?"

"All over the place," Alexandra replied, turning her head away from me slightly. I realized then that she hadn't made eye contact with me since we had buried the man. I tried now, but she turned away from me. "Even a couple up by us in Merseyside. Cumbria, Yorkshire, down south. Around here, probably."

"We can't do anything now," Stuart said finally, standing up and brushing his hands down his T-shirt. "And I'm not digging another grave. None of us have touched him, have we?"

I shook my head, looking around at the others doing the same.

"It'll be like we've never been here. He won't be found for a while. By that time, they won't be thinking of digging around the place. They won't put the two things together. And even if they do, we're still in the clear. As long as none of us talks about what we did here tonight."

"We should move the kid," I said finally, vocalizing a thought that was running through my mind. I went with it. "Think about it."

"Okay. I thought about it. Not a chance."

I gritted my teeth and tried not to rise to Stuart's signature sarcasm. The type that only surfaced when he was hungover or coming down from whatever recreational drug he'd taken the night before. Even in his thirties, he hadn't changed. "Think again. Look, we're not that far away from the other body. If they search the area—which they will—they'll see the disturbed ground through those trees and wonder what it is. They'll dig it up and find him. Then what do we do? We need to put him farther away."

Stuart sighed and put his hands on his hips. He opened his mouth to protest, but Chris shushed him. "Matt's right."

"I know," Stuart said, seemingly coming to terms with what we were going to have to do.

We had already learned where the phrase *dead weight* came from.

This time it was more difficult.

We wrapped him in a spare sleeping bag that I retrieved from my car, that I'd packed in case one of the group had needed it. Brand new in the packaging, so none of our DNA would be inside, we guessed. The first bit of luck we'd had.

Then, as daylight began to creep overhead, we moved him. Stumbling through the woods, sweating and struggling, we carried the dead boy to the other side of the woods.

Finally, we reached it, and we were able to lay him down again. Stuart removed the sleeping bag carefully, then walked away.

I stood over the teenager for a few seconds before I felt Chris's hand on my shoulder. Heard him whisper my name, then we moved back the way we had come.

"Do you think anyone saw us?" I said, surprised I could still talk. My whole body screamed with exhaustion. "I didn't look around us. Anyone could have been in—"

"No one saw us," Alexandra replied, catching up and then passing us in an instant. "I was watching the whole time."

I wanted to say something else. To run alongside her and be of comfort. I simply didn't know what I would say.

She knew what we had all done. What we all were now.

I didn't know if there was a way back from that.

———

I tried talking to Alexandra as we started the drive back home, but she was staring out of the passenger window at the passing scenery. On the single-lane road behind my car, Chris and Nicola were probably having the same trouble. I tried to see in the rearview mirror if they were talking, but they were too far back.

Michelle and Stuart had seemingly forgotten about the argument they'd had before, sitting together in my back seat. Michelle was staring ahead, her eyes tired and unmoving. Stuart had passed out as soon as I'd started driving.

"We had to do it," I said, breaking the silence in the car. I couldn't seem to bear it for any period of time now. "We had no choice."

"Who are you trying to convince, us or yourself?" Alexandra replied, not even willing to turn to me when she spoke. I could hear it in her voice even then. She had been the last holdout. She didn't want to leave the woods behind. In some way, I guessed none of us ever would, but I couldn't see any other choices than the ones we made.

"He'll be found," I tried again, thinking again of the young boy Alexandra had found a few yards from the man we'd killed. "It probably won't take that long at all. There was nothing else we could have done for him. You know that. No one will ever know we were there."

"We will know," she said, her voice flat and dry. "And isn't that enough?"

I didn't have any answer for that, so kept my mouth shut and tried to concentrate on the road ahead. Suppressed a yawn as tiredness washed over me.

I wondered if I'd ever sleep again. Whether I would forever see the battered face of the man, as we rolled him into an unmarked grave.

A grave only we knew about.

Whether we had done the right thing in moving the young boy, I knew there was nothing else we could have done. Not if we wanted to avoid questions that would have been impossible to answer. It was the right thing to do. That didn't mean Alexandra was wrong. That was the problem. What we had done—to save ourselves—would haunt us for years to come.

Maybe forever.

Something had seemed to pass across her eyes at one point. I wasn't sure what it was, or if I wanted to know.

We had placed him in a sleeping bag, but that didn't mean I was sure we hadn't left behind some evidence. Careful wasn't sure.

Once it was done, we had packed up our tents and left.

I could still feel the dirt under my fingernails, even though I'd washed my hands over and over back at the campground.

"I need to stop," Michelle said, and her voice didn't sound like her own. "I need to get out."

"There'll be a gas station on the highway."

"I need to stop now."

I glanced in the rearview mirror, seeing Michelle staring straight back at me. There was a look in her eyes as if she was daring me to disagree or go against her wishes. I sighed and shook my head. "Hang on."

There was a turnout a hundred yards or so ahead; I pulled

into it and shut off the engine. Michelle was out of the car as soon as it came to a stop. Alexandra didn't move beside me. I stepped out, needing the fresh air to try to keep me awake.

The smell of countryside assaulted me as I stepped out and away from the road. Then, the sound of Michelle's throat evacuating her stomach contents onto the grass only compounded the situation.

Everything was hell.

A good few minutes passed and then I saw Chris slowing down. He pulled over and his car went silent. I raised a hand to acknowledge him, then felt in my pockets for cigarettes that weren't there. I really wished I still smoked at that point. I'd never really missed it, but could think of nothing better right then.

I noticed something else wasn't there.

I opened my car door and rummaged around the front seat, sticking my hand down in the gaps that ran alongside it and silently cursing. Alexandra turned her head slowly to me, her brow furrowed in confusion. "What are you doing?"

"I can't find it," I said, not waiting for a response. I ran round to the trunk, hearing the sound of Chris's car door opening and shutting. His voice asking something, but I wasn't listening. I pulled the trunk open, then began shifting things around. We'd left quickly early that morning, barely packing anything up properly at all. There was a mess of stuff piled up, shoved in without regard or forethought. I began pulling things out and delving into half-filled backpacks and hidden pockets.

"What's going on?"

I ignored Chris and continued filling the turnout with various items from our weekend stay. I pulled out clothes—all of them mixed together, to be sorted at a different time. I didn't wait to see if they were mine or not, simply pulling them all out and going through each individually.

The clothes I had been wearing the previous night were buried in a bag near the bottom. A thought came to me then—if we'd been trying to cover our tracks, we should have burned them out in the woods. Or tried to get rid of them some other way. Maybe one of the large industrial-size bins at the festival. Instead, if we were pulled over now, we'd all have clothes with a stranger's DNA on them. A stranger we had killed.

"Matt, what's going on?"

The trunk was empty now, but it still wasn't there. I turned around, surprised to see Chris standing right behind me. "It's not here."

"What isn't?"

I shook my head and jogged toward the back of his car. "Open the trunk, maybe it got tossed in there."

"Matt, you need to calm down and tell me what's going on."

A car blazed past us doing over sixty, but I was only faintly aware of it. I turned to Chris, and he flinched. I must have looked crazed enough for him to take a step back from me.

"It's my wallet," I said eventually, unable to find it anywhere. "It was in my pocket when… It's not here anymore."

Chris sucked in air past his teeth. "Are you joking?"

"Do I look like I am? It was in the jeans I was wearing when it happened. I just threw them on from last night. My phone was in the tent, but I left my wallet in the back pocket."

"Right, right. Well, we were using those woods for the past three days. It's not like we wouldn't have a good story to tell anyone if it was found."

I shook my head. I realized I was wringing my hands together but couldn't stop. When I spoke, my voice sounded alien to me.

Shaking and on the verge of full panic. "I can't just leave it there. They'll ask questions, and we won't be able to answer them all. We're gonna look guilty as hell and that's the end for us."

I heard a car door open and close. Stuart emerged from the side of the car and joined us at the open trunk. "What's going on?"

I looked at Chris, then at Stuart. "We have to go back."

TEN

It was different in the woods, now that it was daytime. The trees seemed to move more easily, there were no dark shadows or strange noises. Or silences.

The stillness of it was almost offensive to me. As if it hadn't understood what had occurred within its tree-lined walls the night before and adjusted accordingly. It should have changed in some way. Instead, it was sitting there like nothing had happened.

I was slowly losing it. I wasn't sure how long I could hold on, without giving up and waiting for the police to take me away. Calling 911 and telling them everything we had done. I shook the thought away and tried to concentrate.

We parked on the other side of the woods this time. Google Maps had informed us that there was another way in, which saved us trying to wade our way through a festival that was now over. The traffic and witnesses would be easier to avoid.

Stuart came with me. The others stayed behind at the cars. We walked without talking for the first five or ten minutes, silently trudging through, as if we were out for a walk, rather than for what we were actually doing.

Retrieving evidence. That's what they would call it.

It took us half an hour of walking before we found the first clearing. We wordlessly took an area each and began searching.

"What's it look like?" Stuart said quietly, after brushing aside branches and leaves for a few minutes. "I mean what color is it?"

"Black, with the Liverpool Football Club badge embossed on the front."

Stuart chuckled, then stopped almost as quick as he'd begun. "Should have guessed."

I was about to respond in kind—it had always been our go-to way of winding each other up, the Liverpool-versus-Manchester thing—but kept quiet when I remembered everything that had happened in the past twelve hours.

It was difficult to believe it had only been that long. I felt like I had aged at least ten years since the previous day.

Perhaps this was how we would be now. This would be our new normal. None of the laughter and the in-jokes we'd had before. What we'd done collectively would be with us always, hanging over us like a dark cloud. Ready to empty and drench us with our sins.

"We shouldn't have buried him," Stuart said, turning to me as he swiped a foot along the ground, his voice cold and wearied. His unlined face and the dimples in his cheeks that kept him looking young now diminished. Now, there was darkness under his eyes and a weathered look to his skin. "I think that was a mistake."

"I think the whole thing was a bit of a mistake…"

"I know, I know. I just wonder if we acted too quickly. We were all running on adrenaline, fear, exhaustion. That's before we get to the hangovers and shock. We were too ready to believe we wouldn't have been able to get through this. I'm sure they would have realized the truth quickly enough. We should have just called someone. We're going to have to live with this forever now."

"Yeah, we are. But that would have been the case anyway."

"I guess that's our punishment."

I looked over at Stuart for a little longer, then turned back to the ground. There was something in his tone that made me look over at him again, but he was getting farther and farther out of sight.

We were murderers. That was all I could be certain of at that moment. Whether we had murdered a serial killer or some random attacker, I wasn't sure there was much difference. Not for me. I had been responsible for ending someone's life. That was enough for me.

"Maybe it'll be like grief," Stuart said, emerging from the tree line ahead. "You don't get past it—you just learn how to live with it, you know?"

I did. I remembered my dad's funeral and how I'd only gotten through that day with the help of my friends. They had picked me up and brought me back to life. Now, I wasn't sure I wanted to see any of them again.

Alexandra…I hoped she was different.

"I don't know," I said eventually, my eyes scanning the ground, my heart pounding against my chest the closer we got to where we'd buried the dead man. "Grief is something that is done to us. Someone is taken from us and then we're left behind. We did this to ourselves."

"He was going to kill me, Matt," Stuart said, stopping and turning to face me more fully. He folded his arms across his chest, and I could see grazes and the beginning of a bruise on his arm, running from his elbow to his wrist. "I don't know why, but I think we can work that out. Problem is, we'll never know for certain, will we? Because even when they find that young boy, they won't know his killer is underground. Literally. So not only did we kill someone, but we also robbed who knows how many people of seeing any justice for it."

"He won't be able to do it again. Isn't that justice enough?"

Stuart shrugged his shoulders, but it seemed as if it took some effort to do so.

We continued on, searching the entire area we had moved through the night before. I grew increasingly desperate as it became more and more apparent that I wasn't going to find the wallet. I imagined some police dog retrieving it in a slobbering mouth, dropping it at a copper's feet, and them opening it up. Seeing the driver's license, the bank cards, all with my name on them.

I traipsed through the ever-thickening forest, scouring every possible place I could. Stuart was beside me the entire way, but I knew he was thinking the same as me.

"I ran off when Alexandra disappeared," I said, grasping Stuart's shoulder as I almost fell over a fallen log. He winced immediately, and I mumbled an apology before continuing. "Do you remember though? When she went off, I ran after her. I don't know where I went."

"I watched you go, mate," Stuart replied, rubbing his shoulder and looking at me with something approaching pity in his eyes. He knew what I knew. "I've... We've looked everywhere. I know it seemed massive last night, but you were running in circles, Matt. If it was here, we would have found it by now."

"Where is it then?"

We both looked around us as my voice reverberated around the trees and settled above us.

"It's going to be okay," Stuart said, making a calm down motion with his hands. "Can you think of anywhere else it could be?"

I shook my head, but I knew that wasn't true. It wasn't where we'd been camping. Not in the woods, as far as we could tell. I looked up at Stuart and he knew what I was going to say without another word.

"We best hurry up then," Stuart said, biting on his lower lip and shaking his head. "If he hasn't been found yet, it won't be long."

It took us another twenty minutes to make our way to the far end of the woods. I had called Alexandra on the way and told her to move the cars farther afield, given how long it was taking us to come back. She gave me a noncommittal grunt in response, which I hoped was agreement.

I ended the call and took a breath in. I didn't think I'd ever be back there. At that place. My muscles felt weak and tired, exhaustion threatening to take hold at any second. I kept my eyes peeled on the ground as we moved, hoping against hope that I'd spot my wallet on the way there.

As the trees began to open and become more sporadic, a large field opened up. We skirted along the edge of it, as we had done the previous night. We could hear traffic more clearly now, as we came closer to the country roads that bordered the farmland here. They connected to the main roads farther down, finally merging onto the highway. In the daylight, the view was something to behold. We were on a rise, meaning we could see across the field and beyond, green belt land as far as we could see.

I wished I could spend some time appreciating it.

Instead, we slowed as we approached the place we had found the previous night, closer to humanity than nature. Hoping the boy would be found sooner rather than later. Now, I hoped he hadn't been found at all.

In fact, I wanted to go back a few hours and run from the woods entirely.

We reached the thin copse of shorter trees and moved into the clearing where we had left the body. I could still feel the weight of him in my hands. The disgust I felt for disturbing his final resting place. It had felt like a final act of despicability, in a night that had been nothing but that.

We had left him near the edge, hoping he would be noticed by someone passing alongside the road. An early morning jogger or a dog walker maybe. We could hear traffic quite clearly now—through the high bushes that almost blocked out the view from the road. A car went past every twenty seconds or so.

I heard three drive by before I took in what I was seeing.

It was almost midday, I hadn't slept, so I still checked with Stuart first. I looked across at him, but he was seemingly struggling with the same disbelief as me.

"Are you sure we—"

"Yes," Stuart replied before I had the chance to finish the sentence. "I remember the way that tree was positioned over there. The way we came in—the way it all looked six hours ago."

The clearing was empty. No disturbance whatsoever.

The body was gone.

We had left him in that clearing, removing him from the sleeping bag we'd carried for an hour. Laid him on the ground and then left him there. Alone.

And now he wasn't there.

I could feel eyes on us.

I looked around, waiting for the inevitable. I knew what Stuart was saying, even as I stopped listening and the world disappeared around me. It went silent as I blocked out what was happening, closed my eyes and waited. I could almost picture them now: a swarm of police officers, emerging from between trees, from the road, from the bushes. They had known we would return, because my wallet had been found. They would be coming from all angles, trapping us in there, so we had no escape. I scrunched my eyes shut tighter and didn't move as the hand laid itself on my shoulder.

It gripped me harder as it began to shake. I thought of my mum. We barely spoke, but I still loved her enough to think about how she would feel about this. The attention it would bring. She'd had me late in life and was in her seventies now. Dad was gone. I was all she had left and even though we weren't close, she knew where I was.

I remembered joking with her and dad a few months before he died, about how it had taken them so long to find each other that they couldn't really moan about it taking so long for Alexandra and me to settle down with each other. I was just following their lead.

I thought about the aunties and uncles and cousins and extended family. How they would have to face scrutiny from all who knew them and me. Whether they could answer the questions that would fly at them.

Did you know he was a killer?

I would need a lawyer. A good one. I didn't know any other than the one who we had dealt with when buying the house. I doubted they would specialize in both house purchases and murder defenses.

I thought about the questions I couldn't answer. When the hand would slip from my shoulder and slide the handcuffs over my wrists. That would be it.

I wouldn't be free for a long time.

I thought about Alexandra.

I thought about Alexandra.

I thought about Alexandra.

When I opened my eyes—as two hands now lay on my shoulders, moving me back and forth—I could feel the wetness on my cheeks.

The world came back in an instant. Noise returned, smells too.

Stuart was there.

In front of me.

Holding my wallet in one hand as he shook me back and forth. A panicked expression on his face.

"He's gone," he was saying, and I could see the same wetness rolling down his cheeks. "We have to get out of here. Now."

I looked around, expecting the police to be there, but there was nothing to see.

There was nothing.

No body that we had moved. No young man, dead on the ground. Mutilated and discarded. Left here, by us, to be found.

He wasn't there.

Stuart grabbed me again, handing me my wallet, which I placed in my pocket in a daze. "We have to go, Matt."

"Where—"

"I don't know," Stuart said, pulling me away now. I didn't resist. "I don't know."

ONE YEAR LATER

ELEVEN

wanted to be home. Safe, surrounded by the familiar.

I didn't need this. No one ever did. It's all a con, a ruse, a way of extracting cash from your wallet. Money for old rope. That's what I was thinking as I booked the appointment. As I left the house that morning. As I drove the few miles to the place. As I waited in the reception area, with the plastic plants and old magazines. As I knocked on the door and entered the office.

"And how did that make you feel, Matthew?"

It took everything within me not to roll my eyes into the back of my head and around again. The idea that any of this would make the slightest bit of difference to my life was beyond any logic I could recognize.

What life there was.

Yet I knew I couldn't go on without *something*.

"It's Matt," I said, hoping the nice woman sitting across from me wouldn't be able to tell that I didn't want to be there. I don't think I did that very well, given the way she peered at me through thick glasses and wrote on the pad sitting on her lap. "I don't know how it made me feel."

I needed to do this, I kept reminding myself. I wasn't going to get any better if I kept ignoring the problem.

Ah, the problem. Except, you can't blurt that out in this room, can you?

It was the only way. The only thing I could think of that I hadn't tried yet.

Everything else had failed.

I needed to be at home. In my own environment. Where it was safe. I could feel the walls moving toward me when I wasn't looking. The air becoming denser and harder to breathe. Until I focused on the counselor and managed to swallow those thoughts away.

"Why have you come here today, Matt, if not to talk about how you're feeling?"

I sat forward in the chair and crossed my arms. Studied the counselor I had chosen from the list of fifty-odd I had found on Google. Fifty quid a session, just to be asked questions I already knew the answer to.

Overworked, overstressed. Constantly thinking. Lost in my own thoughts too often. Playing catch-up on every conversation.

Living in the past.

"I'm sorry," I said, looking across the room and trying to make sense of the painting on the wall. A smattering of colors on canvas, all bleeding into one giant smudge. The entire room wasn't what I'd expected, really. No couch, for one. I'd imagined a psychiatrist's office from a bad sitcom. A long sofa, ready for me to lie down upon and bare my secrets. An older guy with a beard, itching to ask about my sex life, so he could point to a moment in my childhood that would explain everything. Instead, it could have been any small office, for any kind of use. I was pretty sure an accountant would choose the same soft furnishings.

"Tell me what problem you're having that you came for help with."

I knew then that I wouldn't last. That the money I'd spent

on this first hour would be the first and last amount that would leave my account. This wouldn't work for me.

Nothing would.

"What brought you here today?"

"My car," I replied with a smirk. The woman's face didn't change, as if she'd heard the sarcastic remark a hundred times before. "Sorry."

"Go on," she said, her face still unmoving.

"I've tried everything else," I said, leaning back in the leather chair that probably cost more than the entire contents of my house. "I just can't sleep. My brain won't switch off."

"Well, let's talk about what thoughts are running through your mind."

I stared at the woman. She cocked her head to one side and blinked slowly. I imagined it was a look that was supposed to express genuine interest and concern. Only, she had quite obviously practiced it too often, and it came off as patronizing instead.

"All sorts of things," I said, knowing she would see through the lie in an instant. I glanced at the clock and worked out how long I had left. I shifted in the seat and heard the leather underneath my body moan in response. "I couldn't tell you all of them."

"You can be safe in this room, Matt. I'm not here to judge or make you feel anything other than comfortable enough to share."

Maybe if I told her I was a murderer, she would change her mind. Maybe if I told her that what really kept me awake at night was seeing that man's face in the darkness. Just before the dirt, the soil, the mud was poured over his face.

I could try to pretend it was an accident. Self-defense. Whatever. It wouldn't matter. She would still know I was a murderer.

That I was no better than the man I'd helped to kill.

"I don't know what it is," I said, watching as she made a note to herself again. "I just can't switch off."

"Do you live alone?"

"Yes. I was living with someone for a while, but we broke up almost a year ago."

"A long-term relationship?"

I thought about Alexandra and felt the familiar churning in my stomach. "Not really. I've known her since we were teenagers and went out with each other for a while. Split up when we went to university, but we got back together a few years ago. Took us a while to work out we wanted to be with each other. Took us a very short time to work out it wasn't going to last."

"Was it a mutual decision to break up?"

I thought about the days following that night at the music festival. The long silences, only broken by arguments and crying. Of her walking out of the door, not even looking at me as she left. "It was," I said, wondering if I had tried harder, if maybe she would have stayed. "Of a fashion, I suppose."

"Do you think of her when your mind is running away with itself?"

"Of course," I said with a sigh. This was getting me nowhere. "I think of all kinds of things. I think of things that happened twenty years ago too. I think about work stuff, whether I've remembered to lock the back door, whether I paid the bills that month. All of it. My parents, the rest of my family. A TV show I watched that day. I think about it all."

That was true. I tried to think about anything but the one thing that my mind wouldn't let me forget. That it kept returning to, as if it were on repeat.

The dead man's face.

I stayed silent for a few seconds, considering my words as I always found myself doing now. There was a right answer and a wrong answer to everything. I knew that much. "I haven't been feeling *right* for some time now. I struggle to concentrate, keep focus, that sort of thing."

"And why do you think this is?"

There are never any answers. Only questions. "I don't know," I replied, unfolding my arms and dropping my hands into my lap. "That's why I'm here. To find out how to change things. How to cope. That kind of thing."

"Is there anything in particular you can point to and see as a potential reason for this *feeling* you've been having?"

I had a sudden urge to jump up and shout directly in the counselor's face. Scream at her big blue eyes. Wide-open, searching. I imagined the woman thought they were endearing, interested, but I wasn't buying the act. If I was bored with the conversation, odds were so was she.

I wanted to tell her the truth. That my friends and I had been attacked by a stranger in some woods and killed him in self-defense. That when I try to sleep now, all I see is that stranger's face.

All I feel is the emptiness of the woods. The place where we left the young boy who had been murdered. The victim.

The sight of that empty patch of land where his body should have been.

"Not really," I said finally, tasting the lie as it escaped my mouth. It was bitter and filled with bile. "Work is fine. Busy, which is good as a freelancer. I'm paying my bills on time, without issues, which is more than most people can say. I've got friends. My previous relationship broke down, but it was amicable."

Barely. I was also pushing it by pluralizing the word *friend*.

"What do you work as?"

"Website stuff," I said, wondering if it was worth going into more detail. I couldn't see a reason for it. "Boring for most, but I enjoy it enough. I get to work from home, which is good."

"Is it?"

"Wouldn't you rather work in your pajamas and not have to deal with public transport or traffic?"

She smiled briefly but didn't react otherwise. "Do you ever feel isolated by that?"

It wasn't something I'd thought of before. I wanted to answer negatively instantly, but I stopped myself. Thought about the fact that I could go days without seeing anyone else. I liked it that way now, but was that really what was behind me not sleeping?

No.

I knew why I couldn't sleep. Why I couldn't live with the silence.

"Maybe," I said, and this time the lie didn't taste so bad. "I suppose if you don't see or speak to people all that much... Well, you can get cabin fever stuck in a house on your own for days and days."

"Have you always lived around here?"

My forehead creased as I frowned at the question. "I'm not sure what you mean..."

"I just mean did you grow up in Liverpool?"

"Yeah, I understand, but I'm not sure why you're asking, that's all. Is my accent not that strong or something?"

"Just curious is all," the counselor replied, making a note again. I wanted to see what she'd written.

The question had thrown me off a little. Confused me. I

didn't like that. It made me worry about what I'd said previously. Whether she had been able to read something into the words I'd said, knew them to be lies, and was now trying to trap me.

There was a reason I didn't speak or see people all that much. I was scared of what I might say to them.

"And you've been suffering with these bouts of insomnia for how long?"

"I don't know," I replied, trying to remember a time when I didn't feel this out of sync with real life. Tired and wide-awake simultaneously. "Off and on for years, but the past few months have been pretty steady."

"Sometimes it's the smallest moments—the seemingly insignificant occurrences—that turn out to be the ones which cause the biggest issues. If you want to get to the root of your problem, we need to identify those small moments. Build a picture of who you are, what has happened, and help you back to a normal life. Help get you on the path of who you want to be."

Help me on the path... It took everything within me not to laugh at that point. I contained myself, but I wasn't sure it would have mattered all that much anyway. The counselor was on a roll, looking down at her notes, not even maintaining eye contact.

"We have to identify the reasons that are causing the issues you've been having."

"I'm not sure what issues there could be..."

"Yet here we are. You came here for help. You recognize there is a problem and you want assistance for it."

"I just don't know what to tell you," I replied, and I could hear the harshness of my own tone of voice. "If this is about asking me questions I can't answer, I could have stayed at home and Googled this instead. Wouldn't cost me fifty quid an hour that way."

"You don't feel like you're going to get anything productive from talking about what's happened to lead you to these states of mind? You don't feel like there's an underlying issue which could be causing your long bout of being unable to switch off from your own thoughts? The sense of pressure being on you when it sounds as if you're currently in a stable position?"

I held back for a second and composed myself. I didn't want drugs. I didn't want to tell her the entire truth. I shouldn't have been there at all. There was nothing she could do without a full picture. I chose to blur the picture instead, for no palpable reason. "I think everyone has some problems. That's normal though, isn't it? It's impossible to live your life without experiencing some issues. I just...I don't know. I just don't want to feel this way anymore. Maybe I'm just being a snowflake about it all. I don't think anything like this sort of thing is going to help me suddenly sleep better at night. Maybe I just need some sleeping pills and a hot mug of Ovaltine instead."

"I'm hearing hostility to the process, rather than the thought that maybe you have some issues that can be worked through and maybe I can help you with that."

"Maybe, I don't know."

"You're worried about being truthful," she said, holding my gaze now. "Something is holding you back from being completely open about your thinking. I want to tell you that this is a safe space. You can share what you're worried about, what thoughts are running through your head, without worrying about my reaction. I've heard it all, I promise you."

I shook my head, wondering if she could really handle what it was that I was living with. There was no chance of me telling her anyway, but for a moment I wanted to unburden it all. Just to see the patronizing smile wiped from her face.

I was saved by the vibration of my phone in my pocket, followed by the opening bars of a seventies song my mum used to listen to all the time. The counselor tensed at the sound but didn't say anything as I pulled it out and saw Chris's name on the screen.

"I'm sorry. I've got to go," I said, then stood up and walked out before she had a chance to change my mind.

I would have to find some other way.

1992

I was used to being the smallest kid in the class, but that fact only seemed to be compounded by high school. There, I was the smallest kid in an entire building for the first time since I was four years old, and I couldn't remember that far back.

Being born in August was the worst.

Going from year six in primary school to first year at secondary school was almost as bad. In a few weeks, we went from being the ones who ran the place to the bottom of the pile. It was ridiculous.

It didn't help that none of the friends I had in primary school had come with me. I was on my own from day one, and I had to find my place quickly.

Easier said than done.

I went from being popular and never alone to lining up in the canteen at lunchtime, wondering if I'd be noticed if I was sitting on my own in a corner.

Then, I saw him.

He had the same nervous look in his eyes as me. The same flitting look, the same worries. I'd seen him that morning in my English class, sitting in the opposite corner of the room from me. I could have been looking in a mirror. Only, he looked taller and like his uniform wasn't a hand-me-down.

There were a few kids between us. As they began to mess

about and shove each other around a little—dark laughter coming from them—I moved around them and ended up standing next to him. I took a tray and handed one to him.

"Snooze you lose, right?" I said, nodding toward the kids who were still shoving each other and paying me no attention.

He looked around as if I were talking to someone else.

"You know if anything here doesn't taste like crap?"

He grinned back at me, then shook his head. "It's school dinners—it's all crap."

"Right, course," I replied, then remembered his name. "Chris, right? I'm Matt."

Over the next few minutes, we became friends. That easy. He lived a few streets away from my new house in North Liverpool. We'd moved to north Liverpool because my dad got a new job. I had wanted to go to Speke Comprehensive School, like all my other mates in primary school, but we were living at the other end of the city now, so it didn't make sense.

The place was nicer than where we used to live, but it wasn't home yet.

Eleven years old, scared of a new situation, we found each other.

That same day—that same lunch hour, in fact—we found Nicola and Alexandra. They were the only other pair sitting at our table and whispered to each other for five minutes before I turned to Chris. I raised my eyebrows and leaned across the table to him.

"I think we should whisper as well," I said, loud enough for the girls to hear me. "It'll make it look like we've got something interesting to say. Like a secret or something."

Chris grinned back at me and gave an exaggerated nod. "Yeah, definitely. Like we're spies, right?"

Nicola—I didn't know her name yet, but I would discover it

soon—rolled her eyes at us, but Alexandra smiled and gave a small laugh.

"Me mum says it's rude to whisper, but I try to do the opposite of what she says," Alexandra said, leaning across and looking at my dinner tray. "That looks revolting."

"Chicken supreme and rice," I replied, picking up my fork and plonking into the gray and white mess on my plate. "Nothing better."

"I'd rather eat pig's arse and cabbage," Nicola said, pushing her half-eaten sandwich away and grimacing.

"What the hell is that?" I said, glancing at Chris and noticing for the first time that he didn't seem to be able to stop himself from staring at Nicola.

"It's what me dad says is for tea all the time. No idea what it is, but I know I don't want to eat it. That," she said, pointing at my plate, just as I shoveled a forkful into my mouth. "That looks even worse."

"Beggars can't be choosers," I said, swallowing the food down and wishing I hadn't. "Although pigs make bacon, so it can't be all that bad."

"What, even arse?"

"Still the same animal, right?"

"If you say so."

I swallowed another mouthful and tried to think of something funny to say. I couldn't think of a single thing. It didn't matter though, as Chris came to life. He asked them questions, made them laugh, and managed to keep them at the table even though they'd finished eating. I found my voice eventually.

By the end of the day, Chris and I discovered we were in most of the same classes. We walked home after our last lesson, talking about what things we liked, what we didn't like. He'd gotten a Sega Genesis for his birthday a few months earlier, so I ended up going back to his home for an hour. He let me play *Sonic the Hedgehog* and *World Cup Italia '90*.

That was it. We were best friends, just like that.

Over the next few weeks, we'd have lunch with Nicola and Alexandra almost every single day. We'd see them around the school, say hello, but it was me and him mostly. We were inseparable from that first lunchtime. We were eleven- and twelve-year-olds, playing on his Sega Genesis, watching *Power Rangers* on his Sky TV, and eating as much candy as we could get from the store on any given day.

That was the beginning of the group.

TWELVE

The WhatsApp message arrived as a *ping* of noise. Simply a notification on my cell, that I glanced at, then ignored.

That's how we live our lives now. A series of moments, interspersed with cell phones vibrating or dinging away to let us know what is happening around the world. We're instantly contactable. When the world ends, we'll find out from a breaking news notification, I imagine.

I ignored it, thinking it was something as innocuous as a Sky or BBC news banner. An email from a sender I didn't want to immediately check. A message from a friend that I didn't immediately need to see.

I didn't wonder when I'd changed from the Matt Connolly who would snatch up his phone at the slightest bit of noise. I can't imagine being that way again.

Outwardly happy. Ordinary. Nothing special.

My phone buzzed on the desk—a call from Chris coming through. I ignored it, trying to concentrate on my work. I could call him back later.

You never know the moment your life changes forever. Not until later, when you can look back and pinpoint it. Say *That's it—that's when it all went wrong*. Until then, you're just battling against the tide. I sometimes tried to look back and see if there was something before that moment that predicted what was to come later. Some thread on the tapestry of my average life that had come loose, began to fray, threatening to tear the whole thing down if something inauspicious was caught on it.

Memory is never the same for everyone.

An event happens, and six people can experience it differently when they remember it later.

That's what I feel. We all have a certain version of events in our heads. What happened and what our individual part in it was. We imagine ourselves as the hero. The one who made all the right decisions.

I remember the quiet.

I remember hours later, as I washed my hands again and again. Never able to make a difference to the way they felt. I was already changing the way the whole thing unfolded. I could feel myself doing it, but my mind wouldn't stop.

I remember.

I think.

The cacophony of silence would lie there on the edge of my consciousness forever, I imagined. The blurred images, never crisp and clear. I could never escape the silence. It would always be with me, like a dark passenger.

It was already fading away a day or two after that night.

Becoming memory.

My memory.

Fractured.

I remember it in flashes. Every detail a little different each time. A millisecond of change that makes me question the whole. Sometimes, I wonder if it happened at all. Whether I had dreamed the entire thing and that's why no one would talk about it.

Then I remember Alexandra's face in the days that followed and know that can't be the case.

I knew I could ask and find out for certain if what I remembered was reality or not. That would fill in some gaps. Large, open spaces of recollection that weren't there.

Although, doing that would take something from me. I was almost pleased to have something intangible of my own.

I would never ask the question. Chris was the only one who could, or would, answer me now. Alexandra was gone. Stuart had drifted away. Michelle was a stranger. Nicola…I'd rather not open that wound with her. She had been adamant from the beginning that we should never talk about it again.

Instead, I turn the flashes of memory into a narrative and write my own version. Every night a different outcome. Every night a victory.

And every night that same crushing feeling of reality.

I didn't need to wonder at when my life changed.

I lived it every single day.

It was when I killed someone.

I picked up my phone, saw the message waiting, then ignored it. Continued working for a short while, then sat back in my chair and looked outside to the yard. Earlier in the year, I'd been able to sit outside and work in the heat. Now, the leaves from a neighbor's tree were lying on the ground, being whipped up by what I knew would be a biting wind. Magpies landed on the tree as I stared, and I instinctively saluted.

It was late morning, and the second cup of coffee was already wearing off for me. I'd slept fitfully the night before, which was the norm of course, but that morning I was still a little more tired than usual. I could feel the pressure in my temples, the stabs of pain behind my eyes, as looking at the flickering of a laptop screen began to grate after an hour or two.

The sound of music in my ears, emanating from the speakers

on the almost-new laptop I'd bought on credit a few weeks earlier. I'd created a playlist of over four hundred songs twenty-four hours after it had arrived. A day of procrastination, as I put off some job or other. As long as there were enough songs, there would never be quiet again.

The message waited to be read.

Deacon Blue gave way to Childish Gambino as I continued to type. An eclectic shuffle, even for the streaming app I'd downloaded. I wasn't fast, but the words filled the screen at a good enough tempo—mostly in the right order and correctly spelled. Working from home was the dream, no matter that it was becoming increasingly more difficult to find regular paid jobs. It was too easy now to build your own website using templates and stock images. I had enough of a reputation by then to keep ticking along though. And some extra work was always available for someone who could do the fancy design stuff I could do.

My work space was a little sparse, but I'd decorated as best I could. A few framed posters on the wall, a bookcase holding the novels I'd read years earlier, the dresser in the corner. It wasn't a standard home office. Instead, I was in what should have been the dining room, but I'd converted it when I'd moved in a year earlier.

When *we'd* moved in.

My phone buzzed again on the desk, so I stood up, taking the phone with me as I left the office/dining room, and entered the kitchen. Flicked on the coffee machine and began scrolling.

I didn't read the message straightaway, looking at what else my various apps had decided I needed to know about first. More bad reports from two different sources of news, a football manager's thoughts on a previous game, a new friend request from someone I'd never heard of on social media.

I read the WhatsApp message as I stirred sugar into an already sweetened coffee. Dropped the spoon on the kitchen counter as the words began to blur and blend into one another.

"Stuart..." I heard myself say before I placed the phone down next to the discarded spoon and leaned back, a hand across my mouth. I closed my eyes and shook my head.

It couldn't be true.

The message had been scarce on detail, but it had said enough. Sent from Stuart's cell phone, but written by his sister.

Matt, it's Stephanie, Stuart's sister. I'm not sure if you've heard the news (and I think you would have been in touch if you had), but in case you haven't, I'm sorry to be the one to tell you. Stuart died suddenly last Saturday. I know you were friends for a long time, but you perhaps weren't in touch with him lately. He's had some issues, but this has still come as a shock to the family. The funeral is on Friday at 4 p.m. I know you were close, so it would only be right to have you and the rest of his oldest friends there.

It ended with details of where the funeral was taking place and more platitudes. I wanted to read the message again, but I knew it wouldn't change at all. The details would still be the same. Outside, the magpies squawked at each other, piercing the back door, but I didn't salute this time. It seemed too late. The coffee was sitting untouched, so I risked a swig to give me the energy to keep standing. My mouth burned a little at the taste, but I pretended it had given me a jolt of something.

I picked the phone back up and saw the missed call from Chris. Called him back.

"Chris?"

There was a pause, an exhalation, then his voice came through. "All right, mate."

"Is this real?" I said, knowing the answer already. Knowing Chris would already know. I could hear it in the three words he'd said. We spoke often enough for me to recognize that. He was pretty much the only person I still spoke to, if I thought about it. At least that friendship hadn't died yet. "I can't believe it. Do you know what happened?"

"I don't know anything more than what you probably got told," Chris replied, tension in his voice. Sadness too. "I'm guessing there's more to it, but I don't know right now. I'm with you. Wasn't expecting that at all. Unbelievable."

I started to say something but couldn't find the words. Instead, I walked back into my sham of an office and sat down. "I didn't even know he was ill or anything."

"I don't think he was," Chris replied, a voice in the background talking, seemingly asking a question that was quickly shushed. "I've only just told Nicola. She's as devastated as we are. We haven't spoken to him since... Well, it's been a long time."

"'Died suddenly'—what do you think that means?"

"Could be a number of different things...heart attack—not very likely at our age. Stroke, probably the same. Accident or something? I don't want to think of the obvious."

I brought up a new browser window and typed in the name. Looked at recent news reports, clicking on the first one that came up. "So you haven't heard from him at all lately?"

There was a pause, then Chris sighed again. "No. It's been months. Not since he moved to that new job. He stopped replying to messages and voice mails. That must be about five months or so."

"More like eight or nine, I think."

"You?"

I shook my head as I continued to read. "No, not for about as long. I was...I was leaving him to it, you know."

The news report on the screen was a little sparse on detail, but it told me enough.

Police Name Man Found Dead on Merseyside Railway Line

"I can't believe we didn't know sooner," I said, scrolling down and finding his name in the report. Seeing it there, in black and white, brought him to mind instantly. Not as I'd known him recently. When I'd first met him, aged eighteen and a curly mop of blond hair perched on a soft-featured face. The disarming smile. "It's been almost a week since he was found. All it says was he was found dead near the train line south of the city."

"Hit by a train?"

"That's what it says. Police aren't treating it as suspicious. You don't think he...you know? That's usually the case when they say it's not suspicious and 'hit by a train' in the same article though."

"I hope not. He never seemed the type to do that to himself. I suppose we never really know what's going on in people's heads though. What they're hiding and that."

"We should have known about this."

"It's not like we kept in touch with him and whoever he was with lately," Chris replied, a defensive tone creeping into his voice. "We've all kinda moved on. Working hard and all that."

"Didn't stop us keeping in touch though."

"That's different, you know that."

I sniffed an agreement and tried to find more information online. I stopped when I realized it would probably take a little more than a simple Google search to find more. It could wait. "Seems like he was back in the area," I said, leaning back in my chair, rubbing my eyes with my free hand. "He was found close enough. You'd think if he was back around here, we would have heard something from him. It's not like him not to want to see us."

"It's been a tough time. Maybe he didn't want to see us. Dredge up the past, you know."

Silence grew as I turned over the details in my head. Before reading the message, I'd been planning on doing a few little jobs that needed sorting out—a new layout for a website that dealt with designing kitchens, a couple of proposals for some other clients—but now it seemed ridiculous.

"Are you going?" Chris said, and for a second, I assumed he meant ending the call. Then, I realized what he meant.

"Of course, aren't you?"

Another long sigh. "We didn't exactly part on the best of terms."

"We have to be there. He was our friend." Even as I said the words, I could picture Chris's face. His roll of the eyes, small shake of the head. That was the way he always reacted when I was right—which with him wasn't often. No acceptance. Just a roll and shake. That was his way. A small smile that you'd miss if you didn't know to look for it. I'd known him for over twenty years, which was longer than anyone else in my life outside my family. He was more than just a best friend.

"I just don't know what to say to them. We never really met his family. And he never really talked about them."

"We knew him, mate," I said, feeling grief hanging over me now. It was waiting to hit me, it seemed. A dark cloud above me, choosing its moment. I tried to recall the last conversation we'd had. Whether there had been a remark or even a look that I had missed. It hadn't been that long, but then, memory could play tricks on you. "That's enough to...I don't know...pay our respects to his family? We were close to Stuart. It's only right."

I waited to hear the inevitable snort of derision, but Chris was silent. Eventually, he seemed to relent.

"Okay, I'll speak to Nicola now. I'm sure she'll want to be there too."

And that was how it began. A simple message. A few lines about the death of an old friend. An invitation and a condolence.

Only, I knew as I sat back in my chair and tried to think about Stuart once more that it seemed like I'd been waiting for something like this to happen.

Something that would bring us all back together.

I tried working but couldn't concentrate. Instead, I sat in my chair for a long time, wanting a cigarette—despite not smoking for well over a decade now—eyes closed but not falling asleep. Listening to music.

Waiting for tears that never came.

I stayed that way until I couldn't ignore the hunger any longer. I ate a meal that contained more calories than I needed. Ran on the treadmill to burn them off. Watched television for a while, then went to bed.

Apart from the news about Stuart, it was a pretty normal day.

THIRTEEN

I slowly came to full consciousness, a voice purring softly from the outskirts of my mind. It was always the same way—a few moments that resembled panic as my body protested about being awakened.

I was in a bed. It's a double. There's a window to my right with dull winter-morning light struggling to penetrate through the curtains. The noise was coming from the radio, which sat on the dark oak bedside table situated six inches from my head. Through sleep-encrusted eyes, I could see red numbers staring back at me. Static, 8:00. I watched as it clicked over to 8:01 and closed my eyes again.

There was a moment when the dreamlike quality of the morning made me think for a second that I was still asleep. That I was still in the middle of the same nightmare I seemed to have every night.

The cold, the dirt, the blood.

I waited for the shove in the back that would never come to hit me. It was the same way every morning. The absence of something seemed to only make it more noticeable. I used to be a heavy sleeper—a bomb going off outside wouldn't have stirred me. I would have made the worst guard dog this side of Cerberus. Now, I barely slept.

I remembered looking at the time when it had said 4:32 a.m.

A noise from downstairs had made me stiffen. The now-familiar whirl of anxiety and worry quickly followed. When no one came up the stairs and murdered me in my bed, I must have finally fallen asleep.

Every morning was the same. The radio would go on, and I'd wake up and promptly close my eyes again until my body would respond and move. Even against its protests of just a little more sleep.

Sometimes, I would lie there for over an hour. Awake, but only conscious. The rest of me still refusing to move. I didn't have that luxury that morning.

It was the day of the funeral. Stuart. Dead.

It was the day I would possibly see everyone again. I'd seen Chris many times in the previous year and Nicola less often. The rest...the rest of them had become strangers. Even Alexandra, I thought. I hoped she'd be there, but also felt nervous about the idea.

None of that mattered. Stuart was gone.

He had been my friend, but I hadn't been much of one to him.

Since the message, I'd learned that, as I thought, "not being treated as suspicious" was basically newspaper-speak for "he did it to himself." I couldn't imagine Stuart ending his life—not the Stuart I'd known—so surely that should have been suspicious.

Then, I remembered the nightmare and realized I didn't know any one of my friends as well as I'd thought. Had no idea what any of them were *really* capable of anymore.

The body had been released to the family, and a funeral had been organized within a week. I guessed that his parents were religious and wanted to ease the path into paradise as much as it was possible.

I remembered a film about purgatory and decided if they

were religious, I probably needed to stay away from them. I wouldn't be able to deal with the barely constrained anger and sadness they'd hold.

Then, after, a gathering. A wake of sorts. I hoped to be out of there by then. I don't think I could cope with the platitudes and questions.

I crawled out of bed, showered, and took the only suit I owned from the wardrobe while the towel was still wrapped around my waist. It was still in the plastic covering from when I'd had it dry-cleaned after the last time I'd worn it. That was a year or more ago—some wedding in the family—and I hoped it still fit. I decided to put off the inevitable dismay of everything feeling a little looser than it had before and slipped on a pair of lounge pants and T-shirt, took a formal shirt from its hanger, and went downstairs.

I spent ten minutes trying to find a black tie before discovering one balled up at the back of my wardrobe. I did a simple knot, and I was done.

The suit was a size too big. At least. It would do.

By nine thirty, I was waiting at the living room window for Chris and Nicola to arrive. The sky was gray, which seemed fitting for the occasion. I was wondering if I could wear some kind of coat over my suit—and which one of the three I owned would even be fit for the purpose—when I spotted Chris's car turning into my small street and pulling to a stop outside.

I checked my pockets for my phone and wallet. Found my keys. Stood at the front door, willing myself to open it and step outside.

Seconds passed by. I could hear myself breathing. The light coming through the glass panes at the top of the door darkened. I could feel my chest tightening.

I didn't want to leave. Inside the house, everything was okay. Everything was safe. My suit was uncomfortable, and I wanted to change now. I wanted to sit in my office and drink coffee and work and listen to music and forget about what lay on the other side of the door.

I could hear my own breathing.

Nothing else.

I closed my eyes, plunging myself into darkness, and I was suddenly back in the woods. I could hear Stuart's voice. His accent and his pleading for help.

The sound grew and grew until I couldn't breathe any longer.

My hand was on the door, but in my mind, it was against a tree trunk.

I didn't want to leave. Inside was safety.

Outside...

Outside there were woods and trees and my friends screaming for help and blood and death and red candles.

I scrunched my eyes tighter as the silence disappeared and all I could hear and see was Stuart screaming and Chris crying and Alexandra turning the color of snow. Michelle rocking backward and forward and Nicola shaking with anger.

A knock at the door was loud enough to spring me back to reality. I breathed in and out deeply.

I could do this.

I didn't want to.

When the second knock came, I let muscle memory kick in and I opened the door. Chris was standing on the doorstep.

"All right, mate, you ready?" Chris said, his face falling as he looked me over. He looked worried, as if I were about to break down. "All good?"

I nodded and checked my pockets again. Wallet, phone, keys.

I wasn't sure if Chris could hear it, but in the kitchen, music was playing on repeat, so when I came home the house wouldn't be silent.

"Yeah, let's go," I replied, still unmoving in the doorway.

"There's no rush," Chris said, tilting his head to one side, studying me. "We'll be there well before eleven if you need to…"

"No, it's fine, honestly." I watched him hesitate, then purse his lips. Turn away and walk slowly back up the path. I breathed in again and then finally followed him out. Turned around and checked the door was locked. Four times.

"You couldn't find a suit that actually fit?" Chris said, waiting for me before getting into the driver's seat.

"Har har," I replied, giving a tight smile to Nicola in the passenger seat, who returned it. I opened the back door and slipped into the car. Chris followed suit, as I moved a few papers from the back seat and took care not to brush against Chris's suit jacket hanging in the back. His shirt was more creased than mine, but he still looked as well put together as he always did. His stubble more designer than scruffy, his hair intentionally floppy, his build solid rather than the approaching middle-age paunchy that others our age showed.

The car smelled of a mix of expensive aftershave and perfume. I was aware that the only aroma I added to it was Lynx Africa and Head & Shoulders shampoo.

"Morning," I said to the back of Nicola's head. She didn't move, staring ahead now, dressed in a black dress, I assumed, from the limited view I had. "How's things going?"

"They were okay until this happened," Nicola replied, her clipped, southern-money tones still apparent even after all these years spent in the North of England. She had moved up here at around eight or nine years old but hadn't managed to lose the accent. I would have normally tried to joke around with her, but it didn't seem the time. Never did anymore. "Let's get this over with."

Chris nodded at her, but I could tell he wanted to say something more. As if I'd interrupted an argument that had been ongoing. I imagined I was close to the truth. Not that they would ever dream of airing such grievances in front of anyone else.

I couldn't picture them arguing all that much anyway. They'd been together so long that I thought by now they would be immune to the usual niggles that happen in relationships. I wouldn't know, of course, given my history of arguments with partners. *One and out* was apparently my motto. Although, if I took my parents as an example, they could have blazing rows every day about something as small as whose turn it was to wash the dishes—always mum's according to my dad—or something political.

I wondered if that was something my mum missed and made a promise to myself that I'd call her at some point. It had been a while.

The houses faded away, replaced by fields of dirty green and blackening wintertime trees. Roads became smaller, more winding, as we left the town where I lived and drove toward the address we'd been given. A church on the outskirts of Manchester. Some town I didn't know.

The silence was broken by Chris pressing a few buttons and music filling the car. Nicola reached across and turned down the volume almost as soon as he did so. I shifted uncomfortably in my seat, opened my mouth to speak and then thought better of it.

I knew what the atmosphere was about. How could I not?

In the years since we'd first met and become friends, there had been very few moments of discomfort. Of awkwardness. Car journeys had once been filled with the laughter and joy of being together.

Now, the weight of where we were going and the memories of the past year seemed to have destroyed that part of us.

The radio broke into news, then a song came on. An older one, not on the usual playlist I would have thought. A nineties hit I couldn't quite name but seemed to know the lyrics to. I remembered the band easy enough. I'd seen them play live a few times a year ago. All of us somewhere in a field, pretending we were kids again. Jumping up and down and singing along to every word.

Nicola reached across and snapped the radio into silence.

"I can't listen to that anymore," she said, her hand shaking a little as she brought it back and out of my sight. "Sorry."

Chris didn't answer, staring straight ahead at the road, as it began to open up again and more buildings came into view. I kept quiet as well, as the name of the song came to mind, the band...where I saw them play live the last time.

Nothing else needed saying. The conversation was over. We all knew why.

I watched as the time approached ten o'clock and began to brace myself for what was to come. The possible questions I'd be asked, the people I'd see.

The GPS on the dashboard came to life after we passed the only road we'd seen for fifteen minutes and began blurting out directions that Chris took in silence. Within a few minutes, we were pulling up outside a church on a street I didn't know, in a town I knew even less. I could feel the tightness in my chest again as I thought about leaving the car. Walking outside, in a place I didn't know. It was hard to ignore, but I caught Chris's eyes in the rearview mirror, and my heart slowed down again. I was safe. I wasn't alone. We were early, so we settled into the car, which also helped.

"Had to be Manchester, didn't it?" Chris said softly to himself. I sniffed in the back seat, while Nicola shook off her seat belt and leaned forward in the seat.

"It's not technically Manchester, Chris," she said, pulling up a bag, opening it, and rummaging inside. "Don't worry—I won't tell anyone back home that we were here. Not that people on the Wirral care all that much."

"You never did understand," I said from the back seat, hoping to lighten the tone. Chris may have moved over the water of the River Mersey to the Wirral—a mile from Liverpool city center, but because it was separated by the river, it may as well have been a different country—but that didn't change things. We still shared a ridiculous aversion to the major city down the M62. "Remember when we met him? I don't think he realized how long we would go on about it."

Chris laughed quietly, then shook his head. "Remember the arguments we'd have? Always about music. Didn't matter what it was, he thought Manchester was the epicenter of great music. You'd have thought Oasis were the second coming, the way he talked about them. Listening to the Happy Mondays like they were any good."

"That's what it always came down to," I replied, smiling a little at the memory. We were all nineties kids, entering the new millennium. Britpop had been our culture. "Not the Beatles versus the Stones. It was Oasis versus Blur, and we hated both of them."

"That was always a class thing anyway," Chris said, sweeping a hand through the hair that was becoming more gray every time I saw him. In the past year, small flecks had become strands had become blocks. "Working class people liked Oasis, the middle class liked Blur."

"I never understood why he thought going to university in Liverpool was a good idea. He must have known he was going to get grief about where he came from."

"He wasn't bad for a Manc."

"Depends what your definition of bad is," Nicola muttered to herself, quieting us instantly. "Let's get this over with."

I followed them up the path to the church, a few people near the gravestones on grass near the entrance. The temperature seemed to drop a few degrees the closer we got to the building, as always seemed to be the way. A woman around our age was standing in the doorway, looking at us. "Hi, you must be friends of Stuart?"

I cleared my throat and stepped forward. "I'm Matt. This is Chris and Nicola. We were friends of Stuart."

Her demeanor changed in a split second, her features softening, a tilt of the head. There had been an attempt to hide the dark rings under her eyes with makeup, but they were still noticeable. "Of course, I'm Stephanie. Stuart's sister. Come inside."

I let Chris and Nicola go first, struck by how alike Stephanie was to Stuart. I was trying to recall if he'd ever said he was a twin but couldn't remember that far back. I was sure he would have told us, but she looked so like him that I couldn't believe they hadn't shared a uterus at some point.

I wondered if I was the first person to think of the word *uterus* when entering a church for a funeral and suppressed a giggle at the thought.

I was nervous, I realized. My thoughts were racing together, crashing into each other, an uncontrollable train. I knew what was coming. The memories it would bring up, the feelings that would follow.

It had to be done.

Home is safe. Let's stay there. Come on. It's not that far away.

The church was even larger inside than I'd expected it to be from the outside. High ceilings and stained-glass windows that took up most of the walls. We were led into a vast open space— pews on each side, stone pillars in random places—which seemed to stretch back farther than I'd imagined was possible. Various exits to other parts of the church, places the people were conversing and standing around. I heard soft chatter and scuffling feet on the hard floor and clinking jewelry. I followed Chris and Nicola in, stopping at the edge of the hall.

Chris was always much better than I was in these types of situations, but even he seemed a little reluctant to be his usual self in the church. I knew the feeling. We were out of place there. Old friends who didn't know the Stuart who these people would.

We knew a different version than the one who had been driven to do what he'd apparently done.

There were a few introductions to various family members, all looking as vacant and washed out as the next. Stephanie introduced us to a few, then went to speak to who I assumed were her parents.

"I remember Stuart saying you met in university?" Stephanie said on her return. She had guided us away from the larger group of family members and toward an empty pew halfway down the aisle. "Were you all in the same one? Is that how you all met?"

"No," Chris replied, taking the lead, thankfully. "A few of us had known each other since high school. Grew up in the same village. We didn't meet Stuart until university and he just slotted in, I guess. He was a good guy."

"He used to talk about your group of friends like they were some kind of gang. The Avengers or Justice League or...you know?"

We didn't share in her laughter but smiled in turn. "I wouldn't go that far," Chris said, as I continued to glance around, trying to spot any sort of familiar face. "We all just got on really well, that's all. And I suppose we all brought something different to the party. We've all grown up since then."

"He talked about you all," Stephanie said sadly. "Not much recently, but he didn't talk about anything at all I suppose. I don't think he was in the greatest place the past year. That should've been a clue. I guess you don't realize these types of thoughts are going on in people's heads." Then she excused herself to speak to more people who had arrived.

The whole encounter left me feeling on edge, yet it was as if it was only the opening act for me that morning. Like something more was waiting for me.

It was another half an hour before Stuart arrived. Six men carrying his coffin on their shoulders. I recognized one of his cousins but bowed my head as they came closer. Then, we were sitting down, as an older man pontificated from the pulpit up front.

Vicar or priest...I could never remember the difference. Or if there was one.

Stephanie was on her feet, reading from a piece of paper, as her parents sat at the front—straight backs and dead-eyed stares. She talked of Stuart's life, as if she were describing someone I'd never met.

That's all it comes down to, I guessed. When you're gone, someone will read facts from a single sheet of paper in front of a room of people.

It was up to you how you filled it.

She didn't talk of the Stuart we'd known for all those years. A different Stuart in so many ways.

She didn't talk about what we had done.

She didn't talk about the silence that followed it. Or the sleepless nights since. She didn't talk about the teenager and his body being moved.

She couldn't. No one apart from Chris, Nicola, and me could do that. She couldn't recount the moment in those woods when Stuart grabbed hold of me, when we realized the lad's body had disappeared.

I wondered if Stuart had been thinking about that moment while the train came toward him.

It was safe at home. It was safe inside. I had to get out of that church. I could feel my hands shaking and slapped my knee when it started bobbing up and down. Chris gave me a look of concern, and I had the urge to shout out. To tell everyone around us the real reason Stuart had taken his own life. "Excuse me," I whispered, standing up and sliding out of the pew. I received a tut from an older woman in a black hat but barely heard it.

I needed to get out of there. I could almost feel the walls closing in on me. Hidden voices, asking questions I couldn't answer. I walked straight up the aisle and out of the church without looking back.

Outside it was no better. I willed Chris to follow me, so I could convince him that we needed to go. That I needed to get back home. I needed to be safe.

I could almost feel her presence before I saw her.

She was standing with her back to me, staring out toward the grounds of the church. I hadn't seen her in months, but I didn't even need to look her in the eye to know it was her. I could almost smell her, hear her voice, feel her skin beneath my hand.

As if sensing my presence herself, Alexandra turned her head as I stared at her back, and she looked at me.

Then, she smiled.

FOURTEEN

I n that instant, it was as if the past year hadn't happened. I could have kidded myself forever. Concentrated hard—screwed my eyes closed to reality and wished for it enough—so I could see a way to ignore every painful moment since I'd last seen her.

Instead, I watched as the smile slipped from Alexandra's face into a puddle at her feet. The length of time it took to fall, moment by moment...each of them a sting to my heart.

"Hello," I said, as if that would have been adequate. It wasn't, but I tried again even though there was nothing I could say. "I mean, are you okay?"

That wasn't very good either, but it seemed to slide off her. She opened her mouth to speak but didn't get the chance to as the door behind me opened up and Chris and Nicola emerged from the church and made their way toward us. The worried look on Chris's face faded as he saw who was standing next to me. This time, Alexandra's smile didn't fade as quickly, as she looked past me and toward the pair. Nicola and Alexandra embraced, as Chris looked first at me, then shared an awkward hug with Alexandra.

"How have you been? I haven't seen you for a while now," I heard Nicola say, moving away slightly from Chris and I. Chris placed a hand on my shoulder, and we stayed behind as they continued to walk off.

The grass was beginning to brown in the seasonal turn, leaves lying atop it like discarded litter.

"You okay?"

"Yeah," I replied, giving him an unconvincing smile. "I just needed to get out of there. All got a bit much."

"You've not been to many funerals?"

I shook my head. "Try to avoid them as much as possible." I looked across the churchyard at Alexandra and felt my eyes blur. "I didn't think she was going to come."

"How long since you've seen her?"

I looked at Chris, then turned away to watch Alexandra and Nicola talk to each other animatedly. "Ten months. New Year's Day was the last time."

"The drunken phone call. I remember you telling me about that."

"It's why I've stuck to coffee since."

"Not much has changed I see," Chris replied, the beginnings of a grin appearing on his face. "Absence makes the heart grow fonder."

"What?"

"Well, I don't want to say anything…"

"Then don't."

Chris held his hands up but lowered his voice further, knowing I still wanted to hear whatever he had to say. "Nicola still speaks to her occasionally. Off and on. They haven't met up since Alexandra moved over the water. Every time they speak, I hear your name. And the way you two look at each other…it's not over. Just saying."

"I'm not interested in looking backward," I replied, believing the words myself even if no one else would. I knew Alexandra had moved away, but didn't realize it was only across the

Mersey. No more than a half-hour journey, I imagined. In that moment, it may as well have been in a different country. "It's been a long time. Besides, we've known each other for so long that if it wasn't going to work, then it never will."

"So were me and Nicola. We were kids when we started out. We went through that time and we're still together."

"That's different," I said, moving a little farther down the stone path toward the gravestones to the sides of it. I stepped onto the grass, the leaves crunching under my feet almost reverentially. The ground underneath my shoes was a little soft, but there was no mud there. I wondered if Stuart's parents could even make the rain stop, given the gravity of the day. I changed the topic of conversation before I had to explain the unexplainable. "I always knew Stuart's mum and dad did okay for themselves, but I wasn't expecting the whole works like this. I Googled the home address where they're having the wake...it's bloody huge."

Chris turned and shook his head at me. "It's not gonna be a mansion, Matt."

"I know, but this isn't bad for where we are, you know?"

"I think we'd know if he were a millionaire, don't you?"

"If he *had* been," I said and didn't know why it suddenly became important to refer to him in the past tense.

"I'm glad Nicola has something to distract her."

I looked over toward her. She was nodding solemnly at something Alexandra was saying and I could see the tension in her features properly now. The new lines, the dark marks under her eyes. "This is hard."

"I want to get out of here so bad," Chris said, looking up toward the clouds above us as if they would provide solace. "Don't you feel it too?"

"What?"

Chris sighed and shook his head. "It doesn't matter."

I was about to push him for an answer, but he began walking away, toward where Nicola and Alexandra had ended up walking together.

"Have you heard anything more about what happened, Alex?" Nicola asked, as we finally reached where they'd stopped, almost at the church boundary wall. "We don't really know what's gone on."

"I know probably as much as you guys do," Alexandra replied, and suddenly I was a teenager again, hearing her voice for the first time, the soft Liverpudlian accent she had, still the same as it was fifteen years earlier. It had taken us a long time to get together properly, but once we did, it seemed like we'd always known that was going to be the eventual outcome.

And then it was over. In less time than it took to buy a house together, to plan a future. In a heartbeat, we had been done.

I caught her eye and realized she found this as awkward as I did. For some reason, the thought calmed me a little. "Hi. Again."

"Hey," Alexandra replied, then cocked her head to the side a little. "You look tired."

"You look as good as you always did."

She didn't blush at the compliment, but did look away with the ghost of a smile playing across her lips. It was a smoother line than I'd expected to be able to manage. It could only be downhill from there, I thought. She was wearing a black dress that went past her knees, with a jacket draped over her shoulders. Her hair was now brown, rather than the blond it had been the last time I saw her. It suited her better, I thought, but then… it wasn't like I knew all that much. Her hair could have been multicolored, and I would have still found it okay.

She didn't seem to have changed all that much since I'd last seen her, other than the weight of history on her shoulders and a smile that didn't reach her eyes anymore. A hint of darkness within them that was only noticeable if you knew what to look for.

Chris and Nicola moved away and left us alone. I looked across the churchyard toward them, but they seemed deep in their own conversation. I turned back to Alexandra and sighed. "It's been a while."

"It has indeed."

"I wondered if you'd come," I said, and she bowed her head in response. "Still can't quite believe he's gone."

"He was always the loudest out of all of us. Usually they're the first to go quiet."

I looked away, remembering how confident and brash Stuart was when we'd first met him. "He settled into the group like he'd always been with us. I remember we were worried how he would get on with the rest of you, but we needn't have worried."

"He was the life of the party. Just what we all needed at that age. Not that I saw much of him at the start."

"That's right. You were off doing your own university experience."

She hesitated, then sighed, shaking her head. "Is this our fault?"

I stared at Alexandra as she changed tack in a split second. I didn't know how to answer. I opened my mouth, but I had nothing to say.

She shook her head and turned away from me. "How's work?" she said, her hand shaking a little as she brought it up to her face and wiped away an invisible tear. "Still working from home?"

"Yeah, all good," I replied, glad she'd moved away from her question quickly. "Some things don't change. Pays the bills, as you know. And you're still..."

"I actually started lecturing this year. Psychology 101 for the most part. I'll work my way up; it'll just take a little time. Spend most of my days at the university, to be honest. Don't get out that much with all the prep work and that sort of thing."

"That's great," I replied, then wondered where the smoothness of earlier had disappeared to. "I mean, it's really cool that you got the job you were going for."

Seriously? Cool?

"Shaping the minds of the future and all of that?" Alexandra said, and now she was smiling. "Oh yes, I'm doing a great service."

I chuckled softly, then stopped just as quickly, stealing a glance toward the church to make sure no one had seen me. "Probably best we don't laugh too much around here."

"Had you seen Stuart recently?" Alexandra said, shuffling from one foot to the next, as if the mere mention of his name was the wrong thing to do.

"Not for a few months. Things haven't been the same since... well, you know. I guess you can lose touch with people all the time. Still, I wish we hadn't now. I didn't know how he was doing recently. Sounds like he was struggling."

"Aren't we all?" she said, and now she wasn't smiling and the lightness of the conversation evaporated instantly.

I shook my head. "Of course, I guess."

"You didn't lose touch with Chris," she said, seemingly happy to move on as quickly as I wanted to. "Or Nicola. Although I suppose they come as a pair, as they always did."

"I've been trying to get rid of him for years, but I just can't seem to shake him. Stuart...well, that was a different story. I didn't realize how bad he was feeling. He was always a traveler. Remember after we finished university? He was all over the place."

"I remember."

"It's easier to keep in touch these days," I said, hearing the babbling coming out but unable to stop myself. "We seem to forget that it's only ten years or so since we had all this social media in our lives. Can you imagine the photos he would have been posting daily if Facebook had been around in the 2000s? Would have annoyed the hell out of us."

"You remember that party Stuart had for his birthday?" Alexandra said, her eyes dancing at the memory. "Think it was when he turned twenty-two or twenty-three?"

"Yeah, think he was living in Runcorn at the time. Couple of years after we finished school. The big house party that just went mental. Pretty sure that was the last time I got drunk enough that I couldn't remember my own name. There was that game we played..."

Alexandra remembered for me. "Ring of Fire. Only we didn't have a full deck of cards, so it didn't work properly."

"That's right," I said, laughing to myself. "I ended up downing, like, so much I couldn't stand up straight. I remember laughing a lot. And that even though so many people were there, it still ended up being the six of us at the end. That's what...ten or eleven years ago now?"

"It's hard to imagine him quiet," Alexandra said, then we fell into another awkward silence.

I was about to break it when I heard Chris's voice from across the churchyard in some kind of exclamation. I turned to see what had grabbed his attention and saw someone had joined us outside.

It took me a few seconds before I recognized her, but then my mind clicked into gear. "Michelle," I said, looking toward Alexandra for confirmation. She was already moving, the expression on her face changing instantly to one of surprise. I followed her up the churchyard, waiting for my turn to greet the final member of our old group.

"You all right?" I said, stopping as I reached her and saw the expression on her face. She was different from the last time I'd seen her. Thinner and more waiflike. Her eyes were cast downward, to the ground, but when she lifted them slightly, I could see tiredness and weight there. It had been almost a year, but Michelle seemed to have aged many more in the meantime. "How's it going?"

"How do you think I am?" Michelle replied, casting furtive glances over her shoulder toward the church. "Wasn't expecting you all to turn up here today."

"Why wouldn't we be here?" Chris said, stepping forward and rubbing Michelle's shoulder with one hand. She flinched at his touch. "It's not the best of circumstances. I assume Stuart's sister got in touch with you as well?"

"Yeah. Told me it was suicide."

"He was always up and down," Chris replied, wrapping an arm around Nicola as the wind around us picked up. "He was either massively high or totally incapable of movement. Maybe he just had a stupid idea at one of his low points."

Michelle tensed, rubbing at one arm, slow at first, then more vigorously. She would look quickly at us, then avert her gaze. As if she was trying to catch us doing something.

"Maybe if she'd known the truth," Michelle said, spitting out each word with venom. "Maybe then she wouldn't have gotten in touch with you as well."

"What's that supposed to mean?"

Michelle's eyes flitted across the ground away from us, but there was no mistaking the tone in her voice. "Are you kidding me? Do you really think they'd let you anywhere near here if they knew it was your fault he's dead?"

"Michelle, that's not fair," I tried, but it was as if she had been waiting to see us so she could finally unload.

"Fair? You think it isn't fair? I'll tell you what isn't fair. It's not *fair* that what you did a year ago was never spoken about. We never owned up and took our punishment. Instead, we all have to live with it in silence, and now Stuart is gone because of it."

"Maybe this isn't the best place," Alexandra said, but Michelle waved her away.

"This is all your fault."

"Michelle, we can't blame ourselves for this," Alexandra tried again, but it only seemed to make things worse.

"Are you serious?" Michelle said, her voice loud and mocking now. "I'm blaming you. All of you. I wanted to say something, and you all told me we couldn't."

"Not all of us," Chris said quietly, but Michelle ignored him.

"I'm going to go," Michelle said, as the atmosphere darkened and the silence only strengthened it. "I can't be around you people anymore. Stuart's gone. And I can't even go in there and say goodbye because that'll make it real."

"Michelle," Nicola said and tried to put an arm around her. She was shrugged away. "Let's talk about this."

"He's dead because of us, Nicola," Michelle replied, her voice low, almost a whisper, and I could feel the hate emanating from her like fire. "Don't you get that?"

"They found him on the train tracks," Michelle continued,

disgust and hurt in her voice as she spoke. "Hit by a freight train in the middle of the night. There was barely anything left of him. And they're going to pretend he did this to himself. Only, we all knew him. We *knew* he would never do anything like that."

It took a second, but I quickly understood what Michelle was saying and could barely believe she was suggesting it. I hadn't considered the possibility it could be anything other than suicide, how long you could live with something before it finally pushed you over the edge. I shook the idea that there was anything else going on away. A year was long enough for Stuart to make that decision.

I wondered how long I would last. How long *each* of us would last.

"There's no other reason for it," Nicola said, reaching across to stroke Michelle's arm. "Come on, let's go inside. No good, us all hanging around out here. They'll wonder what kind of friends we were. And you'll regret it if you don't go in, Michelle."

"Get off me," Michelle said, pushing her away physically now. Nicola stumbled over, and Chris was next to her in an instant. Took her weight, as the heel on her shoe snapped. Nicola straightened up and made as if to move toward Michelle, but Chris held onto her.

I moved between them, but Michelle was already walking away.

"I can't be around you lot anymore," Michelle spat over her shoulder, and then she was away toward the exit.

I turned back to the other three and could see the anger still in Nicola's eyes. The pain in Alexandra's. I tried to speak to her, but she held a hand up and walked away.

I didn't want to be there. I wanted to be far away, alone in my little house, working in my dining room office, and away from all of this.

I shouldn't have come. I should have stayed at home. I should have stayed away from these open wounds. These bad memories.

This group.

FIFTEEN

The end of the funeral came and went, with promises to keep in touch and polite refusals to go on to the wake afterward. We all seemed to understand that our role in the day was done—the dutiful friends who had probably known Stuart better than anyone else in the place. We waited as Stuart's father, decked out in a suit that probably cost more than Chris's car, made a short speech thanking everyone for coming and where to go on to next.

"It was our fault," Alexandra said, her voice low and hardly audible. I heard it, as she made sure to whisper it in my ear. I turned to answer her, but she was gone. Walking away down the church path and toward the exit. I considered going after her, but I didn't know what I would say to her if I did. It wasn't like I could disagree with her.

Michelle had been as right as Alexandra was now. This *was* our fault. Her words still stung.

Michelle was a world away from the girl I'd known back when we were younger. I remembered how no meetup had been without her constant soundtrack, how she would be smiling and singing, seemingly without a care in the world.

Now, she was different. As if the life had been sucked out of her. I wondered if we all looked the same to an outsider.

A macabre before-and-after photo shoot.

I shook hands with Stuart's father in a daze, feeling the

strength in his palms. His skin was brown like leather, and he looked right through me, as if I weren't even there. I didn't think any of us were for him. He was burying his son. Everything about that day was silent and invisible apart from that fact.

Alexandra left soon after. I didn't see her go, which seemed right. I didn't know if I'd see her again.

I wasn't sure if that was a good thing for my sanity or not.

There was silence in the car, once we got back in again and Chris started the journey home. I fiddled with my tie for a while before removing it and feeling like I could breathe again.

"I should have slapped her," Nicola said, the irritation and annoyance coming off her like steam. "How dare she speak to us like that?"

"She was just upset, that's all," I replied, knowing there was no way I could calm Nicola down no matter how hard I tried. "She didn't mean it."

Nicola snorted, then pulled out her phone, ending her involvement in the conversation, it seemed.

I shifted toward the center of the back seat, so I could speak to Chris a little better. "She didn't look good, you know what I mean? Like there's something more going on. Do you think she could possibly say something?"

"About what?"

"You know."

"Her and Stuart were close," Chris said, staring straight ahead at the road. The traffic was light at this time of day, a few hours before rush hour. "And there was no ending. I think she loved him more than we realized. It wasn't just a simple friends-with-benefits thing between them. That's probably all it was. Getting that news probably brought back all those feelings. She's going to need time. That's all."

"Right, right," I replied, but I knew Chris was lying to me. He was worried about the way she'd been acting, but for some reason wasn't willing to talk about it. "I was worried that it was something to do with what happened...you know?"

"I don't," Chris snapped back, and I could see his grip tighten on the steering wheel. Next to him, Nicola tensed up but didn't look up from her phone. "And now he's gone, we never have to talk about it again, do we? We have to move on, right? We can't change the past now. I wanted to say something at the time, remember? But none of you agreed. Now, it's far too late. I know we're all trying to ignore what might have driven him to take his own life, but we all know the reason. Let's not dig around in the past and make it even harder on ourselves."

"I guess you're right," I replied, turning away and staring out of the window at the passing countryside. "I was just worried about Michelle, that's all."

"Yeah, well, it's unlikely we'll see her again anytime soon."

The music was turned up, and I could see Nicola's jaw tensing as she continued to stare at her phone. I wondered if the two of them spoke about what happened at all. Whether they had gone back to a normal relationship since. Chris and I didn't tend to talk about that side of his life all that much. Usually he was simply listening to my woes, rather than talking about his own. If he had any.

"It was good to see Alexandra though," Nicola said, turning to Chris and smiling a little. "I'm guessing you thought the same?"

I shifted uncomfortably on the back seat. "I'm not so sure about that. Lot of water under that particular bridge."

"I've spoken to her a lot over the past few months. She always talks about you."

"Yeah, but that doesn't really say all that much," I replied, shaking my head and pulling at a stray thread in my black trousers. "I'm sure Chris will have told you that I don't talk about much else either. Doesn't mean I think we will or should get back together."

"It took you a long time to get together in the first place. You had the few years in school, then it was, what? Seven or eight years after we went to university?"

"Something like that."

"And we all know you wanted to be with her for all that time in between. You love her."

"Sometimes love just isn't enough."

Chris smiled sweetly at Nicola, who reached across and squeezed the hand he had resting on the gear stick. "You'd be surprised what love can get you past."

"Yeah, well, given what happened, I don't think it's surprising. Not all of us have what you two have."

I was glad of the silence that followed. I didn't want to think of Alexandra and I being failures for not being able to survive together. I caught Chris's eye in the rearview mirror and looked away.

"Are we ever going to talk about it?" I said, still looking out of the window. The words were out of my mouth before I thought about it, and I could almost feel Nicola tensing again in the front passenger seat.

"What's there to talk about?" Chris replied, the tone of his voice betraying him. "What's done is done."

"Is it though? Especially after what's happened now?"

Chris shook his head, shot a look toward Nicola, who had buried her head into her chest and was breathing heavily. "It's not a good idea to dredge up bad memories. Best we just get past it. Keep moving on."

I clenched my jaw and placed the flat of my right palm against my thigh, moving with it as my leg bobbed up and down. I knew Chris wanted to talk about it more, but Nicola wouldn't have any of it. I wondered how he had dealt with being involved in a murder—because that's what it was—and never being able to talk about it. I could imagine Nicola wasn't willing to share her own feelings at all. I thought about Chris, wanting to talk about what we had done but not being able to. I made a pact with myself that I would catch him alone and make sure he knew I would be willing to listen.

"He'd been acting weird for a long time," Chris said finally, changing the subject a little, toward Stuart. "Even before…you know. He couldn't settle. Was always bouncing from one job to the next. Traveling here and there. He wasn't exactly the type to just have a normal job, a stable relationship, or a house of his own."

"You spoke to him more recently than me. How did he sound?"

Chris sighed, another glance askew toward Nicola. "He was hyper. I think he was on something, looking back at it. This is with the knowledge we have now, of course. Could have been nothing for all I know. Thinking about it, he wasn't himself, that was for sure. Talking a mile a minute, like he was on coke or something."

"He had a history of that kind of thing," I replied, remembering the numerous times back in university when Stuart would still be the life and soul of any party. Even when the sun was coming up and everyone else was ready to stop. I could picture him instantly—jaw moving, eyes wide, and his gums showing as he grinned wide. It was difficult to have a normal conversation with him in that state, but I remember the laughter. "It's not like we've always been clean though. We did our fair share."

"Yeah, but that was a long time ago. We've all grown out of that now."

I hummed a response, thankful that those days were behind us. Didn't mean there was anything odd about Stuart possibly still dabbling. There had been enough moments in the past year when I'd felt like drifting away on some kind of high—leaving reality behind for a few minutes at least. It would make things easier to deal with, for one.

"Anyway, he wasn't himself," Chris continued, slowing down at a junction carefully and craning his head forward to see that his path was clear before pulling away again. "I didn't think much of it then, but I've been replaying that conversation over and over in my mind since."

"What was he saying?"

"Nothing really. He was talking in circles. I tried to have a conversation with him, but it was pointless. Maybe it was a cry for help? I don't know. All I do know now is that I wished I'd listened more. Maybe asked the right questions? If I'd known what was on his mind, there's a chance I could have done something, I think. He used to listen to me. Sometimes."

"I'm sure you did what you could," I replied, knowing it would never be enough for Chris. It wouldn't be enough for any of us. We would all have to live with the knowledge that we could have done more for Stuart.

I pulled out my phone and finally did what I'd put off doing since I had found out about Stuart being gone.

I Googled the news reports and found the place where it had come to an end for him.

1994

I took turning thirteen seriously. I was a teenager now. That meant things were different.

I was the last of the five of us, but that just meant we could celebrate in style over the summer holidays. I convinced my mum and dad to let me spend the day with the gang, and the lot of us went on a day out. It was all planned out—we were going to watch *The Mask* at the Odeon on London Road, then it was McDonald's after that, in town, and then we'd get pick 'n' mix candy at Woolies with my birthday money.

It was going to be amazing.

Chris knocked for me early, a present wrapped up for me to open. He knew I'd asked for a Super Nintendo and had bought me an extra controller so he could play with me. We spent an hour playing *Mario Kart* before we went and got the girls.

Michelle had only started hanging around with us earlier that year. Things were getting serious in school now. They were already talking about "options evening," when we'd decide what subjects we'd study in our high school exams.

"Definitely not geography or history," Chris would say on an almost hourly basis.

We were already planning on which subjects we'd both take, although I was slightly disappointed that he didn't want to take history.

Chris and Nicola had kissed for the first time four months before my birthday. When I asked Chris what it was like, he'd shrugged, but he'd been smiling ever since. I'd kissed one girl in my life before then, a girl in primary school called Alison. I could still remember how our teeth had clattered into each other the first time. The second time was better.

Chris and Nicola kissed all the time now.

We were on our way to McDonald's when the boy with the shaved head dipped his shoulder and pushed into my chest. Hard.

I stumbled backward, not really understanding what had just happened. One second I'm mimicking Jim Carrey, the next I'm trying to stay upright.

"What are you looking at?"

I knew what that meant. I drew myself back upright and looked at where the shout had come from. Three lads, all in tracksuits, shaved heads, and sneers. My heart rate went up a fair few notches.

Alexandra and Michelle had walked ahead of us, so didn't see us stop. Chris and Nicola had been holding hands, walking in step with me. They had uncoupled now and were standing on either side of me suddenly.

"What's your problem?"

"Didn't say anything," I said, taking a step forward. Even as my heart attempted to escape from my chest, I wasn't going to back down. I never did. "Must be hearing things."

There was a moment when I thought they'd just walk off. I don't think they ever got anyone talking back to them—I imagine people skulked off and tried to ignore them. Then, they'd be followed for ages until they found relative safety.

Three lads. Only one of them was the same height as me, and

I was quite small. The others might have been around our age, but something had stunted their growth.

"What did you say?"

Thick accents, swagger, and senselessness. The one in the middle, who just happened to be the shortest one, actually snarled at me. He closed the gap quickly, but I'd been expecting it.

I had been in fights before. On the playground, where you had to fight back early or you'd always be a target. I wasn't going to let myself ever be that.

It grew blurry then, as wild punches were thrown from all angles, and I ended up on the ground. I heard screaming, and it took a second before I realized it wasn't coming from me. I got a few digs in, but also took some as well. I could hear Alexandra and Michelle, shouting my name. Chris's name.

Nicola's name.

The last thing I saw before adults stepped in and separated us was Nicola punching the living daylights out of the biggest lad of the three. She was silent. Focused.

She was dragged off him by Alexandra, who was probably doing the lad a favor.

As soon as we were split apart from them, we legged it. Took a right past the Adelphi and up Lime Street as it became Renshaw Street and didn't stop until we made it past Rapid's DIY store. The five of us together.

We ducked down another side street and kept walking. I didn't hear any footsteps behind us, and it became clear that we were out of trouble.

"What the hell happened there?"

I turned to Michelle, who was flushed and breathing hard. She'd spoken around inhalations, as she bent down and put her hands on her knees.

"They started a fight for no reason," I said, feeling the beginnings of a stitch in my side. The popcorn and Coke from the cinema sloshing around in my stomach. I looked down at the back of my hands and saw reddening on my knuckles. "Thank god you were there. They would have battered me if I'd been on my own."

"I think if Nicola was there, she would have dealt with it anyway," Alexandra replied, and while there was a reddening in her cheeks, she wasn't breathing hard. She was staring over at Nicola with a look of awe mixed with a little fear. "It took three of us to get her off that one lad."

I looked across at Nicola, who was breathing hard but smiling. She had moved closer to Chris, who had put an arm around her.

Blood was drying on Chris's nose, the same color on Nicola's hands as she flexed them back and forth.

"Hands okay?" I said to her, feeling the pain in my own now the adrenaline was beginning to wear off.

Nicola looked up at Chris, moving closer to him as he gripped her tighter. "They'll be fine. They deserved it."

We started walking away from town then, trying to work out a way back home without going back into the city center. Once we had calmed down, we were then wary of every corner we turned, waiting for the lads with shaved heads and tracksuits and sneers and snarls to be there ready to finish the job.

All of us except Nicola.

SIXTEEN

The house was empty, as it always was. Even my presence wasn't enough to give it life. It was supposed to be so much more than this, but now the walls were still bare and the furniture scant and practical.

Still, it was better inside than outside. I could finally breathe peacefully.

I slipped off my suit jacket and threw the balled up black tie on top of it. Placed my phone down on the kitchen counter and switched the coffee machine on. My thoughts were of Chris and Nicola, leaving them in the car, so many words left unspoken. I wanted to know how they were feeling. How they were dealing with things. They had each other, which I guess must have helped them, but I still didn't understand why they hadn't talked about what happened. To me, at least.

As the day ended and night fell, I was sitting in front of my computer reading about what happened to Stuart. The scant details, the distance from the reality. Words on a screen that didn't tell me what I needed to know.

He would have felt that silence again, I thought. Maybe that's all he could hear now. Forever.

His body had been found hours after the train hit him. In the media reports, they took great pleasure, it seemed, in not telling a reader exactly what had transpired that night. Instead, they allowed you to fill in the blanks.

He was alone.

He was unrecognizable when he was found.

His body would have been a mangled mess.

He lay on the train track, and a train destroyed everything I had known Stuart to be.

I closed my eyes and tried to picture him as I'd known him. The smile, the laugh, the way his hair always looked like he'd just simultaneously woken up but also spent hours making sure each strand fell perfectly. The glint he would get in his eyes when he was making us laugh. The way his hands would gesticulate as he told a story. The voices he would put on when he was talking about people he'd met.

He was my friend, and I'd let him die alone.

I knew there was more I needed to know.

The house was insufferably quiet when I went to bed. I stripped and got in the shower, stepping back inside when I realized I still hadn't washed the funeral from my body. I could feel the weight of it all on my shoulders still, even as I increased the temperature of the water and let it burn my skin.

I thought of seeing Alexandra, feeling the old wound reopen anew. I wanted to call her when I'd gotten home, but had no doubt how the conversation would go. There was too much that had been destroyed between us. I would only be hurting myself again. And her.

Michelle.

She looked so lost.

I hadn't thought about her that often in the previous few months. How she'd been or how she was. There was always a little niggle of worry in the back of my mind that she would eventually crack and tell someone what we had done, but I doubted the idea she ever would. Self-preservation was a strong factor in all of this. With every passing day, the judgment became worse. She wouldn't be lauded for coming forward now.

Still, she didn't look like the Michelle I'd known for over twenty years. We were never really close—she had always been part of the group, but we were on opposite sides of it. More friends of friends, who just happened to be together almost constantly.

It was because of Stuart, of course. They had been on again and off again for years. That's all it was. She was hurting and probably blamed all of us for making sure they would never end up together.

And now, it was *really* over.

I knew Michelle loved Stuart. That at some point they would stop playing games and settle down. We all did. Then, that fractured memory of a night occurred and changed everything.

There was no real chance of sleep, but I still went through the motions. Lying in bed, flitting between playing music, playing talk radio, watching ASMR videos on YouTube. None of it worked.

Still, it kept the quiet away.

I heard a noise downstairs. A shift of something. The television settling or the fridge making a *clunk* in the night. I could feel my heart beating a little faster as I imagined someone walking through my house. Opening up drawers, trying to find something valuable. It didn't matter that I knew for certain that I'd locked up correctly and that they would have to make a lot more noise getting in than I'd heard.

I listened for anything else, but nothing came. A tap on the window from the branch of the tree that was outside my bedroom as it moved in the wind. That was it.

I closed my eyes to it all, even as it became lighter outside. The low winter sun peeking its way through my curtains. Counting down the hours of sleep I had left until it was daylight outside and my body would finally give in. Tried to will myself to sleep, even as I felt the hours slipping away.

The next morning, I made a rough estimate that I'd perhaps fallen asleep for as long as two hours. As I was standing in my kitchen, waiting for the coffee machine to kick in, I checked the back door and then the front door, just to make sure no one had been in the house. Everything was exactly how I'd left it the night before. Not a mark on either door.

I drank my coffee, then got dressed. I had made the decision to go without thinking too much about it.

The train tracks where Stuart had been found were a half-hour drive from my house. Forty minutes, tops. A Saturday morning, I thought it'd be closer to forty-five, trying to get through town and then farther south of the city, but it wasn't as if I didn't have the time.

I had all the time in the world. What else was I going to do?

It took me forty-five minutes to finally leave the house. Standing in the hallway, staring at the front door, wanting to stay inside where it was safe. Before, finally, I thought of Stuart dying alone and not being there to help him.

That was enough to make me leave.

The tracks were on the southernmost edge of the city—past Speke and Hale, a few hundred yards until the signs would start to say *Widnes*. Most of the access to where the trains would pass at high speeds was fenced off by metal railings. I had already checked on Google Maps and Street View, finding where I thought Stuart may have started his final journey.

The day was overcast, but not raining, thankfully. I zipped up my jacket as I left the car all the same, as the wind picked up around me and whistled into my ears. The traffic was sparser than it had been in town, but there were still cars passing over the hill that shielded the road from the tracks.

At the end of a lane that ran from a main road into an old yard was countryside on one side, the humming of electricity and power on the other. Overhead, power lines stretched above the multitude of tracks underneath. I could walk directly to the small wall that served as no barrier to the tracks themselves.

Only when the metal gates were open, of course. Which they were in the day, I presumed, but hoped not at night. At the end of the lane, however, I saw how someone could easily gain access at night—three large stones blocked any further route down the concrete path for cars, but were also close enough to the railings that you could hop onto one of them and then launch yourself over to the other side. You might hurt an ankle or two on landing, but that wouldn't matter if you were trying to meet a train at three in the morning.

I parked and walked toward the stones, making sure I was correct in my assumption. There were a few tired-looking bunches of cheap flowers tied to the railings. I stopped to look at the cards, seeing names I didn't recognize underneath Stuart's. The cellophane wrappings were wet and cold to the touch. The railings were the metal kind, with the spikes on top that were dull enough that they wouldn't pierce a shoe if you lightly stepped on them.

In the yard to my left, a couple of vans were parked and workers in high-visibility vests were leaning against the hoods, talking between themselves.

I looked farther up the line and saw the bridge that had been pictured in all the news stories on Stuart's death. A few yards away, if that.

This was planned, I thought. Stuart had found this place and come here. Maybe more than once, so he could get the timing right. It wasn't as if freight trains passed this way every few minutes—especially at that time of night. He would have known exactly when to come and what to do.

"Why? What was going on in your head?" I heard myself whisper. I looked toward the men in the yard, making sure they hadn't heard me. They didn't seem to have noticed my presence at all.

I walked farther past the stones, looking for any other access. Looking for some sign that Stuart had been there.

He hadn't left a note behind, according to his sister. That had been something she'd mentioned at the funeral. More than once. As if knowing what was going through his mind would have made any difference. Instead, we were left to speculate. I tried to picture him in my mind, but nothing came to me.

"I didn't expect to see anyone here."

I spun round, recognizing the lilting voice from behind me. I tried to smile, but found I couldn't. Not there. Not then.

"Michelle," I said, putting my hands in my pockets for something to do with them. "I could say the same thing."

"I've been coming down here quite often," she replied, closing the distance between us but avoiding eye contact. "I'm not sure why."

"Are you still angry with us? With me?"

Michelle smiled thinly, then looked away from me. "Don't worry. I've calmed down a little since yesterday. I shouldn't have said those things."

I waved away the apology. "Is this where…"

"Yeah," Michelle said, before I had the chance to finish a sentence I never would have finished anyway. "But you already knew that. I'm guessing you read the stuff in the papers."

I nodded in response, following her gaze and looking over toward the train tracks. "They didn't say much. I kind of worked it out for myself."

"There's a camera farther up the road. It's the last sighting of him. He was walking over the hill, then turned down the lane. He knew where he was going."

"It didn't say that. It didn't say much at all."

"Well, I spoke to his sister," Michelle said, shivering suddenly as the wind picked up again. It blew across us from the field behind and whipped Michelle's hair from her face. She smoothed it down with one hand. "She told me what she knew. There wasn't...there wasn't much left of him."

I winced internally, wishing I didn't want to hear the details. But I needed to know. I wasn't sure why.

"They found ID in a pocket, driver's license and credit cards in his wallet. She was shown a picture of the tattoo he had on his shoulder. You know the one he got in Thailand?"

"The panther. Or the jaguar. I forget which."

"I'm not sure he knew either," Michelle said with a joyless laugh. "That's all they were allowed to see."

I could fill in the rest myself. I didn't want to picture what they had found of him. What state he was in. I'd never sleep again.

"It's my fault."

I shook my head, surprised how quickly she had shifted the blame from the rest of us to just herself. I looked at her and saw the sleepless nights and endless questions running through her mind. I knew what she was going through, and even though I didn't believe it, I said what you're supposed to in those circumstances. "No, it's not, Michelle."

"Yes, it is," she said, loud enough to turn the workers' heads from the yards. "I could have stopped this. I could have helped him."

"No, you couldn't. He knew what he was doing."

"You don't understand," Michelle said, stepping backward now as her entire body seemed to shake a couple of times. "He reached out to me. Tried to talk to me, and I ignored him. I wouldn't listen to him. I never did."

The wind whistled past us again as a train approached in the distance.

"Michelle," I tried again, but she was turning away from me now.

"It's not over, Matt. It never was. And now we're all going to pay for what we did."

SEVENTEEN

The café was a few minutes from the train tracks—old style, with Formica tables and red-and-white checkered table-cloths. The smell of grease was hanging in the air, so thick I almost held my hands up to part the mist as I walked in.

Tea was served in mugs, plonked down in front of Michelle and me. Sugar from a bowl on the table that looked as if it had been sitting there since the café originally opened decades earlier.

I loved the place.

I wanted bacon on toast, but didn't want to eat alone. Michelle looked as if she hadn't eaten for days but had shaken her head when I'd offered to order something. I didn't want to push it any further.

"We've never done this," Michelle said with a tight-lipped smile. "We were always together in the group. Never alone."

"You're right. That's strange, isn't it? All those years and we were always together, just never *alone* together." I thought about the past couple of decades, wondering if I'd ever made much of an effort with Michelle. We were friends, but would we have been without the others? Probably not. That wasn't to say I didn't like her a lot even so. I knew my life wouldn't be as good without her being in it, even if we hadn't really been that close in the past. I wanted to change that.

"That's not to say I hadn't wanted to," Michelle continued,

looking toward the table and tracing a pattern in some sugar that had fallen onto the surface. "I suppose it's one of those things that happens in groups of friends. There's always a few who don't really interact outside the whole."

"I suppose so," I replied, but I knew there was more to it than that. I remembered twenty years earlier—how Chris and I had met Nicola and Alexandra. It was just expected that once Chris and Nicola had gotten together, and Alexandra and I didn't, that Michelle and I would. It had never gotten to that point though. It was friends and nothing more. We were very different people.

It took a couple of years, but Alexandra and I eventually ended up together. I remembered those years from eleven to thirteen, when I had tried to pluck up the courage to tell her my feelings. Too young to realize, too young to act on them. We had met Michelle by that point, and I knew she was the only one in the group who could see what was going on with me.

Stuart was later, but Michelle had boyfriends throughout high school. None of them had stuck.

I had a memory then—stark and vivid. Sitting on the promenade, down by Otterspool Promenade. A day out, an adventure. Probably the farthest we'd been from our little neighborhood alone.

A clear and bright day. The kind you remember years later as being how all the summer days were. The sun on our faces, Chris and I making each other laugh. Nicola rolling her eyes at us. Alexandra dangling long legs over the side of the promenade wall. Me trying to perfect my impression of Mick Johnson from *Brookside*. Chris quoting *Austin Powers* in the most cringeworthy way imaginable.

It was Michelle I remembered most now. That day, her bouncing around as we sat. Singing a variety of different songs, providing the soundtrack to our day. One day it would be Spice Girls, the next No Doubt. The one I remembered most vividly was the day we heard "Barbie Girl" by Aqua on repeat.

"Do you remember going down to the promenade when we were kids?" I said, wondering if she recalled those times still. Whether they had been diminished and forgotten about. "Summer vacation and all that?"

"Of course," Michelle replied, a small smile appearing, then vanishing just as quickly. "They were good times."

"Every day you had a new song that was suddenly your favorite. You'd sing it all day. Used to drive me mad, but I miss that now."

"I can't believe I used to do that," Michelle said, shaking her head. "My self-awareness wasn't something I was known for, I suppose."

"I thought it would be like that forever. Just a group of us having fun, not taking life too seriously. What happened to us?"

"We all grew up, Matt. Things change."

"I know. I just wish we could go back to that time, that's all I'm saying. Things were changing from the second we left high school. And I'm not just talking about singing in the street. Everyone seemed to become a little more miserable day by day."

"That's being an adult for you."

I shrugged in response, but I wasn't sure. I tried to track the moment when life had begun to become different for us. When we had started not to appreciate what we had—the friendships, the relationships.

It was probably around the time we went to university.

The fact that we were now all responsible for the death of someone had only compounded it. We had a shared secret now. One we never discussed and that had driven us all apart.

"I've never spoken to anyone about what happened," Michelle said, seeming to read my mind. She leaned forward as she spoke, wrapping her hands around the mug of tea for warmth. "I've been waiting for someone to say we got it wrong, but I can't find a single person who has been called a victim of the Candle Man in the past year. It all stopped."

"We know why that is."

"I don't think anyone would understand."

"I agree," I replied, leaning an elbow on the table and itching the back of my head with the other hand. "It doesn't mean we can't think about it. Which is what Stuart was probably doing a lot of, if you ask me."

Michelle shook her head. "It wasn't just that. There were other things happening."

"What kind of things?"

"Have you had anything sent to your house? A message about what we did?"

I shook my head. I didn't really understand what she was asking. I was about to question it, but she continued talking before I had the chance.

"He was messed up after what we did in those woods," Michelle said, looking past me and out of the window behind me. "I tried to talk to him a few times, but he was just numb to it all. Then, a couple of weeks ago, something happened."

"What?"

"I don't know, but whatever it was made him scared. He wouldn't talk to me anymore. He slammed the door in my face and wouldn't reply to any texts or messages. Nothing. He just said it wasn't over and that we were all going to be next. That we weren't alone in those woods, and now we were all going to have to face what we'd done."

I sat back in my chair, trying to figure out what Michelle was telling me. "Someone else knows what we did. And wants what? Some sort of payback?"

"That's what I think. And Stuart was just the first one they got to. But we're all going to be found out..."

"I'm sure that's not going to happen," I said, talking over Michelle. Shaking my head. Even as my leg bobbed up and down nervously under the table. On some level, I'd known this would happen. As if the past year had been spent in a holding pattern, waiting for the fall to come. It wouldn't be a smooth descent either. We were going to plummet to the ground. "No one knows as long as none of us has talked to anyone. You definitely haven't spoken to anyone, right?"

Michelle shook her head. "Of course not. I haven't talked to anyone. Not since that night. I just wanted to forget about it, but I can't. It's always there, just a voice at my shoulder, reminding me how wrong we are."

I'd said the same thing to myself time after time, but that didn't mean I completely believed it. I had spent so many sleepless nights trying to rewrite history—how I would have done things differently if I'd known the consequences. It was impossible though. "We did the only thing we could in the situation."

"You don't believe that," Michelle said, and she was right. "That's just the lie we all told ourselves. Well, now we're going to have to face up to what we've done."

"We saved him." I lowered my voice, even though we were the only customers in the café and the cook-slash-waitress was nowhere to be seen. "He would have died out there. You know that. Stuart saw something he wasn't supposed to and that's why that *man* had his hands wrapped around Stuart's throat. It's that simple. If we hadn't done it, he'd have been dead a year ago and we would never have been able to forgive ourselves."

"Maybe," Michelle replied, but she held no conviction in her tone. "Doesn't mean we still didn't do something wrong. If someone knows what we did, isn't that a good reason to come back after us? And what about Mark Welsh?"

"What about him?"

"Someone moved his body, Matt. Why do we never talk about *that*?"

I remembered when we first learned the name of the boy who Alexandra had found in the woods. The Candle Man's last victim, it seemed. A day or so after the festival had ended, his face was everywhere. A young man, who had disappeared and never returned. His family had never really been out of the news since. "I...I don't know."

"What if the man we killed wasn't working alone? What if someone saw what we did out there, moved that lad's body, and is now out to make us pay for it?"

"What are you saying? That someone hid his body to blackmail us a year later? That Stuart killed himself because he was worried about being outed for what we did?"

Michelle looked across the table, catching my eye for the first time. I found myself wanting to look away.

"No," Michelle said, lifting the mug of tea to her lips and taking a small sip. She set it back down and drew her coat closer around her. "He wouldn't kill himself. All I know is that I'm next. I don't know how, I don't know when, but I'm next."

"How can you know any of this? I think you're letting your imagination run away with you. What happened to Stuart isn't going to happen to you."

"I knew him better than any of you did," Michelle said, her

chair sliding back on the floor. She rose slowly from it, running a shaking hand through her hair. She sighed and shook her head. "I would have known if he were going to do something like that to himself."

"Michelle, wait—"

"I've got to go," she said, cutting me off before I had the chance to ask her to stay. "I can't be here anymore. I just…I just wanted to see if you had anything to tell me. That's all. Maybe I'm just going crazy. Grief can do that to you."

I tried to keep her there again, but she was already out the door. I left some money on the table—too much for a couple mugs of tea, but I didn't have time to wait for my change. Chucked my coat on and left the café, looking up and down the road to see where Michelle had gone.

There was no one around. I thought about trying to find her again, running up and down the road, calling out her name. It would have been useless. She had already told me as much as she was going to, I felt.

And what had she told me? That she couldn't believe that Stuart had killed himself. That someone was coming back for them. It wasn't possible, I decided. Michelle was simply upset and didn't know how to handle it. That was all it was, I told myself. Grief and fear was a chilling mix to have to deal with, I assumed. It could make us more susceptible to ideas we would never soberly think of, thoughts we would usually ignore.

Still, as I walked back down to where I parked my car, I couldn't help but feel that someone was watching my movements. The hairs on the back of my neck rose in response to the feeling.

I looked over my shoulder, but the road was empty.

1996

In the dark, anything is everything. A shadow becomes a monster. A whisper becomes a scream. Silence becomes fear. Yet there was always excitement lying in the darkness too. A sense of facing something and staring it down.

I loved the night.

School had finished for summer the previous day—late July, still a few weeks away from it raining every day of summer break. We'd stopped singing "It's coming home" for now, and even though Chris wasn't that interested in football, he'd still let me take penalty kicks against him.

I scored every time. Gareth Southgate had nothing on me.

I was still not over Manchester United beating Liverpool in the FA Cup Final, but England doing so well had been a nice distraction.

Fourteen years old. All my friends were already fifteen. It annoyed me more every single passing year.

We were too young to be there, but it was something to do. A way of ridding us of the boredom that was always our enemy. And, if we were being truthful, it would make us look good to the girls. We were in the throes of adolescence now, and it burned underneath every conversation we had. Chris and Nicola were in each other's pockets every day, so they were fine. I was still trying to ignore the fact that I liked Alexandra, because she didn't seem all that interested in me.

That night, Michelle had invited Mikey—some lad who lived on her road. He was the same age as us but looked older. He went to a different school as well, so we didn't know him.

He was a bit rougher than us. Said he'd lived in Bootle until recently, which was an estate farther toward the city center than where we lived. Houses closer together and looking a bit worse for wear than ours.

Mikey took the lead, which didn't bother us all that much. He had brought the cider, so it was only fair I suppose. Usually, it was always my ideas that they followed, my path, always had been. I'd come up with something, and everyone seemed to be happy to go along with it. I sometimes wondered what the other four would do without me. Probably stay in every day. It wasn't like they'd be nobodies without me around, but I was the leader of sorts. I was actually happy to have a break from it.

The rumors had started earlier in the week, that someone had been spotted hiding in the scrapyard. Chris had heard it first, then relayed it to us later. Over the week, the story had grown, became something more, until it came to the point where it went from something to be feared to something that could be conquered.

We were deep into high school and people considered us the misfits. The group that was always a little off from the rest. The hierarchy didn't seem to apply to us. We were separate—our own tier of oddity.

"I'm telling you, there's nothing here."

"Then it'll be a boring night and we won't have to worry about it then, right?" I replied, shooting a smirk toward Michelle as I spoke. She was standing with her arms folded across her chest, rolling her eyes at us. I could see fear in them when she finally looked back at me. Mixed with excitement.

"We go down there, we have a drink, then we can tell everyone we got drunk right in this spot," Mikey said, his accent seeming to grow thicker by the syllable. "We'll be legends."

"No one will believe us," Chris replied but didn't stop walking down into the yard.

The story was that bad people were using this yard for shady stuff. Drugs, more than likely, I thought. I wasn't sure what the reason for us being on their patch would be, but it was already too late to back out.

"There's no one here," Alexandra whispered, placing a hand for balance on my shoulder briefly. I tried not to show how much that affected me. Tried to stay cool. I was fooling nobody, I guessed.

"That's what I'm hoping," I replied as quietly as she had spoken. "Don't worry anyway. If there were anyone here, they'd have run off as soon as they heard that lad's voice. You can probably hear him from over the water."

She laughed softly, and the sound almost made me collapse into a heap of teenage hormones.

"Just wait, will yer?" Mikey said, still leading the way. "It's not even dark yet. Got to be patient like. They're not gonna do their business when it's still light out."

I didn't think he was that convincing, but we still followed him down.

"Yeah, but I've got to be back before eleven; otherwise, me mum will kill me."

Mikey shot Michelle a look. She didn't seem to notice, but I'd seen that stare before. It made me tense up. They were on a mission now, and Mikey was the leader. They had to listen to him.

And Mikey wanted Michelle to be impressed by him so much it could only lead to trouble.

The scrapyard was easy enough to get into. There were steel railings on one side, only accessible from the railway line that ran behind it. We'd gotten onto that with no problem—a disused station, left derelict and broken down, easy to cross. The night was quiet and still, the sounds of distant traffic barely making their way over to us.

Behind them, a housing estate we'd crossed quickly. We'd all heard the stories about what happened to people from different postcodes entering. Minutes from the city center, but it might as well have been a different world. This was now our place. We would be legends.

That was the plan, anyway.

"I heard it's that Smith family," Michelle said quietly, as we made our way through the trees and across the rocky part of the entry. "That they take ears as trophies and that they have a load of them collected. Reckon that's true?"

"No, why would they do that?"

"Because it makes a statement, doesn't it? No one is going to try to mess with them if you could lose an ear just by being close enough to wherever they're doing business."

"The whole point is that you piss them off and you're never seen again. How many kids you see walking around with no ears? None. That's how many. They'd kill you, rather than have you walking around with a story to tell people."

I smiled to myself as I listened to them talk. Chris's voice had broken finally earlier that year, but every now and again, it faltered. Usually when he was talking to Michelle and usually when it was to explain things to her that he couldn't believe she didn't know.

I shook my head, kicking a fallen branch to one side, watching it skitter off into the distance. There was a gap in the railings, just wide enough for us to slide through. I was careful not to catch my new track pants on the metal, dreaming about the amount of clothes I'd be able to buy when I started making money for myself. It would be better than waiting for my mum and dad to notice I was growing out of everything I already owned.

The air was still as we dropped down into the yard. Colder too. It was pitch-black, my eyes adjusting slowly to the place. No streetlights permeated. It was silent now, as if we'd stepped into another world. A silent world.

One of the group made some kind of exclamation and then a short beam of light extended from a flashlight. It didn't really help all that much, but it slowed my heartbeat a little.

The shadows began to take form. Broken down cars, big pieces of metal propped up against them. Short, small dirty paths, winding between one wreck and another. From the outside, it hadn't looked that big, but now, I felt as if I'd entered somewhere I could never find my way out of again.

"Did you hear that?"

I turned toward the voice but didn't say anything. I'd heard it too. It sounded like whispers on the breeze. Hanging around us, daring me to keep going.

"I definitely heard something," Michelle said. Her voice was barely audible. I shifted to the center, standing next to Mikey. His breathing mirrored my own—short and stilted.

"What's the plan?" I said to him, hoping he'd make the decision that we'd done enough.

He turned to me in the faltering light, and I could sense his smile.

"Who wants first swig?"

We were in roughly the middle of the yard, I'd guessed. We dragged a couple of old spoilers and car bumpers from the scrap and sat uncomfortably in a sort of semicircle. It was past ten o'clock by then, Michelle checking her watch every minute or so.

Mikey took the first drink. Gulped from the three-liter bottle of Diamond White cider and then wiped a hand across his mouth when he was done. He passed it along until it got to me. I swigged a little and tried to hide how much I hated the taste.

"Do we just…wait or something?" I said as the bottle came back around my way again and I bought a little time before I had to drink.

"We drink this one, then the other, and then see if we can find anything on the other side."

"Don't you think they'd be somewhere else anyway?" Chris said, sitting next to me, shifting uncomfortably on the plastic bumper. "I doubt they do business in some massive scrapyard a ten-minute walk from town, you know? If we know about it, won't the police as well?"

"Hiding in plain sight," Mikey replied, chugging down the last of the bottle as it was passed to him. He was already slurring his words and trying to move closer to Michelle. She either didn't seem to notice or was trying to ignore him. I tensed a little again, wondering how the night was going to end concerning the new lad in our group.

I didn't want to be there anymore.

"Should we even be here?"

Mikey turned on Nicola, grabbing the bag at his feet as he did so. Removed the bottle of cider, and pointed in her direction as he spoke. "You don't have to be."

"I bet you run before I do," Nicola replied, deadpan. Straight. "Just be quiet when you're sprinting out of here, calling for your mam."

I cracked up as the alcohol went to my head a little. Alexandra followed suit, as did Chris. Mikey opened his mouth to say something back, but then caught a look in Nicola's eyes and seemed to think better of it. Instead, he screwed the cap off and swallowed down the cider.

Then, Mikey thought again and decided to go against his first—correct—instinct. "At least I've got a mum to shout for."

Nicola didn't move, but Chris was on his feet in a second. I was up with him, a hand on his shoulder. I didn't think him trying to fight in that yard with someone like Mikey would end well.

"What did you say?"

"It's just weird isn't it? Your mom leaving and never coming back. Doesn't usually happen. Makes you wonder about the woman, that's all. And the dad. How bad it must have been to just up and leave your kids like that."

I held my breath, waiting for Nicola to explode. Instead, she seemed dumbstruck by anger. We all knew how touchy a subject her mom leaving was. We weren't sure of the story behind it, but Chris had once said to me that it hadn't been easy.

I'd seen Nicola's dad recently, and he looked a shadow of the man he'd once been. He'd always been a bit of a drinker, but I imagined that had only become worse in the previous few months.

We never talked about it.

There were a few beats of silence, then Mikey broke out into laughter that no one joined in with. "Just jokin', lad, calm down," Mikey said, holding out the cider bottle as a peace offering. Chris looked at him for a few seconds, as I gripped his arm a little harder. Then, he took the bottle from Mikey's hand and downed a large portion of it.

I glanced at Nicola, who watched the exchange with a passive look on her face.

The night should have been over at that point.

"I've gotta go," Michelle said, breaking the silence that had followed. "I'll just about make it back in time if I leave now. And I haven't had enough for them to be able to smell cider on me I reckon."

"Wait, we've only just gotten here," Mikey replied, a definite slurring to his voice now. "Stay five more minutes, for me."

She didn't even look at him. I stood up, looking at Alexandra briefly and shrugging my shoulders. "Want me to walk you back?" I asked Michelle.

"No, it's okay."

"It's all right. I've got to go as well," Alexandra said, suddenly on her feet and next to me.

And I was fourteen and didn't know what I was doing. Somewhere in the back of my mind, there was a part of me that shouted to follow them. That I could walk back with them, then maybe with Alexandra to her house. We could have been alone for once.

Mikey called them chicken and carried on drinking. I could see the fear in their eyes even as they protested innocence. That they had to go home.

I sat there and watched them leave. Jealous.

Just the four of us were left then.

"Let's go farther in," Chris said, nudging me with an elbow and getting to his feet. "We can really say that we've done it then."

We murmured agreement and stood up. My head swam a little but cleared enough to follow them into the yard. We trudged in silence, save for the occasional nervous laugh or whisper. Walked around the yard, ducking between cars and other pieces of scrap metal. As we moved, the various pieces seemed to grow larger and more enclosing, looming over us like behemoths.

I *really* didn't want to be there.

Then, I heard another noise. Like the first, only louder. I had the thought that maybe it was real. That we had entered a place of myth and legend, and we wouldn't get back out. My heart crashed against my chest as the thought grew and splintered, until the darkness seemed to grow form and creep around me.

It was completely night now. Black. A clear sky above us, somewhere. I couldn't see it for the old cars and metal that seemed to be endless and formless.

"We need to get out of here," I said, turning back to where Chris was behind me.

Only, he wasn't there.

No one was.

I looked around, begging my eyes to see light. To see anything. Only, it seemed to grow darker and darker. I could feel my hands start to shake first, then the rest of my body turned to jelly, as my stomach churned and wheeled around itself.

I forced myself to move. Somehow. I leaned against the shell of a car after taking a few steps, then tried to speak.

I couldn't.

Fear had crawled into my throat and closed it.

I tried again and managed a whisper. "Chris?"

Even I could barely hear it.

"Chris," I said again, and this time it was a little louder. I strained my ears to hear any other sound, but it was silent. I was about to talk again when I stopped myself.

As I moved around another crumpled car, it hit me. A scent

entered my nostrils and almost knocked me over. It was strong, and it made me move quicker.

Death.

It was a similar smell to one I'd had the bad luck to encounter a week earlier. We'd found an abandoned fridge on a green near where we lived, and when we opened it up found an open packet of some kind of meat. I didn't know how long it had been there, but this was what I was experiencing now.

It was like a weight on my shoulders as I moved slower around the wrecks and tried to work out a way back. A way home. I tried calling to Nicola, but got the same silence back.

I didn't shout Mikey's name.

Against my knees, my hands trembled as I crouched behind another car. Tried to will life into my limbs, so I could move. Get away. Forget everything and tear out of there like my life depended on it.

I didn't believe in fairy tales. I didn't believe in myths. In the stories we told one another to scare. The air seemed to sense my thoughts and shifted in response.

It was all in my head.

It was all in my head.

I was seeing, I was sensing, I was hearing things that weren't real.

I could feel ghostlike fingers on the back of my neck. Goose bumps sprouted even farther on my arms and were joined with others. I choked back a sob as I suddenly lost years of my life and became a child again.

I wanted to be anywhere else. At home. On my little estate of houses. Safe. At home with mum and dad.

I was just a little boy.

I was alone.

Then, I heard a scream, and it jolted me alive.

I didn't stop. I didn't turn around. I forgot anyone else existed and thought of myself alone.

I ran.

EIGHTEEN

Stuart's sister was waiting for me at the house when I pulled up half an hour later. I took a deep breath and wiped my face another time, then got out of the car. I had called her from the car, needing somewhere else to go. Now I was outside—away from the relative safety of home—I needed to keep going.

I needed to know what was in his mind.

I'd been there a few times, but not for at least a year now. It was a simple semidetached house, but the street was obviously in a good area. Halfway between Manchester and Liverpool, tree-lined roads and bungalows at one end. The few cars parked there were all displaying newer license plates, and every house seemed to have its own drive.

No one had ever really questioned where Stuart got his money from, but I think we all knew now. He would sometimes mention his family, but it was all about him when he was talking. Now, we understood more. Help with a deposit here, the funding for a few overseas trips there. It would all have come into play, I imagined.

They may not have been in the tens of millions, but I guessed Stuart's family was a lot better off than any of the rest of the group's parents.

I locked the car behind me and walked toward Stephanie, who was waiting on the doorstep. There was an awkward moment, when I thrust out a hand to shake and she looked for a hug. We ended up in a strange half embrace eventually, before she opened the door and let us inside.

"I haven't really been through anything," Stephanie said as I wiped my feet and closed the door behind me. She flicked a hand across her hair and continued. "I don't think my mum and dad are going to want to deal with this, so I guess I'll have to at some point. I just wouldn't know where to start."

"I can imagine," I replied, looking around the hallway and then into the living room. I'd only been there for parties, so the lack of bodies, disco lights, and an inordinate amount of booze made everything look very different. There were photographs on the walls where there would be some kind of banner hastily put up. With Stuart living outside of Liverpool, we were only ever there for birthdays or coming-home celebrations. Now, it looked like a home.

An empty home, but a home all the same.

"I've not really touched anything since...since he was found," Stephanie said, halting over her words but somehow keeping her composure. "We looked for a note or something, but we didn't find anything. Did he...did he say anything to you?"

I wanted nothing more than to be able to answer that question in a way that would give her comfort. I had nothing to say. I shook my head and looked down at the immaculately vacuumed floor. "I wish there were something. We haven't really spoken all that much lately. Both busy, I guess. I wish I had though. Maybe if I'd known, I could have stopped him."

"I've been saying the same thing every day. I suppose we can't think that way, but it doesn't make this any easier. There's always going to be a part of me that thinks I could have done something more." Stephanie turned away, looked at the sofa, then sat down on it. She leaned forward with her head in her hands, but her shoulders stayed still. She was holding it in, I guessed.

I was glad of that. I wasn't sure if I'd hold up anymore if she lost it. "Would it be okay if I had a look around?" I asked quietly enough so as not to jolt her out of whatever silent act she was going through.

She waved a hand in response, and I didn't ask twice.

I walked out of the room and through a hallway to a kitchen-dining room at the back. It was modern built, the tiled floor ending at the edge of the kitchen area and dividing it from the dining room part. When I'd been there last, the table that was sitting there now had been pushed up against the wall and filled with various bottles of alcohol. Now, it was tastefully set—a solid brown oak look that felt smoother than anything I'd ever touched when I ran my hand over it.

I moved back to the kitchen, looking over the fridge door, where a couple of letters had been attached with magnets. I didn't pry but could tell they were nothing of interest anyway. A dentist appointment, a flyer for a local fish-and-chips shop.

I didn't want to start rooting through drawers, but I stopped and thought about what I was doing. What I thought I was looking for exactly, I wasn't sure, and Michelle's meeting with me had only served to veer me farther off course.

I moved back to the dining room, pausing at the table, as something caught my eye. I turned, but nothing seemed to jump out at me. I frowned, looking at the pictures on shelves in the alcoves. It was a mix of what I assumed was Stuart's family and pictures of us.

Stuart in the middle of the group of six—2001, second year of university. Even though he was the last to join, he was the main focus. He was the leader.

Me and Stuart—2004 in Ibiza. I look exactly how I remember feeling: tired, drunk, and wanting to be just about anywhere else at that point.

Stuart and Michelle—I think around 2008. Twenty-four or twenty-five by then. An arm slung around her shoulder, pointing and laughing at the camera. His youth was disappearing with each photograph, but the dimples in his cheeks and glint in his eye hadn't diminished at all.

That's when it hit me. All of these photographs depicted memories—memories that would stay where they were and never be joined by any new ones. That's what had been taken from us.

What *we* had taken from us.

I tore my eyes away from them. Tried to work out what I was doing. Instead of dealing with the grief alone, I had come there for what? An answer to a question I didn't know?

You should be at home. You should be somewhere safe. Not here. Not here. Not outside.

I tried to ignore the pull of the recurring thought in my head and concentrated on what I was there for really.

Stuart had been lost for the past year. Just like we all were. Looking for something that would never come back.

Himself.

When I used to hear people talk about going abroad to "find themselves," I used to laugh, roll my eyes, shake my head. Now I understood why someone might feel the need to do that.

Floor-to-almost-ceiling PVC doors looked out onto a back garden that was almost empty of anything but lawn. I looked out at the rapidly diminishing light outside and thought of Stuart doing the same. Alone in the house, no one to call and speak with.

There were six of us in that group. And none of us wanted to talk about the past.

Other than Michelle.

I allowed myself to realize the truth; I didn't know why I was there. What had made me think that by coming to Stuart's house I would find some kind of answer? There wasn't one to be found. I was simply opening up old wounds and driving myself into a darker place.

Get out. Get in your car, and drive home. Home is safe.

Stuart hadn't been able to live with what we had done. That was all. Michelle was probably struggling with the same issue.

Still, there was that unanswered question that had ruined our lives for the past year.

What had happened to Mark Welsh? Who had taken his body?

We had all ignored it as best we could, but maybe Michelle was right.

I had to leave. I moved away from the doors and turned back into the room. My eye was caught again by an item on the table. This time I knew what it was that had caught my attention.

A candle on the table. In the middle. Housed in a small storm lantern that looked as if it was locked in some way.

It was red.

Burned down, so it was melted wax on a base.

Bloodred.

NINETEEN

I was standing at the table, wanting to lift the candle from it and carry it away. Throw it somewhere it wouldn't be found. *Couldn't* be found. Ostensibly because I knew what it meant. Not just to me—to all of us.

It meant we weren't free.

It meant we never really left those woods.

It meant we would have to go back to a place none of us wanted to go.

My hand hovered over the candle, almost as if I were willing it to relight.

Then, another thought came to me. What if this was just another red candle? What if Stuart just happened to have a candle on his dining room table and I was simply connecting two unrelated events? How many people in the world have red candles in their houses? My bet would be that there would be a large number of them. That's all it was—another house decoration that wouldn't have caught my eye at any other time.

Only, I knew that wasn't the case here.

I knew all of us knew the significance of that color candle. The housing it was within. The relevance to our lives. There was no chance I would have something like that in my house now, so why would Stuart be any different?

Michelle was right.

This was what she was talking about back at the café.

My hands were shaking as I reached back to the candle, wanting to touch it. See if it was actually real. Wonder about its significance now. There was a reason for it being here, but I didn't want to know it. Suddenly, I wanted to be anywhere else.

Not anywhere.

I wanted to be back in my own house. Alone. Away from it all. I didn't want to deal with any of this. It was a mess, and even though it was a mess of our own making, I wasn't sure I could do anything to make it right.

I looked at the candle again, and I was back in those woods. Seeing Alexandra standing over Mark Welsh's body. Seeing the candle and hearing Michelle tell us what it meant. Even now, I refused to believe it. That we had stopped a serial killer. Those things don't happen to people like us. We're normal.

Or we were.

I didn't think we could say that any longer. Our lives had taken a turn in one night, and now we seemed to be trapped in an endless nightmare. The worst thing about it—there was no escape from it. Not alone, in my house. Even there, all I could think about was that night and what we did.

Now, I knew—we had never really left those woods. Something was following us and keeping us in there.

"You okay?"

I moved quickly, banging into one of the chairs pushed against the table and swearing as pain shot through my knee. Stephanie was standing behind me, and I realized it was her voice I'd heard. I turned with a hand on my heart. "Sorry, you startled me. I was miles away."

"You look like you've seen a ghost... What's up? Have you found something?"

I looked back at the burned candle on the table and then back at Stephanie. Shook my head. "No, I was just thinking about when I was last here. We, erm, used to have parties and stuff. Not many here, like, just a couple. Didn't look as nice when we had them. He really kept this place looking good."

"He was always like that, even when we were kids. His bedroom would be spotless, while mine was like any other teenager's room. My mum and dad would get mad at me all the time and ask why I couldn't be more like him. I always thought it was weird though. He liked things in a certain way."

I smiled but couldn't rectify this version of Stuart with my own memories of him. He'd always seemed somewhat...flaky? I wasn't sure that was the right word, but I didn't think of him as orderly. He was always up to some scheme or other. Going off traveling, bouncing around from job to job. Nothing about this seemed to fit with what I knew about him.

I guess I didn't really know him as well as I'd thought.

"What was he like in the time before? I mean in the weeks leading up to him..." I couldn't finish the sentence, but I knew she would know what I meant. My heart slowed a little, as the initial shock of seeing the candle dissipated. The need to run out of there without looking back subsiding.

I still wanted to go back to the safety of my own house, but another part of me somehow gave me the ability to stay.

I had to know everything.

Stephanie closed her eyes briefly and turned her head away. "He seemed okay. A bit more skittish than usual, but you know what he was like. We just assumed he was about to announce some new path he was about to take. I always thought he'd disappear one day and we wouldn't know where he'd gone. He'd do that from time to time—decide on a whim to go to

India or Thailand for a month or longer. We'd get a phone call eventually, telling us where in the world he was."

"That sounds like the Stuart I knew," I said, pulling a tight smile that turned into a grimace of remembrance. "That's how we'd find out as well. Or from a Facebook status update or something. Checking into an airport on his way to some foreign country."

"Yeah, he was spontaneous to the extreme. I don't know. About a month ago, there was definitely something going on with him. I don't know what it was, but he looked like he hadn't been sleeping, so I asked him about it. He didn't really say anything, but he wasn't himself. All he said was that he wished he could tell me more about his life, which didn't make any sense. I knew loads about his life—he wasn't exactly discreet about it."

"That's true," I replied, thinking of the way Stuart could tell endless stories. Always funny, about the scrapes he would get into, the awkward situations, the safely dangerous ones. He always came through them at the end. "He could talk for hours. And he was never boring."

"I suppose we never really know what's going on in people's minds. What they're going through when we're not around. I just wish we did."

For once, I disagreed with her, but didn't say so. I didn't want her to know the truth. No one should hear that.

Stephanie didn't want to know what Stuart was thinking about in the past year.

"I guess so," I said, ignoring the part of me that wanted to tell her everything, just so someone else could share the burden of our collective guilt. "He never told you about anything he was worried about or anything like that?"

"I don't understand," Stephanie replied, her brow furrowing into a frown. "I don't think he did. He wasn't himself, but I didn't take that to mean he was on the verge of...of hurting himself. He was just preoccupied. That's all. Nothing that could have led me to think he was capable of doing that."

At that, Stephanie buried her face in her hands and left the room, leaving me standing next to the dining room table. I thought of going after her, comforting her in some way, but I didn't think I could do that. I needed to think clearly.

The candle was still sitting in the middle of the table—a reminder of what can happen when you don't think about what you're doing properly. A reminder that actions have consequences.

We had killed a stranger.

He was an evil man. Someone who had killed who knows how many people, all over the country. Someone who the police were pretending didn't exist.

Only, we knew the truth, but we couldn't tell people that fact.

I moved quickly around the table, keeping the candle in the periphery of my vision, as if it might come to life. Checked to see where Stephanie had gone, but she seemed to have left him there alone. I took the opportunity. On the display cabinet against the wall, a few notepads had been left on one of the shelves. I flicked through them, seeing various dates and times. Appointments. Reminders.

On one near the bottom, I found something.

> October. A year since—
> Speak to M and C
> Meeting with "Peter"—he knows more
> Eye appt—26th Sept

I continued reading, but I couldn't find anything else that referenced the murder. Or his mental state. Listened for any movement coming from outside the room, in case Stephanie was coming back.

I tried to think of someone called Peter and remembered that being his dad's name. Or his uncle's name. One of the two. On one of the pages, I recognized a sketch of his tattoo. Then, on more pages there were further drawings of it, as if he were trying to get it right. I wondered what that signified to him. A better time? Somewhere he wanted to return to?

I wasn't sure.

All the time, the candle was behind me.

If I listened hard enough, I would hear what was becoming almost like a mantra in my head now.

Someone knows. Someone knows. Someone knows.

TWENTY

We had managed to kid ourselves for a year now. An entire year. Somehow.

How could we have ignored it? How could we have believed it wasn't going to eventually come back on us?

Mark Welsh. The young lad. Dead. We had seen his body. We had moved his body...and then, it was gone.

And we did nothing but run away. Pretend that it didn't happen. Pretend that it didn't mean someone knew what we had done and could reappear at any moment.

I was driving in the dark—something I didn't really like to do—but that didn't stop me from taking my hands from the ten and two position on the steering wheel and smacking the side of the driver's door in frustration.

Was Stuart the first?

We were next. One by one. That's what I was scared of at that moment. That someone had been there that night and now wanted... What? Revenge? Why wait this long?

Questions appeared and disappeared from my head, swirling around and around with no cohesion. I wasn't sure if this was just a manifestation of grief and guilt. The lack of sleep and Stuart's death creating an issue that didn't really exist.

Then I thought about that red candle.

I had to keep going. I knew if I went back home, I'd never leave again.

So I drove on.

———

Michelle lived on the Wirral Peninsula now, over the water and outside of Liverpool for the first time since I'd known her. She was right when she'd said we had never really been that close—I knew she worked for a lawyer's office, but I had no real idea what that entailed. She hadn't studied law at university, so I doubted she had become an actual lawyer, but I wasn't sure of anything further than that.

I didn't think I'd ask at this point.

I didn't know much of the Wirral, but with Google Maps on my phone, it didn't take me long to find the place. It didn't look much different from Liverpool—not that it should have, being only a mile or so away. I remembered when I was a kid, being brought over to New Brighton by my parents. It was on its last legs as a family day outing back then. Early nineties. A fair, with bumper cars, coin-pusher machines, and cotton candy. I imagine it looked tired and on the verge of closing down back then, but I only remembered it being fun and sunny every day. The long promenade and beaches that ran for miles, it seemed.

It had been rejuvenated since then, but the funfair remained. It had just been joined by a supermarket, hotel, and a few chain restaurants. I hadn't bothered visiting. I preferred to keep the memories of my childhood in mind instead.

Michelle lived a few miles away in a place called Moreton. A newly built estate, where every house looked like it had just been delivered flat-packed from Ikea. I almost got lost, even with the aid of the GPS, as the rabbit-run of small roads and tiny road signs only brought confusion.

I parked outside and called Michelle from my cell phone. She answered after a couple of rings.

"We need to talk," I said once she'd said hello. I could hear tension and strain in her voice from a single word. "Do you have time?"

"Yeah, I suppose," she replied, then I could see the blinds in her living room part slightly. "You've not really given me much time to tidy up."

I waved from the car. "Don't worry about that. I'll be two minutes."

The street was small and didn't really give much space to park the car and also leave without turning around in someone's driveway. The houses were all small, weirdly identical, and looked like a strong wind could knock them over. It was quiet though, and I could imagine a fair few first-time buyers were seduced by the seclusion and status. Gravel stones crunched underfoot as I made my way to the front door. It opened as I reached it, and Michelle stood in the entrance. For a brief moment, I saw the teenager I'd known years earlier. Then, she was gone. Replaced by the shell that now stood in her place. There was a hint of the person she had been under the unkempt hair and darkened eyes, but only because I'd known it before, I guessed. She turned and walked back inside without a word. I followed her in and realized I'd never actually been there before. I wasn't sure anyone had.

"If you want a drink, help yourself," Michelle said as I took off my jacket and entered the living room. "I've just made myself one."

I decided against it and sat on the leather sofa that was on one wall, at a right angle to the one Michelle was sitting on. A television was muted in the corner, the wall bracket it was attached to wobbling with every movement I made on the floor.

There was an uneasy silence as Michelle curled her legs underneath herself and then turned slowly toward me.

I grimaced and shook my head. "You okay?"

She rolled her eyes at the question. "You know."

"I went to his house after we saw each other," I said, sitting back on the sofa. I laid my jacket next to me and ran a hand through my hair. I realized I didn't want to mention the candle straightaway. Maybe to pretend things were a little more normal than they were or to see if she was going to mention it herself. I knew she'd been to the house, but she hadn't mentioned what I'd seen there. "It was more difficult than I thought it would be. Everything looked so...normal."

"That was Stuart. He was a different person than most people thought."

"Why didn't you two ever settle down?"

"We were never in the same place as the other," she replied after a few seconds of thought. She shifted uncomfortably on the sofa. "I suppose we were always just expected to and that kind of made us resist it. That's not to say we didn't come close on loads of occasions. We had plans; whenever we were in a good place, we would talk about making a go of it properly. I guess I just thought it would happen eventually. We both saw other people, sometimes for a while, but always drifted back into each other's lives somehow. You know what I mean."

"I do. Even when we weren't together, I knew it was just a matter of time with Alexandra. We spent ten years apart, but I think we needed that. Not that it worked out in the end anyway."

"What happened? Why did you break up?"

That was one of the things that kept me awake at night. Why we hadn't made it work in the end. Not being able to answer the question sufficiently. "After that night last year, it was different. It changed us both. I knew something was wrong within a few hours, but I tried to ignore it. When me and Stuart came out of the woods after going to look for my wallet, I knew that instant we wouldn't last. We wouldn't be able to get through it. When we told you all that the lad's body had disappeared, I could see it in her eyes."

"What did you see?"

I knew Michelle would have Alexandra's version of events, but I didn't think it would differ that much to mine. Still, I treaded carefully when I spoke. "I could see that it was never going to go away. That there would be this thing that would hang over us forever. And sometimes that's okay and you can get past it. Look at Chris and Nicola—they seem stronger than ever. With me and Alexandra, we didn't have that history of facing challenges and then suddenly we're struck with something bigger than either of us could handle. When we got back home, it was like we didn't know what to say to each other. I thought all she could see when she looked at me was what I'd done. It ruined us."

"Stuart and I were never together again after that night," Michelle said, wrapping her arms around her legs as she drew them up to her chest. "It wasn't even spoken about. We just both knew we were done. That it was over. Didn't mean we didn't still speak to each other though. You and Alexandra don't speak."

I hesitated, trying to work out what to say. She was right—we didn't speak. And I desperately wished at that moment we still did. Then, maybe I wouldn't be sitting in Michelle's matchbox living room feeling like I had no way out. Maybe I would have someone to help me through whatever this turned out to be. "I don't think we could talk to each other after all this time. Not the way we used to. It still hurts that it had to be over. I can't speak to her because it hurts too much to think about what we lost and can't get back."

"I think of the young guy a lot, you know?"

I frowned at the sudden shift in conversation, but thankfully didn't answer with my first thought.

Why?

The face came to mind instantly, but another part of me wondered if I had it right. Whether I'd remembered it correctly, or whether I had managed to ignore that as well. I stayed silent and looked at the soundless images on the television screen instead.

"Mark Welsh," Michelle said in a tone that faltered on the last syllable. "I've learned more about him than I know about people in my own family."

"Yeah, I try not to think about him too much."

"You know there's going to be a lot of interest in him, with it coming to a year since he 'went missing.' His mum and sisters are all over social media talking about it. They'll be on TV and stuff. They're out there looking for answers, and there's only us who can give them. Does that sit right with you?"

"No, of course not," I replied, leaning forward, elbows on my knees and hands clasped almost as if I were about to pray. "But we can't say anything now. It would be bad for all of us. I know they'll never get the answers about what happened to their son, but what will it help?"

"It'll give them closure," Michelle said, staring at me as if she were daring me to argue against her. "They've been sitting there for almost a year, wondering what happened to their son, and they haven't a clue. How can we sit back and not do anything about that?"

"Calm down, Michelle," I replied, looking around us. I wondered how thin the walls were in these ridiculous houses. Whether the neighbors could hear what Michelle was saying. "I understand, but there's not much we can do. If one of us confesses, that's all of us going down."

"I can't live like this anymore. Not now."

I shook my head in confusion. "What are you talking about?"

"It's not you who's next," Michelle continued, as if I hadn't spoken. "You don't have to worry about it. You will though. We all will."

"You're not making any sense," I said, but Michelle was on her feet and leaving the room. I followed her into the back room, a tiny dining room, with a smaller kitchen leading off it. She was standing next to her dining table—another flat-pack special that could barely sit two people around it. I saw what was sitting on top of it and forgot everything else.

"You see?" Michelle said, turning to me now, her eyes wide and burning into me. "This isn't over. Not for any of us."

Sitting on the table was a red candle in a storm lantern.

Burning slowly.

Dull red, the color of blood.

I was back in those woods again. Standing over that body.

TWENTY-ONE

I took a step back and found myself with my back against the door frame.

"Where did this come from?" I said, feeling the room get smaller around us. The walls closing in as I stared at the flame. The candle was housed in the same contraption as the one we'd seen in the woods. And the one I'd seen in Stuart's house. "Michelle, tell me what's going on."

"It turned up this morning," Michelle replied, her voice quiet and scared. She had wrapped her arms around her body and was looking at me and then the candle in turn. "I thought maybe I'd bought it when I wasn't thinking straight. I got a bit wasted after the funeral. But I was lying to myself. I wouldn't have one of those things in my house. It was left there—in the middle of the table. And it was burning."

"This makes no sense…"

"Don't you get it?" Michelle said, almost pleading with me to understand. "We've always known someone saw us that night. Someone moved Mark Welsh and now they've come back to finish the job. They couldn't get us all that night, but now they've found out who we were and are going to pick us off one by one."

"Who?"

"Well, obviously someone who doesn't feel the need to tell the Welsh family where their son and brother is."

"Someone connected to...*him?*"

Michelle nodded, but there was no triumph in her expression. Only resignation. She tucked a strand of hair behind her ear with a shaking hand.

"We should tell someone," I said, feeling defeated. "It's over. We don't even know who *he* was."

"Weren't you just telling me we had to keep quiet still?"

"Yes, but this changes things," I said, yet I wondered if I really believed that. Part of me still wondered if this was all a trick—a way of Michelle convincing me that we had to tell people what happened, so she could be relieved of her guilt. Thing was nothing that would alleviate it though. We would carry that forever. "We need to do something. If someone has broken into your house and left this here, it's a threat."

"I know that. Do you think I'm stupid?"

"No, of course not—"

"Do you think I don't understand exactly what this means? It means there's a person out there who not only knows what we've done, but who also killed Stuart and is going to try to kill me next. Did you not see it?"

I hesitated and thought about lying. Then, I decided to answer. "A red candle."

Michelle smiled, but it was entirely devoid of humor. "Exactly."

"Why didn't you tell me about it earlier?"

"I wanted you to see it on your own," Michelle said, looking away from me. "Then you could make your own mind up about it."

"How did you even know I would go there?"

"Because I know you, Matt," Michelle replied, turning back to me and staring into my eyes. "I know what you're like. I knew after seeing me, hearing what I had to say, that you wouldn't be able to let things lie."

"What does it mean?"

Michelle sighed and leaned her head back, closing her eyes briefly. "He came to me, about four days before he died. Totally wired, in shock, and he told me about it. I told him he was mistaken, that he probably bought it and forgot, or he wasn't thinking straight. All the things I've been telling myself for the past three days. I didn't listen to him and look what happened."

"Michelle…"

"Don't, okay?" Michelle said, pushing me away as I crossed the room toward her and put a hand on her shoulder. "This is no less than we deserve. We left that boy there. We were going to walk away, like nothing happened. We killed someone, then as soon as we realized it was a *bad person*, thought we could just hide his body and it was all going to be okay. Truth is, it hasn't been. Not for any of us. And now we're having to face up to that."

"Not by being killed for it," I replied, leaning across the table and pausing with hands near the candle. I suddenly didn't want to touch it. I shook away the feeling and picked it up. "It's just a candle. You should get away for a few days and make sure no one is coming after you, but someone might just be trying to mess with our heads, that's all. We should throw this away. Where did you find it?"

"Exactly where it was just now."

"So they got into the house?"

Michelle nodded and then turned away. She wiped a sleeve over her cheek, then the other one. "He's come back."

"But we…we killed him."

"Again, didn't you ever wonder what happened to that lad's body?"

"Of course I did," I said, even though I wanted it to be a lie. I tried not to think about it because I wanted to pretend it didn't happen that way. I never wanted to think about going back to that part of the woods and seeing that bare patch of land where, a few hours earlier, we'd set down an eighteen-year-old kid's body. All I remember after that is my heart beating against my chest and almost twelve months of waiting for the knock on the door. Not being able to sleep at night, thinking that at any moment, that visit would finally come.

"It's just..." I tried to speak, but I couldn't find the words. I took a deep breath and made another attempt. "I just thought there was some explanation for it. That's all. That's what I've told myself, because the alternative is too much to live with. There were hours between us leaving him there and him disappearing. I thought it was an animal or...or something like that."

"A person took him. Put him somewhere else. Made sure no one could ever find him, knowing that we were the only ones who knew the truth and there was no way we were ever going to say a thing about it."

"But the man who killed him is dead. We did that."

"Which is why we know now that he wasn't working alone."

It was almost as if I were hearing it for the first time, thinking of someone else in those woods, watching as six people descended on that man and took his life. Knowing they couldn't do anything. Waiting almost a year for his revenge.

My throat became wet as my stomach churned and the world spun a little around me. I stumbled backward a little, into the living room where I slumped on the sofa and put my head to my knees. Cradled the back of my head.

I didn't want this.

I just wanted to be normal again.

"Here," Michelle said from above me. I looked up, and she handed me a glass of water. I took a few sips and closed my eyes as I leaned back and turned my head toward the ceiling.

"I don't know what to do," she continued. I heard her crossing the room, then opened my eyes and watched her look through the blinds, gazing out onto the dark street. When she continued, she sounded exhausted. "Do I wait to see if I'm right? I haven't slept properly since. Someone has been in here and I didn't even know it."

"You can't stay here," I said, wondering how she hadn't left sooner. How she had stayed there, knowing that at any moment there could be a stranger in her house. "You have to get out of here."

"And go where? I've got nowhere to go."

"You could stay at my house," I replied quickly and confidently, while another part of me wanted to be as far away from her as possible. "You'd be safer there."

"How long can that go on for though?" Michelle said, shaking her head, turning back away from me. "How long do I keep running?"

I understood it now. Why she was talking in riddles and not running as fast and as far as possible.

She wanted this.

"Michelle, you can't let this happen."

She looked at me through eyes that were no longer alive. The light that had always shined in them was gone now. "Why not? Don't you think we deserve it?"

"No, of course not," I said, getting to my feet and feeling the room spin a little again. "We screwed up. I'm not saying we haven't. It doesn't mean we have to give in. He was evil. If he'd been given the chance, he would have killed us all. He was going to kill Stuart. We did what we had to. That's it. Yes, we have to live with that, and it will mess us up for the rest of our lives, but that doesn't mean we deserve...this. I don't care if someone is out there now, looking for revenge or whatever. We did the right thing."

"I keep having the same nightmare," Michelle said, her voice quieter now, as she moved back across the room and sat down. "Ever since it happened. I'm in the woods and there's a banging coming from somewhere. I'm running, trying to find where it's coming from. Every time I feel like I'm getting closer, the noise moves to somewhere else. I can't find it and I just keep going and going, until I can't breathe anymore. That's what life feels like all the time now. Like I'm just waiting for that noise to get closer, while we all pretend it's not coming. I can't handle it anymore. I either have to tell someone what we did, or just wait for whatever noise is coming to arrive."

"We can get through this—"

"No, I can't," Michelle said, cutting me off as I started to speak. She got to her feet and opened the living room door. "I shouldn't have told you what was going on. I should have kept it to myself."

"It's okay. I can help you," I replied, standing up but not moving closer to her. "It's just a blip, okay? There's no reason to let whoever this is win. We all need to just get together and work this out, that's all. All of us. If we can make some sort of plan, it'll all be okay."

"Because the last time we made a plan worked out so well? There's nothing we can do now. Just...just leave me alone. I'll think about it, okay? That's all I'll say."

"Michelle, come with me back to mine. You can stay a few days until we sort all of this out."

She smiled at me, but I knew there was no changing her mind.

"I'll be okay here," Michelle said finally, stepping aside so I knew it was time to leave. "I'm probably worked up over nothing. Maybe I did buy that candle and just forgot about it. I've not exactly been in the right frame of mind recently. I just need a good night's sleep."

I knew she didn't believe that. Someone had been in her house—had left her the same candle as the one I had seen earlier in Stuart's house. The idea of it shook me again—the unreality of it making me want to laugh.

This couldn't be happening.

I wanted to stay. I wanted to convince her that this wasn't the place she should be right then. That there was another way out of the mess we had created. It would be pointless, I could see, but I should have tried harder.

Instead, I left her there and went back home.

I left her to make myself safe again.

1997

A lexandra."

She looked up at me and her face was blank. I couldn't read it at all. Even as an inexperienced sixteen-year-old boy, I still felt like I could work out some things in life. This wasn't one of those things. We had become girlfriend and boyfriend only a month or so earlier. I was still learning.

Alexandra.

"Why do you call me that?" she said, brushing a finger through her bangs to take it away from her eyes, then not flinching as it settled back in the same place. "Everyone else calls me Alex, but you don't. Why?"

I opened my mouth to give an answer, but my brain didn't seem to want to cooperate. I closed it again, waited a few seconds for it to catch up, then made another attempt. "I like your name."

"I *love* my name, but that doesn't answer my question."

Truth was, I didn't really have an answer. I just enjoyed saying it. Everyone else called her Alex, which was fine, but I felt like I wanted to be different. Maybe that was a good enough answer, but at that moment, I wasn't sure what her reaction would be.

"Do you want me to call you Alex?" I said instead, trying to maintain the eye contact she was intent on giving me. I failed. "I can if you want?"

"No. Keep calling me Alexandra."

The summer was almost over, what there had been of it anyway. A typical August in the north of England. The stress of exams over. The wait for results had been worrying, but we had all done well. Further education awaited us—sixth form and the start of A-levels—although it would be different. No school uniform, for a start. We were growing up. I was enjoying the breeze, which was lifting from the sea—calming and warm. The sun was dipping behind the odd cloud, but I was sitting in a T-shirt and feeling comfortable.

"What did you want anyway?" Alexandra said, turning her head in my lap and looking back out across the Irish Sea.

"What?"

"You said my name...?"

I shook my head, trying to remember if there was a reason. Failing to think of one. "I think I just wanted to say it aloud again." I looked down at her, seeing her face in profile. Her face softened and the corners of her mouth turned upward a little.

"My mum is still going on about this Diana thing you know," Alexandra said after a few moments of comfortable silence. "Talking about going down to London for the funeral. Not sure what she expects to see."

"Queen of hearts, wasn't she?" I replied, wishing I could sit there forever. "I'm just glad it didn't happen while we were at school. Not sure I could have handled all the crying. It was bad enough being woken up at six o'clock in the morning to be told about it."

"It'll be different in high school this year," Alexandra said, sitting up and leaning on her elbows next to me, her long body stretched out on the wall. "First year of sixth form. Got to start thinking about university and all that grown-up stuff."

"Yeah, I'm not sure I'm exactly looking forward to that. At least when it was just us, no one could say a word against us. When we're all apart, it's only going to be harder to keep people from finding out what a complete geek I am."

"Not true," Alexandra replied, pulling herself up and sitting next to me. She leaned close and placed her head on my shoulder. "Plus, if I find out someone is teasing you, they'll have me to deal with. No matter where you are."

"Is that right?" I said, chuckling softly as I spoke. "Alexandra Thompson is going to come to my rescue?"

"Damn right," she replied, laughing along with me. "I've got a mean right hook on me. I could knock out Mike Tyson, me."

We were still laughing as the others joined us. Chris and Nicola refusing to let go of each other's hands as they sat down next to us, Michelle singing a No Doubt song that had been top of her playlist that summer. "Just a Girl," being belted into the skies. She had a great voice, but we weren't about to tell her that.

We were just happy she'd moved on from "Barbie Girl."

"Do you think it'll always be like this?" Nicola said, as wistful as a sixteen-year-old girl could possibly be. "The five of us, I mean."

"I doubt it," Chris replied, sharing a look with me. "Someone is eventually going to be able to put up with her singing long enough to get off with her. Probably just to shut her up, to be honest."

Michelle stopped long enough to aim a wayward kick in Chris's direction. He didn't even flinch, all of us laughing as she placed her hands on her hips in indignation. "I'd like to hear you sing."

Chris needed no further invitation, belting out a tuneless

version of Oasis's latest song. It was barely recognizable, even though it was just the chorus over and over, until we were all screaming at him to stop.

"You just can't recognize talent when it's in front of you," Chris said finally, a smirk of triumph on his face.

When we'd stopped laughing and allowed the silence to creep over us, it was almost a minute before someone spoke again. It was Alexandra who broke it.

"We need to make a pact."

"Not this again," Chris said under his breath, shaking his head. "Every time with the pacts. Remember how we all promised not to get as drunk as we did in the park last New Year? What happened a month later?"

"This is different," Alexandra cut in, standing up now and facing us all. "This is about us. We're mates, right? That comes before everything else."

I didn't like the look she gave me as she said that, but I tried to hide my fear. Chris and Nicola had been together forever, so it seemed redundant for them, but I was starting to worry about something I shouldn't have. A voice inside me, telling me this was just a summer romance for Alexandra and that we had a finite existence as a couple.

"So, no matter what happens in the next year or beyond, we always have each other's backs, right? No. Matter. What."

We didn't disagree.

I thought back to a year earlier. About a scrapyard. About running away, forgetting about Chris and Nicola.

And when I looked at Chris, I knew he was thinking the same thing.

Later, as we headed to the bus stop to go home, Chris and I fell in step. I caught his eye and raised my eyebrows.

We had barely spoken about that night since. I hadn't wanted to talk about it, and it had seemed like he'd felt the same. Now, I wasn't so sure.

"You did what you had to, mate," Chris said, as if he could read my thoughts. "We lost each other. It was dark. We'd filled our heads with silly ghost stories, and you were on your own. I would have done the same thing."

"You had Nicola to look after," I replied, stopping and looking away and out toward the river. I could see Crosby Beach in the distance if I strained my eyes hard enough. "I'm still not sure what happened."

"Neither am I. And that's what I told the police."

Chris and I talked about everything. I knew his life, his dreams, his hopes and fears. I knew him better than even Nicola, I reckoned. Yet we had made some sort of unspoken decision never to talk about that night in the days afterward. At first, it had been all we had spoken about—what we should do, what we should say. Then, nothing. Not until now.

It was as if the worst thing that would ever happen to us had made us shut down. We had instead concentrated on other things. Michelle would try to bring it up, but Chris and I would refuse to be drawn into it. Nicola dealt with her. As did Alexandra. Yet me and Chris...we didn't want to know. "Same," I said finally, turning around and facing him. The girls were still walking to the bus stop, oblivious to our not being behind them. "They reckon that guy will get life."

"So he should. Killing a fifteen-year-old kid, just because he was in the wrong place at the wrong time."

There had been a smell of death in that yard. A few victims of the drug trade, I'd read in my dad's copy of the *Liverpool Echo* in the days after what happened. Mikey had been found killed in the same way. They'd arrested a number of people over the next week, eventually charging someone for his murder. When I saw his picture in the paper, I tried to put myself in Mikey's shoes. Tried to think about his last moments, as a thirty-odd-year-old bloke with tattoos up his hands, up his arms, across his neck, loomed over me. Not blinking, not thinking twice, before ending a fifteen-year-old lad's life over nothing. We'd been foolish enough to think we were invincible, but now, all I could think about was what if that bloke had found me instead of Mikey.

"When they found Mikey's body, they pulled me in again," Chris said, kicking at a stone. "Nicola too."

"Yeah, same."

"Probably wondered if it was us. Glad they got him. Hope he dies in prison. It could have been anyone of us. We didn't even know they were there."

"We heard them. We just didn't realize who it was."

"We shouldn't have been there."

"Just so you know, that wouldn't happen again," I said, fixing Chris with a stare. "I wouldn't leave you behind again. You understand? Never again. We're in a situation where it gets a bit scary or whatever, and I'm not leaving you behind. You get me?"

Chris bit on his lower lip, looking away as his eyes watered. "Yeah, mate. Same."

We wouldn't talk about that kid dying for a long time. Even though someone had died in our presence—even if we hadn't seen it—we never spoke about it.

As if the real pact had been about silence. About never discussing death of any kind.

TWENTY-TWO

After another sleepless night, I managed to leave the house again the following day. Three days in a row. It was a new record. Before Stuart had died, I could go a week without stepping foot outside. With weekly shops now delivering to your door and everything I needed no more than a click of a button away, there was no real need for me to leave.

I could have quite happily gone on the same way forever.

Well, *happily* might have been pushing it.

I'd messaged Michelle as soon as it was a reasonable time, waiting for a response before contacting Chris. She was okay, but I wondered how true that would actually be. Lying awake the previous night, I knew she'd been doing the same.

Someone was in her house and you left her there.

I'd showered, again, then called Chris. Arranged to meet him in the usual place. Left the house a little quicker than the previous day, then sat in my car, trying to work out what I was going to do.

The only answer I had was to keep going.

The usual place was a pub around five minutes from Chris's office. It had been taken over by one of the chains a couple of years earlier, but we'd continued to meet up there at least once a week for lunch. Even as it became more and more difficult to leave the safety of my home, I still kept meeting up. It was as if by doing that I could ignore the fact that there was something seriously wrong with me.

I saw him walking up as I got out of the car and raised a hand in greeting.

"Okay?" Chris said as I approached him. "Sounded a bit urgent on the phone."

"Yeah, let's talk inside," I replied, following him and finding our normal table empty as usual.

"I'm buying," Chris said, as he noted the table number just in case it was different from the hundred other times we had sat there. I'd joked about it with him once, then felt like an idiot a few weeks later when the number had changed.

"You can't take anything for granted, lad."

That was Chris. He was always right and always thinking ahead.

It was why I spoke to him about everything I couldn't work out. It was why when he came back to the table, I didn't pause and told him what had happened in the previous twenty-four hours.

When I was finished, he sat back in his chair and stayed silent for a few seconds. Then a few more. I was about to speak again when he finally spoke.

"What happened last year, it's messed with all of us. Now, there's what happened to Stuart, just to screw us up all over again. We're going to see things, do things, that don't make any sense."

"Someone has been in Michelle's house."

"You only have her word for that, and she's been through a lot lately. Losing Stuart will have hit her the worst. Think of their history—everything that they went through and when they're finally in the right place, last year happens and it all falls apart. Same for you and Alexandra. Michelle's not been sleeping and is living with a grief we can't even comprehend. People in that position…they don't just live a normal life in the aftermath. It affects them for a long time."

"I saw the candle, Chris."

"You saw *a* candle, Matt," Chris replied, shaking his head as he curled a hand around his pint glass and lifted it to his mouth. He set it back down and looked across the table at me. "We all know the story now. She could have bought that thing at any point, then, finds it in the past week and is just forgetting that she lit it in the dead of night or something."

"Why though?" I said, unable to keep the skepticism from my voice. It didn't make sense to me, and I wanted to hear that I was seeing things that didn't exist. I knew Chris couldn't do that. "It just doesn't ring true to me."

"Same thing that Stuart was struggling with."

I was about to ask what he meant just as our food was delivered. Chris wiped down a knife and fork, but I left the sandwich he'd ordered for me where it was. Waited for the waitress to leave and then spoke. "What was he struggling with?"

"Same thing we've all been living with," Chris replied, placing his cutlery back down on his napkin. "Guilt."

"Maybe it's gone on for long enough."

"What do you mean?"

I took a swig from my own drink and looked out at the busy road outside the pub. Watched cars fly past, wondering where all the people were going at that time of day. I turned back to Chris and bit down on the corner of my bottom lip with an incisor. "Maybe it's time we told someone what we did."

Chris breathed in deeply and set his glass back down on the table a little harder than he'd probably wanted to. I didn't let him speak first. "Listen, hear me out, okay, then you can tell me I'm wrong. We've all been living with this thing in our heads for a year. This...knowledge, that we killed him."

"The Candle Man—"

"Yes, but it's more than just that. There's got to be a reason why the police refuse to acknowledge his existence. Maybe they've been waiting for something to happen, so they can finally say it's a definite truth. If we give them the location of where he's buried, maybe that's enough for them to finally close the investigation. The reason we haven't told anyone what we've done is because we buried him."

"And you think a year is enough time for that to be forgiven?"

"Of course not," I said, earning a look from the woman behind the bar in the distance. I lowered my voice again. "I'm just saying look at it both ways—guilt and keeping this secret has started messing with our minds. What we're suggesting is that it's making Michelle see candles appear that she put there herself. *Lit* herself. It's made Stuart take his own life. It broke me and Alexandra apart."

I paused before I continued on, making a quick decision not to lie anymore. "It drove me inside my house, scared to do anything but meet you here once a week. I mean, it's a struggle to leave, mate. I stand at the door for ages, working up the courage. I don't feel safe anymore. I can't sleep, Chris. I can't get that night out of my head. I know it's affected you and Nicola as well. I don't want to live like this anymore. If there're consequences, they'll be better than this life."

"Are you sure about that?"

I thought for a second, but didn't need much longer than that. I simply remembered the lad who disappeared, and it confirmed my first instinct. "Yes. And then there's the other side of it."

"If someone was really there and saw what we did."

"Exactly. Which, of course, is the only explanation for Mark Welsh's body not being there when we went back into those woods. We never talked about that—just like we never talked about that boy back when we were teenagers. Mikey. He died while we were in that scrapyard, and we never talked about it. Not even when that drug dealer got life for his murder. We just pretended like it never happened. That lad's body was moved. Someone took him. I don't know why and I don't know how, but someone had to have done that. He didn't just turn into dust like an Avengers character."

"And you think someone has waited a year for what?"

"He wants revenge or something like that. It has to be someone connected to whoever the Candle Man was. Stuart didn't kill himself; this person did. And Michelle is next."

"So, in either case, we go to the police and that all stops. That's what you're suggesting?"

"I'm saying it's worth discussing," I said, picking up the sandwich on my plate, looking it over, then laying it back down again. My stomach didn't seem to be interested. "We all have to agree to it. That's how we work."

"Then, let me stop you now," Chris replied, swallowing a mouthful of his salad and putting his fork down. He picked up his napkin and wiped his hands. "I'm not doing that."

"Chris—"

"No, I'm not interested," Chris said, an edge to his tone that I hadn't experienced in a long time. "You might have decided that because you and Alexandra couldn't make it through this that you have nothing to lose anymore. Not like on that night, when if I remember correctly, you were right behind the whole idea. If that's different now, it's not my fault. It's not anyone's fault. I still have a lot to lose if the truth comes out. So does Nicola. Do you think we'd just get a slap on the wrist? That they'd let us off because we stopped a serial killer? How do we even prove that was the case? We got rid of everything. The candle in the woods, the boy he killed. It won't work. We kept this secret for a year, while that boy's mum has been everywhere trying to find out what happened to her son. We'd be the new enemy. We'd be *his* stand-in. They can't be angry with the guy that killed that boy because he's already dead. Instead, they'd be angry with us for not saying anything. We'd be pariahs, Matt. No one would want anything to do with us ever again. Everyone would know who we are and what we'd done. That would be our lives forever."

"I understand, but we need to do something."

"We don't *need* to do anything. The plan worked. No one knows what we did. Yes, it's hard to live with, but that's true for everyone."

I scoffed at that. Shook my head and placed the edge of my hand against my head and rubbed a temple with my thumb. "This is a little different. I hope you can see that at least."

"Of course it is, but I refuse to allow it to define me. Nicola too. That wasn't us and all we are. That was a situation we dealt with and came out the other side with our lives. I don't know what happened to that boy's body and I don't care anymore. I'm done with being scared and looking over my shoulder. If someone did move him—which I know is what happened— then that person obviously doesn't want him to be found either. And if he comes after us, then I'm ready for that as well. I'll protect my wife and myself just like I did a year ago. I can't go to the police now because it's just not going to help anyone if I did. It would only hurt everyone involved and why would I want to do that?"

"Someone is coming," I said, standing up and staring at Chris. We had barely disagreed about anything in our twenty-odd years of friendship, but this was beginning to feel like one of those things that could break us. "You know that's the truth. You know Michelle isn't just making things up, that neither am I. I know what I saw. You know what those candles mean."

"They mean nothing."

"You *know* what they mean," I said, leaning on the table with both hands and leaning closer. "I love you like a brother. That's why I came to you first. And I promise I won't go to anyone just yet; I just need you to think about it properly. Will you give me that at least? Speak to Nicola about all of this. You need to be totally sure, I get it, but I don't see any other way out of this."

"There's plenty of ways out."

"Speak to her. And Michelle. She'll tell you the same as she told me. See if that changes your mind."

I left him at the table and walked out of the pub. Paused in the parking lot and looked back. I wanted to go back and let him convince me more that there wasn't anything to worry about—but there was a part of me that knew he couldn't.

No one could.

I kept walking.

TWENTY-THREE

I was driving back home when she called. My phone was in its cradle, linked by Bluetooth to the speakers, so I couldn't even ignore the ringing if I'd tried.

Her name was on the screen as I glanced at it.

"Hello," I said, answering as I looked for somewhere to pull over. I indicated left and stopped the car. "You okay?"

"Hi, Matt," Alexandra replied, sounding like she always did, even if there was a little resignation in her tone. "I'm not bad. Not great either."

If I closed my eyes and forgot everything I knew, I could almost believe it was a year earlier and we were still together. That this was just a normal conversation. Instead, I had to live in a world where that wasn't the case.

"I'm just…I don't know," Alexandra continued, a deep sigh filling the car as I put the phone to my ear.

My stomach lurched as I thought about what had happened to Michelle recently and heard a note in Alexandra's voice that worried me. "What's going on? Has something turned up in your house?"

"No," she replied, the note that concerned me being replaced by confusion. "I guess I'm just worried about you, that's all. Can we talk?"

I breathed a sigh of relief, then thought about what she'd said.

The idea of meeting up with her before that week would have filled me with hope and excitement. Now, I couldn't work out what I felt. Only that I didn't want her around if Michelle and I were right.

"Yes," I said eventually, knowing there was no other answer. "Now?"

"Give me a few hours. I'll come to your house after work."

The call ended, and even though I knew it was true, the words still hurt.

Your house.

It was supposed to be ours. *Our* home, our future. Now, it was a reminder of all that had been lost. A daily ritual couldn't erase it. Nothing ever would.

She hadn't been over since the day she left. In fact, I struggled to remember anyone being in there besides myself or Chris in months. I didn't have visitors. My family—of which there were basically very few—lived far enough away that a simple visit was barely worth it. Everyone was getting older, so it was on me to make the trip to them.

I plugged the phone back in and set off. Outside, rain fell in spots, dusting the windshield and smeared away with wipers. A fine rain that I would barely feel if I were outside, but now was a minor annoyance in a day, a week, filled with them.

That's what I was feeling. Annoyed. I had created a sheltered life, that I now realized I wanted to protect. A bubble, in which I could pretend the outside world didn't exist, so I could live in peace.

Only, there was never peace. Not for me. Not for any of us. I didn't think there ever would be.

Back home, I turned the volume up loud on the music blaring from Alexa and tidied up what needed doing. There wasn't much. Along with creating a shelter, I'd also become more frugal. Mainly because I had to, given I was paying a mortgage I could barely afford and didn't have much left over for any luxuries. No takeout containers littering the rooms, no empty bottles of soft drinks, no clinking bottles of alcohol to hide. I didn't drink, I barely ate, and coffee remained my only extravagance. Even that cost me about a tenner per week.

My phone buzzed in my pocket, just as I finished vacuuming a living room floor that hadn't really been walked on for months. I pulled it out and saw the alarm I'd set a week earlier and forgotten about, then swore under my breath. Wondered if I should reschedule, then thought about the two hours still to go until Alexandra arrived and thought it would save me staring at a wall.

Decided I could at least fill the time semiproductively.

We'd been talking about nothing for forty-five minutes, before her name came up. The counselor doing what she'd tried on my previous visit—opening me up to talk about what she knew was hiding behind the veiled answers of everything I was saying.

I had made a decision to never return, but there I was. Back again. It wasn't just because I couldn't sleep. I was there because I needed help. Because I could kid myself that I was trying by going and speaking to this stranger, as if by doing so I was at least trying. Yet, it was like a game, where I couldn't tell her all of the rules or where the pieces were supposed to move.

So, instead, we danced around subjects, and she prodded and pried, trying to back me into a corner that would have me reveal all. Asked open questions, trying to get me to disclose things she knew I didn't want to.

It didn't work. It *wouldn't* work.

"The ex-girlfriend," she said, flicking back a page or two in her notepad. "Alexandra?"

"Yes."

"Any contact?"

She knew there must have been. I'd told her about Stuart's death—leaving out as much detail as was possible—but she had the knowledge that, of the friends I had, they were all connected. And that included Alexandra. "Briefly."

"How was it?"

"It was…it was nice. Polite. I'm actually seeing her after this."

Her eyebrows raised at this. I felt like, for the first time in that room, I'd actually said something that had surprised her somewhat. "Really? How do you feel about that?"

"Nervous, excited, I don't know. I'm not thinking it's going to lead to anything, but it's the first time we'll be on our own since we broke up."

"How is the sleep going?"

I frowned at the sudden shift in conversation. "Same as it was before."

"And you think it's insomnia?"

"Well, yeah, I guess so," I replied, trying to work out the possible path she was trying to take. I was paying for the privilege of this, I realized. Money I could ill afford. I wanted to laugh at the ridiculousness of it all but kept myself in check. "It certainly seems to fit the criteria."

"Did you do any of the exercises I told you about last time we met?"

"Yes, they didn't work," I lied, knowing that the truth would be too difficult to explain without straying into territory where I couldn't go. "Still can't sleep."

She tilted her head and stared at me long enough for me to look away. The silence grew until I couldn't take it any longer.

"I don't know what it is," I said, feeling a sense of relief when

I could hear the sound of my own voice. "I just can't seem to switch off."

"You seem uncomfortable." It was the first statement she had made. Not a question—she was identifying a fact and she seemed to be happy with the assessment.

"I'm fine. I just don't know how useful this is turning out to be."

"After one and a half sessions?"

Back to the questions. I rolled my eyes in annoyance. Frustration. "I know. I understand that it probably takes a lot more than that, but I'm not a wealthy person. I'm not even a half-wealthy person. I can't really afford to spend a fortune coming back here over and over, just to be told the same things. I tried the exercises; they didn't work. Maybe I should just go the sleeping pills route."

"You told me you'd tried that and it hadn't worked. Do you think anything has changed since then?"

I shook my head. "Probably not. Doesn't mean I shouldn't try again. A prescription is cheaper than these hour-long meetings though." I smiled so she knew I was speaking with some humor, but she was unbreakable.

"When you wake up in the mornings, is it always at the same approximate time?"

I nodded. "I set my alarm. I work from home, so it's important to have some sort of routine. Otherwise, I could end up never doing anything productive."

"The alarm wakes you up?"

"Yes," I said, frowning again, as she steered the exchange in another seemingly odd direction. I wondered if she was intentionally trying to make me feel off-kilter, unsure of where the next turn would be, so she could trip me up and make me reveal more than I wanted to. I was locked into a game now, it seemed. I was sure she knew I wasn't telling her the entire truth, but I wasn't going to give up. "I lie in bed awake for hours, and eventually my body just gives in. Never early enough for me to feel right though."

"What are you thinking about?"

"Now?"

She shook her head, almost imperceptibly so. "When you're lying in bed trying to sleep. You said your brain won't switch off. What are some of the thoughts that run through your mind? Give me some examples."

I sighed and leaned back in the chair. "All sorts of things," I said, running through the images that immediately sprung to me. The man in the woods. The sounds he made. The anger that coursed through him and us. The smell of sweat and blood. Michelle's crying. Alexandra's face. Chris's fear. Stuart's barely constrained panic. Nicola trying to ground herself back into reality. The boy. His body.

The red candle. Burning. Mocking us after what we'd done.

The empty patch of ground where the boy had once been.

"Just normal things," I lied, refusing to catch her gaze now. I looked around the room and settled my eyes on a large oak bookcase that held numerous red-leather-bound books. Thick and probably unreadable to most people. I squinted to try to read some of the titles but failed. "Money worries, social anxieties. Whether I locked the back door before I came to bed. Something I watched on TV before going upstairs. That kind of thing."

"When you did the exercises, did any of this dissipate whatsoever?"

I thought about the list she had given me. All of them had involved the same issue I couldn't deal with—silence. They all required me to turn off the music, the radio, the podcasts.

Everything that I used so I wasn't lying in the darkness in total quiet. I couldn't tell her that though, because it would just lead to even more questions I couldn't answer. Instead, I had to lie to this person and pay for it. Literally. Hand over cash I couldn't spare to lie to a stranger.

Now, I did laugh out loud. A short, sharp bark of laughter, which momentarily broke her blank expression. I recovered quickly and held up a hand in apology. "I'm sorry, but I just don't think this is going to work."

"Matt, what is it about silence that bothers you?"

The shock of the question almost made me shout in response. In truth. I closed my mouth and stuttered around a reply before composing myself. "I don't know what you mean."

"That's the problem here, isn't it? Every time there's a lull in the conversation, you feel the need to fill it. You don't realize it, but when there's quiet in the room, you begin to exhibit signs of some distress. Is this something that happens at night also? Does it become worse then?"

"I have to go," I said, getting to my feet and grabbing my jacket from the back of my chair. "Thanks for trying, but I don't think I'll be coming back."

"Wait, Matt, what is it that you don't want to say?"

I didn't answer, shouting a goodbye as I left the office and closed the door behind me. I didn't breathe again until I was outside the building and leaning against my car. I looked over at the window, where the counselor's office was, half expecting her to be standing there and holding a phone.

Calling who?

I knew the answer and how stupid it was. My breathing slowly returned to normal, as I realized it was just fear. That she hadn't seen through me and knew what I was hiding. The noise filtered back through now—the calming sounds of traffic passing by, the wind in the air, the conversation from someone talking on their phone as they walked past me. It all coalesced into a cacophony of aural pleasure.

It wasn't silence.

It was soothing.

TWENTY-FOUR

I reached home with just enough time to get inside and switch on the coffee machine before Alexandra arrived. The drive back had been a blur. I tried to remember it as I waited for the cup to fill but found myself unable to recall any part of it. Just the sound of the music filling the car as I turned the volume louder and louder, until it hurt.

Her car pulled up behind mine as I watched from the window. I was holding the cup in my hands, cradling it, enjoying the warmth, humming a tune to myself. I breathed deeply as she got out and paused, looking at the house. I averted my eyes briefly, worried about being seen, then checked myself in the mirror.

I walked into the hallway and opened the door just as she was opening the gate and walking up the path. She smiled tightly, then I felt her hand on my shoulder and her lips on my cheek briefly. She murmured a greeting, then she slipped past me and inside. The smell of Armani Code perfume drifted along with her, and I wondered if she was still using the bottle I'd bought her on her last birthday. Then I realized that would have been fifteen months earlier and very unlikely.

There was a moment when I almost said "Make yourself at home" out of politeness but managed to stop myself.

The awkwardness I was feeling wasn't something I expected.

I didn't need to say anything, as it happened. Alexandra

went straight into the living room and sat down on the sofa. As I followed her in and stood opposite, against the fireplace, I realized she had chosen the same space she'd always occupied when we lived together. I chuckled softly as she looked up at me. "At least some things don't change," I said, knowing she'd get it.

"It was always the best seat in the place," Alexandra replied with a smile that showed her teeth. It disappeared as quickly as it came. "Anyway, how have you been?"

"You know," I said, placing the cup of coffee on the mantelpiece and folding my arms across my chest. "Same old, same old."

"Liar."

"Want a drink?" I said before she could say anything more. "Coffee, tea…a large gin and tonic?"

"No thanks."

"Good. I don't have any gin, and the tonic water has been open in the fridge for about a year. Probably less fizzy than water by now."

"I'm fine," she said, looking me over. "Still not sleeping?"

"I get enough."

Alexandra saw right through me, but didn't push me on the lie. She breathed deeply and looked away. "Everything looks the same."

"I never was much of a decorator." I unfolded my arms and moved across the room, back to the window. I didn't want to sit down, wasn't sure why. "So, how are you doing?"

"I was doing okay—not great, but well enough—until a few days ago. Now…now I'm not so sure."

I knew what had prompted the visit now. "Michelle."

"She called me last night," Alexandra said, sitting back and seeming to struggle with the urge to slip her shoes off and tuck her feet underneath her. That's what she would normally do on that sofa, but that was a different time, I felt. Now, she wasn't sure what to do.

"She told you," I replied, as I watched her continue to battle against habit. "What's been going on, what she thinks is happening. All of it."

"Yes. She's scared."

"Wouldn't you be?"

"Of course. Doesn't mean any of it is right though. She said you'd been over. You can't have believed what she thinks is happening if you just left her there."

I hesitated, just long enough for her to read me like a cheap paperback.

"I can't believe you…"

"It wasn't like that," I said quickly, not meeting her eyes as she looked at me. Shame almost drowned me. "She didn't want me to do anything, and I knew I couldn't stay there. She wouldn't let me. And she wouldn't come and stay here, didn't want me to call anyone."

"That doesn't matter and you know it. You're supposed to be her friend. You're supposed to be there for her. How could you just leave her on her own if you thought she was in danger? For God's sake, Matt…even if this is all just your overactive imagination, I would have thought you would care for her a little more than that."

"Have you been over there yourself? I doubt Chris or Nicola have either, and they both know now as well. And I've not heard you once say you believe her. Don't lay all this at my door. That's not fair."

Alexandra made to argue more, then held up her hands in

mock surrender. "Okay, okay, this isn't helping. None of us have done the right thing. Yet."

"I spoke to Chris a few hours ago. I told him what I think we should do."

"I'm guessing it's the same thing Michelle wants to do," Alexandra said, sliding a finger through her hair as it dropped across her eyes. "Bring this all out in the open? To tell them what we did?"

"Yes," I replied, struggling to resist the urge to cross the room and sit down next to her. To place a hand on her leg, like I always did before. I screwed my eyes shut as I turned away from her and folded my arms again. Tried to ignore every part of me that wanted nothing more than to be normal together again.

Absence hadn't made the heart grow fonder. My feelings hadn't changed at all.

I still loved her with every part of my soul.

"We can't do that," Alexandra said, her voice soft but without a trace of doubt. "Not yet. We still all have so much to lose; can't you see that? I don't want to go to prison. None of us deserve that. We all made a decision last year, and now we have to live with it and that means through all of it. No one said it was going to be easy, but that's the call we made."

"We've all been ignoring the important part of this—Mark Welsh." I reiterated what I had said to Chris. What I'd discussed with Michelle. About how he was the important factor we could no longer ignore. "We've all been waiting for the police to knock on our door, but instead, someone else has come. Someone who was there that night. Who saw what we did and wants a different outcome. Not prison. Revenge."

"You think I don't think about what happened every day?"

"It broke us apart, Alexandra." I breathed in and tried to

control the feelings that were simmering away underneath the surface of every word I said. "I know you think about it. We spent years apart after we split before university and then found each other again...only for this to happen and break us. I know you better than anyone—I know you think about it. That's not my point. I just want to do something so we can actually deal with all of this."

"There's still too much we don't understand."

"What is there to understand here?" I replied, feeling brave enough to face her again now. "We're in trouble. We have been since last year, and we've ignored it for too long. Tried to pretend it didn't happen and that we can just move on. Now, we're all in danger—"

"Is that what you believe?"

I hesitated again, but not long enough for her to say anything. "Yes. There's more than just what Michelle has told you. I went to Stuart's house before hers yesterday. Spoke to his sister, who let me look around his place. I thought I could find some kind of suicide note, but if there was one, they would have found it long before I got there. I just thought there must be some explanation for what he did, but there was nothing to find. Instead, I found something else. Want to know what it was?"

"A red candle."

"A damn red candle," I said, finding myself on the other side of the room suddenly. I realized I'd been pacing up and down as I'd been talking. "Same as in Michelle's house."

"It's hardly a rare thing, Matt," Alexandra replied, but didn't seem to have any conviction left in her voice. "People have them in their homes. I bet you've got one in here somewhere, from back when we moved in."

"Are you kidding me? First thing I did when we got back was

get rid of the damn things. All of them. I didn't care what color they were, I couldn't have them in the house." I stopped pacing, moving closer to the sofa where Alexandra was sitting. I perched on the arm of it across from her. Sighed as I locked my hands together and leaned forward. "And both of them in those storm lantern things? Some coincidence. Tell me—do you have any red candles in your house? Do you go out of your way to avoid them now?"

"I—"

"Of course you don't have any. You know what they mean to us now. Chris and Nicola are the same. Michelle too. And Stuart wouldn't have wanted anything to do with them. Such a small, insignificant thing, but it's a symbol of what we did that night. A daily reminder of the man we buried. And Mark Welsh. Moving his body across that field and then it disappearing. Now, it's back in our lives. This is no coincidence. It's been a year this week. It all fits together. We're in trouble, Alexandra. That's the truth of it. How can we live like this?"

"We have to," Alexandra said, her shout bouncing off the walls and around us. She was on her feet in an instant, and I thought for a moment she was going to leave the room. Instead, she turned away, put her head in her hands, and made a low guttural sound.

There was a silence that grew between us. I was about to end it when she lifted her head and looked at me.

"We have to live with it," she said finally, leaning against the door, looking like she was going to collapse to the floor in an instant. "There's no other choice here. If we don't keep going, then he wins. Don't you get that?"

"I just don't see any other way out of this. Stuart's already dead. Michelle could be next. Are we supposed to just sit around and wait for it to happen without doing anything?"

"Of course not," she said, moving back to the sofa and lifting her bag up. She reached inside and pulled out a small laptop, opening it on the coffee table. "We've all read up about Mark Welsh, but how much did we look into the...man?"

"What are you saying?" I replied, moving onto the sofa next to her and looking at the screen. "Believe me, I've thought about him. I've thought about little else but that night since."

"I'm not saying that. I'm saying you've thought about this wrong. You've thought about what happened to him and not who he was. That's the key here."

I frowned at Alexandra, looking away from the boot-up screen on the laptop and trying to read her face. I couldn't. "I'm not following you."

"If you and Michelle are right and there's someone after revenge for his death, then there's a bigger question we need to answer."

"What's that then?"

"Who was the Candle Man, and what was he doing there that night? And I think I'm close to an answer."

1999

Three months into first year at university, it was New Year's Eve. I was still a little too worried about the Y2K millennium bug to really enjoy the night. I'd woken from a dream that morning of a plane falling out of the sky and landing on the student dorms. For some reason, I'd been outside and looking to the sky, watching it crash onto the building. I was confused when I'd opened my eyes and found myself lying in bed, daylight streaming through the thin curtain that covered the window. There had still been a part of me that believed it was actually real for almost a minute after I was awake.

"It's all a conspiracy," Stuart said, handing me another drink. Vodka and Red Bull had become our beverage of choice since we'd started university I reckoned about half of my student loan had gone on the drink alone. We were in the large common room at the student dorm I now called home. Around thirty of us at least, with more arriving by the minute. Once people had seen the prices that nightclubs in town were charging for entry, it became the place to celebrate New Year's Eve for those who hadn't gone home during the break. My parents' house was a twenty-minute bus ride from the dorm, which meant the decision to stay had been easy. I'd seen them on Christmas Day but came back soon after.

"Just a way of keeping us in line," Stuart continued, sipping on his own drink and sighing in satisfaction. Music was playing on someone's CD player they'd dragged down from their room. The more people that arrived, the lower the sound was. I could barely hear the different girls' names that Lou Bega was singing about needing.

"That's all it is," Stuart said when it became clear he wasn't going to be interrupted from going on another rant. "Make us worry about something that won't happen, so we ignore the fact there's something else going on. Probably gonna raise taxes or privatize the National Health Service or something. We'll all be sitting around feeling relieved about the lack of Armageddon to notice."

"Yeah right," I replied, laughing a little now. Stuart had only been a friend for a couple of months, but I had already been wound up by him on numerous occasions. It made me question whether he was ever serious about anything, but I couldn't help but be endlessly entertained by him. And by the glint in his eye, I could tell he enjoyed it too. "I bet Tony Blair is sitting in Number Ten laughing at us all now, while holding onto a big conspiracy lever of some kind."

"Sure it's got nothing to do with the moon?" Chris said, sidling up to us with a smile on his face. When Chris and I had first met Stuart, he'd launched into a half-hour rant about the moon landings being faked. It was impassioned enough to make us interested in listening to him, while also being ridiculous enough to be hysterically funny. "Maybe we'll wake up in the morning with the news that they've really found aliens on a base up there and they've only just found out because we never actually went there before."

"I'm telling you, that flag shouldn't be moving..."

"Thousands of people, Stuart," Chris said, pointing his own

drink toward him, but smiling as he did so. "That's how many would have to keep the secret. And not one of them has ever come out and said a word. That doesn't strike you as odd?"

Stuart bridled and was about to argue when he noticed the look on Chris's face and shook his head. "I'm not getting into this again."

"Only because you'll lose the argument again," Chris replied, looking across the room and then waving toward someone. "Anyway, I predict this whole millennium bug thing will be a bigger disappointment than *The Phantom Menace*. Nothing will happen, and we'll forget it was even a problem afterward. I reckon this is all a distraction from the *real* truth anyway."

"And what's that?" Stuart said, suddenly interested again. I could see from Chris's face that he wasn't being serious, but Stuart didn't know him as well as I did.

"It's simple," Chris replied, leaning toward Stuart as if he were about to reveal a huge secret. "They're going to round up all Mancunians called Stuart tomorrow morning and force them into public demonstrations of penance as an apology for bloody Oasis."

I laughed as Stuart gave Chris a playful punch in the arm. Nicola arrived from the other side of the room, slipping an arm around Chris's waist and leaning her head into him.

"Oasis is the best band in the world," Stuart said proudly, sticking his hands behind him and mimicking Liam Gallagher's signature pose. He began singing "Wonderwall" out of tune. It wasn't much different to the original, to be fair, but still rattled my teeth.

"They're a Beatles cover band at best," I replied, rolling my eyes and pretending for a moment that I didn't own all of the group's CDs and had hated Blur with a burning passion for a long time a few years back. "And probably not even the best one in Manchester."

"What the hell are you lot talking about?" Nicola said, releasing her arm from around Chris to sip from a bottle of alcopop. "It's New Year's Eve. The millennium. Can we have one night when you three don't argue the finer points of Northern music?"

We murmured an agreement, lapsing into silence as the track playing on the CD player ended and Vengaboys entered the fray. A collective groan went up. It was quickly skipped and the Offspring came on to a collective cheer.

"Is she coming?" I asked Nicola, as Chris and Stuart began talking animatedly about something else. "I haven't heard from her."

"Who, Michelle? She's over there chatting up some bloke from Birmingham. I couldn't listen to his accent anymore, but she seemed to be enjoying it."

"You know who I mean," I said with a groan. "Have you spoken to her?"

"I don't know. She knows we're all here, but I'm not sure if she's going to grace us with her presence. Got those new friends in Chester, hasn't she? Not sure she wants to be seen with the likes of us now. Gone all posh probably."

I chuckled in response, knowing it was just the usual sarcasm from Nicola. Truth was, she was probably more than a little defensive regarding her oldest friend. While the three of us had decided to stay in Liverpool for university, Alexandra had moved to Chester instead. Michelle was forgoing university altogether, going straight into work as an office junior. It meant she had more money than any of us, but still didn't mind slumming it with us for parties.

"She's doing okay," Nicola said, looking up and tilting her

head a little. "Seems to have coped with the split well after a month or so of moping. Your name isn't the first thing she says when we talk now."

I wasn't sure if I was happy with that or not, but decided it was probably for the best. I wasn't exactly moving on quickly myself, but if she was doing better, maybe I could finally do that.

There was part of me that thought it was a bad decision, even if it was mutual. We both wanted different things, different experiences. I didn't want to wreck the relationship. She didn't want to resent me for not being able to enjoy university life to its fullest. It simply ended because both of us were scared. That was the reality of it. We were in separate universities, didn't want a long-distance relationship, it wasn't the right time for both of us.

Mutual.

That wasn't true. When we'd started talking, I'd just gone along with it, too scared to fight for us. Too worried about how I looked or being even more hurt.

I had simply accepted it and tried to move on.

"You made the right call at the right time," Nicola continued, laying a hand on my shoulder and giving me a small squeeze. "Both of you. Who knows what will happen in the future?"

She smiled and walked away before I had the chance to respond. I didn't see her again until a minute after midnight. We had collapsed into the street en masse, counting down the seconds before the clock struck, and once I'd checked the skies for any planes coming down, I began shouting and cheering with the rest of the party. Chris grabbed me and pulled me into a bear hug, quickly joined by Stuart, who jumped on top and almost brought us down onto the ground.

We staggered across the pavement, trying to keep our balance, before knocking the back of another small group of people.

I could sense the mood change instantly. The cry of shock and alarm, quickly changing to recrimination. I lifted my head just as the first lad squared up to Chris. I moved toward him, putting a hand on his shoulder, as the stranger in a bomber jacket moved his head in Chris's direction. Pulled him backward as Nicola appeared as if from nowhere and began screaming in the group's general direction. A woman standing with them was quickly in her face, towering over her and pointing a finger toward Nicola. I must have made some kind of noise, as the woman was distracted and looked toward me. Nicola grabbed her finger and twisted it. I was dragging Chris back as bomber jacket aimed a headbutt toward him when it happened.

The guy was suddenly on the ground.

A sound had stopped us all in our tracks and a silence fell over us in an instant. A loud crack, as the guy's head had bounced off the pavement.

Stuart stood over the guy in the bomber jacket, shaking his hand out, as blood began to seep out of the man's head and pool around our feet.

TWENTY-FIVE

On the screen of Alexandra's laptop, she had Google Maps open and was zooming in and out on an area I was familiar with.

"Brock Hope," I said, waiting for her to explain what this had to do with anything. "The forest where the music festival was. I'm not sure…"

"I've been thinking about it for a long time," Alexandra replied, sitting back and leaning her head against the sofa. "When Mark Welsh's body disappeared and wasn't found, I started thinking about the reasons for it. We have the so-called mythological serial killer—"

"The Candle Man."

"Yes, but I wonder if he's not so much a myth, but rather a generic thing that's been made up to explain some missing persons, that's all. Anyway, there're whole forums dedicated to the story. All coming back to the red candle aspect."

"You think you know who the man was. The one we killed?"

"I don't know for sure," Alexandra replied, her expression changing, darkness entering it again. "With all these stories happening across the country, it's difficult to pin down any kind of location. So I started at the end instead of trying to work all of that out."

"The music festival?"

"More specifically, the surrounding area. What do you remember about the place?"

I blew out a breath. "Not much really. Kinda concentrated on events more than the views. Woods, tiny country roads, big field where we watched the bands."

"Farms," Alexandra said, reaching across and scanning the map on the laptop screen. "The whole area is surrounded by farmland. Old places, some of which have been in families for generations. Bits and pieces sold off over the years, but this is countryside proper. That's what I've found. I've struggled to get anywhere with this information, but I'm onto something, I think."

"You think the Candle Man was a farmer?"

"I think he lived on one of the farms close by," Alexandra said, ignoring my sarcasm and continuing on. "Look, I know I've not got enough yet, but what if some of these stories are true? Red candles in storm lanterns are probably a popular item, but when you add in missing persons, it makes it a bit more coincidental. What if he was clever? What if the other murders happened in other parts of the country, just so he wasn't discovered, but this is where his main place was?"

"Great, so we just speak to all the people who live in these farms and see if they're alive or not. We'll find out who hasn't been seen for a year and might have a brother or something that likes revenge."

"Well, you never know," Alexandra said, rubbing the back of her neck with one hand, as if she was trying to massage the stress out of herself. "It's something we should really look into though. I don't really fancy traveling all the way down there and knocking on random farmhouses. What the hell would I say? I don't even know if it's one or fifty-one different farms."

"We might have to."

"That's if you believe there's someone out there hunting us down for what we did. And if that's the case, they saw us in those woods."

"Alexandra, there's no doubt someone was there. The body went missing."

"About that…" Alexandra replied, shifting on the sofa and turning her body toward me. "What's to say there's not some other explanation for that? A coincidence of some sort? It's not like we checked him over properly. He might have still been alive."

"Are you kidding me? Can you not remember the state he was in?"

"Believe me," Alexandra said, her tone suddenly becoming cold and harsh. "I remember every detail about that night. I think about it all the time. I'm just saying, you never know. People can survive all kinds of things. We didn't know what we were doing. We just saw his body and lost our minds. We were scared; we were exhausted. Do you remember anyone checking for a pulse? Because I don't. What if he was still alive, barely, drags himself onto the road, a car hits him and that driver panics? It's early in the morning, no one else is around, and they hide the body somewhere else?"

I began to answer, then stopped myself. It was something I had never considered. Mainly because it was so ridiculous. I stifled a yawn and rubbed some life into my face briefly. "It sounds like something that would happen in some crappy TV show. Not in real life. I think I prefer to go with Occam's razor on this one."

"I'm just saying, it's not out of the realms of possibility. This whole thing has been like a horrible nightmare from the beginning. If there's a chance that there is something deeper to this whole Stuart and now Michelle story though, then it's probably best if we have some sort of plan."

"I do. It's called going to the police and telling them what happened."

"We're not giving up just like that," Alexandra said, smacking the arm of the sofa in frustration and getting to her feet. "Again, I'm not prepared to give up everything I have because of this. I won't let it beat us. Whatever is going on, we can still come out the other side. We just need to stay calm."

"Calm? Calm is what got us into this mess in the first place. We *calmly* made a decision to cover up a murder—"

"It was self-defense—"

"We *calmly* dug a hole," I continued, following Alexandra's movements as she walked over to the living room door and paused with her hand on the doorknob. "We threw a body in there and then panicked when we found another one. No decision we've made since the moment we stepped in those woods was a good one. Simple as that. If confessing doesn't feel like the right thing to do, maybe that's because it'll finally be the right call. We screwed up. Made the wrong choices, and now we have to face up to that."

"You'll ruin all our lives."

"They're already ruined," I said, getting up and moving toward Alexandra.

She was facing away from me, her head dropped to her chest and shoulders moving up and down slowly.

I reached out and put a hand on one of them, but she shook it away. I breathed in and tried to keep talking. "None of us can live with this anymore. No matter what way we look at things, this is it. This is our last chance to do right by everyone involved. It'll be hard, but nothing worth doing is easy."

"You speak for yourself," Alexandra replied, moving away from me, grabbing her laptop from the coffee table and shoving it back in her bag. "You've not considered the fact that there's not just you who was there that night and doesn't want to say a word to anybody about it. You're only thinking about your own selfish reasons."

It was the same argument we'd had when we'd arrived back home a year earlier. Only, we had been in opposite roles back then. Alexandra was the one who wanted to go to the police, and I was trying to pretend it had never happened at all. The fear of that knock at the door had driven us into two disparate corners that eventually drove us apart. Now, we were back in that time.

Only this time, Alexandra was leaving before it could get any worse.

"Listen, I'm sorry," I tried, but she was pushing past me and out of the living room. I followed her into the hallway, still talking. Pleading. "We can sort this out. You don't have to go. Please."

It was no use though. Like the previous time she'd left, I was powerless to stop her going. Even this time, with me at least speaking a little more than I had back then, she was opening the door and on the front path within seconds.

"Matt, get some sleep," Alexandra said, turning around but still walking backward slowly toward the gate. "I'll speak to you soon, when you're more clear-minded."

"Alexandra…" I tried again, but she was through the gate and into her car before I could leave the house. I looked at the blinds in my neighbor's windows twitching as my voice echoed around the street. I ignored them and went back inside.

TWENTY-SIX

I called Michelle as soon as I was back in the house, cradling my phone with my shoulder as I went through sparse cupboards trying to find something to eat. She answered just before I imagined an answer machine would kick in.

"You okay?"

"What do you think?" Michelle replied and tiredness and pressure was dripping from every syllable. "I haven't slept and can't stop checking the locks on my doors and windows. I feel like I'm living in a nightmare. Or a horror film."

"It's going to be okay. You should come here and stay. Or I could come to you?"

"No, it's fine. Why should I drag someone else into this? If it's me first, best they don't get two of us at the same time. If something is going to happen, it's better if it's only me. That way, someone is left behind to stop whoever it is from picking us off one by one."

"Michelle..."

"Did you speak to Chris?" she said before I had the chance to continue. "Did you tell him what we should do?"

"I spoke to him. I think you can probably guess his reaction. Nicola will agree with him, I guess."

"I should just go to the police myself..."

"We can't do that," I said, but I wondered why that was the

case. Michelle was living with the threat of something happening to her, to the point she couldn't even sleep in her own house. Surely that meant more?

"I know," Michelle replied, but I could hear the lack of conviction in her voice. "They're not the ones with a red candle in their bin that won't go away though."

"You threw it out?"

"I had to. I couldn't have it in the house anymore. I don't care if it's got evidence on it—although I can bet there's not a fingerprint on the damn thing—I just don't want to be around it. I don't want it near me."

"You have to get out of there, Michelle," I said more forcefully now. She couldn't stay there any longer, and even if I had to park outside her house that night, I wasn't going to let it happen. "Come and stay here, or ring Alexandra?"

"I spoke to her earlier. She doesn't want to go to the police. She thinks we can deal with this ourselves. I'm not sure if she really believes it's as bad as I'm saying. Makes me feel like I'm going crazy or something."

"You're not crazy," I replied, then steered the conversation back again. "I'm serious, Michelle. You have to leave that house. You're sitting there just waiting for him to come back right now. There's no point. We can get past this. I can convince the others that we need to confess; I just need a little more time."

There was silence on the line that pricked the hairs on the back of my neck. Then, a sigh and Michelle's voice.

"I don't know. I thought this would be easier."

"If you're right, then you're just waiting for someone to come. It's giving up. Right?"

"I know I shouldn't be here. It's just...it's like I've seen a way out of this nightmare. Maybe this is what we deserve. You understand?"

I did, but I wasn't about to say that. "This isn't the end, Michelle. We can beat this. We don't deserve any of this. We only did what we had to."

"I need to get out of this house. It's driving me even crazier than I already was."

I breathed a sigh of relief. "You can come here, if you like?"

"No, it's okay," Michelle replied, something approaching calm entering her tone now. "I'll go to my mum's house. She's always on me to visit more. She won't ask any questions either, if I tell her I'm staying."

"No problem. If you need anything, just let me know. I'll be right there."

"You're a good friend, Matt."

I didn't feel like much of one as I hung up the phone after saying goodbye and laid my cell on the kitchen counter. I thought about Stuart then, something I had purposely tried not to do since his funeral. Since before that, really.

Since the moment I'd been told what happened to him and this all started up again.

I looked again at the empty cupboards and closed the door on all of them. I couldn't stay there, sitting around doing nothing, simply waiting for the next bit of horror to unleash itself at my door. I needed to become more proactive. Not that I knew where to start.

In my office, I switched on my computer and searched for the forums Alexandra had mentioned. Putting *The Candle Man* into Google had given me so many results, it made sense to start at a smaller point.

I pulled a notepad from a pile and found a pen quicker than

usual. Began making notes. The first thing I did was find the forum on Reddit that listed all the possible cases involving the Candle Man. It was an extensive list. Reports were from all over the UK and seemed to have spread from there. Most, you could tell, were simply apocryphal tales. Ghost stories being shared around.

I started making a list of names.

Outside, it became darker, until the only light in the room was the static glow emanating from the screen in front of me. I barely noticed. My stomach growled and grumbled, but I ignored it, along with the pain behind my eyes. The tired headaches were becoming more and more frequent, but that only served to make them easier to ignore. At least, that was what I told myself.

The forum was comprehensive, if nothing else. Numerous disappearances that were then cross-checked, and various theories being put forward. Most of the threads talked about annoyance they felt that no one was taking them seriously. The most prevalent theory was that the Candle Man was a police officer and that was why it wasn't looked into properly. Some thought it was someone in the royal family. Others blamed high-ranking business types. The theories grew and grew, until it was an international conspiracy, it seemed.

I lost an hour to reading through all of these and more. Then two. I checked the time and saw it was approaching eight o'clock

I went back to the beginning and looked at the list of names I'd made. All of them UK based. Those who had families report-ing the existence of red candles after their loved one had gone missing. There were a few newspaper reports about the Candle Man, but they seemed to have dried up pretty quickly years earlier.

I spotted something quickly.

The storm lantern.

This hadn't gone unnoticed by the people on the forum either. In fact, it had also generated much discussion. People arguing back and forth about its significance. With the prior knowledge I had though, it made it much easier.

It *did* have significance.

I began whittling down the list of names. Searched online again for media reports about the disappearances. Found a couple of pieces that mentioned the red candles and the ones that also had pictures, including a storm lantern.

I then went through a whole ream of people who were either eventually found alive or, more infrequently, who had died and were clearly not victims of the supposed serial killer. There were many who had simply turned up after a few days. That fact seemed to be largely ignored for some, however.

I was left with a number.

Twelve.

Twelve people who were missing, who had stories in local newspapers, on social media, which mentioned red candles and storm lanterns. Who had police involvement but a denial of it being linked to a serial killer called the Candle Man.

Mark Welsh wasn't on the list.

I opened Google Maps and began plotting out the areas where the twelve were. Places in Scotland, three in Wales, two near Brock Hope forest. One in Liverpool. Two in Manchester. Peak District. Random places, scattered around the counties.

I added the thirteenth marker in the woods at that damn music festival. Even if Mark Welsh wasn't really considered a victim, it felt wrong to leave him off.

The room seemed smaller somehow, as if something unearthly had entered and settled in the air. Before, I had thought only of it all in an abstract way. I knew the man was a killer and we had stopped him. Now, seeing the red markers on a map made it all the more real.

There didn't seem to be any sort of pattern, but I noticed you could almost draw a straight line up the west side of the UK. No single place. The dates began decades earlier, moving forward in time sporadically. At least one every two to three years.

I looked at the one closest to home. Andrew Pennington. A twenty-six-year-old man from Liverpool, who had been reported missing by his girlfriend. I had a vague memory of the name, but I didn't recognize the face. I looked at the reports in the *Liverpool Echo* online, but after a few articles, there wasn't much else to see. His girlfriend was in the final article, a picture of her sitting next to a storm lantern housing a red candle. The headline didn't bury the lede.

Local Missing Man Linked to Candle Man Myth?

The article contained a few links back to the internet forums I'd already searched, but also contained a statement from Merseyside Police.

A force spokesperson said, "We are aware of the rumors surrounding Andrew Pennington's disappearance and its link to a story that has been swirling around the internet since its inception. The myth of a supposed serial killer has been thoroughly looked into and is not a part of our inquiry at this time. We urge anyone with any information about Andrew's movements in the days before or after his disappearance to please contact us..."

I wondered what was stopping them from finding the information it had taken me only a couple of hours to find and was shared between so many people online. I guessed they had done the same as me and discounted many of the cases they found, that all it looked like was a myth to them.

Or they knew and didn't want to admit they couldn't find him.

What I had wasn't much. Not enough for a court or anything—not that it's possible for a dead man to be put on trial.

The first year on the list I'd made was 1996. There were also names I couldn't confidently add that were much earlier than that. I looked at all the information I'd collected, saw what little it amounted to, and sat back in my chair, wondering what to do next.

While a voice inside me screamed to shut the computer down and forget all of this, another part of me knew I couldn't do that.

This wasn't going to end with me ignoring it.

Instead, I created an account on the forum, posted a few messages, and waited.

TWENTY-SEVEN

It was black outside. Cold. Clouds in the sky that looked angry and filled with dark hate. As if they were waiting for me to step outside, so they could unleash hell upon me. I tried breathing deeply in and out again and remembering it would only be rain. Standing at the doorway, looking at the path that led to my car, parked only yards away.

That path suddenly looked longer. My car even farther away. The street was quiet, the only sound a distant wind chime tinkling in the distance.

I made myself step forward and was outside.

Behind me, the door was still open. Ready for me to go back. Change my mind and retreat. I don't know how I kept moving, but somehow, I did. I pulled the front door behind me, and the noise of it shutting echoed around the street. I breathed in again and began walking. Pushed open my gate and unlocked my car with the fob in my hand.

There was a noise from my side. A shift of feet on the pavement. I turned to look, but there was nothing there. An empty street, dull light emanating from the streetlight a few yards away. An almost amber yellow. A noise again, and I could feel my heart rate increase. Beating against my chest, I could almost hear the pound of it.

Someone was out there.

I didn't know where that thought came from, but it was suddenly stark in my mind. Eyes watching me, unseen, hidden from view. Lurking in what was now a multitude of shadows outside my front door. I heard the scrape of shoes against concrete again and forced myself to walk around the car to the driver's door and crouch. Waiting. My breaths were coming in short bursts, and I willed them to quiet.

I leaned against the car, looking left and right, watching for any movement. The feeling of being watched lingered, as I peered into the gloom of the evening.

Nothing moved, nothing shifted. The only noise I could hear was traffic in the far distance, blown toward me on a wind that increased in strength the longer I stayed there.

I waited for another noise, but none came.

Waited for someone to walk past. A stranger. Didn't know me, didn't know what I was doing.

Couldn't know.

After a minute or two, I shook my head and let myself into the car. Sat down in the driver's seat and placed my hands on the steering wheel. Adjusted the rearview mirror and saw nothing in the reflection. Checked the side mirrors and got the same result.

It was my mind playing tricks on me. That was all. Still, I could almost feel those eyes out there on the street.

Watching me.

I shook the thought from my head, turned the key in the ignition, and started driving.

I had something more important to concentrate on.

Charnock Richard services on the M6 was only a half-hour drive from my house, located between Junctions 27 and 28. I remembered passing it on a drive up to the Lake District that

Alexandra and I had done a couple of years previously—making jokes about a guy called Richard who wrote his name down wrong when they were opening it up.

The memory made me smile as I drove in and parked in a bay. The parking lot was deserted—only a couple of other cars in the place. I wondered which one was the man I was going to meet, if he was already there.

I noticed my hands shaking a little as I took them from the steering wheel and picked up my phone. This was the safest option I could think of when I'd arranged to meet up with someone who I didn't know existed until a few hours earlier.

A highway truck stop that would still be open this late at night. Nice and public, but quiet enough that we wouldn't be noticed.

I closed my eyes and breathed in deeply. Tried to control the butterflies taking flight in the pit of my stomach. Opened them again and got out of the car before I could change my mind.

The parking lot was quiet, almost in complete darkness. The only light was emanating from the large building that lay at the side. A large sign saying *Welcome Break* in green and white adorned the outside of the glass-fronted entrance, but there wasn't much that was welcoming other than the fast food outlets advertised as being inside. Automatic doors opened slowly as I approached them, the noise from inside muted and discomforting. The only greeting an array of slot machines, blinking and flashing red and yellow lights. A couple of big men in high-visibility jackets were standing over the machines, pressing buttons and placing money in them.

I took the escalator that was in front of me up to the bridge, where the various eateries were situated. It crossed over the highway, but I couldn't hear the traffic from inside.

Bored-looking workers stood behind tills at either end. I ordered a Coke Zero and didn't have to wait long.

He approached me, thankfully. I wasn't sure I would have recognized him from the description he'd given me.

"Dave?"

I stood up and shook his proffered hand as he took the seat opposite me. Made another mental note to remember the fake name I'd given him over the phone earlier. "Thanks for meeting up with me on short notice, Peter. And at this time of night."

"No problem at all," Peter replied, shaking a few sugar packets into a large coffee. He was bigger than I'd been expecting— around six foot four inches, I guessed. As big around his chest and waist as he was tall. He pushed glasses up his nose and placed the lid back on his Styrofoam cup. "Got to say, this all feels a bit like some kind of spy movie."

"I doubt James Bond visits many highway truck stops," I said, keeping up the pretense that this was all a normal way of doing things. I pulled out a notebook and pen I'd found in my desk drawer. It had been filled with blank pages, but I opened it to the middle to give the impression I had more notes than I actually did. "Just to reiterate, this is all anonymous. I won't use your name in anything I do, unless you want me to?"

"No, I'd prefer to stay out of any of the stories, if possible. I don't want him coming after me, know what I mean?"

I nodded, writing down a few words. I'd told him I was a journalist working on an exposé of the Candle Man and the police's ignorance or denial of his existence. It wasn't a difficult lie to tell and gain attention—there had been a few similar pieces over the years, after all. "Tell me when you first heard about this story."

Peter made a show of looking into the distance and really

thinking about his answer. I got the feeling he wasn't asked for any sort of opinion in his offline life. Online, he was prolific on the message boards for the pages I'd gone through. He seemed to be first to respond on every post. He was the first person I'd made contact with earlier that evening and his speed of reply had made me sure I could set something up to meet him that night. I needed to do something, my ability to just sit around and wait finally cracking.

"Far too long back to remember, but I really got into it about five or six years ago now," Peter said, nodding to himself as if it was a sure answer. Even despite the year disparity. His voice was a mix of Mancunian and what I suspected was Preston. "I had heard of these killings, but it wasn't like I knew anything about them other than what some of the newspaper headlines said and that. Even those have died down a lot lately though."

"What made you want to investigate it further?"

"Well, there's a whole bunch of threads dedicated to unsolved crimes on the net, right? I was always posting theories and stuff on those, but it wasn't like we ever got any answers for the most part. And they always seemed to be in America—the JonBenét Ramsey case, O. J. Simpson, or that whole *Making a Murderer* series. Then, someone sent me a link to this thread about the Candle Man and it just really appealed to me."

"Why was that?"

"Well, this one wasn't about an actual murder or crime that took place and was unsolved or whatever—this was about whether a murderer actually *existed* or not. That was exciting, you know. I couldn't ignore this thing, and I've been working on it ever since."

I nodded along and made notes that wouldn't make sense to anyone else reading them in my dummy notebook. Tried to ask questions I thought a journalist would ask, but I didn't really have a clue what I was doing. Thankfully, it didn't seem like Peter knew either. We talked back and forth for a little while, as he explained the creation of subthreads and communities, which I didn't really understand but pretended to be highly interested in. He spent a few minutes droning on about a split in the camp a few months back, that was probably the most exciting thing to him and the others online. I was starting to worry I'd made the wrong decision in meeting him at that point.

"So, to get back to it," I said, as he paused for a second or two during a long monologue about characters I didn't have any interest in. Some internet spat or something that obviously still mattered a great deal to him but made me wish I was drinking the same coffee he'd ordered. "At what point did you truly believe you'd discovered a serial killer that wasn't being acknowledged by the police?"

"Oh, a while ago now. When the red candles were first discovered."

"And you never believed the line that it was just coincidence?"

Peter shook his head and laughed. "There's no such thing as coincidence in unsolved mysteries. Everything has meaning. That's how we work."

"What do you think about this Candle Man story then...any theories?"

"Of course," Peter replied, leaning toward me, all sense of joviality leaving his expression. "I think the kill count is even higher than we think. And I don't think he works on his own."

TWENTY-EIGHT

There was a pause, as a worker wiped and cleared a nearby table. A couple entered the restaurant area and moved past us, to the farthest fast food operator. Someone left, leaving only a single other person in the place.

Outside the windows, sparse traffic trundled north- and southbound on the M6.

"You don't think he was working alone?"

Peter shook his head. "It makes sense, even if most of them don't agree with me. I just can't see how one guy can do all these murders and get away with it. I think it's a group of people."

"There hasn't really been a reported link to any crime in the past year though," I said as I finished my drink and slid it away from me on the table. "Does that not strike you as odd? Especially if there's a group of people doing this."

"That's only if you believe that there haven't been any murders. This group is good. There's no bodies found—only missing people. It has taken us years to identify some victims, so it could be that we just haven't caught up yet. There's a few possible ones out there, but nothing confirmed for me. I'm guessing you've seen the maps and stuff?"

I nodded at his response and let him continue.

"Yeah, well, there's two pockets of multiple victims—farther north, encircling the Bowland forest and that. Over in the

Peak District. In the Highlands. And farther down south near Shropshire, Brock Hope, and the Cotswolds. You can draw a circle almost around those places and see what's happening. But there's loads more in other places. It could be that these woodland areas are just where all the bodies are buried, with other victims being taken there or whatever. Or, if you believe my theory, there's a network of people—killers, I should say—who are all working together and have their own patch, so to speak."

"Why do you think no bodies have ever been found? Wouldn't that suggest we're trying to give stories to these missing people, rather than just accepting they're missing?"

"Remember what I said about ignoring coincidences?" Peter said, leaning back in his chair, making it screech in protest. His barrel chest strained at the buttons on his checked shirt. "It's much easier for the police and that to make us believe all these people just disappear for no reason. Much better than the idea that a serial killer is out there and they can't find him. Or, should I say, them."

I pretended to write down more notes, but I was desperately trying to think of the next question. I wanted to know so much more than I did, but I wasn't exactly sure how to ask. "Do you have any theories about who it could be? If there's a main guy or anything?"

"I have a few, but they're all based on psychological profiling, stuff like that. Probably not even close to the truth. I think it started with one guy and just became bigger and bigger. Or I'm wrong, and it's a much smaller group. That's if the number of victims is smaller than we think it is. After all, it is possible that some people have just gone missing. That does happen."

"I heard it's something like a quarter of a million people a year who do just disappear."

"Yeah, but that's a bit of a misdirection," Peter said, puffing his chest out and pushing his glasses up his nose again. "Most of them turn up within a day or two. Can you really be called missing if you only go off radar for twenty-four hours? I'm not so sure about that. The more interesting cases are the ones that don't come back. At all. And there's loads of them."

The word *interesting* jarred me. I'd seen the killer's work. Close up. I wouldn't have called it that. I chose my next words carefully. "Who do you think it is? Do you have any suspects?"

Peter chuckled softly, a nice sound in the confines of the truck stop and given the subject matter. "I wish I did. I'd be a lot more famous than I am online if I'd worked that out."

I couldn't hide the disappointment as my shoulders slumped a little.

"All I can say is that I'm convinced that there's more to this story than even we know about on the threads. For all we know, it could just be a coincidence and there really is no Candle Man. It's been over a year since the story really blew up, but you know, with you coming around to me now and the other guy a few weeks back, I think there's going to be huge interest regenerated in the case. At some point, the police are going to have to listen."

"Wait a minute," I said, frowning at the mention of someone else Peter had supposedly spoken to. "What other guy is this? You haven't mentioned anything."

"Oh, I just figured you knew," Peter replied, seeming to be genuinely surprised by the question. "Yeah, it was some guy who was asking similar types of questions to yours. Said his name was Richard something. I met up with him, but all he wanted to know was who I thought it could be and whether I knew more than I was letting on. I don't, obviously, but he was a bit intense about it. Not friendly, like you. I suppose journalists have to have a thick skin or whatever, but it wasn't like it made me more willing to talk to him or anything."

I had wondered if maybe Alexandra had spoken to the guy before, but this was something else. Maybe I'd just stumbled into a good lie to speak to Peter, but I didn't think the timing was... Well, it was Peter who had told me about coincidences. "What did he look like?"

Peter scratched at his face, looking away from me and actually thinking about his answer this time. "Like, dirty blond hair, bit curly. About your height, maybe a little taller. Scruffy beard, which was odd I thought, because he seemed in shape and still earned some looks, if you know what I mean. If he kept it trim or shaved it off entirely, he could have probably been a bit of a ladies' man."

"Manchester accent?"

Peter nodded earnestly. "You do know him then? I thought you might. Who is he? A rival or something? He seemed a bit scatty and nervous, so I'm sure you're a few steps ahead of him when it comes to getting something down that people want to read."

I shook my head. "Sounds like someone I might know."

"He was talking about an anniversary approaching or something," Peter said, frowning as he tilted his head, trying to catch my eye. "I didn't know what he meant by that, but he seemed... Are you okay? You look pale all of sudden."

"Yeah, I'm fine," I lied, feeling a sudden need to get out of there and away from the man.

He had seen Stuart.

In the days before he'd died, he'd met with Stuart and talked about the same things I was now. I wanted to ask a million and one more questions, but something stopped me.

"Who was he?" Peter said, his voice turning a little now.

More insistent. Something dark underneath. "I want to know who he was."

I swallowed and hoped I would sound relaxed when I answered. "It's like you said, a rival journo. That's all."

"Are you sure?" Peter said, leaning forward, grabbing hold of my wrist suddenly. The grip wasn't tight but wasn't exactly friendly either. "If I'm being conned here…"

I shook my head and managed to extricate my hand. "No, it's nothing like that. Listen, thanks for talking to me and answering my questions."

Peter seemed to blink and go back to the way he had been before Stuart had been mentioned. His tone changing in a heartbeat. "Course, no problem," Peter said, standing up and offering his hand. "Anything I can do to help."

I shook it quickly and placed my notebook filled with gibberish in my jacket pocket and stepped away. "Appreciate it."

"Yeah, no worries. Listen, if you need anything else, just let me know. I'll be there. Waiting for answers. That's all I do now. So, get in touch soon, you hear me?"

It sounded like more of a threat than I thought he would have intended. When I risked a look at his face though, I could see something in his eyes. A brief moment of black, before color returned. I needed to get away from him. "Of course, thanks again," I replied, raising a hand toward him, moving away and toward the stairs that led down to the exit. I looked back as I was about to leave the restaurant area. Peter was still standing at the table, watching me leave. He raised a hand and waved it once. A smile on his face.

I took the stairs two at a time, determined to get into my car before Peter had the chance to follow. The temperature had dropped in the time I'd been inside, and I pulled my coat tighter around me as I jogged across the parking lot. I was inside, with the engine turned on within seconds, pulling away as I was still putting my seat belt on. I pulled out of the space quickly and stalled the car as I shifted back into gear and tried to drive away. Swore under my breath, then stalled again.

The entrance/exit to the truck stop was still empty, but I kept expecting to look over and see Peter standing there. There was something about him I couldn't work out.

Something about the way he spoke about the whole thing.

On the third try, I managed to drive properly. I pulled over once I'd passed the gas station and before rejoining the motorway. Plugged my phone in and called Alexandra.

She answered quickly but didn't sound too welcoming. "What do you want?"

"I'm sorry about before."

There was a sigh that surrounded me from the car speakers, as I indicated to come back onto the almost-empty highway. My heart rate began to slow a little as I finally put some distance between me and whoever that had been back at the truck stop.

"Me too," Alexandra said eventually, but it didn't sound like she meant it all that much. "Are you in the car?"

"Yeah, listen, I need to ask you something."

"What?"

"I've just met some guy I found on one of those threads you talked about on Reddit, about the Candle Man…"

"Really? I spoke to a couple on private message but never in person."

"Did you ever speak to a guy called Peter? I think his online name was something like MysteryBuster70."

I heard rustling in the background and then the sound of a keyboard tapping. I waited as she checked, looking in the rearview mirror for any cars following behind me. I bit down on my lower lip, trying to stop paranoia from taking over me entirely.

"Yeah, I did," Alexandra said, reading names under her breath, then finally finding the right one. "He just gave me a couple of bits of info. Mainly he just redirected me to his posts that were already up there. I don't think I ever asked to talk to him on the phone or anything. Let me just read through our messages… No, I used a different story on him. Told him I was just interested in the case and had stumbled on the message boards. He's one of the main posters on there, so that'll be why I contacted him."

I didn't know if I was relieved or annoyed. It would have been nice to see if he had made her as suspicious as I was now feeling. "Listen, he told me something that doesn't make any sense…"

"How did you get to meet him?"

"I told him I was a journalist working on a story about the Candle Man. He was more than happy to meet quickly and give his take on it. But that's not the point."

"Sorry, go on. What did he say?"

I took a second to check behind me again, then continued. "I don't know if this is right, but I needed to tell someone. He said I was the second person to meet up with him about it recently."

"Who was the other person? An actual journalist?"

"No," I said, taking a hand off the steering wheel to rub some life into my face. The road ahead was too dark, and I had a sudden fear I would drive off the road after falling asleep for a second. "It was Stuart."

"What? I don't understand—"

"Neither do I, but that's who he described meeting. He had

him down to a T, but Stuart had given him a false name. He even mentioned an approaching anniversary."

"Jesus," I heard Alexandra whisper to herself, then silence. I lowered the window to let some fresh air into the car, but quickly closed it when the noise overwhelmed me.

"What do you think he was doing?"

"I don't know," I replied, seeing the exit up ahead. I didn't need the GPS for this part of the journey, thankfully, but wanted to keep driving anyway. To continue north, until I was as far away as possible. I'd always wanted to visit the Highlands. I could picture me living in a tent, growing a long beard, and living off the land. For about a second, before I realized I wouldn't last five minutes without walls around me.

And the silence would be unbearable.

"I wonder if Stuart was just doing what we are," Alexandra said, her voice like a comforting embrace. Bringing me back to reality. "A year is significant, you know. That's probably why it's so strongly in all our minds. For Stuart, I guess...I guess it became too much."

I began to speak but stopped myself. I didn't want to argue with her again—twice in the same day seemed excessive—but I didn't believe Stuart had killed himself now. Instead, I forgot all about driving north and indicated to come off at the junction to turn around. "I'll call you tomorrow. Michelle has gone to stay at her mum's house. Just in case."

"I'm sure she'll be fine," Alexandra replied, but there was a hint of apprehension in her tone that hadn't been there before. "I'll speak to you soon."

She ended the call, as I rejoined the motorway and drove home.

All the time thinking about the man I'd just met and the feeling of unease he had given me.

I wondered why Stuart would meet him and not say anything to us. To not try to speak to a single person in the group about what he was doing.

I wondered why Stuart would hide that from us.

TWENTY-NINE

An hour's drive can be done in forty-five minutes at night.
That's like a law of the road or something that I've always
believed. Still, it was almost midnight by the time I pulled up
outside my house and let myself in.

It was quiet, but I quickly remedied that. The radio was
playing in my kitchen as I cooked some pasta and finally
quelled the gnawing hunger that had plagued me on the drive
home.

I ate it in front of my computer, scrolling through the online
posting history of the man I'd met that night. Peter had a long
record of writing about unsolved crimes. I got back as far as six
months, but that took me a couple of hours.

I then used every bit of internet knowledge I had to try to
find out who he really was but ran into brick wall after brick
wall. That's the thing about fictional representations of people
who work with computers that they never show—it's difficult to
uncover anonymity if the person behind those accounts has even
an ounce of computing savvy.

With a little more time and resources, I could have probably
discovered who he really was in a few hours. Once I'd eaten
though, I knew I had to make the trudge upstairs to lie awake
with my eyes closed until morning.

There was a part of me that wanted to just sit there and forgo the uselessness of trying to sleep, but I was always optimistic before bed.

Some nights, I would fall asleep quickly, exhausted after a few nights of broken, short bouts of sleep. Then, after around thirty minutes, I would wake up with a start and spend hours looking at the back of my eyelids. Counting down the hours I was losing.

Fall asleep now, you'll have five hours.

Now, four.

Three should be okay.

It was an endless war of attrition with my own mind.

I had messaged Michelle to check in with her when I got home, but she was probably asleep already. I didn't blame her—I hoped she got some peace away from her house.

After going through the routine, I lay in bed, my phone on the bedside table playing some American podcast I hoped would bore me to sleep. Closed my eyes and my thoughts immediately overran. The man I'd met, the red candle in Michelle's house. The one I had found in Stuart's house. The things Alexandra had shown me about the Candle Man, the mythological nature of his story.

I tossed and turned, unable to get comfortable, as a droning voice emanated from my cell phone. Some political discourse show that thought it was funnier than it actually was.

The last time I checked the time, it was 4:18 a.m., and I was thinking about a lad's face in the woods.

You never know when you've fallen asleep, but I knew I was dreaming instantly. That eerie quality when you know what is happening isn't real, but you can't do anything to stop it. Your understanding of the unreality of it all is forgotten. The broken images, the blurred scenery, the distorted and warped sounds.

Not that it didn't feel real though. I was aware of the dream, but I still reacted as if it were actually happening. The anxious, nauseated feeling in the pit of my dream stomach was impossible to ignore. The beating of my false heart, the sweat forming on my false skin, the false hair raising on my false neck.

All of it felt as if it were genuinely existing in my world at that moment.

I was walking through my house, the silence almost overpowering me as I moved. I could hear something over it though—a pulsing beat of bass. Not silence then, but that's what it seemed to be. As if the silence somehow had a sound now.

There was a different quality to the familiar—all color had been drained, and I was walking in monochrome. The kitchen was empty—all the appliances, the canisters, the bread bin, the full herb rack, all gone. Empty cupboards and bare walls.

I turned back and into the hallway. Walked into my office and found nothing there. A shell. Dust on the floor where my desk should have been. Brick where plaster had once lived. Light streamed through the window from the yard and then blinked out into darkness. I backed out and into the hallway once more.

Stood outside the living room, tried to push open the door. It wouldn't move. I looked down at my hand but couldn't see it. I tried to move it, but the door still wouldn't budge. Jammed shut. I could feel my shoulder moving before I'd decided to do it. I used it to push against the door, but it refused to acquiesce. I tried again, using my weight to throw myself at the entrance.

It was as if I were moving through water—my movements were all in slow motion and no give was forthcoming. I stepped back and examined the door again. Carefully this time, as the light blinked in and out in time with my heartbeat.

It opened inward independently as I was standing there. The room revealed to me in small segments of space.

I saw him as I always did. Lying on the empty floor where my coffee table was supposed to be sitting. His eyes were closed, his arms folded over his chest, palms flat. They made an X, as if it marked the spot where he had died. Only, it wasn't here. It was in the woods, and with that, I'm there again.

Daylight replaced by the black of night. Words scrawled on the trees surrounding me. White and stark against the black. Every synonym that could be used for the single signifier of what we had become.

Killers.

I know what is different now. The silence wasn't the same. The bass beat was a warning—something my mind had concocted to show me that this wasn't the usual nightmare.

We're usually alone. Just me and him in the woods. Him dead, me standing over his body.

Only this time, someone else is there. I couldn't see who it was yet, but I could feel the presence in the air. He was standing in the shadows, waiting for me to notice him. I could hear his breathing, soundless though it is.

I didn't want to look up. I was looking at the forest floor, at the ground, as it bobbled and modulated into a blurry mess.

There was laughter. Cutting through the silence. The bass beat ended, and I could feel the mocking tone swirl around me and over my skin. My muscles tightened and my biceps seemed to grow until they were straining at my T-shirt.

I shivered, I think. I felt cold, like someone had walked over my grave or I was standing outside in January. I wasn't sure.

I couldn't think properly.

There were words being spoken, but I couldn't understand

them. They're being vocalized in a language I was unable to comprehend. I screw my eyes shut, but I can still see everything clearly.

A mist appeared around my feet, clinging to my legs and knocking me off balance. The man is still on the ground, but he's suddenly alive. Breathing heavily, as if tired from some unseen exertion.

He has never been alive in my dreams before.

I can feel the anger coursing through me now. The same as it had been when I'd been in those woods before. I want to cross the space that divided us in two long strides and pick up the man by his little bare neck. Watch the last flicker of life leave his eyes.

I am my own dark side.

Yet I can't move, even as the mist that has crawled and entwined my legs brings me down to my knees. Still, there's that laughter, mocking me from the darkness.

Then, I'm not myself any longer. Not someone I recognize. I'm a child—shorter and thinner. A scrawny young teenager, who hasn't lived yet. I turn my hands over, staring at the hairless, small things as if they're someone else's.

But it is me, twenty years ago.

Now, I didn't feel anger anymore. I feel fear. I'm scared and I'm sweating and I'm shaking. I can't move my legs and I can't run away. I'm stuck in a quagmire of terror and dread. This is it.

This is what it feels like to know you're about to die.

Someone emerges into the light, and I can do nothing but watch him. Stare with unblinking eyes as the figure goes about his work, whistling to himself a joyful tune. The man is on the ground, still breathing, but the figure is happy about that.

I can feel the life being sucked out of the man. The figure towering over him, enjoying his last gasps of breath.

I can't do anything but kneel there and watch, as my heart races and my skin tightens with cold. Shivering and shaking.

The figure moves back and admires its creation.

Then, the laughter returned. Quiet at first, then louder, until it builds into a crescendo. It stops and turns toward me.

Whispered. The voice is slurred and almost drunken with glee.

"You don't know what's coming. You can't do anything about it."

I scream soundlessly as it comes toward me.

A noise throws me into another place. The dream shifts, and I am standing in my kitchen again. The sound of birds singing, then shots being fired and then silenced.

Bang.

I turn as the laughter comes back, coming from an unseen place.

Bang.

I moved from the kitchen, looking down to see a knife dripping with red in my hand.

Bang.

Bang.

Bang.

I woke slowly from the nightmare as the visions I'd been dreaming followed me into full consciousness. The sound was there too, and it took me a few seconds to realize the noise wasn't coming from inside my head. It was real. And it was coming from downstairs.

I stepped out of bed quietly and found my trousers on the floor. I slipped into them and walked softly to my closed bedroom door. I placed an ear to it and tried to work out what it was I could hear.

It was still dark outside, but I didn't know what time it was. The calm part of me wondered if it was a milkman or the like, but I couldn't remember the last time I'd seen one of them. Wheelie bin collection was my next guess, but that was still days away.

I moved back to my bed and knelt, feeling underneath with one hand. It finally gripped hold of the baseball bat I kept there and brought it out. I held it loosely in my right hand and moved back to the door.

The noise was still there.

A soft *thump* every few seconds or so.

Is this it? Is this the end?

I opened the door as soundlessly as I could, moving onto the landing and stepping carefully on the carpet. I stopped at the top of the stairs, listening again. The noise was a little louder now, and I realized it was coming from the back of the house. I slowly descended the stairs, my back to the wall, carefully stepping on each stair to minimize any creaks. My eyes were focused on the open door that led to my living room, looking for any light or movement.

I reached the bottom of the stairs and followed the path through. Kept my back toward the wall as I approached the living room. I could see better now, as I became more accustomed to the darkness.

The only noise other than the rhythmic banging was my own breathing. I concentrated on it and took comfort in the sound. I could see the outlines of the furniture in the room as I reached the doorway. The kitchen door was on my right, at the end of the hallway.

I swiveled into the room, holding the bat out to my side, ready to swing. Held my breath, as I waited for someone to emerge.

Nothing happened.

I looked around, waiting to see what I'd expected.

No candle.

The banging sound came again, from the direction of the kitchen. My breathing quickened, so I swallowed a few times and took a moment to calm myself again. I willed my heart rate to slow down, tried to soothe myself with comforting thoughts.

Struggled to think of any.

I moved off slowly, rounding the doorway into the hall toward the kitchen door. It was closed, so I placed my palm out and rested it on the door. I was standing off to the side as I pushed, in case someone was waiting on the other side.

I'd have a second, a bat in my hand, and that was about it in terms of defense.

No wonder I couldn't think of anything comforting to think about.

I pushed again, and when nothing jumped out at me, I moved gradually toward the entrance, ready to move at speed.

The back door was open.

Cold air breezed through the kitchen, making me shiver as my chest was exposed to the winter wind and protested. A little light was illuminating the top end of the room, coming from the houses opposite my garden.

I moved quickly, purposefully, outside, careful to not expose my back to any possible hidden attack. Saw the back gate still closed and locked. Faced the backyard and watched silently for movement that never came.

I tried to remember locking the back door and couldn't recall it. I was usually mindful of that, but I wasn't sure I had when I'd arrived back home.

That was it, I thought. I'd left it open when I'd put something out and just forgotten. The wind had picked up overnight and opened it up fully, that was all. Banging against the bin and the kitchen counter. I was relieved suddenly, when I figured it all out.

That didn't stop me thinking the worst.

Then, a scent in the air that reminded me of someone. A sense memory. An aroma.

Aftershave or shower gel. Something of that sort.

I saw Stuart in my mind. Clearly. Laughing at some joke, baring his teeth for the world to see. Bumping me with his shoulder as his body shook with unbridled laughter. The memory faded, but the smell in the air lingered.

I closed the back door, mindful to any noise coming from inside, and hearing nothing. I moved toward the light switch, flicking it on and feeling instantly safer for no apparent reason. I bathed myself in a forty-watt glow, looking for anything that had been moved. Everything looked stark now, edges to peripheral items that hadn't existed in the dark. I calmed myself again, taking deep breaths, the coolness of the room lingering, not warming me up any.

I turned the tap on over the sink and filled a glass. Drank rapidly, soothing my dry and scratchy throat. I placed the glass on the drainer and realized I was still holding onto the bat at my side. I looked at it and wondered how useful it actually would have been if someone had jumped out of the shadows and gone after me. I smiled to myself as I hoped the fact I was half-naked and not exactly small in stature would have intimidated any potential burglar.

Only, I knew that wouldn't have been who was in my house at this time.

I moved back through to the living room, adrenaline still coursing through my body. I wasn't going to go back to sleep anytime soon. I switched on the floor lamp, picked up the remote control, and turned on the TV. Checked the time.

6:42 a.m.

A couple of hours sleep before a door woke me up.

Great.

I hadn't checked the office.

You idiot.

I couldn't live like this anymore.

I switched on lights as I left the living room and walked into the dining room/office. I was expecting the worst, but it was exactly as I'd left it the previous night.

Above me, I could hear music.

I'd left my phone upstairs.

Someone was calling me.

2002

My last exam was over, and that was three years of my life suddenly at an end. There was something unsettling about the process, as I sat at the bar of the cheap pub on campus, downing the dregs of a pint of Carlsberg.

It was two in the afternoon, and I planned on getting steaming drunk.

"Think of it this way—at least there's a chance of retaking them."

I rolled my eyes at Stuart, who was already three pints in by the time I'd joined him. Not that it showed. He was an annoying drunk, who never seemed to show any effect alcohol had on him. The only difference seemed to be an increase in the volume of his voice.

Chris was the other side of me and slapped a hand on my shoulder. "I'm sure you'll be fine."

I grunted a nonresponse and got up to refresh my glass. Chris followed me, as Stuart kneeled on the seat in the booth and chatted to the group of women sitting on the one behind us.

"Isn't he supposed to be seeing Michelle?" Chris said to me, waving the barman over and pointing at the Carlsberg pump. "Two and a Coke."

"You not having another one?"

"No, I can't. I'm not finished yet, remember? Got to keep

myself on the straight and narrow. Don't want to screw up like you might have."

"Cheers for that," I said, but smiled, sensing the attempt to lighten the mood. I wasn't even sure I'd done all that badly in the exam, but it was enough to make me wonder if I'd just wasted three years of my life, only to fall at the last hurdle. It seemed wrong somehow, to make everything dependent on the last few weeks of a student's career. Sadistic, if anything.

"Anyway, him and Michelle, what's going on?"

I looked back at Stuart, who was telling the women some kind of story. They were all around twenty, twenty-one, which surprised me. He usually went after first and second years now, as the older students had all heard his tall tales by now. "I don't know. I think they've been off and on again more times than Ross and Rachel. Did you see that by the way? Apparently Joey accidentally proposes to Rachel after she has the baby."

"Matt, you know I have no idea what you're talking about."

"Right, right," I said, chuckling to myself. "I forgot it's all about the serious programs for you. Honestly, you were much more interesting when we used to watch Power Rangers and WWF. Anyway, as I said, I don't know what's going on with them two. It seems like they're just back and forth all the time."

"They'll work it out," Chris replied, handing over a note to the barman and lifting his glass of Coke up. "Cheers to you, by the way."

I lifted my own pint and clinked it against his soft drink. "I can't believe that's it. All done. Got to start thinking about the real world now. Getting a proper job."

"You'll find something quicker than any of us."

I began to disagree when I noticed a couple of blokes entering and stopping in the doorway. They nudged each other and pointed toward Stuart. I rolled my eyes and poked Chris in the arm. "Look, here comes trouble."

Chris tensed up and turned toward the two men walking straight to Stuart. I couldn't hear what was being said, but from the pointed fingers and chests being puffed out, I didn't think it was anything good.

We didn't need to say anything, placing our drinks back on the bar and walking across toward them.

"…sniffing around something that doesn't belong to you."

"I don't belong to you," a woman from the group protested as we reached them finally.

"Listen, lads, there's nothing going on," Stuart said, his hands up in defense. "I was just talking."

"What's the problem?" I said, standing next to Stuart and sensing Chris moving to my side. "Everything okay here?"

"You his mate?"

"I am."

"Same," Chris said, but his voice was quiet and even I could hear the fear within it. I glanced at him, and he was already sweating. Still, two against two was still good odds, I thought.

"Well, you need to get your mate out of here before I knock his teeth in," the smaller of the two grunted through gritted teeth. He was half a foot shorter than me, but his friend was about the same going the other way. I imagined they were called *little* and *large* by people behind their backs.

"No need for that," Stuart said under his breath, but he seemed to want to avoid anything further.

"What did you say?"

"I said, you're welcome to her, lad," Stuart replied, a smile appearing on his face. It didn't reach his eyes though. He reached down and picked up his jacket. "Got no interest in used goods. Come on, let's go."

I could have done without the jibe at the blameless woman, but I was just glad Stuart was backing down.

"What did you say?"

"You heard me," Stuart said, walking past the bar, grabbing his drink and downing half of his pint in one go. "Got more important things to do than stand around here and have a pissing contest with you."

"Yeah, run along, little boy. Before you get your face smashed in."

My shoulders fell as I felt Stuart bristle as we came close to him. He stopped in his tracks and began to face them. I looked at the door and wondered which one I'd end up fighting, while Stuart took the other and Chris rang the police or something.

I opened my mouth to speak, but Stuart was already moving.

Only, it wasn't toward the two men. It was toward the door, as Chris gripped him by both shoulders and marched him out of the bar.

"Come on," Chris was saying, not breaking stride and pushing the door open. I followed them out, not looking back. "They're not worth it."

"We can't back down from them—"

"I'm not joking, Stuart," Chris said, not letting up on the pace as we walked away from the pub and onto the university square. "We've got more to lose than those idiots."

"They can't get away with that," Stuart replied, his voice low and angry. He was red in the face, his body looking like it would explode at any moment. "No one talks to me like that."

"I know, I know," Chris said, trying to keep the peace, as I fell into step with them.

I patted Stuart on the back, but he didn't seem to feel it.

"I'm serious, Chris. They're not going to get away with it."

"They won't, I agree, but not now, okay? We need to think about our future right now."

Stuart seemed to calm as we continued to walk. Chris placating him the whole way, telling him what he needed to hear, while also making sure he was far enough away that it wouldn't reach the ears of the idiots we'd left behind us.

I didn't see that side of Stuart often—none of us did. Chris was the only one who could calm him down. All of us had tried over the previous three years, but he was the only one who had any success.

We didn't see the two lads again. University was over within a week or so after that night.

Stuart would talk about them though. Every day after that, still unhappy that he hadn't taught them a lesson.

I spent that week wondering at one point if he would lead us into something we couldn't handle.

THIRTY

I ran upstairs, out of breath by the time I reached my phone. It stopped just as I reached it, the screen turning black. I checked the missed call.

A number that wasn't stored in my phone. I checked the time and was about to dismiss it as a telemarketer, then rejected the idea. Even they tended to wait another hour or two before bothering me.

I took the phone downstairs, deciding to Google the number before calling it back. As I typed it in, the phone rang again. I answered instantly.

"Hello?"

A woman's voice I didn't recognize came on the line, sounding tired and as if she had been crying. "Matthew?"

"Yeah, who's calling?"

"Sorry for ringing you so early," she said, sniffing and seeming to compose herself. "It's Val, Michelle's mum."

I was sitting down without realizing, as my legs gave out beneath me. There was silence, but it took a few seconds before I realized she was waiting for me to talk. I cleared my throat. "Okay, erm, is something wrong?"

"I'm not sure," Val said, clearly trying to keep herself calm. "Michelle was supposed to come here yesterday. She was in a right state when she called me and said she'd be coming over to visit. Tried to hide it of course, like she always does, but I could tell. Anyway, I was a little worried because she's been a bit off for a couple of weeks now—well, even longer than that, but that's not important. When she didn't turn up, I tried ringing her back, but I haven't had a reply at all. I've messaged her, so has her sister. And her aunty. No one has heard anything. Her sister has just driven up to her house, and there's no one there. I'm just a bit worried now. She called me the other day and said if anything happened to her to call you and gave me your number."

I tried to remember Val's face, but it wouldn't come to mind. We had met a couple of times when we were younger, but I couldn't see it now.

My mind was trying to drag me away from what was happening in that phone call.

"Right, I see," I replied, scratching the back of my neck with my free hand and trying to keep my voice from cracking. "I spoke to her yesterday and she seemed okay. She mentioned going over to your house, as she's been feeling a bit under the weather. Maybe she's just sleeping it off?"

"Her sister said her car wasn't outside and she knocked loud enough to wake the neighbors, with no answer."

"Right…"

"Do you know where she might be?"

I tried to come up with an answer that might give her some comfort but struggled to think of something. Tried to come up with a thought that might give comfort to *myself*. Failed at that too. I went for platitude. "I'm sure she's fine. Maybe she's stopped off at a friend's and just crashed out. It's only early— she'll call you soon enough, I'm sure. I'll try to ring her myself and see if I can get hold of her."

"I don't really know any of her friends…"

"That's okay. I know a few," I said quickly, wanting the phone call to be over. Wanting so much to tell her everything. Knowing what was at stake. Michelle, alone, out there somewhere. In danger. If I said something now, it could be over. I could save her. Only, I knew it was too late. That this was it. I could stop it now, just by saying something, but I couldn't. I hated myself for it, but I couldn't do it. Instead, I swallowed and tried to sound normal. "I'll get in touch if I hear anything. Let me know if there's anything else I can do."

"Okay, no problem. I'm sure you're right. It's just…you never stop worrying, you know. Even when your kids are older. I'm sure you know that."

I murmured an agreement, then ended the call after saying goodbye. I stared at the phone for a few seconds, picturing Michelle as I'd left her.

I left her. Alone.

This was on me if something had happened to her. And there wasn't much that was dissuading me from the thought that it had.

I navigated to WhatsApp on my phone and sent a few messages. Chris, Nicola, Alexandra. Time was, we had a group chat going on the app, but that had ended a year earlier. No one posted anything on there, but I checked Michelle's name on there and looked for when she had last been online.

Not since the previous afternoon. I checked the time on it—only thirty minutes after I'd spoken to her.

She was in trouble. Or she had been and I was far too late.

I had to resist the urge to throw my phone across the room. I gripped it tighter in my hand and heard a guttural sound in my throat. I scrunched my eyes shut and shouted in frustration.

I think I would have stayed in that position for a long time if my phone hadn't started ringing again. The display blinked into focus, and I saw Chris's name on the screen.

"Hey," he said after I answered. "What's...what's wrong?"

I swallowed down the emotion and attempted to talk. "It's Michelle." I tried to ignore the rapidly forming lump in the back of my throat and faltered through an explanation of the phone call I'd just had with Michelle's mum. There was no holding it back any longer and I let go. "We waited too long," I said when I was done. I was past sadness, past fear; now I was just angry. "If we had just gone to the police yesterday—"

"Hold up. We don't even know if anything has happened to her yet," Chris replied, his voice rising over the phone. "Maybe it's how you said it. She could have gone somewhere else or just be sick or tired. Something like that."

"You really think that? Even after all this? She doesn't have anyone else, Chris. She had *us* and we've let her down."

There was silence for a few seconds, and I could almost hear the cogs turning in Chris's mind as he tried to come up with another reason. Anything that didn't put the blame on our inaction.

"We've got to do something," I said, the phone gripped tightly in my hand now. I could feel the anger and frustration threatening to boil over and tried to control it. "We can't just sit here and do nothing. She's our friend, and she's in trouble. We have to do something. Now."

"Mate..."

"It's time, Chris," I said as firmly and calmly as was possible. I didn't think I quite managed it. I realized I had one hand in my hair, gripping it hard. I let go and forced myself to breathe in and out slowly. "Who's going to be next? What if it's you or Nicola? What if it's Alexandra? There's no time for this anymore."

"Listen, sit tight. I'll be over in a minute."

I opened my mouth to protest, but the phone had already gone dead. I stared at it for a few more seconds, then laid it on the arm of the sofa. I realized I must have sat down there at some point but wasn't sure when. Sat there as the TV in the corner played *BBC Breakfast* on a low volume. Waiting.

Chris arrived in fifteen minutes. Entered the house without the smell of expensive aftershave following him. "You look like you've not slept," I said once we were in the living room. "What's happened?"

"I went home yesterday and spoke to Nicola," he replied with a sigh. He ran a hand through his hair, which was unkempt and the very definition of the term *bedhead*. "I was up most of the night trying to talk her out of coming over here and beating some sense into you, as she put it."

I tried to remember a time when I had seen Chris in anything but a well-kept way. He always seemed like he'd just stepped out of a shower and spent an hour getting ready. That morning, he looked as if he'd just had a night on the booze and slept in a doorway. There was no smell of alcohol, so I took him at his word. "She didn't take it well then."

"Of course she bloody didn't. She can't understand why this has all been brought up again, so long after it happened."

"You know the answer to that," I said, feeling the anger bubble up again. "Did you tell her about Michelle before you came here? About her going missing?"

"Are you kidding me? I left her getting ready for work. I didn't want to make it any worse. Honestly, hours we were going over it for hours."

Something dawned on me then. "You agree with me, right?"

Chris hesitated before he answered, then sighed and crossed

his arms over his chest. "Yes. Yes I do. You're right. There's no way Stuart or Michelle would have a red candle in their home. Stuart wouldn't...you know. And now Michelle. I'm scared."

I put a hand on his shoulder. "It's gonna be okay. We can get through this."

"I just wish he would show himself. Instead of these...these games."

"We spent a year pretending that Mark Welsh's body just disappeared of its own accord. I think we always knew this time would come. It's the only way."

"But only if everyone agrees," Chris said, staring at me now. I could see the lasting effects of the previous night's conversations with Nicola burning in his bloodshot eyes. "We do this together or not at all."

"We need to find Michelle."

Chris swallowed and then nodded his head. "I don't even know where to start."

"Alexandra was here yesterday," I said, waiting for a reaction of surprise from Chris, but he didn't show anything. "She's been thinking about things a lot."

"About you and her?"

"No," I said, shaking my head and shrugging my shoulders *What are you gonna do?* style. "She has been trying to find out who the man in the woods was."

"Right. And how has she gotten on?"

I talked him through what Alexandra had told me. Then, about my own investigation. About the online message boards that covered the Candle Man story and the possible murders. He didn't interrupt until I told him about meeting someone at the truck stop.

"You met someone from the internet on your own?"

"Yeah, in a public place, *Dad*."

He smiled at that, but it didn't last long. I told him about the conversation, but it wasn't until I mentioned the fact I thought he'd met with Stuart that he finally sat down.

"Jesus."

"I know," I said, sitting down in the chair opposite where he was sitting on the sofa. "This guy was weird, Chris. Like, creepy weird."

"You don't think he's...you know?"

I shrugged. "I'm not sure what to think anymore. There's something not right with that guy, but I could just be paranoid about everything right now. It's not like I've been sleeping well and this is all just..."

"Crazy," Chris finished for me. He sniffed and shook his head. "When did life get so complicated?"

"Probably just after we killed a guy."

He stared at me for a second or two and then nodded his head. "Right. Yeah, you're right. I just...I just want things back to normal, you know?"

"I do, but I don't have any other idea how to get back there without trying to get help elsewhere. It just makes sense. Now with this Michelle thing, what should we do?"

"I don't know. We can't go to the police yet. Not until we convince Nicola and Alexandra it's time. Hopefully with what's happened with Michelle, that'll change. I've got no idea where we would even start in trying to track her down."

"It's probably too late."

I opened my mouth to argue with him, but I didn't know what I could say that would change his mind. Plus, I knew it anyway.

We *were* too late. She hadn't made it to her mum's house.

That meant she had either decided to hide somewhere else or was already gone. Those were the only two options I could see. If it was the latter, nothing we did would save her now. If it was the former, by trying to look for her, we could simply be leading a killer to her hideout. I sighed and bit down on my lower lip hard enough to make me wince in pain. Ran my hands over my head and held them at the back of my neck. "We can't do anything unless we're all on the same page. Police-wise, I mean. We have to talk them into it."

Chris winced and tensed up. "That's the problem. I don't think Nicola is going to be convinced."

"Even if Michelle turns up...you know? Won't that be enough?"

He shook his head in response. "She seemed pretty adamant that she wanted us to just forget the whole thing and even if someone was coming after us, that it could be dealt with. I wasn't sure what she meant by that, but I guess she means getting rid of the problem?"

"Don't go thinking that hadn't crossed my mind," I replied, feeling the anger come back into me now. I remembered how scared Michelle had been and was suddenly filled with the urge to deal with the issue myself.

Could you really kill again?

The answer came to me quickly and that worried me.

Someone who hurt my friends?

My family?

Yes.

Yes I would.

THIRTY-ONE

W hat do we do now, then?"

I looked at the clock in the alcove and saw it was coming up on 8:30 a.m. I didn't think Chris would want to sit around all day—especially with me—so I got to my feet. "Go home, get showered, and go to work. I'm sure they'll let you off with being late for once. We need to make sure we lead as normal lives as possible before we decide to do anything. I don't have a boss other than myself, so I can do the brunt of it. I'm going to try to find Michelle."

"You're going to need help with that," Chris said, straightening up and trying to add an inch or two to his height. It didn't help—he was still the least intimidating man I'd ever met.

"It's fine. If I find her or get anywhere near her, I'll call the police. Let them deal with it. I'll give you a call later and let you know what's happening. If I don't get anywhere, we can arrange a meeting between all four of us. See if we can talk the other two into doing what we think is best."

Chris rubbed some life into his eyes and stood up. "You're right. Not sure how useful I'll be, but I haven't missed work in a long time. They'll be okay with me being late. I'll ring them from the car and come up with some sort of excuse. Thanks for...well, you know."

"No problem. That's what mates are for." I gave him a brief hug at the door and waved him off. Closed the door behind me and went back in the house.

I thought about being the last one.

I didn't know what order we were being targeted, but for the first time, I considered the idea that it could be me that was the only one left at the end.

I wasn't going to let it get that far.

My phone pinged with a message just as I was about to shower and try to make a plan. A message from Alexandra.

Just spoke to her mum. Still no sign. Will call soon. x

I wanted to deliberate over the kiss at the end of the message, but I couldn't think about that then.

I thought about Alexandra being next, and that was enough to keep me moving.

A shower is a good place to think, I've heard often. I stood under the water, turning the temperature up high enough to almost scald my skin. The cubicle steamed up and I closed my eyes, enjoying the heat on my body.

I didn't think of anything for a few minutes. Allowed my mind to drift and just listen to the muted music trying to blast its noise over the water streaming down. I would have sang along to it, if I had any sort of voice.

Stuart's face came to me. The way I always remembered it. Earlier twenties, laughing and joking around. Not a care in the world. Always ready for a good time. Then, it morphed into another image of Stuart I'd seen over the years. The guy on New Year's Eve in 1999. Another time after that.

The Stuart from the woods.

What if Stuart wasn't the body on the tracks? What if the reason he was in the woods was because...

I stopped myself before I could think any further.

Still, no major breakthroughs. No bright ideas. No clue as to how I was going to find Michelle.

Just, nothing.

Instead, I tried to think of reasons not to call the police and tell them everything straightaway. Tell them what I knew, who it could have been, and hope they found Michelle alive.

The only reason not to was that I would be going against the rest of my so-called friends. We all needed to be in agreement.

That was the pact.

I was drying off when I heard the doorbell ring downstairs. I tried to look out of the window, but couldn't see who was at the door. I swore quietly to myself and pulled a T-shirt over my top half and pulled jogging bottoms on.

The doorbell rang a couple more times and a bang on the door made me shout from the stairs as I came down.

Whoever it was knocked once more before I managed to get the door open.

"Nicola," I said, hearing the surprise in my voice and then tried to stamp it down. "Are you okay?"

She didn't say anything, pushing past me and into the house. I followed her inside, taking the towel I still had around my neck away and leaving it on a radiator in the hall. I found her in the kitchen, leaning on a counter and biting one of her fingernails.

"You've heard?" I said, stopping at the doorway. She was the only one in the group who hadn't changed all that much in the years since we'd grown up together. Whenever she was angry about something, it seemed to change the atmosphere around anyone in the vicinity. It used to set me on edge—especially when I was the subject of her impatience. Eventually, it became a running joke between us. Not that I spent any time trying to rile her. I reached over and flicked the kettle on. "Cup of tea?"

"No, I don't want a bloody cup of tea."

I left it boiling but switched on the coffee maker instead. "Michelle."

"What happened to her?"

"I don't know," I said, facing her and folding my arms across my chest. "But I intend to find out."

"Yeah, good luck with that. She's probably shacked up with some bloke she's met on Tinder and forgot all about the bullshit that's going on. A quick lay to get over her dead ex."

"Hang on, that's not fair," I began, but Nicola waved me off with a dismissive wave of her hand. I saw her breathing harder, seemingly trying to keep a lid on her anger and about to fail. "What's going on? Why are you here if not because you're worried about Michelle?"

"I don't know. You tell me."

"You're gonna have to give me a bit more to go on than that."

Nicola pushed away from the counter and walked toward me. "Is this all a game for you? Is that what it is? A way of making us do something stupid and confessing to something we didn't even really do?"

Whatever I'd been expecting her to say, this definitely wasn't in the ballpark. "I don't understand…"

"Just because you can't get on with your life, doesn't mean we all have to live in the past. You might have convinced Michelle that someone had broken into her house, but it won't work with me."

It took a second, but it came to me then.

It won't work with me...

My heart started beating harder now. "What's happened, Nicola?"

There must have been something in my expression because she hesitated for a moment, before going on the attack again. "You know damn well what's going on. I don't know what your game is or what you hope to achieve, but I'm not going to crack on this. We're not telling anyone about that man dying or about Mark bloody Welsh and his whining mother on every TV show going. It's that simple. I'm not giving everything up just because you can't handle the guilt. It wasn't just you there that night; we were all there. It's our decision, not yours, and I won't be bullied into doing something because of you. No matter what you leave in my house."

I cocked my head at that, allowing the final puzzle piece to click and turn my blood cold. "What was left in your house?"

"You know damn well—"

"Nicola," I said, my voice echoing around the kitchen as I shouted and stopped her in her tracks.

Her mouth closed instantly.

"I haven't been to your house in a while. I didn't leave anything there, and I definitely don't have the first clue why you think I would do something like that. You know me better than that, surely?"

Nicola peered at me, her eyes softening as the anger seemed to subside a little. It wasn't gone for long. They became mixed with fear, but shone somehow brighter. "Are you telling me..."

"It was a candle, wasn't it?"

She seemed frozen in place, rage barely confined. Staring at me and not blinking.

"Oh my god," I said, moving away and facing the doorway. I

shivered, realized I was barefoot in the kitchen, the tiles burning cold underneath my feet. I turned back to her and she hadn't moved. "When did this happen? Does Chris know? He was only here an hour or so ago."

"He doesn't know," Nicola replied, her voice quiet but with an edge I didn't like. "I found it after he left early this morning. It was just like the one we saw in those woods—in a storm lantern. It was left on the back step. I wouldn't have even found it this morning if I hadn't needed to empty the recycling. Chris is going to freak out when I tell him about this. I didn't even know he was coming here. We...we had a disagreement last night. He wants to go to the police as well. Obviously you were persuasive when you saw him yesterday. I am very much in the not-telling-a-single-soul camp."

"I know. It doesn't matter now. Michelle is gone. Stuart was first. Now he's after you or Chris, and I'm not going to let that happen. We need to come up with a plan. We need to find her before it's too late."

"If he's got her already, then it is too late," Nicola said, and her voice was firm. Decided. "We both know that. I'm not going to the police, Matt. That's off the table as an option. If I have to stop this guy myself, I will. He's not going to ruin my life."

"There's not many ways out of this," I replied, pulling out a chair from the dining table and sitting down. I turned to face Nicola. "We need to think this through carefully. All of us. If something has happened to Michelle as well, then...I don't know."

"We can beat whoever this is," Nicola said, moving across the kitchen and leaning on the chair opposite mine. "I've got no doubt about that. We just have to come up with a way of finding out who it is. That's the first step. If we fail along the way, we always have that backup idea of getting help, but that's all it will be. We'll be asking for help, because we can't see a way out of the problem."

"I can do this," I said, hoping she believed me more than I believed myself. "If I can't, then we have to go to the police and tell them everything. We're in too much danger not to. Does that sound okay?"

Nicola didn't answer, looking at the ceiling and sighing audibly. She dropped her gaze and looked me in the eye.

"Find him. Find Michelle. Then we can talk about what the next steps will be."

I nodded in response, didn't ask what the next step would entail.

I didn't need to. I knew what she meant.

THIRTY-TWO

N icola left me, and I tried to eat something before abandoning the endeavor when it became clear I was feeling too nauseated. There was a battle going on inside my head—one side wanting me to ignore what was happening and go back to work, the other wanting something else entirely.

I got dressed when it became clear that the latter side was always going to win.

I'd already left her alone once. I couldn't do it again.

My phone was still blank with notifications, no word from Alexandra or returned call from Michelle. I tried calling her again but got the answering machine before it even rang for the umpteenth time that morning.

There were ways of finding the whereabouts of where a phone was last switched on, but I didn't have the resources for that. I imagined once the police took Michelle's mum's worries seriously, that would be checked out first. Or they might find her body in the meantime. It hadn't been too long before Stuart had been found.

It was thinking about Stuart that led me to pause. If this was connected to the Candle Man, someone who had killed for years without discovery, it didn't really make sense that he allowed Stuart's body to be found. All of the Candle Man's victims were never discovered. That was why his identity was so easily dismissed and argued for in equal measure.

That would mean this new killer was someone who saw no reason to abide by the original's rules.

The computer was on before I was sitting at my desk, and I went back to research, looking at the same message boards and online threads. I was looking for something I couldn't explain to anyone who could walk into the room at that point, but I knew it was there. I just had to find it.

An email from Peter stared at me from the new inbox I had created the night before. I tried reading the various posts on the web instead of reading Peter's email, but when I'd read the same sentence three times, I knew I had to read whatever Peter had written. I could no longer ignore it.

I had to accept that I suspected Peter was connected to all of this. Putting a face to that—spending time in his company—made the whole thing more real for some reason. I wasn't happy with that.

I clicked on the email and read.

Dave,

Good to meet up with you last night. Hope I gave you some good stuff for your article. I'll keep trying to find out more for you—would be good if I could be known for identifying the Candle Man! That would be some newspaper piece you'd have on your hands. You didn't mention what publication it was for...I've had a look online and can't really find your name as a byline on any stuff. May have got it down wrong though. You know how it is.

All the best and see you soon!

Peter

I wanted to delete the message instantly but managed to control my urge. I wondered if the Google search on the fake name I'd given him had really been done after we had met. Or whether he had known throughout the meeting that I was lying.

Of course, if he was connected to what was happening to our group now, he would have known I was lying all along.

For what reason? Why would he meet you?

The only answer I could think of was he was trying to find out how much I knew. I decided to start making notes, hoping that would help clear the fog that was forming in my head the longer I sat there. When I was finished, there wasn't much that made any sense at all.

The places Peter had mentioned stood out: Bowland forest, which was north, Shropshire, Brock Hope, and the Cotswolds, all south.

Brock Hope was the obvious place.

The music festival we had visited the year before had been where this all began for us. I looked on Google Maps after I spent a minute or so trying to remember the journey down there. All that came to mind was singing songs from our childhood and laughing.

Probably the last time I'd properly laughed was that weekend. It wasn't until the thought struck me that I realized how I had taken that for granted in life. Now, everything was just a little more gray.

I searched for Brock Hope and missing people. Every item was regarding the lad who had vanished from the music festival. Mark Welsh. Eighteen years old, only two weeks before his nineteenth birthday. I punished myself looking and reading through the old articles, learning nothing about the lad that I didn't already know. I remembered doing this same thing a year earlier and the way it made me feel then. If anything, it had only become worse since.

The picture of his mum, holding his photograph probably sitting on the sofa of her living room. I pictured her now—sitting in a quiet house, waiting for the phone to ring or a knock on the door. Knowing that it had been too long and that even though she could never be totally sure, there was no real chance of him being alive.

I ignored the stab of guilt.

The knowledge.

I tried to find other missing people in the area, but didn't get much joy. I imagined Alexandra had the same problem when she was looking into this aspect of it. The Mark Welsh story had overtaken anything else in the area—the salacious rumors about drug taking, the fact that he was incredibly photogenic, the story of his wholesome family background and plans for university.

He shouldn't have been in those woods that night.

There was a thought, sudden and stark in my head.

If he hadn't been there, I wouldn't be in this position now.
It's his fault.

That did not make me feel good. I shook it off, attempting to ignore the fact that I'd really just thought that about someone who had been an innocent victim. It wasn't his fault that he'd crossed paths with a serial killer. It wasn't his fault that we had disturbed the murderer and not even in time to save him.

I wondered about Stuart meeting the man I'd met from the internet forum. What the reason for that could be. Same as mine, maybe? As simple as that?

Did he want to know how much information was out there? *Real* information.

I shook the thought away.

The cursor key in the search box blinked at me accusingly, and I began to type.

Faking your own death

Far too many search results.

Identifying a body when found on train tracks

Not many results that didn't concern actual cases on that one. Someone identified by a fingerprint. Most just reporting that the body had been identified or next of kin had been informed. I kept on until I remembered the tattoo of Stuart's.

That's how Stephanie said he'd been identified.

How easy is it to tattoo

I was going crazy. Stuart was dead. *Occam's razor*, I thought. I was looking for something that was never going to show itself.

I was in the denial stage of grief. That was all.

Missing Dead Brock Hope

I went through pages of Google search results. I narrowed the terms and tried to shorten the dates. Then, I found something.

Months after Mark Welsh had dominated the news in that area, it was there.

The story was brief in detail, and I couldn't find any follow-up to it. Simply a local newspaper story that didn't even seem to be a lead news item. A single mention and then it was gone.

Not even the Reddit forums had this case listed, it seemed. It just wasn't a story that had generated all that much interest, I guessed. Not after reading the story anyway.

LOCAL FARMER SEARCH CALLED OFF

Wednesday 16th May 2019

The search for missing local farmer William Moore has been suspended with no further evidence found.

Moore, 62, has been missing for an undetermined amount of time. He was last seen a number of months ago, and due to his secluded nature, it has proven difficult for police to ascertain when he may have disappeared.

Moore was a keen fisherman, according to a police spokesperson, and his disappearance may be linked to another discovery some months back of fishing gear near a particularly dangerous spot on the River Severn.

His son, George, owned the farmhouse where they both lived until recently. However, he has been unable to help police with their inquiry. Sources believe William got into difficulty at the coastline, and they believe this may be the best explanation at the present time. The small farmhold was only a few miles' walk from the popular fishing destination, and searches along the route have proven unfruitful.

It was just as I'd been thinking, somehow. A local farmer, who didn't seem to have any ties to other people. No quotes from family members or friends. I imagined a loner, who lived with his son.

George.

I tried to make an estimate of the ages. If he'd had his son when he was young, it was possible that the man who called himself Peter was him. Something didn't seem right about that though. Peter's accent had sounded genuinely northern. I imagined those who talked from that area would sound a little Bristolian. Or west country. I wasn't sure.

There was a good chance Peter had been faking it, of course.

A further search got no other hits for the farmer, who now seemed my best lead. If I could call it that.

I messaged Chris.

I think I've found CM. I have a name. He had a son. Call me.

Then, I opened my dummy email account in the name of Dave Richards—the supposed journalist's name I'd created—and emailed Peter.

Or whatever his name was.

I leaned back in my chair and folded my arms when I was done. Closed my eyes and nodded my head in time to the music coming softly from the speakers on my desk and worked out what to do next.

Michelle could be there now. Back in Brock Hope.

I was about to stand up when my phone began sharply ringing. I picked it up, expecting to see Chris's name, but instead, it was Alexandra's.

THIRTY-THREE

Alexandra sounded fed up, tired, and angry. Or none of those things and my read on her wasn't as good as it had once been.

It had been a long time since we'd spoken two days running.

"So we have a name for him. I'm not sure what we do now."

"Neither do I," I replied, stifling a yawn and reaching for the coffee on my desk. The glass it had been sitting in was stone cold, so I paused before tipping it down my throat in one large gulp. I almost gagged on it, but the action was enough to give me a jolt. "It has to help us though, right? At least we know what we're dealing with now. It's a way of finding Michelle."

"You think it's the son who has been leaving candles in Stuart's and Michelle's houses and the reason we can't get ahold of her now?"

"Doesn't it seem the most likely option?"

"I don't know. Maybe the most likely reason is that Michelle is finally getting some sleep—which you should too, by the way—and there are no candles being left for us to find. That's probably wishful thinking though."

I bit on my lower lip to stop myself from telling her about Nicola's visit that morning. She'd asked me to wait until she'd told Chris, which I was happy to do for as long as it made sense. It was something that I wouldn't be able to keep to myself for long—not with Michelle now missing and my fears seemingly realized.

"Alexandra, you can't ignore this," I said once I'd calmed myself. "There's just too much going on that doesn't make sense otherwise. Look at everything. Stuart looking into and meeting the same weird guy I did, then being found dead a week or so later. The one-year anniversary that only we in this group know about, suddenly Stuart is dead and Michelle is missing. Both of them have red candles in their houses, in the same type of metal storm lantern that we found in the woods. It's some coincidence."

"I understand," Alexandra replied, but it didn't feel like she was ready to change her mind as quickly as Chris had. "I'm just saying there's no reason for us to go half-cocked into something we don't fully understand yet."

"We're all going to meet up," I said, still refusing to be drawn into an argument neither of us was going to win. And making a decision not to tell her what I'd decided to do next. "Later on, if that's okay with you?"

"It's not like I have much else going on right now. Other than trying to work while my so-called friends try to convince me a mad serial killer has come back from the dead to get his revenge."

I turned that over in my mind. I'd never believed in ghosts or vengeful Freddy Krueger types, but it would explain certain things.

Maybe I *was* going mad.

No. It wasn't mad. What *was* mad was thinking Stuart had faked his own death.

"I'll let you know what time," I said, ignoring the weird part of my thoughts that were suddenly conjuring up villains from horror films. "Probably be here, but I'll let you know."

"Fine."

I ended the call, placing my phone back on my desk and looking at the screen again. Somehow, the man we had killed suddenly having a name didn't make any of it easier. I wasn't sure why it might have, but I was looking for anything at that point.

I looked at the time. Just past ten thirty.

Turned over the decision I had made in my mind and looked at its pros and cons. I knew it wasn't a good choice, but I wasn't going to sit around and do nothing, while I waited for the rest of them to wake up and realize we couldn't sort this out on our own.

Maybe they just needed a push in the right direction.

Maybe I was just tired and not in the best frame of mind to make any sort of logical decision.

I opened up the Maps app on my phone and tapped "Brock Hope" into the search bar. Pulled on my jacket and left the house after standing at the doorway for twenty minutes.

I was getting quicker.

It was a three-hour drive according to the expected drive time on the Maps app, but once I was on the quiet country roads in Wales, it didn't take that long. I arrived just before two o'clock, stopping off in the last village I saw to pick up a coffee—downed as soon as it wouldn't scald my mouth—and a sandwich, which remained unopened on the passenger seat.

The place seemed to be both familiar and strange. Each road seemed to look the same—narrow and bordered by overhanging trees that made it darker than it should have been at that time of day. The roads dipped and bent in odd ways, as they wound through countryside that hadn't been designed for this kind of travel.

My phone cut the music quieter for a second, telling me to turn right. I was glad it was still talking, as the music I was streaming kept cutting off as the cell signal dipped in and out. It was still working well in the villages, but once out on some of the country roads, it was intermittent.

It seemed like a bad omen.

The farm hadn't been named in the news report I'd read, but I'd decided on the nearest one I could find to the approximate area where the music festival had been held. I could see the GPS counting down the minutes until arrival, while a voice inside my head tried to bring me back to reality.

What are you doing? Turn around, go back, and find a different idea. This is stupid.

I continued to do what I'd done for the previous three hours. Ignore it.

The countryside was like another world to me. I'd lived my whole life in a city, and even though we had hidden woodland areas, I'd tended to only see housing estates and the waterfront. This was a world of different rules and ways of doing things, I'd always thought. The kind of place where, if you hadn't grown up there, you'd always be treated like an outsider. From the windshield, I watched as the road almost seemed to disappear into a lake of greens and browns. Golden squares of pasture, held together by thickets of hedges that kept the modern from the old.

To anyone else, it was probably considered scenic, beautiful, picturesque, but to me, it was just grass and mud and space that wasn't being used in the right way.

I was often wrong about that type of thing.

The road became narrower again, as my GPS informed me we were approaching the destination. I couldn't see any change outside, but as the yards clicked by, I could finally see a sign.

Mentmore Farm.

It was as good a place to start as any, I thought. I hadn't considered if this was the place—whether a serial killer had raised a child there—but it hit me again.

What the hell was I doing?

I pulled the car to a stop and checked the front of the farm. A sign offering fresh eggs and potatoes was attached to the fence that ran along the outer wall. The farmhouse itself was only a short walk from the road, so I moved over as far as I could and then got out of the car. Pocketed my phone and looked at the place.

It wasn't the home of William Moore. That much I could ascertain pretty much instantly. There was a more familial feel to it as I approached the entrance. Then, I stopped myself and wondered what the hell I was thinking. I didn't know anything about the man. I didn't know if his farm was that man's or not. It was my own mind creating the idea that he would have lived in some sort of dark, foreboding place.

A mind that was cracking with each passing moment.

I was about to turn around and leave when a shout made me stop dead.

"Hey, are you looking for someone?"

From behind another wall, a face popped into view. It was a woman in her fifties, short, graying, dark hair and green coat that looked like it had been new when I was a child. As she got closer, I could see she was holding a basket of something.

"I was just looking for eggs," I said, smiling and hoping I looked somewhat normal. "I saw the sign and thought I'd pull over."

"No problem at all," the woman replied, still looking me over and sizing me up. "You're not from around here."

It wasn't a question, and I guessed even if my accent was

local, she would have said the same thing. "No, just down here looking up some old friends. Thought it would be nice to pick up some local produce on the way."

The woman frowned a little, and I didn't think she believed me in the slightest. Still, business from people passing by at that time of year must have been slow, as she seemed to shake it off quickly and beckon me toward an area to the side of the main building.

"A dozen or half? We also have potatoes, tomatoes, plenty of other things. My husband is out in the fields now, collecting more produce, but there's still a lot of choice here."

By the time we were done, I had twenty quid's worth of stuff I didn't need and no cash for a coffee on the journey home. I waited until she was bagging things up for me before I tried to make the whole trip more fruitful than it had been up to that point. "I've been around Brock Hope a few times. It's a massive place though, so I'm not sure where I've been before and that."

"Oh really?" the woman replied, who was more interested in getting a few spuds in a bag, now the transaction was complete. Her hands were lined and red, calloused from hard work. The air was fresh, but bitter along with it. A hint of saltiness behind every gust.

"Yeah, we would come down when we were kids," I continued, trying to keep the lies general enough to not be questioned. "Some friends of ours relocated out over by the coast, but I like driving through this part of the countryside."

"Well, it's a nice place to look at," she said, handing a bag over to me and walking back toward the road. "The scenery can be breathtaking in the winter."

"I'm sure it is," I replied, allowing myself to be led out and away from the farm now. I stopped as we got to the gravel path that led back to the road. "There used to be this other place nearby. Over by where they do the festival camping and that?"

Her face darkened somewhat and I knew that I wouldn't want to cross her at any point. Her shoulders had tensed and she suddenly looked a few inches taller and broader.

"Oh, that thing. Such a shame what that brought to the area. A lot of damage was done to the surrounding land holding that thing. Thankfully, I don't think it'll be happening again. Not after that poor boy went missing."

"Didn't another guy go missing during that same time? I seem to remember seeing the name and thinking it was the farm I'd visited on another trip down here."

She frowned at me, and I could see I was starting to raise suspicions. I kept my face as straight and open as I possibly could.

"I think you're talking about the Moore family," she said eventually, thrusting her hands in her pockets and looking out past me and toward the forestland. "They were a couple of miles through the tree line. Not there anymore of course, after what happened to the father. Terrible business."

"Was he ever found?"

She shook her head, but there didn't seem to be any sadness there. "Lot of rumors, but nothing official. You ask me, he was probably into other stuff besides farming. We never saw him doing any actual work on the land. He only had a hundred or so acres, but no livestock or anything like that. It was always very quiet over there, and we never saw them in the village or anything like that. They didn't mix in with the other locals. It was just him and his son."

"No other family?"

"Not that we ever saw. The story was that his wife died while giving birth to the boy, but we weren't exactly on speaking terms. He never mixed with the people in the area. Kept themselves to themselves. When he went missing, we tried to help out, but the son didn't seem to want anything. All a very strange business, but people were more interested in that boy from the music thing, so he got forgotten about. It can be hard out here. You make a wrong step, and you can be lost for years. The son, he sold up about six months ago and Jim Treador—he owns the place that bordered on his land—bought it up. Now, at least the land will be used properly."

"He has plans to use it then?"

"Oh, yeah, course. He'll be knocking down the old farmhouse that's there now, I imagine. It's not in a good state, by all accounts."

"Ah, right. That's a shame. So, you never spoke to the son after his father disappeared?"

From the look on the woman's face, I'd outstayed my welcome now. One question too many.

"Who are you exactly?" she said, regarding me anew. Her gaze hardened a little. "You're not just passing by, are you? Are you one of those journalists looking for another story about the young boy who disappeared? Trying to link it to us 'simple country folk' like condescending fools?"

"No, nothing like that," I stammered out in response. I began walking away. "Thanks for all this. I'm sure my friends will be very happy with it all."

"Yeah, I'm sure they will," she replied, but there was nothing but sarcasm in her tone now. "Just be sure to watch yourself out there. Not everyone out here is as accommodating as I am."

I waved out of politeness as I reached the car, but she was still standing in the same spot, unmoved, as I switched on the engine.

THIRTY-FOUR

There was no choice. Even if the son had sold the place, it was a possibility. And I couldn't leave without making sure.

Michelle was out there, somewhere. And this seemed like a good enough place to start.

I'm not thinking straight.

I kept moving anyway.

Back in the car, I drove out of sight of the increasingly suspicious farmer. Pulled over to the side of a country road and took my phone out of my pocket. Found Mentmore Farm, where I'd just left, and searched on the Maps app for the farm she'd indicated with a sweep of her hand.

A mile or so behind that farm, there was another place. No street view available, but I could see the overhead image. It didn't look in the best state even from that.

I worked out the best route and programmed the GPS to take me as close to it as possible. Managed to get less than a minute's walk away, down a side road with no name. It contracted as I drove slower and slower down it, until I came to a place that was impassable. The GPS told me I was only a couple of hundred yards away from the marker I'd placed on the map, so even though I couldn't see the farmhouse, I got out of the car and walked the rest of the way.

It was the middle of the day, but the thick tree line covered the sky above me. The path was thick with overgrown foliage and broken branches crunching under my feet as I approached the marker.

A bird chattered unseen to my left, then fell silent. I could hear a breeze lifting leaves from the ground and the sound of my own breathing as it increased in frequency. Nothing else.

I pushed aside a low-hanging branch and saw the farmhouse for the first time. To say it was rundown would be being kind. The outside brick had been white at some point, but with the ivy crawling over it and the weather damage to it, it was now a dirty mix of green and brown. The roof was falling in on one side of it, exposing rotten wood and slate. Attached to the house was a metal lean-to that was being held up by its own will alone it seemed. The rust was a shade of orange-brown I'd not seen before. It rattled a little in the wind.

I was standing there, taking it all in, working out how best to proceed. Whether I should shout Michelle's name and hope for an answer. Or creep closer and find a way inside.

Or run back to my car and get the hell out of there.

On the outside of the farmhouse, I could see the faint outline of a cross. No Jesus figure on it, which was a blessing, I guessed.

I started moving. The ground underfoot was damp, but not overly muddy. I was wearing sneakers that had been white a few years earlier, but were now a dull, almost egg-shell color from overuse. A darker tone would now be added to them.

I checked the metal structure first, glancing inside and seeing a broken-down piece of machinery on the ground. There didn't appear to be my thirty-six-year-old friend lying in there, so I kept going. Walking around, closer to the house.

There was a hole the size of a fist in the first window I came to. I could see cobwebs and dirt and grime covering the inside. I cupped my hands around my face as I looked through, seeing an almost-empty room on the other side. I could smell damp and decay emanating from within. A broken table and a single chair with three legs, propped up against a brick wall.

I moved to the next window and saw much the same. And the next. Whoever had lived there had either lived incredibly sparsely, or the furniture had been removed in a hurry. Every look inside made me more nervous, as if I was going to see something I didn't want to behind each pane of glass.

I didn't want to be there. I wanted to be home.

I swallowed back my fear and moved back to the front door. It was solid and immovable, but I tried the handle anyway. It was stuck tight. Locked. I knocked and the rap echoed around the woodland surrounding me.

No answer. Of course. All I had done was announce my presence if someone was there.

My hands were shaking as I lifted them to try again, and I lowered them now without repeating the effort.

There was only the rear of the property to check now. I walked slowly to the side of it and found the missing furniture from inside. A threadbare sofa, a black stove that would have probably failed health and safety checks of any kind lying on top of it. Two stained mattresses propped up against the side wall of the house, bending in the middle, ready to fall at any moment.

I picked my way through the detritus outside, checking for empty ground with each footstep. I could smell rotting meat and came across a fridge with its door open once I'd gotten past the broken sofa. I glanced inside it and saw yellowed shelves and food packaging I wouldn't want to check the sell-by date on. I lifted the sleeve of my jacket to my mouth and tried to breathe through that instead as I passed it.

I was fourteen years old again. Picking my way through a scrapyard. Scared and wanting to go home. Back to safety.

I had to keep going. Not for me. For her. For all of us.

In the trees to my left—away from the house and back toward the woods—I heard a noise. A sound like footsteps on dead leaves.

I froze in place, midstride, my head cocked to one side. I listened intently for any other sound to follow. Closed my mouth and heard my breathing heavy through my nose. I stood there for at least five minutes, waiting for someone to emerge from the trees and rush me without warning.

I could feel eyes on me. Someone watching. I wasn't sure how I could sense that, but my mind was gone now.

After what felt like an eternity, I started moving again. Made it around the corner to the back of the property. Waited for someone to hit me from behind, but it never came.

I soon forgot about the noise when I looked over the back of the house to what had been a patch of grass in the past but was now blackened by fire. A circular area of burned ground. A firepit, of some sort, I thought. That wasn't what I concentrated on.

On the back step. Sitting on a gray concrete block that served as the way to step up and into the house from the back door.

A metal storm lantern.

I was walking toward it without thinking. Crouching down as I reached it. Trying to open its lid and failing.

I could see inside, although I knew without looking what I would find.

A melted red candle. Only the wax left. It had burned there for an indeterminate amount of time, until all that was left was a puddle of blood.

I looked up and could see a wooden roof that jutted out above the door, protecting the storm lantern.

I was at his house.

There was no doubt in my mind now. The Candle Man was William Moore. And we had killed him a year earlier.

I stood back up and looked across the small yard area and waited. Only, there was no one there. I was on my own. I looked down at my hands and saw they were shaking. I wanted to collapse onto the ground and pretend this wasn't happening. Close my eyes and wake up back in my house. Click my fingers and be anywhere else other than at this damn farm.

It wasn't going to happen. With what little courage remained, I forced myself to keep going. It was a blur now. I was acting on instinct.

I had come this far.

I had to finish.

I tried the back door. Putting my shoulder to it when I felt a little give. It opened with a clunk, and months of neglect escaped, hitting me in the face in a rush of air.

"Hello?" I said, hearing the fear in my own voice. I cleared my throat and tried again. "Michelle, are you here?"

I knew she wouldn't be. Logic told me this place had been abandoned. Sold off, a new place found.

Yet something told me logic had left this place a long time ago.

I moved inside, feeling floorboards underneath my feet groan at my weight. Newspaper was crumpled on the floor, sticking to my trainers as I continued moving. I imagined mice and rats scuttling beneath me and in the walls, but all I could hear was silence.

Silence.

I couldn't breathe.

Still, I kept going. Moving forward, going through rooms without knowing what I was trying to find. Knowing there was nothing there for me.

Everything was gone.

No trace of him left. No trace of Michelle.

It hit me at the bottom of the stairs. Wooden and rotting. Missing posts on the banisters. Cracked walls and peeling paint. Darkness and dust.

I wouldn't hear her sing again.

Ever.

I was too late. I was in the wrong place. I had no clue where she was and she was already gone.

And I could hear something in the darkness as it grew around me and the shadows took form and tried to claw at me.

It was the sound of my own voice. Saying the same words over and over.

"I'll kill you. I'll kill you. I'll kill you."

THIRTY-FIVE

I left the house. Left the trash piled up outside. Left the rickety metal lean-to, the building covered in overgrown ivy, the abandoned pathways and ill-maintained grounds.

Left the candle.

Left it all behind, with my body shaking uncontrollably and each step a risk of falling to the ground and screaming at the sky.

Managed to get into my car, sitting where I'd left it; untouched, it seemed, at first sight.. Pounded the steering wheel until my hands hurt and my head screamed with pain.

It took a good twenty minutes until I felt calm enough to drive.

On the drive back north, I got ahold of everyone on the phone. The bag of potatoes and tomatoes and eggs I'd purchased gave the car a sickly earthy smell, so that I had to crack a window to breathe through after an hour on the road. Then, I pulled over and threw the food over a hedge after I'd checked the coast was clear.

They were all prepared to meet, and when I finally arrived back at around five thirty, Chris and Nicola were waiting outside for me. We greeted each other awkwardly and I let them inside, the whole time trying to ignore questions about what was wrong with me. Telling them to wait until Alexandra arrived.

She arrived a few minutes later, walking into the house like it was death row. We were sitting in the living room, silence growing by the second, everyone refusing the offers of drinks or takeout even. My stomach rumbled in protest, but I wasn't sure I'd manage to get through more than a few mouthfuls. I could still feel that farmhouse on my skin and wanted to get in the shower and wash the stain of it away.

"I can't remember when we were all together like this," Chris said, breaking the tension finally. "Just the four of us."

"Stuart's funeral," Alexandra replied, sitting back on the sofa and crossing one leg over the other. "Although I suppose that doesn't count."

"The week before the festival," I said, sitting on the armchair opposite the sofa and leaning forward. I was itching to tell them where I had been, but another part of me wanted to try to get my thoughts in order first. "We had that meal to christen the stove. We'd only just moved in, and I couldn't get the oven to work properly, do you remember?"

We all smiled thinly at the memory, but just like everything else, it seemed tainted by what happened after now. That's how it would always be, I guessed.

"Did you tell Chris?" I asked, looking at Nicola and trying to gauge a response before she gave one.

"Yes, I did."

Chris's head was hanging down now and his shoulders hunched over. At first, I thought he was about to break down in tears, but when he looked up, there was something else in his eyes.

"We need to work out what we're going to do about this," Chris said, a hard edge to his voice that I hadn't heard in a long, long time. "This is it. Michelle has disappeared. And now…"

"What are you talking about?" Alexandra looked at Chris and then me. She finally settled on Nicola. "What is it?"

"I found a red candle this morning," Nicola said, her arms cradled around her body. "Same thing that Michelle had. And Stuart, apparently. It was in a storm lantern, so it could still be burning, even outside."

"Bloody hell," Alexandra replied, her voice quiet as she closed her eyes briefly. Her shoulders sank into her body a little. "Maybe you were right after all."

She looked at me as she spoke, but I couldn't maintain eye contact with her. I shifted uncomfortably on the chair and looked up toward the ceiling.

"Well, that's why we're here," Chris said, putting an arm around Nicola and pulling her closer to him. "I don't think we can just pretend that there isn't someone after us anymore."

"I agree," I replied, waiting for Alexandra to argue, but she stayed silent, which I took for agreement. "So, what do we do now?"

"Has anyone heard anything from Michelle?"

I shook my head at Chris and looked at Nicola and Alexandra who both slowly did the same thing. "I found his old house."

"Who's house?" Chris said, frowning at me. "What are you talking about?"

"The man from the woods. The Candle Man."

There was silence as they waited for me to continue. I swallowed and found the words. "There was a story online about a missing farmer in the area. Only a short thing, but it all tallied up. I've been down to Brock Hope today."

I told them what I had found and when I got to the discovery of the candle in a storm lantern, everyone in the room took a deep intake of breath.

"She wasn't there though," I said when I was done. "It didn't look like anyone had been there for a long time. Apparently, the son sold the place to another farmer. I don't know who the son is yet."

"So we know who he was," Chris said, then cleared his throat, as his words got caught in it. He shook his head, his face filled with tension. "Is it the son then?"

I shrugged my shoulders. "That seems the best guess."

"What do we do then?"

I turned to Nicola, who seemed to be taking it in better than anyone else in the room. "Try to track him down, I guess. I'm not sure where to start with that."

"In the meantime, Michelle is still missing," Alexandra said, picking at a thread on the arm of the sofa. "Have you spoken to her mum?"

"I called her just before I got back here. She's rang the police now. She waited twenty-four hours, the poor woman. She had a key for her house and went over to check if she was home or not. House was empty. Car's gone and her phone goes straight to voice mail."

"It could still be the case that she's decided to hide instead," Nicola said, but it didn't seem like she was believing in that any longer. "Maybe she was worried about putting her mum in danger or something?"

"I want that to be the case." I bit down on my lower lip in order to quell the rapidly forming lump in the back of my throat. I coughed and continued. "I think there wouldn't be another candle if that was the case. And they're coming more frequently."

"It's the year anniversary in two days," Alexandra said, and I could hear her struggle to keep her composure too. "Do you think he wants to deal with us all by then?"

"He's got some way to go," Chris replied, removing his arm from around Nicola and wiping a sleeve across his cheek. "There's still four of us left. He's taking his time."

"Maybe he's also going to get a little sloppy. You have to remember that we're not dealing with the original man here."

I nodded toward Alexandra and told them more about what I had learned, how sure I was now about what we were facing. "It's the son. The apple doesn't fall all that far."

"Some things I don't understand," Chris said, sitting forward and allowing his hands to hang in front of him. He ticked each item off on his fingers. "One, we are forced to defend ourselves against an attacker in the woods and we learn that the reason he was out there was because he had killed someone a few yards away, right? We all think it's this supposed serial killer because of the red candle thing. Only, we don't know for sure, because he's never been identified by police as actually existing. Secondly, we…erm…we move Mark Welsh's body and then that disappears. We spend a year pretending that we weren't all just waiting for a knock on the door because someone knows what we did. Then, Stuart is found dead. Now Michelle is missing. Both of them have these candles in their homes. Another one shows up this morning. And we're all just convinced that this man's son—who must have known his dad was a serial killer, by the way—has just been, what? Waiting for the one-year anniversary to deal with us all? Why wait until now? It doesn't make sense."

"Maybe it's taken him this long to find us?"

I shook my head. "I think it's more than that, Alexandra. The whole thing is ritualistic. The thirteen names I narrowed down as being the most likely victims of the Candle Man, they all have a certain thing in common. They all went missing between

October and January. You read about how important rituals are to some of these serial killers, I'm guessing that was passed down. You could be right though. It's not like we left a lot of clues behind about who we were. It could be that it's just taken him this long."

"Or Stuart sticking his head above the parapet has given the game away," Nicola said quietly, but with enough malice in her tone that we were sure of her feelings. "And put us all in danger."

"It doesn't put us any closer to figuring out a way to deal with any of this though," Alexandra replied, shifting her body on the sofa and groaning to herself. "What the hell do we do?"

"I think we know my stance on it," I said, getting to my feet and stretching my arms out to the sides. My muscles ached from the long journey. The tension I had felt as I'd looked around that farmhouse. It was taking an age to slip away, even as the feeling of being safe at home grew. "I believe there's only one sure way to stop this. Bringing it out in the open. Secrecy isn't helping any of us."

"I agree," Chris replied, avoiding Nicola's stare as he spoke. "I'm done with all of it now. I just want it over."

Nicola and Alexandra began speaking at the same time, as Nicola turned on Chris and began telling him what they had to lose and Alexandra backed her up. The crescendo of noise built, as everyone began to talk over each other, until we were all shouting to be heard. I stopped as Alexandra turned on me and began pleading for us to find another way out.

"I can't believe this is our lives," I said, then repeated myself again. The shouting stopped and they turned toward me, as I started laughing. "Listen to us. We're supposed to be normal people and instead we're having a serious discussion about how we avoid being killed off by someone who uses candles to choose his victims or whatever they mean."

Once I'd started, I couldn't stop, until I was hysterical. I could almost see myself, doubled over as I collapsed in the chair and put my head in my hands. I didn't calm down until I felt a hand on the back of my head. I looked up to see Alexandra shushing me as she stroked the back of my neck.

None of it was helping. I wasn't sure what it was meant to do anyway—a meeting of the four of us who were left. I was sure within a day or so, there would be fewer, as the hours counted down. We were all marked.

"We need to fight back," Nicola said, but didn't get much further as I stopped her with another bark of laughter.

"Fight back?" I said, shaking my head at the ridiculousness of it all. "We don't even have anyone we can fight back against."

"That's not true," Nicola replied, her jaw tensing as she spoke to me. "If it's the son, we have his name, and I'm sure we can find someone who could give us a description of him. Then there's the bloke you met online. What if it's him?"

I shook my head and thought of the usefulness of trying to find someone with the surname Moore. It wouldn't take long to show her how futile that would be, but I could already see that she knew that. I opened my mouth to say so, then changed my mind. "Let's just accept that we're in over our heads here. We have been since this all began. We made a bad choice back then, and we've made a series of them since. We're not going to fight our way out of this."

There was silence between us all then, as Alexandra rested her hand on my shoulder and stroked her thumb against it.

"We're never going to agree on the best course of action," Chris said finally, slapping his knees with a crack. "I think the only thing we can do now is to stay on guard for the next day. I'll go to Michelle's house and see if I can find anything. Maybe try to speak to her workmates or something? See if she spoke about going somewhere. In the meantime, me and Nicola should check into a hotel. We can both take time off work, right?"

Nicola nodded next to him, but I wasn't sure she was too happy about the idea. She was tense, I could see. A ball of anger and fear rolled into one.

"I'll do the same," Alexandra said, taking her hand away from my shoulder and standing up. "I'm sure they can handle things without me for a couple of days. I'm probably safe at home for now, but I want to be ready at a moment's notice."

I looked up at her, trying to work out exactly what she would be ready to go for, but decided to stay quiet.

We were delusional. All of us.

"That's settled the immediate response for now," Chris continued, getting to his feet as Nicola did the same. He tried to put a hand on her back, but she was already moving out of the room. "We can work out what we do next later."

I walked them to the door, aware of Alexandra standing behind me. If I tried hard enough, I could imagine for a few seconds that we were back to normal, showing our friends out of our house. Ready to carry on our lives in the way we'd always imagined.

Chris hugged me as he left, but Nicola was already out and near the car.

"I'll make sure she's okay about it," Chris said quietly in my ear. He grimaced toward me when we broke apart.

I nodded in response, then left the door open and turned toward Alexandra. "You could stay, if you like? Get something to eat or talk…"

"I don't think that's a good idea."

There was a pause, as I tried to find the right words. "You should stay here," I said eventually, deciding my need to make sure she was okay was enough to override any thoughts of awkwardness. "We both shouldn't be on our own right now. There's security in pairs, right?"

She didn't say anything, but I could see her weighing up the idea and trying to decide what was best.

"Honestly, I'm not suggesting anything else," I continued, moving closer to her now. "I just think we need to think practically here. We're in danger. If we could look out for each other…"

"Matt, I can't stay here," Alexandra said, stopping me in my tracks. "You know I can't. We'll be okay. There's a way out of this. We just have to work it out, just like any other problem. Everything has a solution."

I wanted so hard to believe her, but I couldn't make myself accept it. As I watched her leave, I came to the conclusion that had been on the periphery of my mind all week.

The only way this was going to end was with more death.

THIRTY-SIX

Once everyone had left, I put some music on and finally ate a proper meal. I ignored the protestations from my body and forced it down, knowing I wasn't going to last much longer if I didn't. The lack of sleep, of food, of normality was all coalescing to make everything around me seem a little blurred and distorted.

The partially completed map I had started since speaking to Alexandra one day earlier—was it really that short a time?—was on my desk. I liked order. Enjoyed it. My thoughts may have been running around in a dark room, crashing into unseen objects and fading away, but words and markers on a computer screen made things easier.

I knew there was something that would make everything come together for me. A part of the story I wasn't seeing. There was suspicion inside me that was gnawing away my insides, pleading to be noticed.

A significant portion of me was refusing to see and question what had been nagging me for over a week now. I let it wander and aired the thoughts for the first time.

The son.

The father.

That night in the woods.

Stuart.

There was a phone call I knew I had to make, but it needed to be done in the right way. I tried Michelle again first. Same result as it had been all day. Instantly to voice mail. I called her mother, but she only told me there was no word and rushed me off the phone. I imagined receiving a message in the coming hours or days, just like we had after Stuart's body had been found.

If I couldn't find her first.

And with every passing second of not telling the police, I was giving her less and less of a chance of being okay.

That brought me back to the phone call I needed to make. I breathed in deeply, scrolled through my phone, and found the number. She answered just before I expected another voice mail to kick in.

"Hello," Stephanie said, the grief still so present in her voice. Her brother may have been our friend for the best part of two decades, but he was her family.

"Hi, Stephanie," I replied, hearing the strain in my own voice. I cleared my throat and continued. "How are things with you and the family?"

"You know. Pretty much the same."

I thought for a moment, then remembered something I'd read in a book once. "I don't want to tell you the same platitudes you'll have heard nonstop for the past couple of weeks, but there is something I've been thinking about. Grief doesn't go away. It'll be with all of us, always—that's how it works. We'll never get over what happened to Stuart. We'll just learn to live with it somehow. How long that takes, I don't know, but it will happen. That's what he'll have wanted. He'd never want to be forgotten, but he'd want us to carry on."

There was silence on the phone, then I heard a sound that made me close my eyes and pray I could keep it together. A sob, choked off. The room had become darker, until all I could see was the glow from the screen and my own hand against my face.

"Thank you," Stephanie said, a few more seconds passing before she spoke again. "He knows anyway. He could never be forgotten."

"He was a good guy," I replied, then engaged in some small talk with her. Asking about the family, seeing how they were all dealing with the shock of Stuart's death. All the while trying to find a way to attain information I had no reason to ask about. Stephanie seemed to relax the longer we talked, which only served to make me feel worse about what I was starting to think about her brother.

"I just wish I could have seen him one last time," Stephanie said, a sniff cutting off the last word.

This was what I wanted to know. The dread of fear in the pit of my stomach. The thoughts I wanted to ignore.

I just wanted to know why Stuart had been in those woods that night. Why he had gone to see the man who called himself Peter, to learn more about a serial killer called the Candle Man.

I needed to know it was just an overactive mind and lack of sleep.

"Anytime I think about it...well, let's just say I can't," I said, choosing every word as carefully as I could. I was on the thinnest of thin ice. "I can't imagine what that was like for your family. I only know what I've read in the paper and that was enough."

"It was...it was something that no one should ever have to go through. I just don't know what he was thinking. We couldn't even see him properly one last time. There was just... We saw a photograph. That was it."

I gritted my teeth at the words. I wanted to feel pain. The idea that I was now complicit in making Stephanie feel these things again. To picture it.

I just had to know.

"His tattoo, that was it?" I said, trying to keep my voice calm and steady. "I just wish there was something more that would tell us what was going on in his head."

"I know," Stephanie replied, and her voice had changed a little. The image of her in my head changed a little in the darkness— the tears subsiding and her forehead creasing into a frown. "A photo of his tattoo and that's all we could see. There was talk of doing DNA or something, but apparently with his ID, that photo, other…things, that was enough. And not a single note to tell us why. No last text, or WhatsApp, or email. Nothing."

I thought about the tattoo. How easily that could be placed on someone else's body, if you were trying to pass off something destroyed as another.

What the hell are you thinking?

"I know, I guess I'm just trying to make sense of it all," I said, but I could feel the conversation slipping away from me. "I'd known him for almost twenty years. I guess that it's something we'll have to live with that we'll never know why he didn't reach out to any of us."

"I get it, believe me," Stephanie replied, her voice softening again. There was a low voice in the background that said something that was unintelligible. "Listen, I've got to go, but feel free to call anytime. It would be nice to keep in touch with his friends. As I've said, he spoke about you all a lot. He didn't really find his way in life until he found you and the rest at university. He was a bit lost as a teenager. Was always in a mood, didn't have any friends really. Yet, with you all, he seemed to find his way. You should take comfort from that."

I found I couldn't answer properly, so I managed to croak out an acceptance and then ended the call. Sat back in my chair and placed my hands over my face, trying to work out exactly what I was thinking.

It wasn't such a stretch to think that Stuart was just interested in finding out more about the man we had killed. The truth behind the "Candle Man" moniker. We had all gone our separate paths to an extent over the past year, so it made sense that he wouldn't have told us what he was doing.

It seemed like the finality of the way Stuart had died was starting to make me feel uneasy. The thought of being identified by a tattoo—something that could easily be faked.

Perhaps I was simply still in the denial phase of grief. Yet Stuart's body was identified by something that could be constructed if you needed to disappear.

I was grasping at straws, but was it so out of the realm of possibility that there was a chance they were both still alive?

There was really no hope of that, but with everything that had happened since the year before, I could almost make myself believe it.

The man from the online forum. Peter. Someone who had seen Stuart in his final days. That's who I needed to find.

It came to me five minutes later.

I opened up his last email and found the IP address that had been used to send it to me. Then, I opened a new browser on my computer—one I tried to avoid using if possible—and began searching for someone.

Illegal searches weren't something I did often. Never, I thought. The IP address narrowed down the search area, but once I saw the name, I knew I'd found him.

It took me longer than I'd wanted it to, but eventually

I managed to get the info I needed. I was taking a risk, but I thought the element of surprise might work in my favor.

The idea that anyone could be found if you looked hard enough sometimes scared me.

"Ribchester" was a place name that would have made me giggle in normal circumstances. That's what I had been known for in our group—a childish sense of humor. I would be the single person laughing at a terrible joke in any given situation.

It was a fifty-minute drive, and despite the driving I'd already done that day, I decided I had to do it now; otherwise, I may have talked myself out of it by the morning.

It was almost ten o'clock when I pulled up outside the semidetached house my GPS led me to.

An IP address from an email. Land registry records and some other information that was illegal to have access to. That's all it took.

It was farther north than Liverpool, on the edge of Preston. If I'd traveled any longer on the road, I'd have ended up in the forest the town bordered.

In a ten-mile radius of this town, four people had been reported missing.

I switched off the car engine, silenced the music blaring from my phone, and unplugged the USB charger from it. I didn't make a habit of going to strangers' houses at night—couldn't remember a time when I had done it, to be fair—and wasn't sure if I should have taken more precautions. I stopped outside my car, after I'd closed the door softly behind me, and looked at the house. At the street. At the surroundings.

It looked normal enough.

Still, that's how bad things happen: underestimating the threat of places that seem normal before turning into the opposite.

"You really need to get some sleep," I whispered to myself, as my thoughts began to make even less sense than normal. I swiped a hand through my hair and, at the last second, texted Chris with the address I was standing at, told him to save it for me. If anything happened, at least he could point them here.

I breathed quickly and deeply once, then opened the gate at the end of the path. The squeak it made on its hinges was loud enough to make me jump a little. I let it swing closed behind me and made my way up a well-kept flagstone path. There was running water coming from nearby, and I realized it was a fountain on the front lawn, surrounded by stones.

Not what I had been expecting at all.

I breathed again, then knocked softly on the door. It felt wrong to ring the doorbell at that time of night, as if I were intruding in his life somehow if I was wrong about him. There was no answer for a good few seconds, but as I raised my hand to knock again, I heard movement behind the door. The sound of keys being sorted and then entering the door before it opened up.

"Dave?" the man behind the door said, holding onto the door between us. He didn't look as shocked as I'd expected, but was perhaps hiding it well. "How did you…"

"I need to talk to you."

THIRTY-SEVEN

I thrust my hands in my pockets, so he couldn't see that they were shaking. I couldn't hide the sweat on my forehead or my pale pallor though. I just hoped he wouldn't notice. Then again, if he was who I suspected, he would probably be able to recognize it in an instant. Looking for any weakness to exploit. I was waiting for him to turn in an instant—to become the man I believed him to be. Still, there was a part of me that wanted him to. To show himself.

If he was the Candle Man's son, I wanted to see it.

I didn't think "Peter" was the man's real name, but I'm sure he knew my name wasn't "Dave" either. I decided to let him have the veneer of anonymity a little longer.

"Of course," Peter said, and opened the door further for me.

I moved inside, the heat from within the house hitting me in the face like a blast of steam. I hadn't realized how cold it was outside and quickly undid my jacket. I was unarmed, I realized. I had come there with nothing to protect myself.

I really wasn't cut out for this.

"Just through on the left," the man said, moving behind me. "It's only me in tonight—my wife is out at her club until eleven. I'll have to go pick her up then, so I'm afraid I haven't got much time."

"That's okay," I replied, wondering how long he'd let me stay for anyway. How long he'd pretend his wife was ever coming back. "It shouldn't take long."

He followed me, sitting down on a floral-patterned sofa that was out of sync with the rest of the more modern living room. I stood near the mantelpiece, casting a quick glance at the array of family photos littering not only the surface, but also the walls of the room.

"You're not his son."

Peter couldn't have looked more confused if he'd tried. "I'm sorry?"

"Nothing. Just something we were trying to ascertain for the, erm, story," I said, hesitating over my reply. I could see from my response that he no longer believed me anyway. "Who are you really?"

He peered at me for what seemed an eternity but was more like a few seconds. "I don't understand the question."

"You're all over everything I read about the Candle Man. Your username, or derivatives of it, seems to be on all things I can find online. Why are you so interested in him?"

Peter didn't respond, but instead got to his feet and crossed the room. He came toward me and I tensed up in response, but he reached past me and took a photograph from the mantelpiece.

A photograph of a teenage boy I'd seen in very different circumstances.

"This is my son," he said, showing me the picture and then turning it back around to look at it anew. "His name is Mark. He was nineteen years old the last time I saw him. He will have turned twenty a few months ago. August 12. A year I've had to sit here and wait for him to walk back through that door. We both know it's not going to happen, but it's as they say—it's the hope that kills you. How many people go missing every year?"

"Quarter of a million, like we talked about last time."

"He's one of the ones that didn't come back."

"What happened to him?" I said, but I knew the answer already. In every news item, every *This Morning* appearance, every social media post about Mark Welsh, there was one person missing other than Mark himself.

His father.

"You're Mark Welsh's father," I said, realizing I'd made a mistake. I remembered his name instantly. Geoff. "Why don't you say that on the forums?"

"I'd get bombarded with messages," Geoff replied, nervously fiddling with a frayed thread on the arm of the sofa. "I'd get accused of all kinds of things. It made sense to stay anonymous. Have you seen some of the things they say about me on there? I wouldn't get anywhere if people knew who I really was."

I had seen a few mentions about Mark's father, and none of them were kind. I remembered seeing his name mentioned in one news item. He had never met a journalist, it seemed, until I had come along and pretended to be one.

And Stuart, of course.

"You know about Mark, of course," Geoff said, placing the photograph back on the mantelpiece. He walked over to the sofa and sat down with a sigh. "His mum told them I hadn't seen him for more than ten years. None of the kids. Didn't even know where they lived."

"Is that true?"

"Yeah, sadly."

"So, she didn't want you involved in any of the media stuff."

"Not at all. I didn't have the right, apparently. I'd walked out when they were younger and didn't know them anymore. Even that photograph is one I've printed from the internet since.

All of them are. I tried talking to the police, but they took her side, so it didn't leave me with much else to do. When they made sure I had nothing to do with his disappearance, I was just a nuisance to them. They were useless anyway. I know what they think. That he's just buggered off with some girl or decided to go abroad to work. Like that's the case."

"When did you know?"

"That he had been taken by the Candle Man? It was a while later. I'm not sure. I spoke to my ex-wife briefly, and she told me something strange. Something that was found in his bedroom that had annoyed the police..."

"A red candle."

"Exactly. It didn't make sense at the time, because the rest of his room was an absolute mess, she said. Just computer games and clothes everywhere. It's the only time she told me anything about who he was now. Then, there's this nice red candle in a storm lantern, just sitting on his bedside table. I asked her if it was hers, but she'd never seen it before. Then, she rushed me off the phone and didn't talk to me again. Neither will the police now."

"When did you make the connection?"

"After a few months, I was desperate. I was online, looking at missing people in the area when I stumbled on this Candle Man story. I found a couple more who had gone missing within a few miles of here, then it just spiraled."

I turned away from him, scratching at my increasingly stubbled chin. Whatever I had been expecting, it wasn't this. "Did you go talk to the police about what you'd found?"

"Of course," Geoff said, scoffing and shaking his head. "They treated me like I had gone crazy. They didn't take it seriously at all. Of course, by this point, while the rest of them still had hope, mine had gone. My son is gone, Dave. He's been taken from me."

"So you've spent the past few months becoming an expert on the Candle Man."

"Yes. There's nothing I don't know about his movements, his actions. Everything. I've talked to other people who might have sons and daughters and brothers and sisters who are victims. Many, many people. Most of them, I'm pretty certain don't have a connection to him at all. Some...I know some of them do."

"How do you know?"

"The red candle—it's not just a typical thing. Not one of those glass Yankee Candle things, or tea lights, or cheap sorts. It's housed in a storm lantern that keeps it alight in any situation."

I knew then what the difference was for the others. The candles that were found in these victim's houses after the fact.

It was the last thing those killed would have seen.

"That's what makes the cases different," Geoff said, looking older and more frail than he had been back in the truck stop, when I'd first met him. "The candles. I've been narrowing it down, further and further each time. I've had some doors slammed in my face, some tough conversations, but I think there's some kind of pattern. Only, I've run into a brick wall recently."

"How so?"

"I've not found anything concrete for a while," he replied, spitting it out in frustration. "Not since Mark...not since Mark went missing. I felt like I was getting close to him, but with no new leads, I don't know. It's not like it's an official thing. Maybe Mark was the last one and that's it. Now we'll never find out who he was. I doubt that though. He'll be back. I just need him to make a mistake."

I tried to stay as stone-faced as possible, but I could feel the mask slipping. "I can't imagine what you've been through…"

He waved me off before I could finish the sentence. "Platitudes. I've had enough of them. What I need now is answers. And I think you're not telling me everything."

I moved to the smaller sofa against the other wall opposite the window and sat down. Placed my hands on my knees and leaned forward. "The man you met a few weeks ago. He was my friend."

"Was?"

"He died a few days later," I said, speaking slowly so as not to dissolve in front of this man. "We'd known each other since we were kids. His death was very unexpected."

"I'm sorry to hear that," Geoff replied, then rolled his eyes. "Now it's me with the platitudes. What happened to him?"

"He was hit by a train. They reckon it was a suicide, but…"

"You're not sure if it really was."

I shook my head. "He had a candle in his house. Red. In a storm lantern."

Geoff's eyes lit up as the information hit home. "You saw it?"

"Yes."

He slapped his knees, getting to his feet quickly and pacing up and down in front of the bay window. "He's back. This is huge. I mean…I know what price it's come at, but I don't think you're just here for your own health. You want to know what I know. But this is unbelievable. I've waited so long for this. Of course, I hoped it wouldn't happen, but now at least we're not in a cul-de-sac of noninformation anymore."

Geoff continued talking, his words spilling out at a rate I couldn't keep up with for the most part. It was the most energetic I'd seen him and a world away from the broken man he'd been a few minutes earlier. I looked at the clock on the wall and saw I'd been there for twenty minutes already.

"Wait," Geoff said suddenly, stopping and facing me again, as if he'd just noticed I was still sitting there. "You say his body was found?"

It took me a second to find my voice again. "Yes, it wasn't easily identified, but the family managed it."

Geoff frowned and then his shoulders sagged a little. "Maybe I'm mistaken then."

"What do you mean?"

"Well, the obvious—none of the other victims have ever been found. Why would he wait a year and then leave a body behind? It wouldn't make any sense."

No. It wouldn't. Because he's bloody dead and this is someone else.

I wanted to shout the thought in his face, but managed to control myself somehow. He could read my intentions, however, as his expression changed a little. Softened.

"Listen, I'm sorry if I'm being thoughtless," Geoff said, sighing as he did so. He looked at the ceiling, shaking his head. "I just get a little overexcited. You have to understand, I've spent a year in the dark waiting for something to happen. I'm sorry about what happened to your friend, but maybe he holds the key to all of this. The Candle Man's first mistake."

I didn't argue with him, but I couldn't agree. Instead, I waited for him to come to the conclusion himself.

"They never know before," he said quietly, dropping back onto the sofa, his large frame making the old furniture squeak in protest. "Why did he come and see me? Has he changed his methods? Has everything I learned become irrelevant?"

I didn't want to hurt him anymore, omitting the facts as I

knew them. I wanted nothing more than to tell him that he didn't need to keep searching for his son's killer anymore.

Only, I remembered the stories of the Moors Murderers. About the child who was never found. How his family could never move past their tragedy until he was.

For Geoff and his wife and the rest of the family, this nightmare would be forever.

"I'm sure that's not the case," I said, standing up and preparing to leave. I shouldn't have been there. I wasn't sure I should have been *anywhere* in my current state. Spots in my vision, a growing pain behind both my eyes that would eventually become too difficult to ignore. "I'm sorry to make you bring this all out again."

Geoff peered at me, his eyes turning a deeper shade of gray. He seemed to accept something that had been obvious to him. "You're not a journalist, are you?"

"I have to go."

"Tell me the truth," Geoff said, rising up, and he suddenly looked a foot taller than me.

I thought if it became physical, I could have defended myself, but in that moment, I wasn't sure. "I'll see myself out."

"I deserve to know what's going on here," Geoff said, and he was pleading now. He took hold of my arm and stopped me in my tracks. It wasn't a hard grip, but it was still enough to make me pause. He looked at me through watery eyes and said one word. "Please."

I couldn't. I wanted to. More than anything I've ever felt in my life before. I wanted to give him the closure that he desired, but I knew it wouldn't change a thing. All it would do was ruin all of our lives. My friends.

I needed them more than giving him closure.

I had never felt more selfish in my life.

"I knew my friend met with you," I said, hoping he would believe me. "I thought you might have been someone else. I can see you're not now. I wish I could help you, I really do, but we're looking for the same ghost."

"There must be something you can tell me."

I shook my head and pried myself away from his grip on my arm. He didn't look a foot taller than me anymore. He looked exactly like he was—a man ten or fifteen years older than me, who looked at least a decade more than that. Someone who had been beaten by grief and the worst of not knowing the truth.

And shame. And guilt. Guilt of not seeing his children as they grew older. Always thinking he'd have one more chance to connect with them. Then, Mark disappears, and that chance goes with him.

He would be in my nightmares, I thought. The look in his eyes. It would join the others.

"I think the reason it was different this time is because it's over," I said carefully, placing a hand on his shoulder briefly before moving away from him. "I just need to make sure, that's all. And I promise, you'll be the first to know if I learn anything."

I left the room, feeling his presence following me. I took hold of the door and looked back. He was standing in the shadow of the living room doorway, looking at the floor. He lifted his head and looked at me with a blankness in his eyes now.

"I knew from the start you weren't who you said you were," he said, leaning against the doorjamb and folding his arms around himself. "I knew you were carrying something like what I am. I hope you're right. I hope I don't have to think about that *thing* anymore."

I nodded and left, feeling my phone in my pocket vibrating a couple of times.

Outside, the temperature had dropped further, spots of rain falling as I jogged to the car. Even inside the vehicle, the cold seeped through and into my skin. It spread across my body like the numbing tide of an icy sea.

I willed myself to look back at the house, but I couldn't.

Instead, I pulled out my phone, switched on the music, tried to blink some life into my eyes, and turned the ignition.

It wasn't until I was a mile or more away that I glanced at my phone again. I saw a missed call and messages. I pulled over and took it from the cradle.

Missed calls from Chris.

A message from Chris. Not a voice mail.

Two words in a text message.

The world turns and spins on phone notifications.

Two words.

Nicola's gone.

THIRTY-EIGHT

I made it to Chris's house by eleven thirty. I was pretty sure I'd have some speeding fines landing on my doormat within a few days. If I made it long enough to receive them of course. I had gone my whole life without a single point on my license and was probably not going to be around to finally receive one.

Ironic? Not sure. I'd have to check with Alanis.

He opened the door before I even had the chance to knock, swinging it back on the hinges, the bang against the inside wall echoing around the street. I followed him, closing the door behind me carefully and finding Chris in the living room.

"What happened?" I said, stopping short of moving any closer to him.

He was a ball of energy, hands clenched into fists and banging against his thighs.

"Chris, tell me…"

"I'll tell you what's happened," Chris shouted, turning on me now, the distance between us closed in a split second. "This is your fault."

"What do you mean?"

"All of this crap," he said, his voice still bouncing off the walls around us. I tried to place a hand on his shoulder, but he shrugged it off like an annoyance.

"Calm down, mate. We can fix this."

He laughed at that. I didn't blame him.

"There's nothing to fix, mate," he spat at me, then paced away from me. Fists still flexing and finding a home on the mantelpiece. A vase crashed to the laminated floor, landing with enough force to smash it into pieces. Chris crunched through them with his shoes. "This is your fault."

"Tell me what's happened, Chris," I tried again, my own jaw clenching now. We had never fallen out, the two of us. Everything that happened couldn't be my fault. I couldn't take the blame for it all. "Where's Nicola?"

"She's gone. I don't know where."

"Gone how?"

"I haven't the first idea," Chris said, a sarcastic laugh preceding it. "We were all set to go to the damn hotel, and she has to go get something or other, I don't know. Next thing I know, I get a text from her."

His phone was on the coffee table, and he picked it up and threw it at me. I looked at the screen after swiping it to unlock it. No password or security. I had an urge to point that out to him, but it didn't feel like the right time. When the screen came alive, the message was there.

I've got to go away. We can't be together while this is going on. We're too much of a target. I will call you. Love you x

I looked up, and Chris was standing a foot away.

He snatched the phone from my hand and threw it across the room.

I moved quickly, placing my hands on his shoulders as he screamed in frustration.

"It's going to be okay…"

"Liar," he said, pulling away from me. He was breathing heavily, facing me with a look of violence in his eyes. He wanted to inflict damage on someone, and I was starting to wonder if it was going to be me.

"She's probably just gone to another hotel," I said, keeping my voice low and steady. "That's all it is. Maybe it's better that way. She can handle herself, Nicola. We both know that. We've seen it enough times over the years."

"I'm supposed to be by her side through everything. I don't care if she could kick all our heads in if she wanted to; I'm still supposed to be the one there with her."

"I know."

"You know? How could you? You and Alex split as soon as you possibly could. You have no idea what it is we have. You couldn't possibly comprehend what we share. We're a team. It's always been me and her. Now, we're arguing and she's disappeared. That hasn't happened in twenty-odd years, Matt. And it all starts with Stuart throwing himself in front of a train, just because he can't take a little bit of guilt."

"You were onboard with what we talked about earlier," I said, sensing I had lost an argument I hadn't even been part of. One he'd had with himself before my arrival. "You agreed with me."

"What the hell do I know? This isn't right. We've all panicked because of what we did last year. What if there was no one in those woods? What if someone is out there, but is just messing with our heads, so we do something stupid? What if, what if, what if?"

By the final repetition, Chris was in my face screaming, spittle flying from his mouth and hitting me on the cheek. I could feel his breath on my skin, and I placed my foot back, waiting for the punch to land.

It didn't come.

I would have let it.

He knew that as well. The thought seemed to land inside his head and began to crumple.

I'd never seen him cry in the twenty-five years we'd known each other. Not when his dad died a decade ago. Not on his wedding day, when I stood next to him at the altar as his best man. Not when he told me he and Nicola couldn't have children, after years of trying.

He did now.

Chris dropped to the sofa in a heap, and I moved quickly to fall with him. I grabbed him and held tight, as his cries of anguish filled the room.

We were sitting like that for a minute or so before he finally began to calm. I let him go and shuffled to the side to give him room. He breathed in and out deeply a few times, then seemed to gain control again.

"It's going to be okay," I said, putting my hand on his upper arm and squeezing once. "We can all get through this."

"How?"

"Well, if you're going to ask questions I can't answer, then I don't know how I'm supposed to get you through this without crying myself."

He chuckled a little at that and wiped his face with a sleeve. "It's always been me and her, you know? We came as a pair. I don't know how I'd have fared without her. She makes me a complete person."

I nodded in response, thinking of Alexandra and the way we had been until a year ago. She had always been independent, freethinking, and self-sufficient. I had been the same. Yet once we were together, that was it. We were entangled. Our separate lives had become a whole. Now, I felt like there was always something missing.

"Before all of this, we were okay," Chris said, his voice barely above a whisper. "Sure, we still carried some guilt, but we got through it. Since Stuart died, I've felt her slipping away. She's been colder. The other day, some guy cut us off at a roundabout, and I swear if she'd had a gun or whatever, that bloke would have been dead. She's always had a short temper, but I don't know...lately, she's been different."

"It's the stress of the situation—"

Chris shook his head in disagreement and spoke before I had a chance to finish the thought. "It's more than that. I'm worried about her state of mind. All of this, it's breaking us apart. Not just me and her, but the rest of us too. Those of us who are left, anyway."

"We can fix this. He's not going to beat us."

He seemed to nod in agreement, but I didn't feel confident that he believed me. I wasn't sure I believed me either. I looked around the room and felt my stomach fall a few floors. "Chris, where's the candle?"

He looked up as if he were seeing the room for the first time, then got to his feet quickly. He banged into the coffee table, leaving the room in a rush. I followed him as he went into the kitchen-dining room and began moving things around the room.

"Did you throw it out?" I asked, hearing the desperation in my voice. "When you got back or something?"

"No," Chris replied, now ransacking the room, pulling things from cupboards and then running out.

I could hear feet pounding on the stairs, so had a look around myself. I didn't find anything.

He returned quickly and jogged through the kitchen, tearing open the back door and going outside.

I could see him through the window, opening up each wheelie bin and checking through its contents. I closed my eyes and felt the sense of sadness wash over me.

"Maybe she took it with her," Chris said, coming back into the kitchen and looking at me with pleading eyes. He took one look at me and began to shake.

"Yeah, maybe," I replied, but even I could hear the doubt in my voice. I cleared my throat and tried again. "She probably wanted to make sure she had it, for evidence or whatever."

He looked at me again, then moved to the side and gripped hold of the kitchen counter. "No, she wouldn't have done that. She didn't even want to look at it. I've got to find her."

I was almost pushed off my feet as he moved past me, not even grabbing a jacket as he picked up his keys and pulled the front door open. I chased after him, finding him getting into his car.

"Wait," I shouted, wondering just how much his neighbors would be listening in now. If they hadn't already had a glass to the wall as he'd first screamed at me in the living room, then smashed up his dining room looking for the candle, they would be getting a front row seat now. "Chris, let me come with you."

He wasn't listening to me anymore, slamming the car door shut and turning the engine on. The car was moving up the road before I'd even had the chance to shut his front door behind me and get to my own vehicle.

By the time I was driving, he was long gone.

I slept that night.

I'm not sure what it was that made my body shut down without a problem, but maybe it had just had enough. Chris's phone would ring and ring as I tried to contact him. Alexandra was doing the same for Nicola's. We spoke a little after midnight, but she ended the call when she realized I was beginning to make little sense. Told me to go to bed and try again in the morning.

To lock up my doors and make sure I was safe. I told her the same.

I remembered turning on classical music on my phone—a ten-hour collection I found on YouTube—and not hearing more than a few minutes before the world turned black.

A dreamless sleep.

I was so out of it—so deeply asleep—that when the banging started, it seemed to only exist in a void of darkness. A black space with just a rhythmic sound. A song started playing. One I recognized. It stopped after a few seconds, letting the silence grow again, before starting up again.

Silence.

Banging.

I woke up confused and bewildered. I could hear knocks and banging, so I pulled myself out of bed in a daze. Still half-asleep.

A crash against wood made me jump, and I was suddenly alert again.

I pulled on lounge pants draped over the end of the bed and grabbed the baseball bat that had been lying under the duvet as I slept. Crept downstairs and realized the knocking was coming from the front door.

There was someone there.

It was still pitch-black outside. I rubbed my eyes and moved slowly to the door.

"Who's there?" I said, but it only came out as a whisper, fear cutting off my voice box. I coughed and cleared my throat before repeating myself. "Who's there?"

A muffled voice that was instantly familiar to me answered. I didn't hear what was said, but it made me cross the final few feet between me and the door in one long stride. I unlocked the door and swung it open.

The first thing I saw was Alexandra. She was red-faced and shaking in the cold.

The second thing I saw was what she was holding in her hands.

A red candle.

In a storm lantern.

Still lit. Still burning.

THIRTY-NINE

I managed to get Alexandra inside before she poured out what had happened right there on my doorstep. I checked there was no one following her, then locked up behind her and moved her into the living room. Sat her down on the sofa, as her shaking continued, and tried to take the candle from her hands.

"No, don't touch it," Alexandra said, gripping it tighter and holding it to her body.

I broke away and took a step back. "You're freezing. You need to warm up."

I did the good British thing and flicked the kettle on. Raced upstairs, chucked a T-shirt on, and grabbed my phone.

A few minutes later, Alexandra had finally let go of the candle and its metallic housing. She was sitting huddled over it, both of her hands wrapped around a cup of tea.

"He couldn't get into my house," she said, her voice so quiet I almost couldn't hear it.

I was kneeling on the floor near her, so I moved closer and placed a hand on her knee for comfort.

"I heard him trying to break in, I think," Alexandra continued, her shaking hands lifting the cup to her lips and seemingly risking a sip of the drink. She blew on it at the last moment instead. "I barricaded the doors before I went to bed and all my windows are well secured. You can't even get into the place with a key, once I'm inside. He settled for ringing the doorbell for a few minutes instead to get my attention."

"Did you see him?"

She shook her head in response. In the dim light from the lamp I'd switched on, she looked so different from a few hours earlier. Her eyes were flat and listless. Skin pale and taut with tension. I had to stop myself from embracing her and never letting go.

This was my fault.

"I didn't even open the door until half an hour had gone by. I didn't want to go out, but I had to be sure, you know? After all, I was the last one pretending this wasn't going on, wasn't I? Aren't you going to tell me I told you so?"

"I think that's below even me right now," I said, grimacing and smiling in equal measure. I rubbed my thumb against her kneecap and looked her in the eyes. "What happened after that?"

"I checked about four thousand times, but I think he was gone by the time I opened the door. It was still on the chain, but I could already see it anyway. Feel it, almost."

"Did you see anyone?"

She shook her head. "I couldn't stay in the house anymore. I got dressed, picked it up, and did the twenty-yard dash in about half a second to my car. Came here. I didn't know where else to go."

"You did the right thing," I said, but didn't believe it. It seemed everything was falling apart, and I included myself in that. There was a part of me that wasn't even really sure that this was real or if it was some lucid nightmare.

My whole life felt like that though.

"What do you think we should do?" Alexandra said, her

hands no longer shaking, her eyes becoming steelier by the second. "We have to work this out."

"I think any way we dress this up, we're still in the same boat."

"One without a paddle, a million pin-size holes, and on a river of shit?"

"That's the one," I replied, smiling without humor. "What we're dealing with here...I don't think there's an easy way out of it."

"What do we know?"

We sat there for twenty minutes, as misty light began to enter the room from outside, going over everything we knew. The facts as we understood them, what they meant and how they fit into the whole picture. It wasn't long before we came to the same inevitable conclusion.

It had to be the son.

It had to be revenge.

"Okay, but that doesn't help us figure out what we do next," Alexandra said, a hand going to her forehead and massaging it in thought. "Do you think the police would believe any of this? We have no more evidence than the rest of the online community, and the police have managed to ignore them successfully enough."

"We have a body."

She looked at me for a second, then shook her head. "All that would show them was that there was a dead guy. It's not like they would be able to figure out anything from that. If there were bodies out there of his victims, then maybe we have a shot in the long-term. For now though, we'd still have the same problem. I mean, unless you want to be arrested and denied bail?"

"Would that be a bad thing considering the alternative?"

"Yes, prison would be a bad thing," Alexandra said, rolling her eyes at me and leaning forward to put her empty cup on the coffee table. "You wouldn't last five seconds in there. Too clean-cut."

"Oh, and you would?"

"I'd do a damn sight better than you."

I let out a short bark of laughter, and Alexandra sniggered next to me. I sighed and leaned back into the sofa and turned my body to face her properly. "This is all my fault."

"No it isn't..."

"I killed him," I said, saying it out loud for the first time. In an instant, I could feel the rock in my hand as I brought it down on his head. "If I had controlled myself better, Stuart and Michelle would still be here. I dealt the final blow, as they say."

Alexandra sat forward on the sofa suddenly, perching on the edge and staring at me intently. "What are you talking about?"

"What happened," I replied, letting my head fall into my chest, unable to keep her gaze any longer. "We were all fighting with him, but he would have survived if I hadn't finished the job. Things would have worked out a lot better if I had been able to control myself."

"That's not what happened."

I looked up at her, my forehead creasing in confusion. "I think I remember what I did."

"Obviously not," Alexandra said, shaking her head and moving closer to me. She laid a hand on my knee. "You weren't the one who did that. I watched the whole thing. He was already gone by that point."

"Alexandra, it's not the time to try to make me feel better."

"I'm not," she said, becoming more vehement by the second. "He wasn't moving at all when that happened. It was one of the others who ended it. Not you."

I was back in those woods, seeing his eyes as I crashed a rock onto his head. The pleading look he gave me.

Then, the memory became distorted, blurred. I placed my hands over my face as the night came back into focus. It was like I was there again. The sounds and smells. The fear and panic.

The silence.

I didn't realize I was rocking back and forth until I felt Alexandra's hands on my shoulders. I leaned into her, shaking my head as the memories faded and became fractured.

I wasn't sure what was real or not anymore.

"Matt, what's going on?"

I pulled away from her, standing up and putting some distance between us. "I've spent the past year believing what happened that night was my fault. That's what I remember."

"But it's not true."

"Maybe you're not remembering it right," I said, feeling myself calm down now. That's all it was. She was mistaken. It was dark that night—everything was chaos and she wasn't sure of everything that happened. "There was a lot going on."

She shook her head sadly and glanced at the clock on the wall. "I remember it perfectly. I'm not trying to minimize any of our roles that night, and yes, if he were still alive, we'd all be in a much better position now. That doesn't mean you're to blame for it though. It's not your fault Stuart is gone. Or Michelle, if she is. Or Chris and Nicola or me."

"Why did you leave me then?"

It was a question I had never asked her—not even when she walked out the door. I had sat back and let it happen, the fight gone from me. We had spent weeks arguing about everything except for what had happened that night, but knowing that was what was central to it all.

When it had come down to it, we just couldn't live with that knowledge between us.

"You think I left because I thought you were a murderer?"

I looked at her and shrugged my shoulders. "That's what I've thought, yes."

She blew out a breath and motioned to the seat next to her.

I waited a second and then sat down next to her. We were a foot apart, but it felt like more.

"I left because we were going to end up destroying each other if we'd stayed together. It became a toxic atmosphere. I left because I was making it worse for you, and you were making it worse for me. We were never going to make it through if we couldn't deal with it alone. We were only making it harder on each other by being in the same environment. We couldn't work it out in the same way as Chris and Nicola."

"We could have made it."

"Maybe," Alexandra said, resignation in her voice. Maybe regret. "We'll never know."

I could see where the conversation could lead. A path I could take, which could change our lives again. Put us back to where we were supposed to be.

It was there in front of me.

I couldn't take it.

Instead, I told Alexandra about meeting Mark Welsh's dad. Who he was, how he was. How he told me about looking for a son he never knew. Waiting for closure that wouldn't ever come. When I was done, I closed my eyes and spoke softly. "Stuart. Why did he meet that man?"

"Because he's feeling guilty and couldn't let it go."

"What if there's more to this than we first thought? What if it's not because of what happened, but because of what he was."

"I don't know what you're saying."

"Neither do I," I said, running both hands over my head and then interlocking them behind my neck. "I just, I don't get it. I can't accept that the Stuart we knew would do that. It doesn't make any sense. What if that's because he *wouldn't* do that?"

I told her about my theory. That Stuart had possibly faked his own death, how easy it would be to tattoo a body, knowing that would be used to identify someone quickly. If that body held Stuart's ID, but he had been left unrecognizable, how easy it could be for this to work. As I spoke, I heard myself believing it less and less.

"You really haven't been sleeping well have you?" Alexandra said when I was finished. She looked at me with kind, disbelieving eyes. "You know how crazy that sounds?"

I opened my mouth, but having voiced my thoughts, I no longer trusted what I'd been thinking in the last few hours before I'd returned home.

"I mean, let's get this straight," Alexandra continued, speaking softly but with no less a straight tone of voice. "You're suggesting Stuart may have what? Faked his death because he is the person behind these candles being left?"

"Well, it sounds ridiculous when you say it like that."

"That's because it is."

"It would explain why Michelle hasn't been found," I tried, but I knew I'd lost the argument without a shot being fired. Mainly because I heard it out loud and knew it was stupid. There was something there though.

Another memory.

Stuart in an explosion of violence. A lad lying on the ground. Blood and shouting. Footsteps running away. New Year's Eve 1999. A police investigation that didn't get very far. No one telling the truth. A lad who sustained heavy injuries, but thank-fully nothing lasting.

How close it might have been to death.

I didn't know if I could trust my memories anymore.

"We've already agreed we know who is coming after us. We need to concentrate on that. I know you want Stuart to be okay, but we know he isn't."

"You're right," I said, dismissing my thoughts, my recollec-tions, my gut feelings. I looked for my phone and tried to call Chris again. When I got nothing, I tried Nicola and Michelle, watching as Alexandra was doing the same. I messaged Chris, making it easily double figures since I'd watched him drive away.

Call me. I can help. You don't need to be on your own.

I let my mind drift, gazing over at the clock on the wall. An ugly red thing that Alexandra had picked out and I had never liked. I kept it after she left.

Almost six o'clock

I was still looking at it as I dozed off with her head on my shoulder.

FORTY

woke up with a start, having been asleep for a couple of hours.
I had been dreaming, but it faded in the early morning light.

It wasn't the nightmare. I wondered if Alexandra being there
had been the reason it hadn't come, but I wasn't sure. Perhaps
my mind had just decided to give me a little respite.

I found my cell and gave Chris a quick call. It was early, but
I still expected him to answer. It went straight to voice mail, so I
sent him a message instead.

The next course of action was in my mind almost as instantly.
What I needed to do next. I was annoyed with myself for not
thinking about it sooner, but it had been a series of moments like
those over the past week.

I left Alexandra sleeping on the sofa and walked quietly into
my office. It didn't take long to find the information I needed.

Jim Treador. The farmer who had bought William Moore's
place after he went missing. His son had sold it, which struck me
as the final confirmation that he had known all along that his
father was dead. Why sell it if he was just missing?

I heard movement from the living room and waited for
Alexandra to appear. I turned in my chair and saw her in the
doorway.

"I can't believe we slept," she said, yawning and stretching. While we hadn't lived in the house together long, I still

remembered her doing the same a few times. Getting up for work and finding me already in my converted dining room, a look of glee on my face, I imagined.

"You still make weird noises when you're asleep. Like a hamster or guinea pig."

"How would you know what sounds they make?"

I shrugged my shoulders and took the defeat. "The son sold the farm to a guy called Jim Treador. I've just found his contact information. I think he's our best bet of finding him."

She walked over to me and looked over my shoulder at the screen. "He wouldn't have sold it if he thought his father was still alive."

"That's what I was thinking. A little later than I probably should have, but it's been a bit of a hectic twenty-four hours."

"What should we do then?"

I leaned back in the chair and swiveled it a few times. Picked up my phone and held it in the air. "Call him."

Alexandra left to put the kettle on, leaving me to dial the number I'd found. A man answered after a couple of rings.

"Hi, is this Jim Treador?"

"Speaking," a gruff voice said, the sound of traffic in the background. "I hope you're not going to try to sell me anything."

"No, nothing like that," I replied, discarding lie after lie before I settled on one. "My name's David Clarke. I work for the BBC producing documentaries."

"Right…" Jim said, a hint of surprise and wariness in his voice. "You sure you have the right number?"

"We're currently making a program concerning missing people," I continued, allowing the lie to spool out and take form. "I understand you have a connection to one of our main subjects."

"I doubt it. I don't know anyone who is missing."

"Ah, I was under the impression that you now own the farmland that once belonged to William Moore?"

A moment of silence followed, which I allowed to go on for a few seconds.

"Of course," Jim said finally, his voice lower and deeper. "I was approached by his son a few months back. I felt it was only right to make sure it was kept in good hands."

"Well, we're hoping to bring some more publicity to the case, given it was a little overshadowed by a more high-profile one around the same time."

"The boy from the music festival. Yes, we know all about that one."

"Right, so that's the main focus of the documentary—the missing persons cases that aren't featured as prominently as they perhaps should be."

"I'm not sure how I can help out with this."

I paused, hesitating on how to proceed. With caution, seemed to be the best bet. "Well, we're trying to make contact with Mr. Moore's son, but we're finding it a little tricky."

"Uh-huh."

"So we were hoping you might be able to help us out with tracking him down. He's unaware of the documentary at this time, and we want to make sure he's happy with his father being featured and that he has as much chance to assist as possible."

Another period of silence. I imagined Jim standing on farmland now—a big, burly man with arms that were bigger than my entire body. I had no idea where it came from, but the image stuck. He could have been a much smaller guy, sitting in a field wearing a tweed jacket, surrounded by cows for all I knew. Behind me, I felt Alexandra's presence again. I looked over and saw her standing in the doorway, holding a cup of tea in her hands.

"I'm not so sure about this," Jim said, more than suspicion in his voice now. "We've had a few of you journalists sniffing around for the past year now."

He said the word *journalists* like it was the worst insult you could say to someone. I ignored it. "Look, we have a vested interest in this project, hoping it brings a lot of publicity to cases that are overlooked."

"And get publicity for yourselves while you're at it, no doubt."

"That is one of the by-products of these types of shows, I'm willing to admit," I said, guessing correctly—I hoped—that Jim Treador valued honesty above anything else. "We want to make a show that is watched by people, talked about on social media, the subject of much discussion. That's how this business works, after all. Word of mouth and all of that."

"It was a shame what happened to William," Jim said, his voice softening now. He made a tutting sound before he spoke, as if he were talking about the price of something rising, rather than someone going missing. "He wasn't exactly well liked around here, given he didn't talk or mix in with his neighbors. No one really knew anything about him. It was just bad timing, because of what happened to that boy. They couldn't care less about him when they had a fresh-faced lad to concentrate on. First time I met his son was after that. He seemed a good sort, if a little quiet. Older than I'd been expecting. The house is in a right state, but that was expected. We heard William's wife died years ago, but that was all we knew really."

"That's why we're hoping to get in touch with him. I'm sure he'd like as much help to get details of his father's story out as possible."

"I doubt you're doing this for nonselfish reasons though," he said, a deeper tone coming over the phone. Mildly mocking, but a hint of menace underneath it. "Tell me, is this just another ploy to get more behind that young lad from the music thing on TV? Only, we had to deal with all kinds of underhanded stuff last year. Is this *documentary* going to really be about what you're saying?"

"You have my word on that."

"You know, I haven't even got a TV. Couldn't put up with the right-wing bias on your programs."

I frowned, catching a questioning look from Alexandra. I waved it off but couldn't hide my surprise at the political leanings of the man. I wasn't exactly good at reading people, and it turned out I was even worse when it was just over the phone.

"I'm just asking for any help you can give to help us contact Mr. Moore's son," I said, trying not to sound too desperate. The more he talked, the less I was convinced he would actually tell me anything I hadn't already heard the previous day. "I promise we will treat him with respect. If he doesn't want to participate, then that's our involvement over and done with."

"Good. The guy has been through enough as it is."

I gave a thumbs-up to Alexandra, who nodded and handed me a pen. I noted down an address and checked it over with Jim.

"That's the forwarding address he gave me," he said, ready to hang up now, it seemed. "I don't have any more than that. I paid him a fair price; we dealt with it between us without any other hassle."

I paused, then wrote down underneath the address the words *paid in cash* and underlined it. Pointed to it to get Alexandra's attention.

"Thank you, Mr. Treador," I said, looking at the place-name he'd given me. Something about it rang a bell, but I wasn't sure what it was. "You've been very helpful."

"Just make sure you don't cause any trouble for the bloke. He's had enough of that in the past year, with his father going and leaving him behind on his own. I'll see you."

The phone went dead, and I turned to Alexandra. "Well, that wasn't as difficult as I'd been expecting."

"A TV producer?" Alexandra said, raising an eyebrow at me. "Some story, that. Where did you pull that one from?"

"I have no idea. Seemed to work though." I picked up the address I'd written down and studied it again. "I feel like I know this for some reason. Does it ring any bells with you?"

Alexandra took it from my hand and looked it over. Tilted her head, as if that would shake free a memory, but then shook her head. "Not at all."

I took it back from her and opened Google Maps on my computer. Put the address in and was none the wiser. "It's about an hour from here."

"What do we do?"

I thought about it and knew I'd already made a decision. I had no doubt Alexandra would disagree with it, but it didn't make any difference. There was only one way out now.

Well, two, if you didn't discard the more sensible idea of going to someone a little more professional.

"What's our thinking about going to the police now?" I said, knowing the answer but needing to hear it one last time. "Do we have enough to make them see things from our perspective?"

Alexandra gave me a wearied look and leaned back against the wall. She mimicked holding a phone to her ear. "Hello, Officer? Yeah, we killed a bloke a year ago who we think is a serial killer that you don't believe exists. Buried his body in the woods, and remember that missing lad from Brock Hope? We moved his dead body and then it disappeared. We think the serial killer's son is now trying to get revenge on us."

"I take your point. It doesn't mean we couldn't tell them a different story though."

"Is there any version where we're not carted off to an institution?"

I thought about it and couldn't come up with anything. "If you need an idea about how to trick some bloke into thinking I work for the BBC, apparently that's the only lie I have."

"Then what do we do?"

I wanted to tell her what I was going to do, but that way would only lead to arguments and division. Instead, I picked up my phone and tried to call Chris. This time it rang a few times before it went to voice mail. I placed it back down and looked up at Alexandra. "Remember that place we stayed at in Blackpool?"

"The place we stayed one night and then came home because it was so bad?"

"Exactly," I said, standing up and feeling the stiffness in every joint. My muscles ached, but I didn't feel as tired as I had been. "Who would think to look for us there?"

Alexandra smiled at me, and I wanted to scream with anger at myself for lying to her.

For pretending I would be there with her.

FORTY-ONE

It's only an hour's drive across the M58, north on the M6, then the M55, and Blackpool reveals itself in all its nostalgic glory. The B&B was somehow still standing. I pulled up outside, and it took us five minutes to be shown to a dingy room. It overlooked an alleyway and was possibly last redecorated in the seventies.

We had gone there a few years earlier—a weekend break that we had a voucher for or something of that sort. We probably should have looked at the reviews for the place before going—we would have learned that the B&B, which boasted about having color TVs, wasn't exactly rated all that highly. Still, we had stayed for the experience. And the stories we could tell about it for a long time afterward.

"I'm going to go find some stuff for the room," I said, after we had settled in as much as we could in a place like that. We had twin beds, but I didn't expect to have to sleep on them. Alexandra had brought nothing with her, deciding against going home before the journey north. She had her phone, and I had a spare charger. That's all she needed, she'd said. Now, she gave me a list of things. When she was done, she seemed to change her mind.

"I'll come with you."

"No, no, it's okay," I said quickly, eager to leave. "Probably best we don't walk around together all that much. Just in case."

"What? In case we were followed?"

I grimaced, biting down on my lower lip. "We need to be careful. Until we work out what we do with this address. Agreed?"

Alexandra thought for a little longer than I'd have liked, then nodded. I hesitated, then crossed the room and embraced her.

She pulled me tighter, and I could have stayed there forever. Terrible online reviews be damned.

Instead, I left her sitting on the bed, switching on the television and flicking through channels.

Once outside, I prayed that I would get the chance to do that again.

I got back in my car and pulled out my phone. I didn't want to go alone, but with Chris not answering, I didn't have much choice. I tried again one last time, but after a few rings, the same voice mail kicked in.

I was about to pull the car away when my phone trilled its song. I half expected it, so my shoulders sagged in resignation as I pulled the phone off the cradle and looked at the screen.

Not Alexandra.

"Chris?" I said, hearing relief and fear mixed together in my voice. "Where are you? Are you okay?"

"I'm fine," he replied, and I could hear only despondency in his. Resignation. "I can't find her."

"But I've found him," I said, unable to keep the excitement hidden any longer. Of approaching an endgame. Of finally taking control of our story. Of not being alone when it happened. "Chris, we've got him."

"Who? The son?"

I nodded enthusiastically, then realized he couldn't see me. "Yes. Someplace near the Peak District. Not that far away. He sold the farm to a guy and left a forwarding address and has apparently been in touch since. He's going to be there, I can feel it. Where are you? We can go together."

"I'll come over to yours and meet you. I just need a little time..."

"I'm not there," I said, pulling the phone away from my ear and placing it back on the cradle with the speaker turned on. I turned the engine over and shook on my seat belt. "Me and Alexandra decided to hide out. Remember that terrible place we went to in Blackpool?"

"How could I forget? It's all you would talk about for weeks."

"I'll come get you. Whereabouts?" I drove away from the curb, signaling left and turning onto a side street that led me back toward the main road. "Chris?"

"I've got call waiting," he said, then disappeared for a second. When he came back on, his voice was different. "That's Nicola. I've got to go. Listen, don't go there. Stay in Blackpool."

"Nicola, is she okay?"

"I've got to go. Stay where you are. I will sort this out. Don't go anywhere. I can handle this. Wait for me to deal with it. Don't go alone."

"Chris?" I shouted, but he was already gone. I pulled the car over again and tried to call him back but there was no answer.

I took the address from my pocket and looked at it again. The odds were that it was a bogus place—either it didn't exist, or he wouldn't be there.

Still, there was the feeling that I had come that far. I couldn't turn back and hide in a bed-and-breakfast, waiting for it all to blow over.

It never would.

I had lived for a year with the weight of what we did in those woods.

I couldn't do it any longer. I didn't like the way Chris sounded and had a vision of him going off on his own, walking into a situation he couldn't control. All in the mistaken belief that he could *handle it*.

That's not how things would end. He didn't know what he was dealing with.

I plugged the address into the GPS and drove off.

Blackshaw Moor was on the outskirts of the Peak District; a ninety-minute drive from Blackpool. Halfway through the journey, I stopped at the same truck stop I had met Geoff Welsh in Charnock Richard. Picked up a coffee and messaged Alexandra.

> I've gone to finish this. I'll try to come back. I can't live in fear anymore. The silence has to stop. I love you. Always have and always will. X

I switched my phone off for the next hour, when the calls and messages wouldn't stop. I didn't look at any of them.

As I drove into the countryside, the roads narrowing and nature trying to claw back what man had lain, I felt my insides begin to churn. My heart was beating fast, as the road dipped and bent round, as I left the main highway and moved into denser and denser forest.

I had been there before.

I thought hard as I turned the radio down to try to hear my memories. There was something there, but I couldn't grasp hold of it. On the periphery of my mind, refusing to share the answer with the rest of me. A bird swooped down past my side mirror, just as the tree line fell away and my ears popped as I went uphill.

The view was spectacular. Green and bronze fields as far as I could see. The hills turned into mountains it seemed, as the land opened up and nature won its battle. Trees in the distance swayed in the wind, as the road became smaller and stone walls became its border.

It was like nothing I'd ever seen before.

Only, I felt like I had. I felt like I had driven this same road and had the same reaction.

I continued on the narrow road, passing cows in the grasslands around me. Farther up, I noticed sheep on the hills, red numbers marked on their bodies. A few cars had pulled over, people in walking boots and hefty coats readying themselves for treks through the countryside.

I had seen all of these things. It was possible that I was simply merging it all with other places I'd visited over the years, but with every moment that went by, I couldn't shake the feeling of flashing back, rather than forward.

Remembering, rather than foreshadowing.

I had to slow down for a couple of riders to trot past on horses. The quintessential English country pursuits on a single stretch of road. A few spots of rain fell on the windshield and turned the sky darker overhead. The clock on the dashboard clicked over to four o'clock, and I could feel the night drawing closer.

I didn't want to be there without daylight.

The GPS told me it was less than a mile to my destination, as I took the right turn of a fork in the road and entered a path that didn't seem to exist on the map. I could see the route on the map change, but the place was still marked. Driving became more difficult, as the disused ground beneath me became more unsuitable for the car. Potholes and broken concrete. Gravel replaced normal tarmac, as the GPS decided I'd arrived without anything in sight.

Only, I knew where I was going.

I followed the path only traveled by those who knew the place existed. The tree line returned, broken branches littered the way, and I felt myself ducking down every time I passed the thicker forest.

The road climbed higher over the final hundred or so yards of the journey, until it came to a stop.

I knew where I was.

I guided the car through a stone wall, with a narrow entrance-way, until an old farmhouse was revealed. You could barely see the windows for the ivy, which was overgrown, creeping over every available surface. It clung to the brick, twisting and squeezing its prey.

Another view of the house came to mind. One that looked more inviting, coming to life in the summer sun and the sound of an excited child's laughter.

I stopped the car, parking twenty feet from the front of the farmhouse.

The front door didn't open at my arrival. There was no twitch of curtains, not that I'd have been able to see them anyway. The sky overhead drizzled down on my head as I got out of the car and heard my feet crunch on the gravel lying on the ground. To the side of the farmhouse, a crumbling structure of wood peeled and cracked, and a memory flashed in my head.

I was a child. Or a little older. I wasn't sure. I was standing in the same place. The house was different in the blink of an eye. Filled with people I knew. Recognized.

Liked.

Loved.

It was a home.

I walked into the lean-to at the side of the house and ducked through a small opening. Inside, tiny pinpricks of light came through holes in the roof, not enough to make it completely light. Still, it didn't matter.

There were candles dotted around the entire room.

Red candles. In storm lanterns. On every available surface.

And that memory came again. As if I'd stood there before. Seen the same things before. Only this time, it was more distorted. More blurry. My mind was filling in blanks that didn't exist before.

I wasn't breathing. The silence wasn't silent.

There were sounds. All around me.

I couldn't move.

I couldn't speak.

I could only stand there, waiting.

And when the blow from behind me came, I welcomed the darkness that followed it.

1993

We were sitting watching WrestleMania. Chris had managed to get a VHS copy of it somehow—probably managed to convince his mum that he desperately needed it—so we had made a plan to have a sleepover at his house. It was July, last day of school, and we went straight around to his place.

It was ace.

"If Bret Hart puts Yokozuna in a sharpshooter, it wouldn't hurt him at all. His legs are too fat."

"The sharpshooter can hurt you whatever size you are," I said, grabbing a black licorice from the pile of candy we had in front of us. "Anyway, he's gonna get Banzai Dropped before that anyway."

"You don't think Bret will win? It's WrestleMania...the good guy always has to win."

"Not always."

We watched it, giggling at the girls in bikinis that came to the ring with Lex Luger. Laughed until it hurt when Bobby Heenan came in riding a camel backward. Shouted along with the crowd when the Mega-Maniacs threw money into the air.

"We're going to this farmhouse during summer vacation, and my mum said you could come too. Do you want to?"

"Yeah, should be okay. Where is it?"

"Somewhere called the Peak District. Never heard of it."

"Neither have I."

"It's my nan's place. Been in the family for years, but no one stays there anymore. I think they're gonna try to sell it."

That's how things were organized between us. Easy and stress free. We spent every day together, it seemed. Usually at his house. Now, I would be going on vacation with him. I just hoped it would be soon. I didn't fancy spending a week on my own during summer break.

"Do you think that good doesn't always win?" Chris said, as the commentators built up to the main event on the screen. "You know...can bad win as well?"

"I guess," I replied, then glugged down another glass of Coke. "It would set it up for SummerSlam."

"I'm not talking about the wrestling."

Something in Chris's voice made me tear my attention away from the screen and look at him. He was staring out his bedroom window as the daylight outside began to give way to the summer evening.

"What do you mean then?"

The room became smaller and more quiet, as Chris shifted uncomfortably on the floor and away from me.

"Sometimes, I think there's only bad, and there can't really be any good without it, you know?"

I didn't, but I nodded along anyway. Chris sometimes went quiet for long periods and I wondered what he was thinking half the time. I knew he didn't like our status in school—that he would say things sometimes about what he wanted to do to those who picked on him.

"I just wish there were a way of getting the bad thoughts out," Chris said, reaching over and picking up the last piece of candy in the pile and breaking a Refresher bar in half. He handed me the other piece. "If we did that, then it would be good all the time, don't you think?"

I wasn't sure what to think, and the match was about to start on the television. "Macho Man" Randy Savage in gold and white. Yokozuna following Mr. Fuji holding a Japanese flag. Bret Hart in his pink shades and pink-and-black costume. "Yeah, you're right," I said, leaning forward and readying myself for what was about to happen. Excited and nervous. "If we only had to do something a little bad to make things all good, then maybe everything would be great."

"Exactly."

I turned my attention back to the screen, but something next to the television made me frown. "What's with the candle? Can I blow it out? I hate those things."

"No," Chris shouted, startling me into silence. He was on his feet, standing next to the burning red candle, a hand out as if he were protecting it. "You can't mess with this. I need it."

I shrugged, thinking he was just being a weirdo, as he sometimes was. He started murmuring something under his breath, but I was already engrossed in the wrestling. As he was, eventually. Sitting next to me and shouting and hollering alongside me. After it ended, we argued for hours about whether it was right that Hulk Hogan came in at the end of the show and won the title in like twenty seconds or something, after Bret Hart had been cheated. I forgot about the conversation that happened before it.

The words he'd said, as I stopped listening and tried to watch the main event.

"Here comes a candle…to chop off your head."

FORTY-TWO

F lashes of darkness. Consciousness fading in and out. The sound of grunts and moans. My body being moved without my say. The smell of rain and mud in my nostrils. Trying to gain control of my senses but failing every time.

I could hear my own voice, but I didn't think it was under my control.

The sky darkened each time I managed to open my eyes. I tried to move, but my limbs wouldn't respond. My eyes felt covered in a film of fog.

My head was stuck in a vise. Squeezing it until all I could hear was the sound of my own pain. It had taken form and was now all there was. Pounding and throbbing.

It began to subside, as I felt the ground underneath me begin to solidify. The world was spinning, and I couldn't move.

I can't move.

I tried to speak, but all I heard was a gasp of agony. My head felt as if it were being split in half. I could taste copper in my mouth. Pennies. Blood. Wetness on my face. Sharp, stinging pain in my left temple.

All my senses returned in stages. I opened my eyes carefully, blinking rapidly in the darkness.

Someone was singing close to me. A rhyme that reminded me of being a child. Of primary school and tuneless songs.

Oranges and lemons...

There were pinpricks of light surrounding me. I could feel dampness and cool air rushing over me. I tried to speak again, but my throat simply croaked and snapped shut.

Say the bells of Saint Clements...

I moved my head, and an explosion of pain came with it. It blurred, and I was above myself in a split second, hovering outside of my body and looking down.

You owe me five farthings...

It came to me piece by piece. A spark of recollection.

Of the smell of expensive aftershave. Drifting toward me from behind. Of someone standing over me as I struggled to stay conscious. A face so familiar suddenly becoming alien. Strange.

My friend becoming a stranger.

Then, there's nothingness. A clean slate where memory should have been.

Say the bells of Saint Martin's...

I opened my eyes and stared into the face of death. The smell became overpowering. Decay and putrefaction. Desolation and destruction.

She was lying on the ground a few yards away. Her face turned to mine. Eyes open and staring lifelessly. In the flickering light, I could see dirt and blood dried on her face and neck.

I didn't want to believe it was her. I had failed her. Failed us all.

I should have known. I should have protected us.

Michelle began to move slowly. Being dragged away. A grunt of effort around the words in the song. I tried to follow where she went but couldn't manage it.

Michelle was dead.

Stuart was dead.

And Chris was a stranger now.

That was when I saw them again. Red candles in storm lanterns. Two candles. Three. Four.

I continued to count them until I ran out of vision.

The slide and scrape of a body being dragged. A tune being hummed still. I didn't remember the words past the opening lines.

A distinctive *thump*, as Michelle was dropped somewhere. Then, the sound of a shovel being driven into dirt and poured over her.

I could almost see it.

"Stop, please," I heard myself whisper. The tune stopped and the sound of footsteps came closer to me.

I felt his presence over me and turned my head slowly to look up.

"You shouldn't have come here," Chris said, a look of anger and disappointment on his face. "You should have stayed away."

He was close enough to me that I could smell the sweat and expensive aftershave mix of him.

"Why did you come here?" Chris continued, a mark across his face, a shovel in his hand. He laid it down on the ground and crouched over me. "I didn't want you to see this."

"What...what's going on?"

"If you had all just let me deal with this, nothing would have happened," Chris said, his voice exactly how I'd always heard it. No darkness, no evil in it. Normal. "I just had to take care of the ones who were going to say something. Not you. Not Nicola. Not Alexandra."

"Who are you?"

"I'm your friend," Chris said, and I felt his hand on my shoulder. "I wish you hadn't come here. It would have been okay."

"Nicola?"

He looked away quickly, and I could hear something approaching emotion in his voice when he spoke again. "I don't want to talk about that."

"What have you done?" I tried, strength returning to me in stages. I still couldn't move, but I knew why now. I could feel the ties binding my wrists and legs. They kept my body in place. "Where is she?"

"I said I don't want to talk about it." His voice close to my face, my ears ringing suddenly with the force of its scream.

I tried to breathe in and out. Calmly. There was no calm. Not there. My insides felt as if they were being churned around and my heart was crashing against my chest.

There was no way out from this.

"You killed her," I said, louder now, as my voice came back little by little. Word by word. "You loved her and you killed her."

"Stop."

"How could you? Who are you?"

"I said stop."

When the blow came, it was almost in slow motion. A crunch of something unseen against my body exploding into a billion stars of pain. I cried out, but I couldn't hear it. My vision went dark again. It returned quicker this time, and Chris was still next to me.

"I didn't want to do this," he said, softly again, like the Chris I knew so well. "This isn't what was supposed to happen. I thought we could deal with all of this."

"Why? I don't understand..."

"You've never understood, Matt," Chris said, talking over me as I continued to try to work out a way out of this. "You thought everything was okay when we were being treated like shit at every turn. When we were being forced to be people we weren't. All those people out there who think they can treat us like we're nothing. I couldn't take it anymore. I was going to explode. You were always able to shrug it off, but I never could. So I found a way out of it. I found a way to feel better."

"Tell me then," I spat out, turning my head to face him. His eyes were bloodshot and dark. The red candles flickered around us, and I could smell wax and blood. "Talk to me. Don't I deserve that at least? What happened in those woods? What happened to Mark Welsh?"

He sighed and stood up. I watched him walk away and then come back, something in his hands. Outside, I heard rain fall onto a corrugated iron covering above our heads, and the wooden structure creaked and moaned in response.

"I'm not who you think I am."

I stopped myself from saying anything, but I wanted to scream in response. Twenty-five years of friendship and I didn't know him.

Of course, I did, on some level. Had missed the signs, but read them all the same.

"I always thought the Candle Man was a ridiculous name."

And there it was. Finally, I could see what had happened. No Stuart killing Mark Welsh and being discovered. Then covering it up by faking his own death. Tattooing another body, as if that was ever the likeliest option. No son of a serial killer we had murdered in the woods.

No Candle Man.

Only my friend. Only Chris.

"Why?" I said, and it wasn't enough. It would never be enough. "Why would you do this?"

"I need a release every now and again. That's all. There's nothing wrong with that. I've learned to keep myself under control, but sometimes…sometimes I need more. Every now and again, that's all. It's no big deal. Always people that deserved it. I get what I need, and they get what they deserve."

I tried to follow his twisted logic but failed. Tried to accept what he was telling me and failed again.

"Do you remember that night a year ago?"

I croaked a response, which he took as an agreement.

"The way Michelle spoke to me. To all of us. And Stuart, standing there and taking it. For you, it was nothing. An argument, quickly forgotten. That's because that's who you are—you're a pushover. You accept the unacceptable. You respect the disrespectful. I don't. I can't. After something like that, I need to do it. I can't live with the anger inside me. It has to come out; otherwise, I can't go on."

"Mark Welsh…"

"I saw him earlier that day. He barged into me and Nicola and didn't apologize. Spilled our drinks everywhere. I followed him around after that. Watching every step he took. After Stuart and Michelle argued and divided us, I found him. I knew where he was camping. I took him into the woods. It would have ended there and no one would have been the wiser, only I was interrupted."

"William Moore," I said, picturing the farmer walking through the woods with his fishing gear. That was the weapon he had. A hook of some kind, fighting for his life against us. "He saw what you were doing."

"It was an unfortunate thing. Stuart had heard me leave though—that was even less fortunate. He came looking for me, and it all became chaotic. I managed to get away from the

THE SILENCE   359

farmer, but he came across Stuart and thought it was me. I didn't
have time to do anything. Thankfully, you all came too and it
made things a little more manageable."

"His body?"

"That was me. I moved it before you came back, so it
wouldn't be discovered. It would have been found where we left
it. I couldn't have that. It didn't take me long. When you went
back to look for your wallet, you almost stumbled onto where
it was, as a matter of fact. I went back later and gave him a
proper burial, close to the road. A few others over the years are
in those woods. In fact, I heard about the festival when I was
on another trip down there. Then, there was the man's son... I
buried him with his father. I got lucky. No one knew who they
were. I sold the farm to a nice guy named Jim, and that was it.
It was a mess to deal with, but I dealt with it. Just like I always
have."

My mind refused to accept all of this—confusion reigned
within me, as I tried to comprehend what he was telling me. It
didn't make any sense. There was no part of me that thought
Chris was anything like this.

That there was evil in him.

He was just my friend. How could he be...this?

"I thought it was all over," Chris continued, quieter now as
he moved out of my eye line. "Then, Stuart starts poking around
where he wasn't needed. I wish it hadn't gone the way it had—and
in the manner it did—but I had no choice. He was always suspicious. Kept asking questions about where I was when he left the
tent. Then, he called me and asked to meet me. I knew why. He
wouldn't listen to reason. Wouldn't hear me out. It was...it was
an accident."

"You killed Stuart."

"It wasn't supposed to be that way. I didn't even hear the train coming. I wanted to deal with it in a different way. He fought with me and then...and then it was over. I almost went under with him, but I got out of the way in time. If he had just disappeared, maybe he would have been the only one. If I'd had more time to speak to him, I could have ruled everyone else out. I couldn't be sure that he hadn't said anything to Michelle though. That's when it all fell apart. Now, you all have to go. You all know too much. I have to protect myself."

I could hear sadness in his voice, but I didn't believe it. I moved my head, so I could see him again. He was six feet away, his face in shadow as the candlelight burned around me. "You said you wanted to go to the police. We can still do that. I can help you."

He chuckled, but there was no humor to it. A sad sound in the silence. "If only it were that simple. I wanted *you* to go to the police. I would have disappeared. Now, I have to do something I never wanted."

I tried to move again, but it was no use. I was stuck there, and I knew this was it. I had no option left if he wouldn't listen to me.

"You were my friend, Matt," he said, coming closer now, and I could see the knife in his hand. It glistened as the low light caught it here and there. "I want you to know that. You were always my friend. I...I just have to do this."

I could see a tear forming in his eye, rolling down his cheek as I opened my mouth to speak and he shoved something down my throat. I mumbled a scream from behind it as he raised the blade above me.

"I'm sorry," he said, his breath hitching and breaking. "It has to be this way."

I screamed as the knife came closer. Felt the blade across my neck. Then, I screwed my eyes tight, tensed my body, and waited for the darkness to descend.

FORTY-THREE

I remembered being in that place before. The house where I'd found Chris burying Michelle. Where he had already buried Nicola, I imagined. And countless others probably. Twenty-five years earlier. A summer holiday with Chris and his family. We would go up the nearby hill and watch the sun go down together.

Throw rocks and pebbles into the abyss below.

We had called it a cliff, but it wasn't that, of course. We were in the middle of nowhere, so there was no coastline. It was simply a long drop down, as the hill came to a point, rather than a gradual drop on the other side. A strange feature of this countryside.

We would sit there and imagine jumping off. Laughing together about it. Working out how we would survive. What we could do.

He told me he would like to watch someone try to do it. Maybe push someone off just to see what it was like. I remembered laughing, thinking he was joking.

That memory was the one I had now.

I almost felt the knife enter my body, I was so ready for it to happen. I braced and tensed and hoped that it would be quick and as painless as possible. Screwed my eyes tightly shut and wished for it to be over.

I couldn't take it anymore.

The only fear I had was the after. The silence I would hear and live in for eternity.

Only, there was no pain.

There was no after.

I opened my eyes slowly and heard Chris's cries of anguish. I tried to move, but I was still groggy and my body took an age to respond. My hands were tied. Literally.

"I can't do it," Chris whispered, talking to himself. "Why can't I do it?"

I wanted to feel relief, but I knew I had only bought myself a little time. Eventually, he would pull himself together and be able to finish what he started. He was a killer, after all.

I tried not to laugh at my situation.

"Chris, we can stop this," I said, trying and failing to move myself closer to him. "I've known you most of your life. I know this isn't you…"

"That's just it," Chris sniffed, shaking his head and stopping me from continuing. "It is me. This is what keeps me going. If I didn't do the things I do, I wouldn't be here. I just never thought I would have to hurt people like you. People who have always been there for me."

"Where's Nicola?"

Chris shook his head again, more forcefully this time. "I can't talk about that. I won't talk—"

"Okay, okay," I said quickly, wondering where her body was. Whether she was dead already, like I feared, or whether I still had time. The way he spoke whenever he mentioned her name made me think I was too late for that. "We don't have to talk about her."

"I thought you would be easier," Chris began, but then stopped himself. He stood and picked something up from a shelf above me. "She's been calling you for the past hour. Alex. Or *Alexandra* as you always called her. I've always wondered why that was. Why you had to refer to her as something different from everyone else? It never made sense."

"This can end now, Chris. Mate. Just listen—"

"I think it's a control thing," Chris continued as if he hadn't heard any interruption. "Like, if you have just that one single thing that you own—a name for someone—then it's enough for you. No matter that you can't control anything else in your life now. You still have that one thing. I don't know. Maybe I'm overthinking things. It just…it never made sense to me why you wanted to be my friend when no one else did. Why all of you wanted to be my friend. I was so scared you'd wake up and realize one day that it was a mistake that I never brought it up."

"You're a good man," I said, wishing I still believed that. Surrounded by the smell of death and red candles. There was no good there. "This is just a mistake. You can get help and stop this…this part of you. I know you can."

Chris chuckled softly to himself. "Don't you think I've tried to stop? I haven't killed as many as they say I have online, but there's enough of them. I can't go back. There's no help for me."

"Wait…"

"I can't kill you, Matt. Not like the others. But you're not leaving here. You can stay and keep Michelle company. I'm sorry."

I tried to say something more, but Chris moved quicker than I could react and then there was an explosion of pain across my chest. The knife in Chris's hand came back into view and it was slicked red with my blood.

"Just something to get the ball rolling," he said quietly. He had something else in his hand. "I hope it doesn't hurt and that you're asleep when it happens. I remember that place in Blackpool well. You wouldn't stop talking about it for days after you came back. I'll make sure she doesn't suffer."

"No," I managed to get out, but my mouth wasn't working properly. My body wasn't either. The pain began to dull to a screech, but it was still there. Pounding. Pounding. *Alexandra. Chris. Stuart.*

All of them. Pictures in my mind.

"Goodbye," I heard a voice say—Chris? Michelle, back from dead? Alexandra come to help me? I wasn't sure.

Then, there was only silence.

And my blood. Dripping to the floor, like wax from a candle.

I came around in stages. I was lying on my front, and for a moment, I thought I was lying in bed. Listening to classical music, or TalkSport, or an ASMR video, or some boring podcast about American politics.

None of those things.

I was on hard ground. Not soft mattress. I was in hell, rather than safe at home.

I had to free my hands.

My mind had decided to wake up first. My body, on the other hand, was less willing. It didn't want to move. It wanted to stay where it was and let more blood escape. Let it all go. Just lie down and wait for it to be over.

No. We're not doing that. We're getting up and going after him.

I grunted with the effort, but I managed to move my unwilling body around until I was sitting up. Every movement was agony. I needed to stop the bleeding from the slash across my chest, but first I had to free my hands. I could feel the cable ties digging into my wrists. My legs tied together at the ankles were the same. My shoes had disappeared at some point—probably removed when I was tied up, I imagined. I wasn't sure.

My head was still pounding. Concussion, I assumed. The world spun with every movement, my stomach churning along with it. I tried to take a few deep breaths, think of Alexandra, and ignore the fact that, only yards away, Michelle was buried in a freshly dug hole.

Somewhere in my muddled mind, that last thought broke into an idea.

I shuffled slowly across the dirt floor, glancing over my shoulder and seeing the glint of metal in the candlelight. Kept going, as my nausea subsided and the jackhammer in my head diminished a little. Reached the shovel Chris had used to bury Michelle and tried not to collapse at the weight of that image.

I had to keep going. I had to keep going.

I had to…

It took me at least five minutes to make my way to the shovel leaning against the wall. Then at least double that to hack my way through the cable tie with the edge of it. Finally, my hands came free, and I instantly put them to my chest. Put my hand up my T-shirt and carefully felt along the wound, wincing at every touch.

It wasn't deep, but blood was thick on my fingertips when I withdrew my hand. I picked up the shovel and had my legs free after a little more effort.

I allowed myself a minute's rest—my head resting against the cold brick. Tried to keep my eyes from falling shut again and, when that became too difficult, cut the rest short with an image of Alexandra in my head.

I was probably already too late.

I placed a hand against the wall and rose to my feet. I wobbled a little, and gravity tried to take me down to the ground again, but I managed to keep myself upright.

The car may as well have been in another country. It didn't matter. With each step, my mind cleared an iota more. Adrenaline kicking in and helping me for once.

I wanted to be back at home.

It was safe there.

I made it to the car somehow. I barely remembered any of the short journey to it, but I could see darkness in the sky above and realized I was still holding the shovel in my hand.

My keys.

He'd taken them.

I almost fell to the ground then. Screamed at the sky and wondered if I had the energy to reach the top of the cliff behind me and throw myself off it.

I was too late. It was over. I was at least thirty minutes behind Chris, and I had no way of getting to him in time. Of getting to Alexandra in time.

It was over.

I thought back to a year ago. The week before the music festival, when everything was perfect. Alexandra and I, moving into the house, so happy, planning for a future we'd always wanted. A future that would be filled with contentment and pleasure. Children and companionship. Love and laughter.

Gone in a flash of violence.

And now, that future was simply darkness and destruction. Chris was going to find her. She would never be seen again. He would come back to that house and find me still sitting against the driver's side of my car. He would be able to finish the job he'd started and that would be it.

The spare. The box.

I was thinking of that day we'd left for the music festival when I finally remembered—the small contraption that I had scoffed at when Alexandra gave it to me. I'd fixed it underneath the car and then forgotten about it.

A spare key.

I turned and knelt by the wheel arch. Ran my fingers under it, sure that it would no longer be there. I went back and forth, becoming more certain by the second that it would have fallen off in the past year. Caught on something and been torn away.

Finally, my fingers found purchase, and I pulled the box away with a guttural sound of triumph.

It was a small thing, the size of the palm of my hand. I closed my eyes and remembered the combination.

12 05 15

I would never forget that date.

If I got out of this, I would make this another date to remember.

The box opened, and there was the key.

I could have cried, but instead I rose to my feet, unlocked the car, and got in. My head was still pounding with pain and my chest leaked blood over my T-shirt, but I could barely feel any of that.

I wasn't going to be late. I was going to make it.

I didn't have my phone, but the GPS in the car was thankfully built-in. I rarely used it, but was glad of it now. I would have become lost in the hills and country roads without it, but instead I was on the major road in minutes, and then the M60 and M61 followed quickly. A trip that was an hour and forty-five minutes was going to take much less. I weaved through traffic as the sky darkened and became blacker by the second.

I was there in an hour and change. Pulled up to the hotel and saw Chris's car first. Then the dirty white walls of the hotel, as I left the car—door wide open and forgotten—and ran toward the entrance.

My hand was on the door when I heard the scream.

It came from above me. The roof. I looked up and thought I saw movement. I waited there for a second. Frozen in place. Waiting for what I thought was the inevitable.

There was nothing else.

Only silence.

Instead of being afraid of it, like I always was, something broke in me. I felt anger instead of fear. Hate instead of terror.

He wasn't going to win.

I shoved the door open and ran inside.

FORTY-FOUR

I t had started raining at some point, but I wasn't sure if it was before or after I'd reached the roof. My clothes were already wet, but that could have been sweat, blood, the rain, or most likely a combination of all three.

I breathed rapidly in and out as I stood with my back to the door of the rooftop. From behind me, alarms rang. I hadn't heard them on my way up the stairs, but the race up had been done in a blur.

The rain fell harder, and I wanted to close my eyes. I didn't want to know what was happening. What was about to go into her. What was about to slice her flesh.

The shovel was in my hands still. I didn't remember taking it with me from the car, but some part of me was still working without me knowing. My arms felt heavy, and suddenly any movement made me want to shout in twisted agony. I could feel the bruises and splinters in my hands. I could feel the angry slash across my chest, tearing apart a little more with each breath.

I could smell her perfume in the air.

I could see Chris. Standing with his back to me. His arm around Alexandra, as she knelt on the rooftop, looking almost like he was embracing a loved one.

Alexandra.

Kicking and squirming with every last ounce of energy she had left.

I moved forward, raising the shovel with both hands, and then when I was close enough and heard his voice, I screamed with everything I had.

The wave of pain hit my hands first, then up my arms into my shoulders, and I fell to the ground. My face hit the floor and my eyes met his.

Chris.

On the floor, his eyes opened for a second before they glazed over and closed. Blood seeping from his head onto the dark ground and disappearing into it.

I almost felt myself slip away. Then, her smell and her voice came through the fog.

"Matt…"

I wanted to answer, but I could say nothing. Could feel nothing. I wanted to sleep. I wanted to wake up and forget about all of this.

I felt her hands under my arms and was lifted to my knees. My body wasn't responding, my mind not much better. I retched and felt the world spin around me. Saliva filled my mouth as my stomach churned and threatened to overpower me. I swallowed, trying to keep some semblance of control.

"We have to get out of here," Alexandra said, looking around I saw the storm lantern and the red candle. Even up there, he had needed his talisman.

"Is he the…" she said, before stopping, unable to finish the sentence. Unable to accept the truth.

I managed to nod my head and set off another bout of nausea. I breathed a few times and managed to calm. The word *concussion* bounced around my head, and I wondered what would be left of me if I got out of there.

"He can't be."

"He is," I said, twisting to see him. All I could see was the end of his leg before Alexandra pulled me again. My chest throbbed in pain, and I tried not to dwell on it. Tried to stay lucid.

I wasn't winning the battle.

I held onto her arm as she turned and pulled me away. My legs groaned in protest. I could see the way out ahead. The door that led from the rooftop came into focus. I didn't think this was real. My mind had slipped into delirium. I was still back at the house where Chris had buried Michelle and he was still slicing his way through my chest.

My best friend. Someone I considered closer than family.

This was him.

The feel of Alexandra's hand on mine brought me back somewhat. She looked back at me, and I could see in her eyes that it was going to be okay.

Then, they changed. They darkened in a moment, and I suddenly dropped to the floor. I heard a scream. I heard footsteps scraping against the concrete. I heard my name, then a screeching feeling in my back.

I tried to speak, but my mouth wouldn't move. My body went limp and I could feel a wetness under my upper body as I lay on the floor.

I saw her.

I saw him.

I saw the knife in his hand, something dripping from its blade, and Alexandra disappearing from view. Chris staggering after her.

The last thing I saw before I blacked out into the silent darkness.

The rain was still hammering down above me when my eyes came back into focus. I put my hand slowly underneath my arm and against my chest, flinching rapidly with the pain it caused. When I pulled my hand away, I could see the blood on it by the candlelight.

I wanted to lie there forever and accept it was over. Lie there in the evening darkness and let it wash over me. Take me away. Allow my life to seep from my body and onto the dirty ground. Wait for the silence to consume me and not worry anymore.

Alexandra's face came to mind then, and in an instant, I shook my head to try to forget.

It wouldn't happen.

It *couldn't*. I wasn't going to let it.

I dragged myself up to a sitting position, my right arm limp across my lap. I groaned with the effort as I managed to get to my feet and start moving.

With every step, a fresh wave of pain hit me, and my head swam as the world threatened to flip over me. The pain stabbed into me, down into the depths of my body. I put a pale hand against the wound and screamed in response.

I kept it there and continued moving.

I hadn't been unconscious long this time. I could still hear their voices on the other side of the rooftop. My vision was darkening by the second as I dragged myself along.

I heard a shout from ahead, and it seemed to help.

I moved quicker in the open air. The freshness and cold hit me and seemed to wake me up to the reality of what was going on. The world became more solid around me, and I focused on what was ahead of me. The rooftop was long, and I kept moving toward the distant shouts and struggles.

I fell to my hands a few times, as I dragged myself along the roof. With each moment, I felt another minute of my life end.

They eventually came into view ahead of me. Two figures

in the darkness, as the lights from the front of Blackpool shone ahead.

"Stop," I said, but it came out as a whisper. I coughed and continued to move slowly up. "Chris, it's over, stop."

He turned toward me, and I could see the man I had known for so long wasn't there anymore. This was someone else—a stranger in familiar disguise.

"I just can't get rid of you," Chris shouted across the rooftop. He had hold of Alexandra, who was fighting against him with everything she had. He still had the knife in his hand, but was too close to her to use it. "Don't come any closer. It's over."

I kept moving as Alexandra managed to dodge another blow and then struck Chris in the chest. He stumbled backward, dropping the knife to the floor. I broke into a half run, trying to get closer to them.

Alexandra looked over at me and then aimed another forearm at Chris, who absorbed some of it with his hand in the air in front of his face. It was hard enough to make him lose his balance, falling to the ground and away from her.

I was only a few feet away now and could almost reach out to Alexandra. She turned toward me and ran the distance between us. I grabbed her and tried to pull her away, but she resisted.

"We have to get out of here," I said, having to take a breath after every other word. Splinters of pain shook through my body, and every muscle was weakened by effort and agony. "Please…"

I glanced behind her and saw Chris moving groggily side to side. Only conscious because he hadn't taken the full weight of her elbow into his temple. I stepped ahead of Alexandra and faced him again. "You're not going to win."

"This isn't a game," Chris said, getting to his feet slowly.

One side of his face was a mask of blood, a thin laceration on his forehead the cause of it. What had once been a light shirt was now a mix of browns and reds. Still, he came forward. Off balance at first, then more purposeful. Behind us, the drop below was a chasm of possibility.

I pivoted around, trying to keep the distance between us, but I managed instead to leave no way off the rooftop other than through him.

"I'm not going back," he spat at me.

Alexandra's hand found my shoulder, but she was no longer behind me but at my side.

"We can still get through this."

"You never knew me." Chris wiped a sleeve across his brow and winced at the pain it caused. "This is my life. I'm not going to lose. You don't know what it's like. You could never understand this. There is no black and white. There's only gray. I'm both people, Matt. You won't take this away from me."

I blinked away sweat that began to sting my eyes, sucking in a breath as another sharp bite of fire shook through my body. "Chris, there has to be another way."

"There is no other way."

I had taken my eye away from where the knife had fallen and Chris was faster than me. Faster than Alexandra. I saw him move, but it was already too late. He pounced forward, knocking me to the ground in one movement before tackling Alexandra. I turned groggily to see him above her. The knife in his hand. In the air and moving toward her. She struggled underneath him, bucking him one way and another, one hand gripped on the wrist holding the weapon. I tried to crawl, but my body protested against any movement.

I watched as his free hand formed a fist and he pounded it

down into Alexandra's face, her struggling becoming weaker. I tried to move again, hearing my screams coming from another world.

Reality slowed down. I saw the knife in the air. I saw the fight leave Alexandra's body as unconsciousness gripped her. They were on the edge of the roof—an unseen drop of at least forty meters. One hundred and thirty feet. I saw the universe shift into the abyss and roared with one last effort.

I didn't see the drop below us.

I didn't care.

I used the last remaining strength I had to fling my useless body at his and take us over the edge.

The last thing I remember is the sound of shock escaping his lips.

And then, it was only screaming into the abyss.

LATER

don't know how I'm still alive.

It took a long time to accept I wasn't dead. That I am lying in a hospital bed and not on the concrete at the bottom of that hotel. Lying next to Chris, experiencing the same darkness he is. Every time I fell asleep, I kept expecting to never wake up.

When I wake, Alexandra won't tell me what happened. She says I have to wait. That we can talk about it another time. All that matters, she thinks, is that I get better. I lost a lot of blood, and the important thing is to make sure I'm well enough to go home.

I know I won't go back there.

Everything is tainted now. All my life has a dark stain on it.

I won't be able to live in a place where he was so present.

She seems okay. She knows I did it to save us both, even if I will never be the same person I was before.

I killed a man. I somehow survived. I didn't go over the edge of the roof with him. It was only luck that saved me.

I was prepared to go over that abyss with him.

There have been questions from those in authority. Men and women in uniforms, with doubting faces and suspicious expressions. Most we can't answer. We have told the truth as much as we can, but there are some we haven't given the full story to.

We want William Moore and his son to have justice, but when it came to it, we couldn't accept the blame.

There's no one left but us now.

Stuart is gone. Michelle and Nicola. Chris. The group that had once existed is now only the two of us.

I don't know what the future will be.

Mark Welsh was found an hour ago. On the television in the corner of the room, Sky News has a yellow ticker running along the bottom of the screen. A woman is standing in front of crime scene tape as a uniformed police officer stands guard. The woodland behind them looks normal from my hospital bed, but I know what secrets it holds.

They would find more.

A picture of Chris appears on-screen, and I close my eyes to it.

Too painful right now.

They found Michelle's body buried on the farmhouse grounds. They were still digging around the property, I imagined. Soon, they would find Nicola and that would be it. I told police that Chris told me a few locations when I found him there. They intimated they had more evidence after combing the farmhouse and his own home.

I'm waiting to see if any of it comes back to us.

He was my friend.

He was a serial killer.

I wonder how I can make those two disparate ideas work in my mind. How I can live with the knowledge of them both.

We both wanted to know he was gone. That he wasn't going to come back. They assured us there was no doubt.

He is dead. His body is in the morgue. There is no coming back.

No one can survive a fall of that height.

I should have gone down too.

I am a killer. Just like him, I felt. We should both have been found on the pavement.

I am not sure what will happen next, but for the moment, I just want to sleep.

Alexandra is sitting next to me, watching the television and holding my hand. I don't know how long we'll be allowed to do that. I don't know if we'll be allowed to be free.

I don't know what will happen to us next.

I do know there will be no more candles.

I know there will be no more death.

No more lies.

No more silence.

NOW

In the beginning, there was a girl.

She met a boy in school and fell in love. Teenage love, of course, but that only grew into something more over those first few years. Until she couldn't imagine a life without him in it.

The cell phone she had bought earlier that day vibrated in her pocket. She had set it up with a pay-as-you-go SIM card, downloaded a few apps while she waited, and charged it up in the lobby.

She was waiting for him.

That's how we live our lives now. A series of moments, interspersed with cell phones vibrating or dinging away to let us know what is happening around the world. We're instantly contactable. When the world ends, we'll find out from a breaking news notification, she imagines.

And that's all it was. A news notification. She didn't look at it straightaway.

She was alone and running away. From the life she had once had. That she worked hard to build and never wanted to change.

If everything had gone to plan, like she knew it would, then they would think she was already dead. They had planned well for this moment. Had an escape route worked out. A way out if it all fell apart.

She had dyed her hair and put in colored contacts. At a

cursory glance, a change of hair and eye color would be enough. Every day would be a struggle, but she was well prepared for that.

If he didn't come, she knew what would happen. They would want her secrets. They would ask her questions and demand answers. She would be on the front page of every newspaper, talked about online, accused of being the Rose to his Fred. The Carr to his Huntley.

The Hindley to his Brady.

It didn't matter that she didn't know who he was. Not until recently.

Okay. Maybe a little longer than that.

Maybe she'd always known on some level.

The boy in the scrapyard, twenty years ago. The one who had insulted her mum. She'd known about him. Had been there when Chris hurt him.

Killed him.

It was an accident, he'd told her later that night, when they'd run away and left the boy to die alone. He'd just gone too far. It would never happen again. And anyway, he was only doing it to protect her honor.

They were kids.

She had believed him. She loved him.

She hadn't known about the others. Not until that night in the woods. Then, it all made sense. Why he kept the candles burning all year round. Why he could never rest.

They had moved Mark Welsh's body together. So it wouldn't be found. That's when she was brought into his world for real. That's when she'd had to make a choice.

She'd chosen him.

He'd asked her to tell Matt about finding the candle. Hoped

it would be enough to tip him over the edge and run to the police. Put him out of the picture. No such luck.

A dye job and a foreign country. A bit of cash stored up.

A simple notification on a phone. She lifted it from her pocket and read the headline. Read the two that followed. Watched two ferries depart without her aboard them.

They had found bodies. She recognized the place that was pictured on the news app. The family home that had become a burial ground.

She read there were two survivors being treated in the hospital.

Finally, she understood that Chris was never going to meet her.

Her world ended in a breaking news notification.

It was over.

She was on her own.

She remembered the last thing he'd said to her as she boarded the train and left him behind to finish cleaning up the mess they had made.

"No matter what I've done, I really do love you. If I don't make it, please don't look back. Go far away. Never come back."

Inside her mind, the words made sense.

In her heart, she wanted to go back. To hurt the people who had taken him from her.

Nicola sat there for a long time, trying to decide what to do. Whether her heart would overrule her head.

Let the anger build and build inside her, until it became all she could feel.

There is no black and white. No good and evil.

There is only gray.

Hate and love.

In all shapes and forms.

READING GROUP GUIDE

1. Even before the incident in the woods, Matt feels like long-term promises are impossible. Do you think we can make commitments without knowing how circumstances may change? If not, how do you navigate that uncertainty?

2. If you were a part of the group, would you have avoided calling for help? Would you be afraid of the authorities turning on you?

3. How do the members of the group differ in their reactions to the crime? Who handles it best? Who do you relate to the most?

4. Michelle argues that the group is getting what they deserve for the murder. Do you believe people always get what they deserve in the end?

5. How would you describe Matt's reluctance to leave the house? As he investigates the Candle Man further, he struggles less with leaving. What do you make of that change?

6. Throughout their lives, Matt and his friends always

seem to find themselves at the center of "random acts of violence"—fist fights, accidental deaths, jealous arguments. Do you think any of them found that suspicious? If you found yourself in that kind of pattern, what would you do about it?

7. As the characters discuss Michelle's disappearance, Matt thinks, "We were delusional. All of us." What exactly is he referencing? Do you think you could break the delusion in his place? How?

8. Matt's insomnia haunts him at every turn. How do you think it alters his reasoning and judgment?

9. Who did you expect the Candle Man to be? Were you surprised by the truth?

10. By the end of the book, Matt thinks that he and Chris are essentially the same. Do you agree?

11. If you were to continue Nicola's story, what would happen next?

A CONVERSATION
WITH THE AUTHOR

How did you come up with a figure like the Candle Man? Any real-life inspirations?

He's a representation of what a media-influenced serial killer often is. A mythical figure, that bears little relation to what it usually tends to be—a seemingly normal man, whom neighbors would describe as "keeping themselves to themselves." While I draw on real-life examples, the Candle Man is very much a fictional creation. I wanted to have this somewhat otherworldly, almost mystical apparition running through the novel, with a very ordinary explanation as to what he is in reality.

Matt and his group of friends have been close since childhood. Do you still keep in touch with your anyone from your childhood?

Weirdly, not many. I grew up in various housing estates where everyone knew everyone, but I don't really keep in close contact with people other than being Facebook friends with a few. It's for no reason other than moving in different directions once we became older. Many of them are very surprised I became a writer!

If you had to cover up a crime like your characters, who would you want on your side?

Well, I hope this never happens, but I think you want someone trustworthy on your team. Someone who isn't going to crack under the first sign of pressure. Alexandra is my representation of that kind of person. She closely resembles my wife, who is definitely someone you want in a crisis. Plus, she knows how to dig a big hole quickly.

There's a lot of music in the book, from the festival to Matt's various attempts to fend off silence. Did any of your go-to bands make their way into the book? Do you listen to music while you write?

I have a growing playlist running whenever I write and a lot of nineties music is found on there. All of his musical tastes match my own. The nineties are really where I found my own music, rather than just listening to everything my dad put on when I was younger. I still love the same bands he does—Pink Floyd, Jimi Hendrix, etc., etc.—but I complemented with my own choices. I love music—it really is my first love—so I've been waiting for the right book to start listing some of my favorites in. The nineties was a great decade for music, so it was great to remind readers of some of my fondly remembered songs.

Your books often center around detectives, but the characters in *The Silence* **resist the involvement of investigators over and over again. How did that change the way you reveal the mystery to the reader? Did you have to adjust your writing process at all?**

It was a definite choice to write a book without any police characters appearing, and there were often times when I wished I hadn't done so! It's much easier when you have a character who can simply kick a door in or question people with authority behind them. It was a challenge but one I relished. Having a non-detective as the lead character possibly makes it easier for a reader to picture themselves in that position, which means the mystery unfolds in a different way. With a detective character, it can almost seem like sometimes a reader is waiting for them to solve the clues, the puzzles, and that's the joy of the book. With this kind of character, the mystery is unfolding around you, which I hope means a more involved read. It was the most enjoyable experience I've had so far writing a story, mainly because there were so many puzzles to work out. It's one I'll be repeating again a fair few times in the future.

What first attracted you to mysteries and thrillers? Were there any particular authors that were instrumental in capturing your attention?

I was a horror reader as a teen, then went through a stage where I didn't read much of anything. It wasn't until I was in my early twenties that someone passed me the first novel by Mark Billingham—*Sleepyhead*—and said I should try it out. I was hooked on the genre from that moment on. I think because it's a genre in which there are so many aspects to it, you can never be bored by it. I went from Billingham to other British authors, such as Val McDermid, Ian Rankin, Steve Mosby, and Denise Mina. Then, I became a voracious reader, devouring anything I could get my hands on. Harlan Coben, Linwood Barclay, Laura Lippman, Dennis Lehane, and Megan Abbott all became firm favorites.

What have you been reading lately?

I'm almost finished reading an advance copy of a debut from Richard Osman called *The Thursday Murder Club*. It is spectacular. He is an incredibly well-known TV presenter in the UK, whom I've had the pleasure of meeting, so I know his love of the crime genre is very real, which really shows in the book.

Do you have anything new in the works?

I visited Connecticut earlier this year as research for a future novel. I stayed in a town called Mystic, where some of the action takes place and did a lot of walking (which is difficult when there aren't sidewalks everywhere!), took hundreds of pictures, and talked to some great people. And ate my way through many diner menus. The book is set in a small village in the south of England before moving across the Atlantic, with the main character searching for answers to a long-held mystery. That book has consumed me for almost a year now. It's a real departure for me with a much broader setting, being set in both the UK and USA. I can't say too much more, but I'm really excited about sharing it with readers.

ACKNOWLEDGMENTS

As always, this book wouldn't be in your hands right now without the support of a bunch of ace people. Here's as many as I can fit into these end pages without making the book Stephen King length.

Thank you to:

Craig Robertson, for always having an ear to lend, a beer to share, and an insult to bestow. I'm blessed to have the friends I do, and you're one of the best.

My agent, Phil Patterson, who is always there. Always. Has never let me down, has looked after me in the best way. Listens to me rant, calms me down, and makes me laugh endlessly. A better agent would be hard to find.

Jo Dickinson, editor extraordinaire, who never blinked when we ran into issues with what turned into "the difficult sixth novel." You continue to make me a better writer every day. Bethan Jones, who appeared as if by magic and came up with some outstanding suggestions to make this book multitudes better than it once was. Thank you and hope to hear more of your brilliant ideas. Jess Barratt, who is just the best, ever. Alice Rodgers, for her keen eye, and Clare Wallis, for excellent copyediting. And to the Simon & Schuster team, who make these words real and tangible by getting them into readers' hands.

Kate Moloney, for reading an early version and easing my worries. I love your husband.

All the readers who have followed me into the world of stand-alone novels and enjoyed them just as much—if not more—than the series books. You're the best. Special mention to Dona Pattison, who is the best reader a Scouser could find. I will never forget that. Also the bloggers and reviewers who are fantastic champions of books.

No thanks to Mike Hale, who went to the Champions League final without me.

My bandmates, Mark Billingham, Chris Brookmyre, Doug Johnstone, Stuart Neville, and my road mum, Val McDermid. This thing of ours is awesome. The best thing ever. May the Fun Lovin' Crime Writers last for eternity...or at least until you gits can make it onto a stage.

My dad, who gave me many things, but most importantly a love of music. Even if he can't agree that the nineties were the best decade.

Thanks to my family, who support me endlessly.

Finally, to the three most important people—Emma, Abigail, and Megan. My life. Alton Towers season passes and walking up hills. Life could never be better.

ABOUT THE AUTHOR

Luca Veste is a writer of Italian and Liverpudlian heritage, husband, and father of two young daughters. He studied psychology and criminology at university in Liverpool. He is the author of five previous novels: *Dead Gone*, *The Dying Place*, *Bloodstream*, *Then She Was Gone*, and *The Bone Keeper*. He is the co-creator—alongside fellow crime writer Steve Cavanagh—of the acclaimed podcast *Two Crime Writers and a Microphone* and a bass player in the Fun Lovin' Crime Writers band. Follow him @LucaVeste on Twitter.